A Woman of Marked Character

A Woman of Marked Character

The Imagined Portrait of Sarah Ridge Paschal Pix

1812 - 1891

BOOK ONE
1812 - 1848

by
Nancy Stanfield Webb

The song "This Good Life" copyright 1978 by Luke Wallin.

A Traveler in Indian Territory: the Journal of Ethan Allen Hitchcock. Edited and annotated by Grant Foreman 1930. Foreword by Michael D. Green © 1996 by the University of Oklahoma Press, Norman. Used by permission.

This book is a work of fiction. While some of the characters and incidents portrayed here can be found in historical accounts, they have been altered and rearranged by the author to suit the strict purposes of storytelling. These characters and incidents, despite their resemblance to actual persons and known events, are therefore the products of the author's imagination.

Copyright © 2024 by Nancy Stanfield Webb
All rights reserved
Printed in the United States of America

Cover and book design by Nancy Webb and Andrea Reider
Author photograph by Adam Himber Photography

Except for reviewers who may quote brief passages in a review, requests for permission to reproduce material from this work should be sent to the publisher:

Requests for permission to reproduce material from this work should be sent to the publisher:

Crimson Peony Press
Little Compton, Rhode Island 02837
Email: publisher@crimsonpeonypress.com
Website: nancywebbwriter.com

Library of Congress Control Number: 2024905580

ISBN 979-8-9896098-0-2 (paperback)
ISBN 979-8-9896098-2-6 (hardcover)
ISBN 979-8-9896098-1-9 (e-book)
ISBN 979-8-9896098-3-3 (audiobook)

Dedicated to my children, Jarret and Jessica

and to the memory of
Sarah Ridge's great-granddaughter
Kathryn Agnes McNeir Stuart
1906 - 1998

CONTENTS

Epigraph... xiii

Author's Note... xiv

Maps.. xviii

The United States 1840.................................... xix
Cherokee Nation & Removal Routes to Indian Territory......... xx

PART ONE, GEORGIA 1811 - 1837

1	Sarah Speaks...................................	3
2	*Gado Alitelvhvsgv*............................	7
3	Listening & Learning...........................	14
4	Words & Letters................................	22
5	Another *Donadagohvi*..........................	28
6	A Friend Found.................................	35
7	Sarah Speaks...................................	41
8	Eagles & a Raven...............................	46
9	Miss Corbett Regrets...........................	55
10	Lasting Mementos..............................	63
11	Sarah Speaks..................................	68
12	The Winds of Change...........................	74
13	Strangers on the Road.........................	84
14	A Talk in the Parlor..........................	91
15	A Later Talk in the Parlor....................	96
16	Sarah Speaks..................................	100

17	Time Runs Out	105
18	Lamentation for a Dying Nation	111
19	The Treaty of New Echota	120
20	Ashes	127
21	What Is Happening to Us?	132
22	A Multitude of Decisions	141
23	Questions & Sealing Wax	150
24	The River of the Cherokee	158
25	My Dearest Mother	166
26	The Suck, the Boiling Pot, the Skillet, & the Frying Pan	174
27	Twice-dead	179
28	The Promised Land	185

ILLUSTRATIONS

President Monroe Indian Peace Medal 1817	194
Major Ridge	195
John Ross	196
John Ridge	197
Elias Boudinot	198
Stand Watie	199
Sarah Ridge	200
Sarah Ridge Paschal	201
Susan Agnes "Soonie" Paschal	202
George Paschal	203
Ridge Plantation House, Rome, Georgia	204

PART TWO, ARKANSAS 1837 - 1848

29	Sarah Speaks	207
30	Letter to Hester	213
31	This Good Life of Mine	217
32	A Stained Slouch Hat	222
33	Peonies & Chrysanthemums & Poor Joes	229

CONTENTS

34	The Daughter, the Sister, the Cousin	236
35	Answers Great & Small	245
36	Poultices & Notes Payable	250
37	Holy Bible, Holy Moccasins	256
38	Rumors	267
39	Thornes of Revenge	276
40	Sarah Speaks	284
41	It's All About Hair	288
42	From Mud Pies to Blood Ties	294
43	Lilacs for the Dead	298
44	Sarah Speaks	307
45	Snakeskins	314
46	Go or No	318
47	An "Eat-crow" Face	329
48	Portraits & a Word-Picture	333
49	A Friend Appears	338
50	A Letter Received, a Message Conveyed	343
51	Sarah Speaks	348
52	Pursuit of a Dream	354
53	Eggs & Barbs	360
54	An Eagle Flies	368

Afterword 376
Acknowledgments 379
Illustrations & Map Credits 381
Sources & Further Reading 383

A Woman of Marked Character

The Imagined Portrait of Sarah Ridge Paschal Pix

1812 - 1891

BOOK ONE
1812 - 1848

by
Nancy Stanfield Webb

EPIGRAPH

"She was the daughter of a prominent Cherokee chief and was a woman of marked character."

Quoted by Ben C. Stuart, editor of the *Galveston Citizen & Gazette* and later the *Galveston Daily News*, referring to Sarah Ridge Paschal Pix in a memoir published in that newspaper on February 2, 1911. Stuart was born in Galveston, Texas in 1847 and attended school with Sarah's sons.

A woman of "marked character" as described in the 1800s was a woman of remarkable ability and intellect, strong in her friendships as well as in her intolerances, and a most useful member of society.

Author's Note

I believe in magic—call it coincidence, happenstance, or Fate. Smith's Point, Texas. Sunday, January 8, 1991. I stood under an ancient live oak tree beside the grave of Sarah Ridge Paschal Pix. It was, coincidentally, the hundredth anniversary of her death.

Some months before at a historical society meeting in Orange, Texas, where I was living at the time, Kevin Ladd, former director of the Chambers County Museum at Wallisville, presented a lecture on a woman who had lived and died at her ranch on that point of prairie jutting into the east side of Galveston Bay.

As a freelance writer, my curiosity took hold. Why did this Cherokee woman have a Texas historical marker commemorating her existence in this world?

I gathered as much printed information as Kevin could provide me. Then, armed with a few facts, I set out to answer that question. On that chilly January day, a friend and I went in pursuit of Sarah's grave. Asking around at the Smith's Point community, we gained permission to walk through a cattle pasture to an oak grove where a small family graveyard lay near Sarah's historical marker. I parked on the side of the road. Pulling on our muck boots, we slipped through a barbed wire fence and trudged across the prairie.

The live oaks were overgrown with Spanish moss draping and resurrection fern clinging; wisteria vines dangled and poison ivy entwined a battered chain link fence surrounding a smattering of family headstones. My photographs show a foggy haze hovering over coastal marshlands. Sarah's marker was a worn tan stone incised with faded black letters reading "Sarah Ridge Pix, 1814 - 1891." (Today, the McNeir Family

Cemetery is trimmed and manicured, and a more recent pink granite slab marks Sarah's life.)

I had read that the live oak trees under which Sarah was buried were planted near their homeplace by her last son Charles Forest Pix, from acorns given him as a child. Grand spreading limbs rose and arched over their graves, but that day I envisioned smaller trees planted a quarter of a century before her death. Forest lies near his mother, curbing outlining his grave.

I stood in the hazy mist imagining Sarah walking through mustang grapevines, dodging palmettos pointing sharply; the browns, the grays, the greens. The crackle of winter leaves.

That January day standing over the stone that marked her time in this world, I told Sarah that I would write her story.

Sarah's life—I was to learn through my decades of intense research—survived in her letters, family memories, and a few portraits; court documents; and occasional paragraphs in books and dissertations written about her well-documented Cherokee father, brother, cousins, and first husband. A university press to which I sent an early proposal of Sarah's story replied if I could provide a footnoted biography, they would consider publication; I felt there was not enough documentation to write such a book.

So I give to you here Book One of my two-part biographical novel, a word-portrait of Sarah imagined by me—researched with diligence and devotion with a bit of magic tossed in along the way. The answer to my long-ago question rests within *A Woman of Marked Character*.

Nancy Stanfield Webb

Maps

Facing page
The United States of America 1840

Two-page spread following
Cherokee Nation & Removal Routes to Indian Territory 1838 with Sarah Ridge's Locations

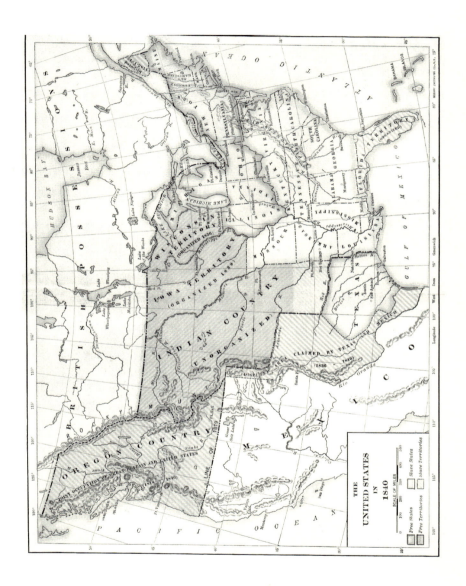

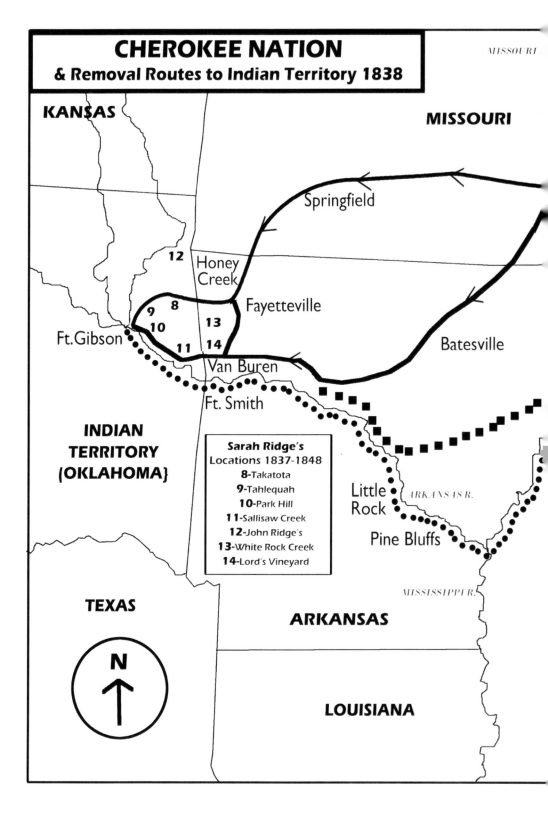

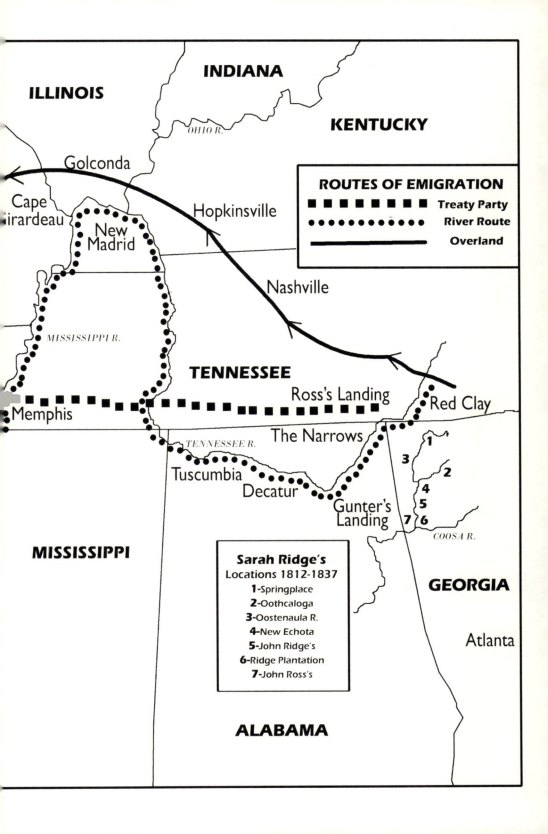

Part One
Georgia
1812 - 1837

. . . the background out of which Sally Ridge came to Salem Academy was, in many ways, little more primitive than that of her white schoolmates. The truth is, she had moved in circles far more cosmopolitan, probably, than any of them had experienced.

Less Time for Meddling - A History of Salem Academy and College By Frances Griffin, writing of Sarah (Sallie) Ridge's tenure during 1826 - 1828

Chapter 1

Sarah Speaks

January 8, 1991

Today marks a hundred years from the day I died. My bones have long since moldered to dust.

Look around at this coastal prairie of mine as it eases into Galveston Bay. Some of what you see remains the same as when I lived: this pale winter sun, the chill that hangs at day's end. The *V*s of waterfowl seeking an evening resting place. Mustang grapevines, palmettos pointing sharply; the browns, the grays, the greens.

I have witnessed much over my lifetime, yet even with a century of rumination I, Sarah Ridge Paschal Pix, recognize the imperfections and limits in comprehending human actions and events.

I speak to you now from my grave since I, unlike Ishmael, did not survive the sinking of a whaleship by a great white leviathan to float on an empty coffin and return to narrate his own tale of obsession and greed, of hatred and tragedy.

As I hover here under these live oaks, I should add that within my tale of tragedy are love and laughter as daughter, mother, wife and friend. Yes, there are happy times interspersed amongst the sorrow.

Yet how very interwoven is my story with the political maneuverings of others. Politics, the art of the inexplicable. "How can *they*," I used to rail, "do this to us?" To me?

I learned. Not by acceptance, no. I learned to fight when necessary. At other times, quietly acquiesce, moving on with my silent anger simmering.

I learned about truth, about what is real. I learned that within many truths, there are also many lies. But within these entwined absolutes there is but one certainty: what you believe is true is true to you. Though another person believes the matter to be as false as you believe it to be true, *your* truth to you and *his* truth to him are true truths unto yourselves.

Who, then, you might ask, is the arbiter of wrong? To the multitudinous evils; brutality, murder, grievous crimes? Again, principles are set by one party's beliefs to which the other party adheres or chooses to refute.

I have concluded there is no one true truth: there is but what we choose to believe.

Congress lied to the Cherokee. The Presidents lied, too. Their treaties. What farces! Oh, those honorable men with their honorable promises! Do you know that of the over three hundred treaties we native peoples signed not *one* was ever honored?

No, government leaders had other means of getting what they wanted. Spanish, French, and British soldiers and colonists left behind a swath of death more potent than gunfire as they passed through. Smallpox and measles wiped out entire tribes along eastern shores from the Algonquian in the Maritimes to the Seminole in the Everglades. Following the American Revolution and into the next century, they of their God-given Manifest Destiny expansion westward did not stop there. Creek and Choctaw, Shawnee and Sioux; all the tribes in all the hills, deserts, and plains were routed from their homelands. And along the way the whites turned upon themselves, fighting North to South.

I am Cherokee, so I tell our story.

George Washington and Thomas Jefferson told us we could be equal to the white man if we became civilized like them, spoke their words, dressed as they did. These Great Fathers diplomatically addressed the

"Cherokee problem" to our leaders while ordering troops into the forests to slaughter our warriors and burn our villages.

Yes, *they* wanted to civilize *us*.

Christian missionaries encouraged by federal authorities taught us American words to help us progress from savages to colonials. Along with the word of their God, they taught our men to farm, to plant crops in rows on plantations using slaves. Our women learned to spin and weave.

The words of the Presidents, and those who followed, were contrary to their actions when the states encroached on our tribal lands. Engorged with greed, Georgians asked why the Cherokee should live in fine cabins on farms and plantations, amid rich hills filled with gold.

Early on we traded peltries for goods that made our lives easier: knives, gunpowder, and muskets; iron hoes and plows to till our corn and cotton, so much lighter and more durable than stone; stroud and calico to cover our bodies, simpler to wrap and sew than scraping and tanning deerskin. Trade goods made our lives easier, but oh, the price we paid when white traders included whiskey with the deal.

Greed. Trade. Whiskey.

For decades my Ridge family and other leaders battled with words against the Presidents, but we lost. In the final moment of accepting the government's promises, we believed our truth. Principal Chief John Ross, as I shall tell you, believed his. History most often is viewed through the eyes of the victors; my family's story has been told and retold from a partisan point of view. I now tell you *my* truth about those times.

We, the Cherokee—the Real People—we claimed our mothers' blood. Women owned the lineage. We owned the lodges. We owned the crops. We planted, we harvested. We were the traders—until European merchants refused to accept women as trading partners. We chose our warrior husbands and if later we chose to go our separate ways, we placed his blanket and belongings outside the door; he returned to his mother's lodge with only those items he had brought into the union. His children remained and always, always we—the mothers, the grandmothers and aunts—*we* guided the lives of our children and they inherited our blood.

I now share with you these recollections of my life and loves, my cohorts and enemies, and the tumult that unfolded around me as I aged. I beseech you to open your eyes to buried truths.

Some of these stories I lived, others I learned by questioning. All are *my* truth. You may conclude your own.

Listen, listen. The leaves crackle like parchment.

Chapter 2

Gado Alitelvhvsgv

Oothcaloga Settlement, Cherokee Tribal Lands

Northwestern Georgia

December 16, 1811

The warning of a screech owl fractured the frigid night.
    In the third hour before dawn mid-way through *vsgiyi*—the cold moon—daytime animals roused to sense a restlessness already disturbing their neighboring night creatures.

In the pen beyond the cabin the buckskin mare slowed her pacing, then stopped. Starting again, she placed one tentative hoof after another as if walking on a frozen pond. Again, she stopped. A wretched groan rolled up from the depths of her gut as she hung her head, then spread her legs to keep from falling.

Sharp yaps from the yellow hound guarding the pigs changed to a mournful howl. Echoing through the darkness, the howl blended with the horse's groans. Pigs snorted and shuffled and dug their hooves into the muck.

In the orchard tips of young peach trees fluttered. Tiny waves ruffled the surface of Oothcaloga Creek, located near that area where the state of Georgia abuts Tennessee. Canebrakes lining the creek began to rustle, their tops whipping together as if buffeted by a windstorm.

7

There was no wind.

On a rise near the creek sat the cabin—not a pole lodge of the old Cherokee way, but a sturdy log house built in the manner of the white man with a coveted glass window in front. Inside the progressive home slept a progressive Cherokee family: the mother, Susanna, also known as Sehoya, a woman of the Wild Potato Clan, and her warrior husband of the Deer Clan, no longer called Kahnungdatlageh but The Ridge, whose name early European traders translated from the man who walks on mountains. The couple, in embracing the white man's manner had put aside their children's tribal birth names calling them in the new way: Nancy, ten; John, approaching eight; and little Walter—Watty, Susanna called the child who was her blessing to take away her sadness when another baby born after John had died. Watty though, now almost two, was not right, not right in learning to walk and speak as did his older sister and brother. And now within Susanna, another baby grew.

Alerted by the animal calls, Susanna awoke. Shifting her position, she touched her rounded belly as if to reassure the child quickening within that the strange sounds filling the air were merely rumbles of wagon wheels on a road passing over river stones.

But there was no nearby road.

When the earth could no longer contain its quivering, the *gado alitelvhvsgv,* the earthquake, exploded from its depths. The cabin trembled, then shook. A smoldering log rolled from the hearth onto the floor. Chimney stones loosened and tumbled. The Ridge jumped from bed. Susanna sat up. High-pitched screams from her children sliced through the deafening roar that filled the air like thunderous war drums.

The floor fell away as Susanna ran across the room. Panes in the window near the children's bed imploded. Nancy rolled onto the floor, crawling toward her mother, her hands and knees bleeding. Grabbing for support from the spinning wheel, John tried to stand but his legs crumpled beneath him. Watty screamed from his pallet.

The Ridge shouted for his family to get outside. He shoved the log back into the hearth, beating sparks from a smoldering braided rug.

Susanna seized Watty, carrying him toward the door just as it pulled away from the frame and fell open. Nancy grabbed John. Planks in the floor pitched and parted. Gathering her brother in her arms, Nancy ran out into the yard. Behind her, Susanna stumbled under an avalanche of roof shingles. Batting them away, she clutched Watty and ran to the cornfield, drawing her children around her.

A great *crack!* broke through their terror. Chickens fell from their limb-roosts in a shower of feathers and squawks. The upper trunk of an enormous white oak separated as if cleaved by a tomahawk. A smaller section began to lean and toppled toward the cabin. Susanna screamed, pleading with her husband to come out.

Falling, crawling, pulling the now-flaming rug, The Ridge reached the cornfield just as the porch roof disappeared beneath a limb. Stomping fire from the rug, he turned his attention to his wife and children. The family clung to each other as the land rocked and shook beneath their feet.

Four hundred miles west of the Cherokee settlement, the flow of the Mississippi River slowed and seemed to reverse. Uplifts in the mighty riverbed created a series of rapids near the earthquake's epicenter between Memphis, Tennessee, and the settlement of New Madrid in Indiana Territory just below the confluence of the Ohio River and the Mississippi.

The powerful quake rerouted the powerful river. Seismic uplifts created fissures, some five miles long; great bluffs of red clay tumbled into the water. From the river bottom, trees sunk for a century rose like dreadful corpses. Alongside the banks and even in the center flow, geysers—foul-smelling like rotten eggs—exploded into the air disgorging coal and sand, creating a pocked landscape of sand boils and craters twenty to thirty feet deep. Ducks and geese sought out keelboat masts and landed on the heads of horrified flatboatmen who cowered on deck in the deafening noise and turbulent water.

New Madrid residents were thrown from their beds. If they survived to run outside, they watched their cabins roll over or sink into the sand. For hundreds of miles around, cradles rocked and church bells rang. In the unmapped Indian country, unrecorded by white men for their newspapers, unknown damage ravaged the land. In Washington City, President James Madison and his wife Dolley woke to the clinking of clock pendula on glass door-fronts. From as far east as Boston came reports of chimneys cracking and chandeliers swinging.

In New Madrid during the day preceding the quake, it would be reported, the atmosphere had been dark and hazy with red clouds in the evening sky, a day unusually warm for December. As far back as August, the night sky had been lit by a bright comet with a split tail, one side straight, one side curved. Strange times. Prophesies abounded. Christian preachers issued warnings: Repent your sins! God will punish the wicked!

Upriver in Cape Girardeau, the Shawnee Tecumseh—whose name meant "panther passing across" because it was said that at his birth another great comet streaked the sky—recognized these warnings. He implored the Delaware and the Wyandot, the Potawatomi and the Miami: "Unite! Fight against the white man! Restore the ways of your ancestors!"

Fire in the sky. And now the earthshaking, the *gado alitelvhvsgv*.

The land of the Cherokee had at times trembled since the days when the Old Chieftain drew on his pipe and blew his smoke across the eastern mountains to veil them in blue haze, but never in the memory of the wise ones had such a rocking occurred.

Susanna closed her eyes, one arm cradling Watty and the other caressing her belly while Nancy and John clung to her nightdress. She invoked her ancestorial mothers and prayed to the God of whom the Springplace missionaries read stories from their book. Her husband begged the benevolence of the Great Spirit. All through the darkness of early morning, the earth rumbled. Dawn brought another shock, more fearsome than the first.

As tremors rocked the land beneath his feet, The Ridge remembered last month. He and other Cherokee leaders had gathered at the Creek town of Tuckabatchee with Choctaw, Chickasaw, and Seminole. They had told Tecumseh not to include Cherokee warriors in an alliance against the white man. The council had advised the Shawnee orator not to visit their people with his message of tribal unification. An angry Tecumseh threatened to stomp the mountaintops.

The Ridge did not believe this *gado alitelvhvsgv* was Tecumseh's promised earthshaking, his signal that the time had come to repel the white invaders in full-out war—

Or was it?

Three weeks into January—*unolvtani*, the moon when the cold wind blows—another violent quake struck the Oothcaloga settlement. Powerful upheavals created writhing creekbeds and shattered forests. The springs at the Moravian Springplace Mission went dark and failed to bubble; sinkholes filled with green water. Days and nights grew long while the Cherokee lived outside, afraid to rebuild their homes, moving into caves or broken cabins away from thunderstorms and flooding cloudbursts. One day was so warm they un-barred their windows; the next saw a frigid snowstorm.

Then two weeks later in early *kalagi*, the greatest earthquake yet destroyed what remained of New Madrid and crumbled the remaining chimneys in St. Louis. It swallowed a Shawnee village in Tennessee; it submerged the woods and people beneath a lake that white men would name Reelfoot.

One evening the sky darkened over the Cherokee wilderness at Oothcaloga like the draping of a black shawl; in the west was a small white stripe on the horizon. From the east shined a red light that lit the land like a full moon. Why? Why these warnings from the Great Spirit? It was said that these signs appear before a great day.

Rumors ran rampant. Prophets promised storms of hail the size of rivercane baskets.

Medicine men and the tribal beloved woman spoke at council meetings. Word passed along streams and into the hills that the Great Spirit of the Cherokee was troubled and was shaking the land with his wrath. His children had displeased him. They had taken the ways of the white man.

"The *yonega*—the white man—is different from us," the medicine men said. "He signs his name to treaties and says he will keep the promises for as long as grass grows and water flows. Then he does as he wishes and takes our land. We cannot trust him."

"We, the *ani yvwiya*—the Real People—are made from red clay, firm and hard," they sang as they danced around their council fires. They made promises: "The *yonega* is made from sand and will wash away."

But the white man did not wash away and the Real People did not go back to their old ways. The land of the Cherokee continued to experience upheaval as the lives of the people were torn apart with change.

The earth shook again one night a few months later, but this quaking was brief. Inside the re-braced cabin beneath the cleaved white oak, Susanna's mother and four midwives—the *adagatidisgi*—attended her, assisting her own tremors. The women spooned blue cohosh steeped in warm water to speed their sister's delivery; they pulled inner bark from wild cherry trees and boiled a tea to ease her pain. Susanna leaned against the footboard of the cedar bed and squatted on a deerskin, pressing her baby from her body into her mother's hands, the tiny corded frontside and wrinkled face upturned. A good sign: an infant who fell onto its breast was a dark omen, but Susanna's good fortune prevailed.

Now they handed her the child of her body.

The Ridge stopped his pacing near the porch and raced inside at a call. He smiled at his wife, stroked her sweat-soaked hair, and gently touched his child's forehead. Old Kate Wickett, Susanna's mother, welcomed him as the midwives and her other daughter Betsey Lassley finished swaddling the birth remnants in the deerskin and tied the packet with a beaded strap Old Kate had woven. With a blessing from the midwives, Betsey handed the packet to her brother-in-law. Following the old tradition, The Ridge received the remnants and left the cabin. He picked up a spade from the porch and walked across the hill to bury the bundle—not so deep that no more children would be born.

With her other three children secure nearby in their aunt's cabin, Susanna, surrounded by women of her clan, smiled at the child in her arms. A girl. In a week—if her baby lived—Susanna would bestow her daughter a Wild Potato Clan name, Sollee, and a name in the white man's manner: Sarah. To family, she would be Sallie.

The day of her birth unknown and the year uncertain, family lore recounts that Susanna's daughter was born during an aftershock of the great earthshaking, an omen that would foreshadow Sarah Ridge's tumultuous life.

Chapter 3

Listening & Learning

Oothcaloga Settlement

September 1818

"Our Nancy has left us to be with her Little William. Come. We gather in the woods to say *donadagohvi*." Until we meet again.

Sallie woke to a cascade of Cherokee words rippling from the foot of her bed. Back-lit by the sun, her mother seemed to float on the morning's rays. Crawling from beneath the quilts, she burrowed into the warm folds of her mother's calico skirt. In this her sixth *dulisdi*—the moon when leaves turn red and breezes blow cool—she shivered with cold and the chill of dread: Nancy was gone.

During her sister's days of bleeding, Sallie gathered chokeberries in the woods with Aunt Betsey and helped her spoon the black juice into Nancy's lips to thicken her blood, stop it running out. The women gathered, some chanting to the Great Spirit, others praying to the missionaries' Jesus. With her eyes closed, Sallie pleaded with Nancy not to leave, not to join Little William, her baby who had come to her asleep and who neither Susanna nor the *adagatidisgi* tending her sister could wake.

Clinging to her mother, Sallie remembered how the family had cried last year when her baby sister Jane had sickened with a hot, wet fever and melted away.

"Where is everyone, *Etsi?*" She used her loving name for her mother.

"Everyone is downstairs," her mother said. "Flying Bird is here. And your Watie cousins. We must get you ready."

"Is Stand here?" Her cousin Stand Watie as twelve. He and his brother Buck who had gone far away to the missionaries' school were the sons of her father's brother.

"No. We hear that the fever is upon Stand at Springplace. Your Uncle David and Aunt Susie with Dawnee and Thomas are here, but they soon leave to bring him home."

As Sallie folded her sleeping blanket her mother took from a peg her tunic of tiny gingham flowers, red with green leaves. Tying the drawstring at the neckline, Susanna stroked her daughter's dark skin, so like her father's and much darker than her own. Sallie stepped into her skirt—her favorite, woven by Etsi in red with stripes between browns and greens—and drew the waist-string tight.

Her mother completed the girl's ceremonial dress: a long blue scarf tied above her hips; a small headscarf of amber flax intertwined with ornaments and loops of trailing beads falling above Sallie's ears and down across her thick black hair; a necklace of silver medallions threaded with freshwater pearls.

Susanna went back to the cherrywood chest and removed Sallie's best doeskin moccasins, ones she had softened and sewn to decorate her younger daughter. Tall and beaded in red and blue patterns with circles of tiny snail and mussel shells, the shoes spoke with a voice of their own.

Sallie stomped her feet and the shells rattled. "I can dance for Nancy."

Her mother smiled a sad smile. "Yes. We go now to the woods where we buried Jane and Little William, to lay Nancy next to her baby. Flying Bird will sing and dance."

"Is William coming with us? Or is he broken?" Yesterday Sallie overheard William Ritchie, Nancy's white husband, speaking his ragged Cherokee words, telling Father that if Nancy died his heart would break.

"William will go with us." Sallie followed her mother down the stairway feeling as if she were stepping into a forest of family and friends.

Leaves of words fell around her. A man in tribal dress whom Sallie had not seen before addressed her father as Major Ridge, the name General Jackson gave him when he came home from fighting the Creek Red Sticks. "The time is not right," Sallie heard her father say as she passed him in the main hallway. "We must first mourn our daughter's passing, John Jolly. Come again in seven days."

Sallie looked up in time to see her mother give the chieftain her angry face, then Susanna bent close and said, "Watty will need you beside him today. He's in the parlor."

Winding her way through the people forest, Sallie found her older brother sitting in the horsehair chair near the mantelpiece. Watty smiled his happy smile; he was thick of body with heavy brows, his complexion was dark like hers. Outlined by the mantel's colors of deep red and turquoise, he looked to Sallie as if the sun had set behind him, leaving the bright greenish flash as it fell.

Whispered word-leaves now falling around her were attached to her brother's name: "Feebleminded." "Slow." Watty, although six years older, was in many ways younger than she. As his overseer when their mother was busy Sallie leaned in close, her Cherokee words precise. "We're going up the hill," she said, "to say *donadagohvi* to Nancy."

He rose. Towering over his sister, his black eyes as dark as hers, his full lips parted in a grin as Watty said, "*Donadagohvi* to Nancy."

"Yes." She straightened his loose muslin tunic, brushed dirt from his tannin-dyed breeches, and retied his moccasin strings. Taking Sallie's hand, Watty lumbered behind her to where their older brother John stood on the porch.

The contrast between brothers could not have been more startling. At fifteen, John Ridge was slim and pale of complexion with gray eyes and dark brown hair that lay in waves, not thick and mane-like as his sister and brother. He wore a white cuffed shirt tucked into gray breeches, those tucked into tall boots.

As Sallie and Watty approached, John shifted his weight to his good leg and pulled himself upright. Frail since birth, as a child the skin on one hip had developed a mottled, bluish-purple mass. The accompanying fever, chills, and weight loss had taken its toll on the boy. Susanna had treated him with a soothing ointment made from the root of bear corn and prohibited John from eating turkey meat since the wattles on a gobbler's head resembled the splotches on his hip. A white doctor passing through had diagnosed the ailment as scrofula, a tubercular condition often seen on the neck and face. Charles Hicks, a family friend and fellow council leader with Sallie's father, also walked with a limp from the condition. Like Hicks, the educated second principal chief who served as *linkister*—official translator for his people—John was his father's dream of an educated son. Although Major Ridge accepted Watty's incapacity, his son's slowness tested his patience.

In times past the mother of a deformed or weak infant would take her babe into the woods and leave it. Life was for the strong, the warrior, the trackers of deer, the tillers of corn. To keep the clan safe and whole was crucial. As guardians of the lineage, women decided whether the child of a woman's body survived. After acquiescing to the white man's world, though, tribal councils replaced the old truths with new ones and wrote laws prohibiting infanticide.

On this day Susanna's remaining three children prepared to say farewell to her fourth. They walked across the porch and waited beneath the old cleaved white oak, still standing as a reminder of the earthshaking, still shading the rebuilt and enlarged cabin, now a two-story log and clapboard house with glass windows, the center dogtrot hallway enclosed with solid doors. About a dozen or so families lived on separate farms within the hills and woods known as Oothcaloga, near where that creek merged with the Connasauga River, then the Oostanaula, which in turn merged with the Coosa some twenty miles south.

"They're coming!" Sallie said, squeezing Watty's hand to make him stop squirming.

Susanna and Major Ridge walked to the far end of the porch near the wagon where Nancy lay. Her aunts had washed her slender body with a cleansing essence of boiled willow root, then wrapped her in a fine winding sheet Susanna had woven and dyed from goldenrod blooms and walnut bark. The lid of the coffin had been tapped down with but a few nails. In the old way of burial, Flying Bird, a wise and revered woman, and Adohi, a medicine man, would sing chants. In the new way, Charles Hicks' brother William would read from the missionaries' book.

Lithe and graceful, Susanna wore a calico tunic and skirt she had sewn and a cap-like headdress beaded in a row of small silver loops; ropes of colorful beads and silver draped from her neck, hoops from her ears. She of amber complexion and blue-gray eyes harkening back to a Scottish trader ancestor walked in moccasins.

Major Ridge, tall with his head held high, took his wife's hand. Dark of complexion with black eyes, he was dressed in an Army uniform. A blue short-cut jacket edged with gold braid topped his gray pants and high black boots; a tall beaver hat topped his head above gentle waves of black hair. Following his warrior years with General Andrew Jackson at the Battle of Horseshoe Bend on the Tallapoosa River while fighting the Creek, Susanna's husband chose the officer dress of the Americans to augment his once-assigned military rank.

The couple, in their late forties, epitomized the changes the Cherokee faced.

They valued education, yet neither could read nor write. They sent their children to mission schools but spoke Cherokee at home. They owned a dozen black slaves and no longer worked the fields, having learned to live where land was cordoned off. Susanna and Major Ridge were the bridge from the past to a future generation, one that would not roam the forests they hunted and tilled in their youths.

The medicine man came now and led Sallie and her brothers to their parents. Dressed in deerskin leggings and a bright woven vest and shirt, his turban wrapped tight and silver bands hanging from his slotted earlobes, Adohi walked to the horse and caught the lead.

The family stepped behind: William Ritchie and the Ridges, the Waties, the Parrises, the Lassleys, the Fields. Friends: the Hicks, the Vanns, the Browns, the Walkers. Following came the black slaves: Doll, Big Tom and Little Tom; Luther and his wife, Lucinda, and others who worked the Ridge farm. A medley of dress, ages, and skin tones, the chanting procession followed the wagon up the bluff to the woods where Nancy would again be near her baby.

Major Ridge and William lifted the coffin from the wagon bed and leaned it on the pile of fresh red soil next to the tiny mound raised only the week before. Sallie leaned into Susanna's skirt as the grieving mother began a doleful lamentation. Other women joined in.

"*Ah que tsa. Ah que tsa.*" "Oh, my daughter. Oh, my daughter." Birds stopped their chatter as the woods echoed the haunting chant. Adohi raised his gourd filled with pebbles and shook it to the beat of the lamentation. Singers sang and Flying Bird danced in a small circle, her green tunic swinging over her doeskin skirt, mussel and turtle shells on her moccasins and around her neck bouncing. Up and down, the medicine man's rattling gourd kept time. Then with a *hiss*—the net of beads quivering against the gourd—all were silent.

Adohi lifted a large wooden bowl filled with water and offered it first to William, then to Susanna and Major Ridge, John, Sallie, and Watty. Dipping their hands into the bowl, each rubbed them together and then rubbed their faces, washing away tears and the past. Sallie made sure Watty followed the ritual as she and John did. The medicine man moved through the crowd of mourners as all repeated the ritual.

Flying Bird took Sallie's hand and led her near the coffin. Reaching back for Watty, Sallie pulled him along. John stayed with his father as Susanna stood beside Adohi while he removed the nails and pried open the pine box, then leaned the lid against a tree. Again, the ceremonial gourd hissed and the chant began; women's voices filled the silence. "*Ah que tsa. Ah que tsa.*"

At Adohi's direction, all were silent. With tears trailing her face, Susanna reached into the coffin and unwound the sheeting from Nancy's right arm. Sallie glimpsed skin no longer the clear red-tan of a piney stream. With loving tenderness, Susanna lifted her daughter's gray-brown hand and shook it as if in welcome or, in this ritual, *donadagohvi*. Holding Nancy's arm above the edge of the box, Susanna stepped back beside the coffin. William and Major Ridge moved forward and each bent to shake one last time his wife's and daughter's hand. John next, then Flying Bird directed Sallie and Watty. Watty grabbed his sister's hand in both of his, smiling and saying, "*Donadagohvi*, Nancy."

Knowing mourners did not utter the name of the deceased at a burial, Sallie glanced at her mother. Susanna smiled and nodded her head as if adding a blessing to her son's innocence. Adohi scowled Watty's way but said nothing.

Reaching forward Sallie grasped not the gentle warm hand of the sister who had tied her ribbons and fed her, who threaded her needle and brushed her hair. Instead there was a coolness she'd never known, fingers with no softness, a hand that did not grasp back. Sallie shivered. Stepping back, she clutched Flying Bird's warm hand as the line passed by, each shaking Nancy's hand in their final farewells until they would meet again.

Replacing the lid, Adohi tapped in nails with a stone. Uncle David Watie stepped forward and he and others lifted the coffin and lowered it into the grave. Adohi again took his gourd, raising and lowering it in a haunting rhythm. Flying Bird danced a mournful, slow beat, chanting to the cadence. Each mourner again passed the grave, picking up a handful of dirt and dropping it into the hole. Sallie heard the soil hit like rumbles of distant thunder. Taking Watty's hand, she led him back beside their brother.

Uncles and friends removed hoes and shovels stashed behind trees and filled the grave. Susanna, her farewell made, turned and with her husband led the group back to the house.

Guests overflowed the dining room and parlor, into the hall and out onto the porch. The traditional ceremony now completed, Susanna asked William Hicks to read from the missionaries' book for the sake of Nancy's Christian husband and her own growing education in the stories from the Bible, as well as for other friends and family who believed in the new stories.

Feeling like a sapling in the forest where she was pushed behind Watty into a corner, Sallie listened to Mr. Hicks' English words, then his Cherokee.

She quit trying to follow the words and looked up through her people-forest thinking about roasted venison. Everyone here, she thought, will eat our feast. Doll's been cooking for days and she had Lucinda stripping beans and baking sweet potatoes. Aunt Betsey and the girl cousins will all stay here. Mother said for another seven days while we sing to Nancy, others coming as they wish.

". . . these shall go away into everlasting punishment, but the righteous into life eternal. Amen."

That word means the end. Good.

Huzzahs and grunts, cheers and smiles. William Hicks closed his Bible.

Sallie gave Watty to John and went up to her room. Lying across her bed she felt again Nancy's cold hand within her own, and she cried.

Chapter 4
Words & Letters

Oothcaloga Settlement

September 1818

For a week following the funeral relatives and friends sat cross-legged on the front porch at Sallie's house, singing and chanting or silent as they mourned Nancy and her baby. The Great Spirit also cried. Rain poured for days, heavy with flooding. Finally everyone went home. Today was clear and warm and Sallie played alone on the porch.

"Stay right here, Nancy. I'll make a Little William for you." Sallie held a little corn husk doll Watty had tried to make for her. His knots of twine would not stay so she had retied the neck and waist using her mother's quilt scraps. Through the open parlor window, she could hear the voices of her father and his chieftain friend.

Barefoot, Sallie tiptoed off the step, found an acorn cap under the oak and scooped a finger-full of rich red clay. Back on the porch she took a walnut from a basket near the door and returned to her play area under the window. She filled the acorn cap to overflowing with mud, pressed it against the top of the nut, and anchored it. Then she tied another scrap around the walnut.

"Here's your baby, Nancy." She laid the cornhusk doll on a piece of calico she had stitched as a tiny quilt and nestled the walnut next to it.

"No one will play with me today," she complained to her sister-doll, not whining just thinking aloud. "Doll and Lucinda are in the kitchen making a big supper. Mother and Aunt Betsey took the wagon to Flying Bird's house to meet with the women. They're writing an important letter and will come back later to finish it here.

"John's writing a letter, too. To Cousin Buck in Cornwall, to tell him Father asked the missionaries if they will send him away to school in Cornwall, too. We're all waiting for a letter to come. John's so happy. I don't want him to go away.

"Watty wanted to brush horses so John quit writing and took him to the stables. John told me since that was Watty's favorite thing and since this might be the last time they could play before he goes away, then he would brush with him. Everybody's busy. And you're gone." Sallie stretched her apron across her knees, smoothed the little quilt, and laid her dolls side by side. "Are you happy wherever you are? Next to your Little William?"

"You call on me to remove? How can you ask that, John Jolly?"

Angry Cherokee words hurtled out the window. Her father's voice.

"Last year you signed the treaty at the Hiawassee Agency that relinquished all right, title, and claim to an area of our lands for land given to those on the White River in the Arkansaw!"

"But Ridge, we have established the Western Cherokee Nation—"

"You gave up over a million of our acres! General Jackson and Agent Meriweather in this treaty provided for enrollment to remove to the Arkansaw. Those by signing accepted. The law of the Cherokee Nation deprives citizenship for whoever enrolls in the removal!"

"Yes. But the new Western Nation is thriving. The Arkansaw land is good!"

"That I do not deny, John Jolly. But it is dangerous talk. Dangerous for you to be here even now. Not after this summer's council. Any Cherokee who agrees to sell our common land without the approval of the entire council is subject to death. *That* is the law.

"To gain our land is the government's only ambition. Twice now I have traveled to Washington City for talks with the War Department and President Madison. They speak like the serpent with its split tongue."

A serpent is a snake! Sallie thought. Father talked with a snake! She lifted her dolls and scooted unseen nearer the window.

The chieftain's voice softened. "I know our nation's law, my friend. But you don't have to remove. In the treaty are provisions to grant citizenship in the states to those headmen who wish to reserve a six-hundred-forty-acre section in the states. Over three hundred heads of families signed. John Ross, his brother Lewis, many others. Even John Gunter signed to receive reservations."

"I know! But it is folly, my friend! Those brethren signed agreements for sections of land to occupy and enjoy permanently. Should they uphold that treaty they are no longer Cherokee, but Americans!"

Sallie soothed her dolls, silently patting them to reassure them—and herself. Words flew, but few landed; many she did not understand.

Her father's voice softened. "We have known each other a long time, my friend. We have fought together as brothers. I say to you now with sadness, what does citizenship mean for the Cherokee in the State of Georgia? In Tennessee and South Carolina? Nothing. Less than nothing.

"In those states we are men of color. Less than slaves as we have no owners who value us! Their laws say we like black slaves have no rights. We can own land and pay their taxes but we cannot vote, we cannot hold office, serve in the militia, or testify in court. Our children cannot go to public schools or marry their white children. Who in the federal government will enforce our citizenship in the states?"

"You call Jackson your friend, Ridge! If you believe him, you could own land on which to work your slaves."

"No. Cherokee do not own the land on which we walk. It is a gift from the Great Spirit. Think what that would mean to a poor warrior, now a farmer. The white man gives him whiskey and he signs away his farm!"

"The entail provides, Ridge. A life estate to pass on to his son! It keeps him from selling in his lifetime."

"Yes. So he dies and the white man gives his son whiskey—and *he* sells. Either method, our people lose their land. There has to be a better way."

"Ridge, no! You must look with open eyes. The white man will take our land no matter what promises they give. Come west, my friend."

"There will be great talk at our council meeting next month. We'll find a way to keep what is ours—our last remaining five million acres—for all of us. We shall remain here."

"We've known each other long, Ridge. I wish you well. My adopted son Sam Houston the Raven we can trust. Yet he holds little trust in his friend General Jackson who as well is your friend. We will welcome you and your family when you come to the Arkansaw."

Sallie jumped up as the front door opened and the men stepped out on the porch. Her father smiled, his voice soft. "My daughter, John Jolly. My little Sallie."

The chief was tall, as tall as her father but his complexion reddish brown to her father's dark brown. His red turban wound above his ears, his short and tousled black hair escaping beneath. Silver bands inlaid with turquoise looped through his earlobes. He adjusted his loose blue coat, woven with rows of browns and reds and trimmed on one side with a long white ruffle draped across his wide-collared white shirt. A wide red sash wrapped around his waist; his deerskin breeches were tucked into tall moccasins. Sallie thought John Jolly's troubled face looked like pictures the missionaries at Springplace showed her, pictures of their God's son only without the blood. Sallie knew her father's friend was a fine chieftain. But now they had argued and looked like sad friends, sad like everybody who missed Nancy.

Chief John Jolly smiled and nodded. "This daughter will grow tall like the daughter you lost, my friend. I wish for her a peaceful life."

Sallie's father hugged the man and walked him to where his horse was tied beneath the white oak. From her place on the porch, she heard her father wish him a peaceful trip blessed by the Great Spirit, then he walked toward the barn.

"All this talk of going to the Arkansaw. Where is the Arkansaw? I'll ask Doll. Maybe she'll let me pat out the bean bread for Mother and the women," she said to her dolls. Picking up Nancy and Little William, Sallie rolled them in their quilt and walked through the mud to the kitchen cabin.

After the women ate, Sallie helped carry the dishes out to the kitchen. Mother had told her friends how Sallie had made the bean bread and they all said how good it was while they filled up on ham smothered in honey, squash and onions, green beans, and baked apples. Now Mrs. Hicks, Aunt Betsey, Flying Bird, and many others, gathered again to talk about their letter. They moved candles to the center of the table. Mrs. Hicks set papers and quills and John's inkbottle before her.

"Nancy Vann Hicks who is our best scribe," Sallie heard her mother say, "will write in English the issues we discussed earlier. We'll present our petition at our next council and ask our leaders to carry it to Our Father President Monroe when next they travel to Washington City."

Other voices joined in, some with Cherokee and some in English words Sallie couldn't understand. She listened and whispered to her dolls until her full belly made her sleepy. Leaning against the stair banister she dozed, but awakened to hear Mrs. Hicks reading back her words in Cherokee.

"Beloved Children," she read, "we the women of the Cherokee Nation have met and counseled among ourselves over the many issues relating to our national affairs and concerning the welfare of our people. It is with great worry and sadness that we see our lands now being diminished to a tiny portion of those given to our ancestors by the Great Spirit. We have lived and raised our children on our common lands, but will we retain it for ourselves and our coming generations? The Cherokee were the first settlers. Our generation must not be the last. Therefore, we respectively petition our Great Chief Pathkiller, our headmen and warriors to hold out to the last and do not deny our children the right of their soil."

Sallie sat up straighter, her dolls on her knees. "Listen, Nancy. This sounds important," she whispered.

"We have through many years accepted the advice of Our Father the President to take on the ways of his white children. We have moved from our villages to farms, taken up the plow, and laid out our corn in furrows . . ."

Sallie's mother taught her the old way of planting the Three Sisters: corn in the center of a circled dam, beans next to it to grow tall and climb the stalks, squash and pumpkins around the edges to spread and bloom. But now straight lines surrounded cabins.

"...we pick our rows of cotton," Mrs. Hicks continued, "we card and spin our threads. We weave and work the loom and stitch our clothes. Some of us send our children to missionary schools to learn to read and write American words. We have followed Our Father the President's counsel and have done as he wishes as far as we are able.

"Yet the thought of being removed to the Arkansaw beyond the Great River fills us with dread. We do not understand how Our Father the President asks this of us, he who only a few years past gave us gifts of plow and hoe and said it was not good for his red children to hunt, that we must cultivate the land. Now he tells us there is good hunting across the Mississippi and offers us rifles and beaver traps, blankets, and brass kettles. He says we must become savages again and throw away our enlightened lives.

"This is wrong. We, the women, agree that we must hold our Nation in common for ourselves and our children's children.

"We ask Our Father the President to respect our people and acknowledge the path we have taken to advance our Nation. Protect us from those who would send us back to a savage state.

"We the undersigned unanimously offer this petition to the leaders of our Nation to hand to the Great Father in Washington City."

"Yes!" "*Ve-ve!*"

Sallie smiled as she heard the women agree with Mrs. Hicks' words. A shuffling of chairs. She watched her mother and all line up to take the feather quills and scrawl their names and make their marks on the parchment.

Hugging her dolls Sallie whispered, "Our land is safe, Nancy. I can always visit you and Little William on the hill."

Chapter 5

Another *Donadagohvi*

Oothcaloga Settlement

September 1818

A few days later John limped into his sister's room, his smile wide, his gray eyes sparkling. "Good news, Sallie! Brother Butrick received approval for me to go to Cornwall! Father convinced Mother that I could not get a better education than there so I'm leaving!"

Sallie jumped up and made a circle dance, then sat back on the edge of her bed. She blinked away the wetness filling her eyes. Nancy was gone forever and now John was going to a place so far away that it was only a word everyone used. Cornwall. Going to Cornwall. Last year their cousin Buck Watie went to Cornwall. He changed his name to Elias Boudinot.

"Will you change your name?"

"No, no. I'll always be John Ridge. Don't you worry. Cornwall is a great opportunity for me. I'll learn the ways of the whites and come back to our nation and help Father speak to Our Father the President. Someday I'll be Principal Chief John Ridge!"

ANOTHER *DONADAGOHVI*

Cornwall.

All of John's schooling—the years with the Moravians at Springplace, the months at Brainerd Mission, and the tutoring school in Knoxville—had not been enough to please his parents. Nor John himself. Major Ridge knew if his son was to become the tribal leader he and Susanna wanted—and who John wished to be—he would need to live among the whites and learn the subtle meanings of their ways.

The American Board of Commissioners for Foreign Missions School at Cornwall, so very distant in the northern state of Connecticut, offered that opportunity. Heathen boys the world over were brought to the seminary—from the Sandwich Islands and Ceylon, Siam, and Persia—to learn the Word of God. The Board's goal was for these young men to return to their homelands where they could convert their tribes and fellow heathen to the Second Great Awakening, the growing Protestant revival.

Last year the Board commissioned two missionaries Cyrus Kingsbury and Daniel Butrick to minister to the Cherokees, and sent them—adding soon William Chamberlin—to establish Brainerd Mission on the Tennessee side of the great river near Ross's Landing, some sixty miles from the Ridge's home. With the permission of the council, the missionaries were welcomed into the neighborhood. Cherokee living nearby began sending their children to the school, a few at first, then more. They helped the white men clear forty acres, and erect a sawmill and blacksmith shop, corn crib, and stables. In separate schoolhouses with dwelling cabins—one for boys and one for girls—the teachers instructed the children in reading and writing the English language; foremost the Word of God from the Bible. The boys worked to learn the rudiments of husbandry, plowing, and raising livestock; the girls spun cotton and linen into threads for their looms, stitched clothing, and knitted. Major Ridge and Susanna supported the school by enrolling John and Nancy.

When the missionaries found heathen boys who might be suited for the rigors of the ministry, such as Buck Watie and now John, funds were sent from Cornwall and arrangements were made to bring the candidates to the seminary.

With additional recommendations by Father and Mother Gambold at the Moravian Brotherhood mission school at Springplace, John received an invitation to join his cousin and a half dozen other Indian boys already there. Dr. Dempsey, a visitor to the Brainerd mission who was returning to Cornwall and who had presented a letter of reference from the mayor of New York, would oversee the boys on their trip.

Sallie lay in the wagon wrapped in a blanket. The day was cool this last week of September when the family drove to Springplace with John's horse tied behind. Susanna, with the help of Doll, Lucinda, and other house servants had spent the past week sewing new clothes for her son that were now packed in his father's valise. Lucinda's husband, Luther, who served as driver and linkister, guided the reins of the draft horses across rutted wagon trails to reach the Federal Turnpike, then on north to Springplace. Watty happily shared the driver's bench.

The trip, about fifteen miles, would have been shorter had father and son traveled overland by horseback or up the Conasauga River by canoe, but Susanna insisted on accompanying John as far as she could before she said her final *donadagohvi*. And, of course, bringing her other children. John would have to travel horseback for so many weeks, she said, and riding would be difficult with his ailing hip. He needed this part of the trip to be as easy as possible.

Looking up at the sky, Sallie watched cotton clouds swirl into shapes behind the points of loblolly pines; red dust stirred and settled. She had been to Springplace many times, she and Watty, with Mother when she took Nancy and John to school, walking or in the buckboard through snow and showers or clear days like today. Now amid rumbles and creaks, jangles and squeaks, she listened as her parents gave her brother instructions on how to conduct himself among the students and townspeople of Cornwall.

"Now, John." At the sound of Major Ridge's deep voice, Sallie could feel John sit up straighter on his cushion of blankets. Her mother, next to her father on the back-facing bench behind Watty and Luther, moved her hand to Major Ridge's leg and patted him gently as if to remind him to keep his lecture on a positive basis. "You will see sights we have only heard of in your cousin Buck's . . . uh . . . Elias's letters. The teachers at the Cornwall School are welcoming, accustomed to foreign boys, the Cherokee, Choctaw, Abnaki boys—"

"Yes, Father, and the Chinese and Hawaiians. Now they have two boys from islands called the Marquesas, Elias wrote me. I haven't found a map with those islands on it—"

"From all over the world the boys come," his father continued. "They come to learn the gospel of the missionaries, but also to learn American ways. It will be important for you to watch your white teachers. Mingle with the townspeople whenever you can. Walk through the town, observe the shops, the tradesmen, and especially the printer. You and Elias must visit with him whenever you can. Also with lawyers and merchants. Your English is gaining depth, but you must improve it. You, my son, and Elias represent the future for our people. My dream is for us to establish a new capital town for the Cherokee Nation with a Council House for meetings, a building to seat our Supreme Court, a shop with a printing press for a newspaper to keep our people informed of their Nation's business. It will be the center of the Cherokee."

"Yes, Father. I'll learn all I can. I'll come home to help you save our nation."

Susanna leaned forward and patted John's shoulder. "And learn you must. Pay close attention to your studies and your health, my dear son. If you were merely going away to make your fortune I would never give my permission. But you're going to this distant country to further your knowledge of white ways. Listen to your teachers. And above all, listen to your heart."

At Springplace the missionary couple John and Anna Rosina Gambold—Mother and Father, the Cherokee called them—welcomed the Ridges. After a small feast, the family walked across a meadow from the mission to visit their friends the Vanns. Up close, the red brick house with its tall white columns frightened Sallie. How could anything be so big? Inside was better. She saw the bright yellows and greens, blues and reds that her father also had used for their parlor.

Coming back from visiting Mrs. Vann, they could hear the revelry of whiskey drinkers coming from Vann's tavern on the Federal Turnpike. Sallie had heard the story of how years ago Mrs. Vann's husband James, notorious for his whiskey-drinking rages, stepped out of Tom Buffington's tavern near the Chattahoochee River one night. A man hiding in the woods shot him! Joseph Vann, his son, now ran the plantation and tavern here. Each night the Gambolds prayed for the souls of the nearby whiskey drinkers, but the Vanns helped support the mission with their funds. Tavern money aided the good missionaries.

At nightfall, lying on her pine straw pallet as everyone slept nearby, Sallie kept squeezing her eyes tight, willing them to stay shut. On the wall above her hung the large painting of the man the missionaries called Jesus the Son of God. Oh, the blood! A big stream of blood ran out of a hole in his side. He was nailed to a tree and blood dripped from his hands and feet. Someone had wrapped a turban of thorns around his head; blood ran down his sad face. Every time she came into the mission house, she covered her eyes. The missionaries told about him, the man of five wounds who can save your soul. Now Sallie knew blood kills: blood ran out of Nancy and she died. Poor man! Sallie tried to forget him, forget Nancy, forget they would leave John at Springplace and he would go away.

When morning came, Sallie stayed close to John, wishing he wouldn't leave. Mother had told her she did not know how long he would be gone, but it would be a long time.

Tomorrow three boys and their sponsor would head toward the Moravian town of Salem in North Carolina to deliver letters from the

Gambolds, then to Philadelphia and New York, and on to Cornwall in Connecticut, a trip of over nine hundred miles. But not to Washington City to meet President Monroe, as cousin Buck did last year. That group of heathen boys also stopped in New Jersey to meet the president of the American Bible Society who had served as president of the Continental Congress. Now an old man, Elias Boudinot was so impressed with Buck that he invited him to take his name.

This trip would be three fifteen-year-olds: John; George Vann, Joseph's younger brother; and Dawzizi, a full-blood Cherokee student of the Gambolds, who, though poor, was given funds from the Brainerd missionaries to go to Cornwall. The Gambolds, Major Ridge, and "Rich Joe" Vann entrusted the boys' money to Dr. Dempsey as their keeper.

As the family stood near the mission barn, Dawzizi ran to them, homespun tunic flopping, his cropped hair tousled and his dark face aglow. "The dear Savior blesses me again! I had no saddlebags so I made a sack for my clothes. But this morning a traveler passing told me he needed money and sold me his new saddlebags for only a dollar! But still, I needed a halter for my horse. And riding over today I found a halter in the woods! I am so blessed!" Tears of joy poured down his face as Mother Gambold embraced him.

Brother Butrick, just arrived from Brainerd, immediately removed his wool drab-color short coat. He gave that to the boy and as well his pocketbook. Joseph Crutchfield, the overseer for the Vann's plantation ran back to his house, bringing with him a checkered hunting vest and breeches of his own. Mother Gambold returned from her cabin with two shirts and pantaloons the mission kept for boys in need.

Susanna took leave of the group. Walking with John to the spring at the foot of the meadow, she said *donadagohvi* to yet another child. Knowing she might never see her son again, she wept as she gave her final blessing and prayed to the Savior for his return.

Brother Butrick led a prayer service to bless the boys; Father Gambold read one last time from his Bible to the little group. Gathering around the wagon, the family readied to depart for home. Watty climbed in front, Sallie in the back. Susanna took a step forward, but Major Ridge touched her shoulder. "He'll be safe. Let him be."

His face beaming with excitement, John stood next to his friends with whom he would spend the next two years of his life. Not willing to let her brother see her tears, Sallie blinked them away. As the wagon pulled out for home she smiled and waved, secretly relieved that Father Gambold hadn't said anything about blood.

Chapter 6

A Friend Found

Oothcaloga Settlement

September 1818

No one spoke on the drive headed home, only the wagon with its dialect of squeaks and creaks and clatters. Sallie lay on the blankets, but the clouds above her were no longer of interest. Her parents swayed with the buckboard's bounces in the back-facing seat; Luther and Watty drove in silence.

Shortly after they turned off the Federal Turnpike onto the trail toward home and bumped down the side of a draw, Watty's yell of warning shattered the forest.

"*Yo nv! Yo nv!*"

Luther jerked the reins and stomped the brake. Sallie rolled forward and hit the food basket; her parents bounced hard against the backboard. One horse reared and one lurched as Luther yelled and pulled the reins.

Her father grabbed his long gun and draped his powder horn and shot pouch across his chest. He jumped over the sideboard and ran toward the direction Watty pointed. The bear lay on a ledge in the tangled roots of a washed-out tree.

Everyone stared as Major Ridge stopped and loaded the flintlock. At a slow pace, he stalked the dark brown mound at the base of a scarlet-leafed tupelo.

The bear shrugged. Her father moved nearer, then stopped. With the bear in his sights, he aimed for the head.

But it had no head. It was a bearskin robe!

"Come out!" he called. "Show yourself!"

Luther repeated the order in English and grasped his tomahawk, poised to throw.

Sallie gripped her mother's hand as they watched. The bear moved; one human arm poked out, then another. Father reached over and jerked the pelt, revealing a young mulatto girl. She scooted against the tree while tugging at her ragged dress. She looked at the musket pointed at her, then at the wagon.

"Please dinnae shoot me, master! My wish ha' been to shelter here in th' hide, hoping somebody kind would come bye 'n bye. Are ye folks kind?"

Luther called from the wagon, "Yes, child. We are kind! Let the man help you!"

He repeated the conversation in Cherokee. Referencing a Scots trader who often came to the house, Luther added, "She does not speak like a slave girl. She speaks like MacLeish!"

Susanna climbed down and walked to the girl as Major Ridge backed away, looking around, suspecting a trap laid by bandits with the girl as bait. He ran across the draw and into the woods, hunting for danger.

Sallie stared as Mother offered her hand. The girl hesitated, glancing back at the tree. Then she put her hand in Susanna's and followed her to the wagon.

The girl looked to Sallie to be a bit older than she. Her tan calico dress was the color of her skin. Her hair was a dark tussled mass of curls and twigs; her eyes golden-amber like the sun just before it turns red and goes down. One sleeve was torn at the cuff, a darker sash tied her tiny waist, and her skirt hem was dirty and ripped. She had no shoes.

"What is your name, child?" Luther asked.

"I'm called Lettie, sir. Me ma named me Violet, but I go by Lettie." Her English words were tinged with a Scottish lilt.

Susanna repeated the name she heard.

"Ask why she is hiding?"

Lettie answered Luther, but faced Susanna. With a quick curtsey and bow of her head, she rose and began her story. "Two cruel white lads bought a mess of us in Knoxville. Herdin' us to sell in Savannah. Me ma's fearsome ill. When we camped last night, she made me run off with th' bearskin. They hunted me for a time, but I hid good. Me ma told me to hide an' walk 'til I came 'cross a Cherokee place. They are kind to their slaves, she told me. I heard the wagon a'comin', so I slinked around in the bearskin to see yer. Yer looked like Injuns all dressed up. Are ye Cherokees?"

Luther answered, "Yes, Lettie, these folks are Cherokee. They're called the Ridges."

As Luther translated Lettie's story, Sallie saw her father return and circle the tupelo. He leaned over and touched something in the roots.

Lettie called out, "Och!" and ran to the tree.

Father raised his hand. "Ask her who is the baby?"

Luther translated to Lettie. Sallie waited, confused.

Major Ridge stood on the tupelo's tangled roots. Reaching around to the side he released a rivercane basket, long and tapered like a cradleboard. Sallie could hear what sounded like birds chirping.

Susanna ran to the tree and took the basket from her husband. Cradling it in her arms she moved the swaddling blanket and revealed a small face. Walking back, she smiled, gently running her fingers around the tiny mouth. As she pulled the sugar-teat from the infant's mouth, a loud wail filled the ravine.

Susanna anchored the cradleboard and told Luther to ask about the infant. Lettie stepped forward, took the baby, then swayed and caressed the baby as she continued her story. Luther relayed fragments to the family each time Lettie paused to wipe her tears on a fold of the green-and-blue plaid swaddling blanket. Sallie, too, wiped her tears as Lettie related a childhood so different from her own.

"Mistress Ridge, ma'am. Master Ridge, sir. Young Master. Young Lady. Mister Linkister. I stand before ye a lost lass holding me wee brither. We are perhaps by this time orphans.

"Me ma's story begins when she were brought from Scotland with Master MacKenzie's household some twenty years ago before me was born lo' these ten years. Master established an estate in th' hills outside of Knoxville an' there he lived 'til his untimely death two months past when falling as his horse jumped a wall whilst riding to hounds in chase of th' fox.

"Me ma were raised a house servant in Scotland until the owning of black slaves ended. Master came to buy his own land, he being the second son of a baron an' not to inherit as landed gentry. His mistress bore him several fine sons, but th' master had a special place in his heart for me ma. She being house-trained an' educated, from when I was born of him, he allowed me ma to teach me proper manners an' schoolin'.

"But when th' master passed, th' mistress told me ma, large though she was with th' master's child, that she could remain on the estate until the babe was born. Och, then! Just a few days after birthin', a slave trader came an' took us from our cabin. He drove us to Knoxville town an' there we were bid upon by th' two lads from whence I now escaped.

"Me ma was weakly, not well enough to walk. For some distance she rode in the merchant wagon, me walkin' beside. But she would bleed, pardon, ma'am, an' then her milk went dry. Th' mistress packed sugar-teats an' tobacco plugs to keep me wee brither quiet an' calm. But when he turned to cryin' from cravin', me ma held me to her, bid me farewell with love, an' sent me into the gloamin' last evenin' with me swaddled brither an' the bear hide. I know not how the cruel men punished me ma this morning, but I fear somethin' awful for her."

Lettie wiped her tears for the final time. Looking directly at Sallie's mother she said, "I am well taught an' can work in yer household. I can care for me wee brither. I'd be obliged to ye if yer will accept us, please?"

As Luther repeated Lettie's plea Susanna looked at her husband who nodded. The girl, though slim, had carried the cradleboard and heavy bearskin all this time. Such strength, such determination. So desperate. She told Luther to tell the girl she could live with them, and ask what was the baby's name.

"Robinson," Lettie replied. She reached into the cradleboard and pulled out a book. "Master gave me ma this volume to teach me to read. Th' wily an' shrewd ways the sailor Robinson Crusoe taught himself to survive on his island gave me ma th' idea to have me disguised as a bear. Only she may not have reckoned that bears get shot at."

While Luther described the story of a British sailor wrecked on a deserted island, Sallie looked at the green book, its leather worn, the gold embossing on the cover faded to brown. Susanna handed the book to her. Sallie opened it to lines of markings she hoped someday to read.

Putting the volume aside, Sallie guessed Lettie would be hungry and pulled some pork, a biscuit, and a jar of peach jam from the basket.

Susanna helped the girl and babe into the wagon. Cradling the baby, she dipped a finger-full of jam and touched the baby's mouth. He quit his crying and sucked her finger. With hands scratched and dirty, Lettie took the food Sallie held saying, "Thank ye." She smiled as she bit into the pork chop.

Sallie spread her blanket and helped Lettie settle in. Father stowed the bearskin at Watty's feet, then climbed next to Susanna and the baby. As Luther urged the horses up the bank, the girl tore the meat and took another biscuit Sallie offered.

Sallie looked at Lettie's pretty face, smeared with streaks long unwashed. Edging her way to the water jug, Sallie poured two cups. One Lettie quickly drained and from the other, Sallie soaked a rag and handed it to the girl to wash.

While the buckboard bumped along, Sallie imagined Lettie playing dolls with her on the porch, the two girls brushing horses with Watty now that John had left. Sallie felt she had found a friend.

But all the sorrow in Lettie's story! Her mama sold! With a baby and little girl! Now Sallie felt sad. She tried to picture her mother being sold. Oh! Sallie didn't understand. She had heard stories of how old

James Vann had been so cruel to his slaves, beatings, and whippings, but she had never seen anyone on a farm hurt a slave.

Mother and Father owned slaves. Many Cherokee planters did, as was the way of the white planters. On the farms where Sallie's family visited, black people—and mulattos like Lettie—worked in the fields or as servants in houses. But black people's color was a different dark than dark Indians like her father and herself.

We live in big houses and don't work so hard as black people do, she thought. I'll ask Mother to tell me why. What is a slave?

Late that evening after Doll and Lucinda took the new children to Doll's cabin, Sallie went to bed not so lonely. She was glad the sadness of John's leaving had been eased by the excitement of finding Lettie and Robinson.

Sleep, though, would not come. Happy thoughts of a new friend were erased by images of the big painting of Jesus at the mission. Last night it rose above her pallet; now it hovered above her bed. His bloody gash, his turban of thorns. The story of Lettie's mother added to Sallie's vision of Nancy and her days of bleeding.

Wrapped in her blanket, she walked quietly to the closed doorway of her parents' room and ended the night curled on the floor outside.

Chapter 7

Sarah Speaks

Oh, the terror of seeing the glorification of the Moravian God's son's bleeding wounds! It frightened me so, the blood in that painting—though I went on to see much blood spilled in my lifetime.

As you learn my story in the present days, I wish you not to have suffered life experiences that relate to blood. For the Cherokee, though, blood permeated our lives from the nomenclature of "full-blood" and "mixed-blood" to barnyard animals, chicken necks wrung and hogs stuck, to loved ones who died as did my sister and Lettie's mother or were brutally murdered. For all who lived in my times, life was brutal.

That night at the mission at six years of age, when I viewed the bleeding stab hole in Jesus' side—the church's focal point—was an experience that shaped the spirit of the woman whose words you hear as I speak to you from my grave.

You see, the Cherokee, having no conception of sin, could not comprehend how the Savior's blood would absolve us of our bad actions.

We believed blood belonged inside the body as did other fluids. We lived in a world of balance and order where blood possessed mystical powers. Menstrual periods were a time of awareness of a woman to be away from the tribe. Possessing heightened spiritual powers during this time, she went alone to a hut beside a stream to bathe and connect with her spirits. When a man shed blood it indicated death; when a woman bled it meant life.

We had the Blood Law. An eye for an eye in the Biblical sense. If a member of one clan killed—even accidentally—a member of another clan, then the victim's relatives had the right to punish the killer by taking his life. Call it revenge, call it justice, but through the ages the Blood Law represented balance. The spirit of the victim, without balance restored, wandered the land, unable to enter the peaceful forest. Belief in the Blood Law prevented feuds between the clans; accepting the inevitable restored balance.

A story:

A chieftain named Doublehead who held the position of Speaker of the Nation—a title my father later held—profited from a treaty he signed in 1796, ceding portions of our hunting grounds. His bribe was well known, shown blatantly with his two dozen slaves and his stable of fine horses. He was arrogant and insolent, and his unpopularity increased with every negotiation. Resentment against Doublehead built. His actions caused good men to die.

Then in August 1807, Doublehead beat his pregnant wife until she—and her baby—died. His wife was a sister to one of James Vann's many wives and that wife insisted that she would avenge her sister's death. She rode with Vann and others, including my father who was then a member of the Lighthorse Guard, riders who enforced Cherokee laws. The men were chasing Doublehead when Vann, so drunk he couldn't ride, fell off his horse. His wife stayed with him and she and Vann delegated my father and another man Alexander Saunders the honor of retribution without them.

They found Doublehead in McIntosh's tavern at Hiawassee where he had brutally taken yet another life, a man named Bone-Polisher. My father shot him in the head. But Doublehead wasn't dead. In the struggle that followed, Doublehead whipped out his knife. My father and Saunders shot him again. Both pistols misfired. Doublehead sprang. Father grabbed the knife and stabbed him while Saunders drove his tomahawk deep into the murderer's head. Retribution had been served.

But Father was Deer Clan, not of the Wild Potato Clan as were Vann's wife and sister, and as so not entitled to invoke the Blood Law. Father addressed the crowd that gathered saying the killing was retribution not only for Vann and his wife but also for Doublehead's illegal signing of treaties ceding tribal land. Those words would later return to haunt our family.

Blood, so much of it. Real and what I saw in the Gambolds' painting. That good missionary couple came to Springplace to save heathen souls through the blessed blood of their Savior.

The brethren were fervent Christians, members of a Protestant sect established in Moravia who immigrated to the British colonies along the Hudson River in the early 1700s to convert Mohicans. They later settled in Pennsylvania at Bethlehem, then moved southward, purchasing their large Wachovia Tract in North Carolina. The town of Salem rose as their religious center with a school for disciples' daughters from across the land.

For church decisions, they used a system called "The Lot," long practiced for almost every decision—great and small—that consisted of three sticks or pieces of paper placed in a bowl, one marked "Ja" for yes, the second "Nein" for no; the last remained unmarked, indicating the decision be deferred until later. The brethren considered each matter thoroughly, then laid it before God. As a brethren drew, God gave His sign through the Lot.

Springplace with its hodgepodge of white missionaries and travelers, black slaves, and red Cherokee was a vital component of our nation and to my upbringing.

Among the rites taught us at the mission, Mother and Father Gambold's baptismal ritual of immersion in water was familiar to us, we being a people of the streams and rivers. As children, we romped naked in the streams, much to the consternation of those good teachers. Their belief in washing away the ills of the world and making it clean was not hard for us to believe. Our women did this following their bleeding cycle.

But sin was difficult for us to grasp.

The Cherokee knew no shame. We had no word for it. We were a happy people, young and old. We danced and laughed. Some of the new and strange things the missionaries told us seemed ridiculous. When they spoke of their solemn and momentous subjects, they would later write in their diaries that we laughed like mere idiots. They didn't understand.

Shame and guilt; those burdens were taught us.

After Nancy died and John left, I remember my mother wanting to learn more of the stories the missionaries told. She'd been a casual participant in the mission for years, but after John left, she changed.

Later that year of 1818, Mother visited her friends the Crutchfields at the Vann farm. She and Peggy Vann Crutchfield—James Vann's long-suffering wife now remarried and a fervent Moravian convert—stayed up late talking heart to heart. Something happened. I guess the missionaries' Holy Spirit entered my mother.

I did not, I will say, experience a religious conversion until much later. Although Protestantism was woven deeply throughout my life, I was never swept up into the bleeding arms of the Savior as was Mother. Mother could not get enough of the talk while she cried and cried. The next day she and Peggy went to the mission and Mother Gambold joined the discussions. She gave Mother a small engraving of the crucifixion painting, Jesus bleeding on the cross.

When Mother came home and proudly showed it to me I ran and hid in my room. She never brought the picture out again but kept it out of sight in her and Father's bedroom. Over the next year, evidentially, the missionaries believed her heart fully contrite and on November 14, 1819, they baptized Mother at the spring.

With her contrite heart, did Mother abdicate her role as matriarch of the family? Or did she bring in a Spiritual Helper, perhaps yielding her single yoke for a double one? I don't know.

She continued to look after the farm and manage the house and slaves, even to the details of bringing Lettie and Robinson into the household and seeing that they attended local mission schools.

I learned then as a child of six about ownership of human beings. Mother told me slavery had always been a part of Cherokee ways—warriors brought back prisoners from raids on other tribes and later captured frontier trappers who killed our game and white settlers who stole our land. Prisoners became tribal possessions. When the Presidents encouraged the Cherokee to accept European methods of farming our people followed their system of buying black slaves for field hands and house servants. We did as they did. Slavery in my lifetime always *was*—until it wasn't.

Mother's Moravian conversion changed not only her life but mine, and changed the way she viewed my upbringing. She renounced and repented her traditional beliefs—Nancy's heathen burial—and sent me to the Moravians for instruction. I learned to pray before a portrait of a bleeding, suffering man.

Thus began my transformation into a little red-skinned white girl, a Christian girl, one who wore dresses and shoes and spoke German-accented English.

Yet my Cherokee soul remained within me.

Chapter 8

Eagles & a Raven

Tennison's Hotel, Pennsylvania Avenue

Washington City, District of Columbia

January 1824

Mud. Smelly mud. Everywhere. It stinks of dead fish and horse dung. No trails to go around. Not like on the paths from the Coosa to Springplace, or even the big Federal Turnpike, Sallie thought as she looked out the window of the hotel's drawing room. She pulled her tapestry shawl higher on her shoulders against the chill of the afternoon. The unceasing rain had not yet turned to snow.

During her long stage trip over the past weeks, the coachmen drove around the mud; when they got stuck they got out and cut limbs or dragged logs over it. But here in Washington City wagons and carriages, mules and horses churned the thoroughfares day and night. Although the streets were wide, boardwalks and buildings with new rows of planted trees formed dams on each side leaving rivers of mud.

So many buildings! John told her the story about the big war with the British ten years ago and how in August of 1814 the invading troops set fire to the city. The President's House and the Capitol building! The roaring blaze destroyed where the Senators wrote laws at the Capitol and burned all books and documents in the Library of Congress. The fire was so hot it reduced the marble columns in the Senate chambers to dust. Mrs. Dolley Madison and her servants barely saved the silverware and red draperies from her house! The invaders turned all but one of Washington City's major public buildings to smoking rubble. If not for a drenching rainstorm the entire Capitol building would have turned to ash.

As the stagecoach passed the sheep's meadow in front of the new Capitol yesterday, Sallie gasped at the size. The round domed roof shone like a shiny copper one-cent piece John carried, where the lady's headpiece spells "Liberty."

Tennison's Hotel was a long way up Pennsylvania Avenue from the Capitol, but close by the President's House and the houses of the War and State Departments. Her father and the others would meet with the President and his leaders. Sallie hoped they would give liberty to the Cherokee Nation, like on the shiny penny. Liberty from the thieving Georgians who wanted to steal Cherokee lands.

The delegation was writing their letter now. From her place on the settee Sallie observed her father, Speaker of the Council, in his blue major's uniform and the others: tribal leader, George Lowery; John Ross who was president of the National Committee; and Elijah Hicks as clerk. They addressed the letter to Mr. John Calhoun, Secretary of the War Department. The note would let the Secretary know that the Cherokee delegation had arrived and request a time for an audience to present him their credentials.

She looked at Elijah, their scribe. Such a dandy. Sallie smiled. His scarf was oak green and ruffled, his white shirt smocked. Although she could see the slit-like piercings through George Lowery's ears and nose, today he chose not to embellish himself with silver ornaments to compliment his tunic and turban, dark blue with tiny yellow leaves embroidered throughout. John Ross was dressed in simple white man's clothes, his pale, ruddy Scot's complexion evidence of his seven-eighths white blood. He spoke Cherokee badly. Luther, dressed in dark livery, stood near Father and translated as Elijah wrote.

Her brother John sat in a wingchair near the fire, his gray waistcoat unbuttoned. His hip was hurting, although he felt much better than when he came back from Cornwall two years ago. He left the loving care of the Northrup family to return home to heal. He had sailed from Connecticut to Charleston, but the remaining stagecoach trip inside the lurching and jolting carriage was painful. Everyone was aware that John was returning to Cornwall next week, but only the family knew he was going to ask Sarah Bird Northrup to marry him. Sallie loved holding that secret.

Elijah rested his quill and read the letter in Cherokee; Sallie was relieved that John's presence was mentioned. Father had instructed Elijah to write that she, Miss Sarah Ridge, had accompanied the delegation. He mentioned, too, that Colonel Thomas S. McKinney, their friend at the Indian Office, had recommended she be placed under the benevolent tutoring of a lady in the city. That would be Miss Corbett, Headmistress of the Quaker Girls' School who was sending one of her teachers, Miss Ashley, to tutor Sallie at the hotel. Father planned for Colonel McKinney to sponsor her schooling and arrange funds for her tuition.

Sallie's thoughts ran all over; she was excited and scared at the same time. At the Springplace and Oothcaloga missions, Mother and Father Gambold had been well pleased with how she had learned to read and write from their English Bible and reader books, but John said she must work hard to change the way her words came out of her mouth. Here she was, almost thirteen years old and she sounded like a little German girl! He worked with her when he could and forbade her to say, "*nein* and *ja*." No and yes from now on.

Lucinda was late arriving today. A drayman on Fourteenth Street almost ran her over and covered her with mud. Now she had to walk back to the rented shack near the canal to get her other skirt to wear.

So very sad, Sallie thought, that Lucinda and Luther had to stay so far away. Though to the family they were servants, here they were slaves unless they were freedmen. John had told Sallie that coloreds weren't allowed to live anywhere near the Capitol and fine houses unless their owners kept them in the cellars or attics. All the slaves working to build government offices and houses had to sleep in swampy shantytowns. The delegation's breakfast was cooked and served by slaves, but at night, they had to walk through the mud for long distances.

Another sadness passed over Sallie as she remembered how far she was from her home. "Etsi," she whispered, missing her mother's touch.

Mother continued to oversee tasks at their plantation, and they built cabins for all the field hands, no shanties. Farther downriver was Ridge's Ferry, where others worked. Ridge slaves numbered about thirty, all told, along with the house servants who lived near the kitchen of their new family home recently built near the area called Head of Coosa, on a bluff above where the white man George Lavender ran Father's trading post.

Within a clearing of sugar maples and chestnuts, John had overseen the carpenters and stonemasons. Sallie loved watching the way their old cabin had risen higher and higher into two floors with many rooms and windows, and covered in white-washed clapboard. John called their new home "a New England house."

Sallie was glad that John was sharing her room while he was here but wished Lettie could have come on the trip. Oh, how she would have loved seeing the city!

Lettie's colored, she thought, so she wouldn't be able to stay with me anyway.

Yesterday when Sallie opened the trunk of new clothing in her room, her fingers flew across silks and muslins and lace. Softest Morocco leather slippers and kid gloves! Mother had measured her and John had posted those measurements to the store where he had purchased a ring for his Sarah Bird. The dressmaker had stitched three frocks plus petticoats and chemises. Lucinda had placed the new attire in the wardrobe; Sallie managed to dress this morning, but John had to tie her backside lacing before he left for breakfast.

She fiddled with the tiny red ribbon that circled the neckline of her undyed muslin day dress. She'd picked this simple one to wear because Father and John said they'd remain in the hotel today writing letters and securing arrangements for meetings with the Secretary of War and the

Secretary of State, the man with the three names: John Quincy Adams. The Cherokee delegation would also be invited to present their credentials to Mr. James Monroe, Our Father the President.

Tomorrow, her father told her, the delegation hoped to go to the War Department building down past the President's House to meet Secretary Calhoun. But, come Wednesday, the dressmaker would return to fit Sallie's new dresses so she could accompany Father and John to Mrs. Monroe's evening soiree at the President's House! She would wear the saffron yellow silk gown under her dark green pelisses cloak, and her green silk slippers. Lucinda would braid her hair with ribbons and Sallie would wear her yellow velvet bonnet!

Sallie removed one glove and ran her hand across the crimson silk cushion of the sofa on which she perched, letting her fingers follow the embroidered eagle centered within a border of green laurel leaves. Threads of gold—a true gold and a rose gold—built up the image to where it seemed to Sallie that the eagle might fly. A golden flying eagle!

From now on when I see an eagle in the sky, she promised herself, I will remember this night at the President's House.

She looked up. No eagle flew amid the glittering chandeliers where beeswax candles flickered, but the ceiling was so high one could, she supposed. With walls that curved! She had never imagined a round room, though John corrected her saying it was but a half-round room named the Elliptical Saloon. Red velvet draperies bordered with loops of gold tassels fell across tall windows.

Just then a tall man leaned over her. "Why Miss Sallie. You have truly blossomed into a young lady since last we met." No eagle he.

"Our friend, The Raven," her father said in Cherokee as Sam Houston, now a congressman from Tennessee, lifted Sallie's ungloved hand and kissed it.

Smiling, she jumped up unladylike. Her glove fell to the floor. The Raven bent to pick it up and bowed to her when he placed it in her hand. Surrounded in the tall room by tall men, Sallie wriggled her fingers into her glove and busied herself buttoning the wrist, listening, glancing at the long-haired Raven as he spoke, his hands gesturing and blue eyes flickering, his cheeks flushed with enthusiasm ... or perhaps the rosiness of rum. From his visits and tribal stories Sallie knew him by his Cherokee name, *Colonneh*, the Raven. The storytellers sometimes used his other name, *Ootsetee Ardeetahske*, the Big Drunk.

Continuing his conversation with her father and John, Houston said, "I told my friend Congressman John Randolph of Roanoke, that you, John, reminded me of himself. You and Major Ridge here are not inferior to the white man in thought or action. Note those around us ... "

Sallie cringed as a stream of amber landed in a spittoon near the end of the sofa. A purported gentleman with slick-oiled hair chewed vigorously, his dirty white collar buffeted by his tobacco-stained chin whiskers. Next to him stood another man who had failed to wipe his boots and left clods of mud on the polished floor.

Earlier the room seemed regal, the ladies wearing gowns of colors Sallie never imagined as they stood beside their husbands: the secretaries of the government, the consuls and foreign ministers. But most had departed, as had John Ross and Elijah Hicks.

When her brother presented her upon their arrival, Sallie shook hands with President Monroe and his attractive daughter Mrs. Eliza Monroe Hay, receiving for her mother who, John had whispered earlier, was often infirm. Sallie thought Our Father the President a distinguished man and knew he was sympathetic to the Cherokee cause. Mr. Secretary Three-named Adams introduced the council members all around and inquired of the purpose of her accompanying the party to the Capitol city, to which she replied in precise words—hoping no tinge of German edged in—of her expectation for enrollment in the Quaker Friends School.

"So, John, how goes the ofttimes-turbulent process of requesting governmental appointments?" Houston asked.

Sallie noticed the muddy-boot man easing closer between her brother and Houston.

John, too, saw the eavesdropper slipping in and answered in Cherokee, "A great success thus far. We'll be received in two days by the President."

Sallie sighed. Now she could listen more easily.

"What will be your request?" Houston asked, glancing around and also shifting from English.

"We are authorized by our council," John answered, "to request an adjustment to the Compact signed in 1802 by President Jefferson and the State of Georgia."

John leaned in closer as his voice rose with frustration. "Colonneh, you know that the Cherokee did not sell our lands to Georgia! The Federal government *bought* Georgia's Yazoo lands for over a million dollars, lands Georgia had claimed—Creek and Choctaw lands—from the falsely-drawn Georgia line west to the banks of the Mississippi River. Bought the huge parcel from the Georgians and promised them they could have also our Cherokee lands."

"Colonneh," her father said, "help us! The Cherokee had no say with the legislators from Georgia! Blinders, all! President Monroe must reject the promise Jefferson made without our permission. On Friday we will request him to rescind the Compact."

"I admire your efforts, my friends," Houston said, shaking his head, "but I fear it will not happen. As congressman from Tennessee, I will work to support Cherokee concerns as well as I can in matters of State. But I advise you as my brothers—as I did my father John Jolly so many moons ago—that the only means to save the Cherokee is to remove west. Negotiate! Acquire from the federal government the very best treaty and demand the greatest sum of recompense, then leave your homelands. The Western Cherokee under my father's leadership thrive in the west. You must join John Jolly as soon as you can."

Houston lowered his voice should Cherokee speakers hover nearby. "You know the General's view . . ."

Sallie's father nodded a slow, thoughtful nod.

Houston continued. "You and I fought as brothers at Horseshoe Bend. General Jackson laid upon us rewards and honors. But now he desires the Presidency. When he makes good on that endeavor he will make good on the promise to Georgia in the Compact, that the United States government will extinguish all Cherokee land titles in the State of Georgia. He *will* enforce it.

"I do not wish to set before you more distress," Houston added, "but President Monroe will not rescind the agreement. Though he genuinely admires you Ridges and the Cherokee cause, he has not the power nor the votes."

Sallie crossed her arms across her gown and clutched her gloved elbows as the room spun. The candles in the chandeliers seemed to waver on an unfelt breeze. Sallie couldn't believe Colonneh's words! He was such a friend to the Cherokee! How could he be telling the truth? We are the Real People! The land is ours! She leaned against her father.

Major Ridge looked down at her, then thanked his friend for his words and for speaking from his heart. He added, regretfully, it was now time to take Sallie back to Tennison's. She nodded and tried to retrieve the happy smile she wore when she greeted The Raven, but his words buzzed in her head, stinging like bees.

As the party moved to the cloakroom, she heard the stranger with the muddy boots ask John if her father would be attending Mrs. Louisa Adam's soiree tomorrow night, the big celebration honoring General Jackson on the ninth anniversary of the Battle of New Orleans.

"No," John answered. "Although my father fought with General Jackson at the Battle of Horseshoe Bend, he did not assist in the glorious victory of New Orleans."

"But Jackson calls your father his friend, does he not?" the man replied, taking a notebook and pencil from his pocket.

"Indeed he does," John answered. Ever the diplomat he added, "The Cherokee have many powerful friends in Washington City."

Sallie watched the muddy-boot man write in his notebook, then John slipped her soft pelisses around her shoulders. As she buttoned the cloak's collar she hoped the rented carriage would be pulled up nearby so she wouldn't step in a puddle and dirty her new slippers.

John trailed his finger down the page of the *Capitol Intelligencer* newspaper. "Sallie! A column on Mrs. Monroe's soiree!" They sat in the dining room having breakfast.

He continued. "The Wednesday sundown affair at the President's House was this evening brushed with the exotic feather of the Cherokee Delegation, visiting here from the woodlands of Georgia in hopes of rerouting the Stream of Removal so long-flowing from our Seat of Government. Yet, as this reporter observed, not a single real feather among them!

"Each of the Chiefs, dressed as bankers or well-appointed country gentlemen, stood out only with their tawny, chiseled faces. Young Elijah Hicks, handsome in a purfled scarf and flowing lace cuffs, cut a dashing figure. Outfitted in the latest cut of Army officer uniform, Major Ridge's full figure and rugged aboriginal features made a great impression on Mr. Secretary Adams who introduced the Cherokee leaders to other notables. In attendance with the aforementioned Chieftain, was presented his daughter, Miss Sarah Ridge, who looks forward to attending school in our City—"

"John," Father called, "the carriage is here. It is time to lay our cause on the table of the President.

"Sallie! Miss Ashley from the Friends School will arrive soon to begin your tutoring. Be ready!"

Chapter 9

Miss Corbett Regrets

Tennison's Hotel

February 1824

In mid-January shortly after John arrived at Cornwall he sent good news to his father and sister at Tennison's that Mr. and Mrs. Northrup had given their blessing to his marriage to their daughter Sarah Bird and the banns had been published. A secret no more, the ceremony was set for January 27th at the Northrup home.

Miss Ashley walked several days a week from the Quaker Friends School and instructed Sallie on her diction and preparation for her acceptance to the school.

Sallie was delighted with the books! So different from the ones at the mission. Even those shelved in Chief Charles Hicks' library at home. At night before Sallie blew out her candle she read her lessons aloud, identifying words she'd stumbled over and now heard pronounced in Miss Ashley's perfect New England phrasing.

Each morning after breakfast Sallie entered the drawing room with a book and her embroidery basket to fill her days at Tennison's, seldom venturing out but for carriage rides with her father and once when The Raven drove her around the city.

During her time in the parlor, she met a lady, the wife of a Charleston merchant, who enjoyed correcting the little Cherokee girl's accent and instructing her in embroidery skills. Over the weeks Sallie graduated from simple cotton cross-stitch samplers to silk threads on fine linen. The woman encouraged Sallie to use her imagination in her designs; for one larger piece, she created a rich diverse scene of several stylishly dressed ladies standing on an imagined green lawn before the President's House—not the true mud-filled swamp.

Before John had departed he had met with a Dr. Anderson on 10th Street and arranged for Sallie to visit the following week. Luther waited in the rented carriage and Lucinda stood a step below as Sallie turned the bell with shaking fingers. The doctor opened the door and greeted her.

"Are you prepared for your kine pox variolation, young lady?" the doctor asked.

John had explained that kine pox matter was taken from the sores of cows and known to protect from acquiring the dreaded smallpox that had brought death, blindness, and scarring to so many Indians since Europeans first stepped on their shores.

While still home on the Oostanaula, John's pleas to his mother for permission to allow Sallie to receive the inoculation helped Susanna overcome her fears. Even President Thomas Jefferson years before had supported variolation for American soldiers, John informed his mother and saw to his own family's protection.

He assured his mother that Sallie would most likely not fall ill, a little fever, perhaps a few pustules, but those would be a small payment for not contracting the disease later in life. Though many missionaries felt this scraping of the skin was an act against God and others feared contagion, Susanna agreed.

John vouched for Dr. Anderson's well-reputed system of variolation and told Sallie that to keep a supply of fresh pox matter, the doctor kept an infected cow in a backyard pen.

Standing as instructed with her left sleeve rolled high and her elbow resting on a marble-topped stand, Sallie watched as Dr. Anderson took an ivory quill from his desk and opened the back door. Through the windows, she and Lucinda saw him squat next to the cow. John had told her the doctor would secure matter from a pustule on the cow's udders. When he returned Dr. Anderson scraped Sallie's upper arm with a small knife and smeared the pox matter into her wound.

The procedure hurt somewhat, but more irritating was the protective walnut half-shell he placed over the wound. Wrapping the shell with linen strips, he tied them off and said, "Now you'll be as pretty as a milkmaid!" John had told her the doctor would say this, that he'd said it several times when John interviewed him. Long ago it was discovered in England that milkmaids did not get smallpox because during milking they received natural inoculations from an infected cow's teats.

In her room at the hotel, she was careful not to sleep on her left side. For several days her forehead felt warm to her touch. Whenever she passed a mirror she peered at her face; no spots yet or on her chest, but several eruptions appeared on the tops of her hands. Sallie tried not to scratch them, but that was difficult. She wrapped her hands in linen, then pulled on her loosest gloves.

When her sores healed, the eruptions left circular scars and created a life-long tradition: Sarah Ridge, whenever with others, wore gloves until her dying day.

On a frigid day in early February, the hotelkeeper handed Major Ridge two letters left earlier by the post. Seeing one in John's handwriting, he sent for Luther to assist in translation and for Sallie so she could enjoy the news.

Standing near the settee in an alcove Luther carefully broke the seal and unfolded the first letter. Sallie squirmed with excitement as he read John's hurried script:

Thursday, January 29th, 1824
Cornwall, Connecticut
My dear Father and Sister,
This trip I have taken to Cornwall was met with much affection from my dearest Sarah Bird Northrup and her esteemed Mother. However, unforeseen and much-unexpected resentment against myself and the Northrup family has arisen in the community.

Major Ridge leaned forward. "Continue," he said to Luther, who lowered his voice although the room was empty.

Rev. Stone, the Foreign Mission School agent who has been encouraging of my scholarship for so long, declined two days ago to perform our marriage ceremony. In his stead Rev. Walter Smith, a fine teacher and colleague, read the service. We are wonderfully married!

However, I am delaying our aforementioned plans to depart for the Nation at this time. Mr. Northrup is concerned with residents of Cornwall rising in indignation against him for allowing his daughter to marry an Indian! Col. Gold and his wife, who have so encouraged Elias in his courting of their dear Harriet, are persevering against the outrage. Elias is so fortunate to have this fine girl as his beloved. In a show of faith, Col. Gold will conduct Sarah Bird and myself to the meetinghouse this Sabbath where we will be seated as a married couple next to his family on the deacon's bench. He honors me with my removal from the scholar's pew to the first pew of the church. His friend, Capt. Miles, entertained us at his farm, and praised my time at the Foreign Mission School. However, rumors and occasional shoutings from windows as Sarah Bird and I walk the Town Green have caused us to turn inward, and we fear reprisals. She, as much as I, is determined to see our marriage bloom.

We leave by coach on Monday for the Nation. I will write when first I can. Pray for us, dear family. I worry that you—and my dear Mother at home—will read newspaper reports, as the adverse news from Cornwall flies on the wind while letters of peace and affection travel slowly on the post.

Luther handed the open letter to Major Ridge who then stared at his son's handwriting. After a long period, he raised his head.

Sallie waited for her father to say something, but his vision was fixed on the distant wall.

How can this be? she wondered. Brother Butrick, Brother Chamberlain, those missionaries who came as friends to the Cherokee, who promised her cousin and brother that if they learned Christian ways and learned how to live like the whites, they could become as them. And now? Now? John and his dear Sarah Bird are the objects of scorn as they walk in the street!

Shifting beside her, Major Ridge ripped open the other letter. It unfolded under the weight of several creased newspaper clippings; the papers fell to the floor. Luther bent to pick them up as Sallie's father said, "Take them to my room. You can read them to me later."

As Luther headed for the back stairway Major Ridge turned to Sallie. His sonorous voice soft and mellow, he said, "Your mother and I welcome Sarah Bird into our family. But it seems the path to our home for her and John may be fraught with distress."

"Why Father? John has done nothing wrong."

"No, he has not. Nor Sarah Bird. But it is complicated on both sides of a marriage between a Cherokee to a white woman, Sallie. You, of course, are of the Wild Potato Clan because you are your mother's daughter. Sarah Bird Northrup's white mother has no clan, so Sarah Bird has no clan. She will come into our family, but she will be known only as John's wife. The council has written new laws to honor these unions."

Sallie sat silently, then said, "I know of others with no clans, using only their father's names. But why do the people of Cornwall not want Sarah to come to the Nation with John? She will have a beautiful house like ours, and field hands and servants . . . and our family will welcome her like a sister."

"They question a marriage to an Indian, that he is not worthy of her."

"Well, Father. They are wrong! We will learn the ways of the whites and prove to them we can walk beside them!" She added with confidence, "I'll learn that walk at the Friends School and come home to help you and John."

Sallie's dark eyes sparkled, and as she rose her father took her hand. "I wish for you, my daughter, to always hold the innocence of your time here in Washington City." Then he turned away before she could see doubt in his eyes.

Some weeks later in early March on her tutoring day, Sallie rushed into the parlor to find Miss Ashley standing near the door still wearing her black cloak and bonnet, a letter in her gloved hand.

"I am sad to say that I cannot stay for thy lesson today, Sallie," she said. "Miss Corbett asks that I give this letter to thy father to read."

Holding her embroidery basket and the book they were to study, Sallie replied that her father was not here, but at the War Department.

Miss Ashley handed Sallie the letter. "Then I am asked to instruct thee to give this to him upon his return, sealed. Good-bye, Sallie. I am pleased to have known thee and wish thee a blessed life." With a nod of her head and the saddest of smiles, the young woman turned and walked out the door.

Clutching the letter Sallie rushed to the window to watch her teacher walk along the hotel boardwalk, then down the steps. Miss Ashley lifted her hem as she tried to avoid the mud and snow slush of Pennsylvania Avenue. A cold wind rattled the window.

Sallie returned to a chair near the fireplace and set her book and basket on the floor. She looked first at the letter's seal and touched the spot of dark blue wax embossed with an indistinguishable emblem. On the front side, she traced her finger along the swirling script and identified enough familiar characters to recognize, "Major Ridge, Tennison's Hotel."

Knowing it would be hours before her father returned, Sallie retrieved her scissors from her basket and carefully ran one blade under the wax.

Unfolding the letter she identified the English salutation to her father and traced Miss Corbett's first words: "I regret—"

Sallie squeezed her eyes tight closed. A picture formed in her darkness, a picture of her standing before a dark blue door and beating on it while white women in black bonnets hammered nails into the door . . .

"*Wena!*" Stop! she called out.

"Miss Ridge! Are you ill?" The hotelkeeper started walking from his counter near the front door.

"No . . . yes," Sallie said. "Yes. Ask Luther to come." Father had said Elijah would be translating today and Luther would remain at the hotel should she need him. She stared at the rear stairway door.

When Luther walked into the room Sallie, her voice now controlled, handed him the letter. "I cannot read her script. Read it to me." He glanced at the salutation and text, then folded the paper.

"It's addressed to your father, Miss Sallie. We should wait 'til he gets back."

"Read it to me now, Luther. I know it begins with 'regret.'"

"Yes, Miss Sallie, it does, but it's still not right—"

"Read it. Please. I'll tell Father I asked you to."

"Yes, ma'am." Luther began reading: "It comes from the Headmistress of the Religious Society of Friends School . . ."

Sallie knew that much. "Go on."

Luther took a deep breath. "Miss Corbett writes, 'I regret, that following much discussion, the governing members of our Friends School have reached the conclusion that for us to accept the sister of John Ridge, whose words and actions we consider an active hostility toward the State of Georgia and general morality, would be incompatible with our religious beliefs against any form of violence.'"

"Violence?" Sallie exclaimed. "John doesn't want violence!"

Luther shook his head and bit back his words. He, of course, had read the lascivious newspaper reports chronicling John and Sarah Bird Northrup's marriage.

Sallie picked up her basket and book. "Tell Father I won't be coming down this evening."

"Yes, Miss Sallie. I'll see that Lucinda brings you up some supper."

Alone in her room Sallie opened the wardrobe door and looked at her new dresses. She walked to the window and for a long time watched the people of the city going about their business. A snow shower began to cover the dark mud.

She removed her dress and hung it with care on its peg. As she shut the wardrobe door the tall mirror revealed an altered reflection: the girl was no longer. Dressed a little girl's chemise stood a wise and strong woman. In addition to the scars on her shoulder and hands, Sallie now felt a scar on her heart.

Taking the sleeping blanket her mother had packed, she rolled herself into a ball on the bed and fell asleep wrapped in the love of home.

Chapter 10

Lasting Mementos

Tennison's Hotel

Spring 1824

During spring John wrote from the Oostanaula sharing his and Sarah Bird's happiness, and relaying Susanna's love for her new daughter. His house at Running Waters six miles north of the family's was nearing completion. Listening to his stories Sallie's heart ached for home.

Major Ridge had dictated a letter for Luther to send to the Moravian Academy for Girls at Salem, North Carolina. Surely as the daughter of a devout Cherokee Moravian woman Sallie would be welcomed there? The brethren wrote back that they were at full capacity and taking no applicants.

Was this refusal based on speeches and published articles by John, explaining the situation with Georgia, imploring supportive whites in the Northeast—who purported to be sympathetic to the Cherokee cause—for help in funding and in turning the tide of removal? Or was it the scandal of John's marriage to Sarah Bird Northrup?

Supporters of the Indian cause wrote letters countering the salacious newspaper columns fanning out across the country. One account related how pious citizens had thrown eggs and rocks at John and Sarah

Bird's carriage as they'd left for the nation. Poems were written and published. One—"The Indian's Bride"—romantically praised Sarah Bird Northrup's love for her husband. Others ridiculed and denounced predatory Indians for taking white women as brides and disparaged the women as lewd, God-forsaken, and filthy. The upcoming marriage of Sallie's cousin Elias Boudinot to Harriet Ruggles Gold added fuel to the fire.

For the Cherokee delegation the months of meetings in Washington City produced few successes except for the resurrection of the Treaty of Tellico signed and agreed to in 1804, but long lost in the records of the War Department—and still unpaid. When George Lowery presented the tribe's copy, Secretary Calhoun sent his clerks to find the government's agreement and at once prepared to make good on the five-thousand-dollar annuity for land purchased.

John Ross, in the council's final meeting with Secretary Adams and the President, addressed those leaders by reminding them of the provisions in President Monroe's Doctrine, issued last year. The Doctrine served as a warning to the kings and queens of Europe and beyond that the "New World" was no longer to be considered subject to colonization by the European countries.

John Ross read from a copy of the verbose document:

"'. . . the occasion has been judged proper for asserting, as a principle in which the rights and interests of the United States are involved, that the American continents, by the free and independent condition which they have assumed and maintained, are henceforth not to be considered as subjects for future colonization by any European powers.'"

"Your Honors, can you not see," John Ross asked, "how this philosophy applies to the Cherokee Nation? That the Cherokee were here first and were colonized by the Americans? And that we want no more land taken from us?"

A hush filled the President's office.

John Ross read on: "'We owe it, therefore, to candor and to the amicable relations existing between the United States and those powers, to declare that we should consider any attempt on their part to extend their system to any portion of this hemisphere as dangerous to our peace and safety.'

"Your words, gentleman," Ross stated. "You warn the Europeans that *you* will consider an attempt on *their* part to take any more of the North American continent as dangerous to America's peace and safety. Can you not see that the Cherokee feel the same as you? And yet, we are not countering your treaties with war-like actions. We only ask that you stop. Take no more of our land!"

Ross's words fell on compassionate but deaf ears.

In the halls of Congress, the Georgians wreaked havoc. Angry that the government would even consider discussions with the Cherokee delegation, Georgia legislators repeatedly reminded the President and any who would listen that there only two choices: Cherokee removal beyond the limits of the State of Georgia, or total extinction.

That May afternoon, John Ross and the delegation returned to the hotel filled with hope that the highest leaders of the land would consider his argument. To celebrate his protégé's reading of Mr. Monroe's Doctrine to the President himself, Major Ridge asked Mr. Tennison to prepare a fine meal in the dining room.

Sallie was seated between her father and John Ross. As the conversation turned to preparations for leaving tomorrow, John Ross pulled a large coin from his waistcoat pocket and handed it to Sallie. "President Monroe gave the delegation each a commemorative Indian peace medal struck when he came into office."

The medal looked like a bronze coin, though much heavier and larger than the Lady Liberty penny. On one side Sallie saw the words "*President of the U. S. A.D. 1817*" raised around the edges. In the center was Mr. Monroe's embossed profile image, looking much as she remembered him at his soiree with short, wavy hair and a ruffled necktie. She looked closer: encircling him beneath his shoulder was a big scarf-draped wreath that looked almost as if the President was rising from a bird's nest!

She turned the coin over and read the word "Peace" at the top above a tomahawk crossed by a tobacco pipe. The word "and" was embossed in the middle, then two hands were grasped in greeting, one showing a cuff of braid with buttons and one naked. The forefinger of each man's hand pointed to letters embossed near the rim below that spelled the word "Friendship."

"Peace and Friendship," Sallie said. John Ross nodded.

She stared at the hands for a long time and reckoned that the one with the cuff was the President's hand, but whose was the other hand, the naked one? Not John Ross's. He always wore sleeves with cuffs. Her father, too. Perhaps this was the hand of another Cherokee, one of the people from the hills who wore a breechclout and tunic at the Green Corn dances. Or maybe a Shawnee or another band of Indians.

"Did you get a medal from President Monroe, Father?"

"Yes, he gave us all one. I and others left ours off at Mr. Keyworth's shop. He said he would have his jeweler attach loops to the tops before we leave so we can wear them as decoration."

"Do you not want to wear yours, John Ross?" Sallie asked.

"No, Sallie. I want you to have it, to carry with you always as a reminder of the evening you met Our Father the President in his house."

"John Ross!" Major Ridge said. "The medal is a great memorial to your speech before the President! Surely—"

"I will always remember my speech, my friend, but I want Sallie to have a lasting memento of her visit to Washington City."

He leaned in closer. "Sallie, I know you have been saddened by not being received by the Friends School, but I want you to keep this medal as a talisman. Remember, if you truly believe in something you must do everything you can to make it happen. I know you want an education so you must go to the local schools until you can find a way to be accepted into a higher school. Never give up on what you truly believe."

Sallie could barely breathe. "Oh, thank you, John Ross!" Then she turned to her father. "May I keep it, Father? Please?"

"Of course, Sallie," he said. Then to Ross, he added, "Your unselfish generosity is greatly appreciated. I value our friendship and that of yours to my daughter."

Sallie couldn't put the medal down. She touched each raised letter, followed the pipe stem to the bowl, and ran her gloved finger down the bumps of the President's nose and mouth and chin. She memorized each rise and recess and would not have put it down at all if the servant hadn't placed before her a dish of former First Lady Dolley Madison's raspberry ice cream recipe.

Sallie knew, though, she would treasure this gift from her friend John Ross all the days of her life.

Chapter 11

Sarah Speaks

From those days onward, whenever I saw an eagle fly I remembered sitting on the sofa in the Elliptical Saloon of the President's House and how I felt that evening. As if I could soar. As if all doors were open to me. I treasured John Ross's gift of President Monroe's medal, the memento of my happy times in Washington City and sadly, of my awakening to the contradictions in the white man's world.

In the months following my return home, chieftains, councilors, and Congressmen pursued all means of negotiations to save our land. The State of Georgia boiled like a tempestuous kettle; our people were hounded and coerced.

My father asked Brother Butrick if the violent opposition to John's and Elias's marriages with white women was justified in scripture. The pious preacher could offer neither chapter nor verse.

My parents continued their pursuit of a white girl's education for me. I was in and out of mission schools. A rudimentary education. My spelling was always weak; I learned to depend on a dictionary.

But imagine this if you will:

Frustrated with my local schooling Mother, in the fall of 1826, dictated a letter to John requesting my admittance to the Moravian girls' school and had him post it to Salem. Did the brethren of the school pray over this pious and devoted Cherokee woman's plea for her daughter's attendance? Did they ask The Lot? Did the stick named "Ja" fall face upward?

It must have because in early December Lucinda and Mother sewed new dresses and let out seams of old ones.

We packed my trunk, she wished me love and *donadagohvi*, and Father took me to Salem in North Carolina! We rushed. The trip of four hundred miles could take ten days, more with treacherous storms, and we had a goal of Christmas Eve. Father loved the Moravian Christmastime.

Father had Tom and Luther drive us in our large coach. The trip varied between bright skies and blizzard gusts. Lettie sat inside next to me. I cherished her presence for conversation and companionship.

We arrived on Christmas Eve day in time for the celebration. My head spun at the sight of Salem and the school's large estate. Father, who had passed through the town on his first council trip to Washington City in 1808, pointed out the bakery that was firmly imprinted in my childhood: so many times he had told of following a scent he'd never smelled before. Walking Salem's main street he—in buckskin and turban—followed his nose to peer through a window. The baker invited him in and gave him a loaf of *Früchtebrot* filled with dried pears. Lettie and I hoped we could share a piece of the fabled bread before she had to return home.

Arriving at the school, Father and I were ushered into a great hall and seated on the front row, I with the women and he with the men. Before a painted backdrop of the Nativity scene that captured the glow of Mary's face as she cradled baby Jesus, several girls performed a lively conversation describing the Savior's birth.

Suddenly in the dialogue, though, in front of the backdrop of joy at the Savior's birth, the girls' words turned to his death. I wanted to press my fingers to my ears, but I couldn't. One girl described how the tortured Jesus stood in his purple robe, meek and patient, adorned with a crown of thorns. She told of his flesh torn by the lash, his body bruised by rocks, his face streaked with the spittle of sinners mixed with blood from his wounds . . .

Oh! I would live here for the next two years?

I should not have worried, though. While I was lonely for my family, my Salem years were good years, cloistered years.

The Moravians loved children and were genuinely concerned for our happiness since all of us came from elsewhere. We were divided into "room companies"—like a family with two parents only ours being two female teachers. About a dozen of us shared a sleeping room; we ate, we played, we sat together in church, and we shared celebrations and chores. Each room company was assigned a plot in the academy's elaborate terraced "pleasure garden." When spring arrived I learned to care for blooming flowers, my favorite being luscious crimson peonies and in autumn, the vivid colors of chrysanthemums. We were assigned classes according to our ability, but otherwise lived with our room company. We received plain but adequate food and excellent medical care. Should we need to be corrected for our errors there were no canings or beatings, merely reprimands for broken rules.

The school believed in physical fitness and outdoor exercise, throwing balls and brisk walking, at which I excelled. And skipping rope, at which I did not. I learned reading and grammar, writing and arithmetic, and history; our teachers spoke with minimal or no German accents. Books held secret discoveries for me. I perfected my needlework and sewing and learned to paint, although never the piano.

The good Moravians emphasized strength and integrity in women; from my time in Salem, I gained character and learned that the decisions we make throughout our lives create circumstances that affect our destinies. Each day augments—for better or for worse—the person who we become.

So how did the Cherokee girl fit in and assimilate? Well, truth be told, at sixteen I was nearly the same age as some of my teachers. Had any other girl in attendance visited the President in his house? Joined in conversation with leaders of the government? Spent their days in the center of Washington City observing the Congress, learning the pitfalls and prejudices of power?

Mother had instructed me not to speak of my family's life, the public scandals of John's and Elias' marriages, and the ever-growing treachery of the Georgians encroaching upon our nation. I could answer questions describing how I lived—not in a hut woven of rivercane, but in a New England house similar to other girls' homes with servants—but not speak of tribal politics.

During my last year there Hester Cole, the daughter of a whaleship captain out of New Bedford, Massachusetts, joined our room company. We were the same age, older than many, and became such friends: she of the coastlines and I of the forests and streams. The daughter of a seafaring father and a devoted Moravian abolitionist mother, Hester was as light of complexion and hair as I was dark. She found in me a sympathetic cause and I found in her a friend with whom to share my innermost thoughts. I told her those things of which Mother preferred me not: the perils of the Cherokee. Hester took them to heart and empathized and counseled me, told me of her mother's abolitionist meetings aimed not only to free southern Negro slaves but to help thwart Indian extinction—even to the point of raising money for the Cherokee to purchase a printing press and lead type in the shape of Sequoyah's syllables!

I shared with Hester how Sequoyah, turbaned and lame and always with a clay pipe in his hand, would visit with Father in our home. I described listening when he spoke of his talking leaves, determined to draw Cherokee words onto bark. He worked for years until he found eighty-six sounds to scratch into syllables. Now from bark to lead! Such good news Hester shared with me.

My room company was my family and I was set apart from the other girls only by the darkness of my skin—and the fact that as we undressed for our bedtime after nightly prayers, I wrapped in my sleeping blanket, not a nightdress.

A story:

Father—who had left an account with the brethren for my benefit—had John write to a local painter to contract him for my portrait. I enjoyed so dearly my outings in the company of Hester, walking into Salem town for my sittings at the studio of Mr. Daniel Welfare. Afterward, we would stop at "Father's" bakery for a sweet and linger as long as we dared without causing alarm to our room company.

The artist was skilled and painted an acceptable rendering of me, my face full-on, my hair parted and tied back with a blue band, curls falling to my shoulders. I wore a green gown with a laced yellow bodice to disguise my growing bosom. A red shawl Father left with me was draped across my left shoulder in the Cherokee style of adornment. Mr. Welfare captured my eyes with some proficiency, but my nose and lips he romanticized, displaying little resemblance to my mirror image and depicting my skin color more like that of my friend Hester's than my darker tint.

Still, I treasured the painting, commemorative of my several fortunate years of education, although later it passed from my possession and disappeared.

When my parents arrived for my Examination Ceremony in May 1828, they were honored with seats on the first rows of the chapel—men on one side, women on another, of course. I was as proud of them as they were of me. Father looked stately in his uniform. Though other ladies of her faith wore silks and satins, Mother was plainly dressed but for a fashionable bonnet made of soft gray fox fur, the tail positioned as a plume.

Hester and I hugged and cried as we parted, promising to write until the end of our days. I returned to the Oostanaula and she to New England, and we began our lifelong correspondence.

As our coach brought us nearer home, talk concerned the progress of our new Constitution and resolving our land ownership and borders with Georgia. John Ross was now President of the National Committee and Father was Speaker of the Council. The Cherokee had pulled together and risen to a nation with a written Constitution printed on the national printing press.

In the coach, Father handed me the first issue of our newspaper, the *Cherokee Phoenix*. Rising from the flames, the masthead heralded a great rebirth of the Cherokee. Reverend Samuel Worcester, sent to Brainerd by the Foreign Mission Board, had worked tirelessly to assemble funds from Northern missionaries and abolitionists' groups such as Hester's mother to purchase the press and have it shipped from Boston where he had spent two years overseeing the creation and manufacture of Sequoyah's syllabary into metal type.

What an accomplishment for our people and my cousin Elias Boudinot as editor! The first issue was printed February 21, 1828, and it was in the coach that I saw that issue with our hereditary language in print, side-by-side with columns in English. The first American newspaper ever printed in an Indian tongue, which I quickly learned to read. How proud I was of everyone who had created this grand achievement.

I left home a young girl and lived over two years immersed in the customs of the whites; I returned an educated woman prepared to join in the fight for the rights of my nation and my family. Leaving behind the confines of school, I now experienced a spiritual faith cobbled together—much like my years of education—by my mother's early teachings of tribal rituals and her newer belief in God. I felt a close allegiance to neither, but now I was relieved to no longer need to pray before paintings of Jesus' face streaked with blood.

Soon, though, such faces would be real and they would be Cherokee.

Chapter 12

The Winds of Change

New Echota, Northwestern Georgia
Capitol of the Cherokee Nation East
March 1832

A cool wind left the Blue Ridge Mountains and followed the Coosawattee River to its confluence with the Conasauga where the rivers formed the Oostanaula. Here the wind raced through the new town named for the ancient tribal village of Chota—a place of refuge—and turned down the wide streets, blew past the Council House with its two chimneys and the tall log-built Supreme Court, weaving its way between crisscrossing rows of young pines and poplars planted to border new homes and businesses. Entering the newspaper building, the wind rustled fresh editions draping from the rafters.

Sarah tossed her head letting the welcomed breeze slip around the collar of her indigo dress and cool her neck beneath her braid. She beat the type with the leather ink ball, then pulled the bar that lowered the platen, pressing a sheet of damp paper onto the lead characters arranged in the type frame. Her face glistened with sweat and smudges of ink.

Sarah raised the platen on the cast iron press, slid back the carriage, and removed the wet sheet. She eyed the remaining stack still needing the front side printed; if she didn't finish, this edition of the *Cherokee Phoenix* would run late.

During her four years home from North Carolina, under the tutelage of her mother Sarah's instruction turned to plantation life. She learned to manage a household and assign duties and tasks to servants, plan meals, and entertain visiting chieftains, Indian agents, and military attachés.

She now enjoyed the assigned work left her by her cousin Stand Watie who with substitute editor added to his other commitments as Clerk of the Supreme Court, had fallen behind and sent word to enlist Sarah's help. Today he'd ridden to meet the stage on the Federal Road and should return soon.

She laid another sheet in the carriage. Front side down. Slide the carriage, pull the bar. Hang the paper. Repeat. From the masthead of the newspaper, an etching of the Phoenix—the sacred bird of Egypt— rose from a nest of flames and ashes, the mythical representation of the Cherokee Nation in its bid to rise as a sovereign government.

"Or," Sarah said aloud to no one as she reached back for another sheet, the bird's eye searing into her brain, rekindling her ceaseless anger, "at this point merely to survive as a people."

Above the bird waved a banner with the word "Protection," invoked by the Cherokee Nation to the larger United States surrounding it. On each side of the bird boldly stood the symbols ᏣᎳᎩ and ᏧᎴᎯᏌᏅᎯ, *Cherokee* and *Phoenix* in Sequoyah's syllables, and beneath repeated in English.

Within its four pages, columns in both languages enlightened readers with poetry, literature, and scripture, and terrified them with the latest raids on homes and farms by Georgia's "pony clubs"—the carefree name for malicious white thieves who banded together to steal horses and cattle and terrify helpless farmers.

As her pages were pressed, she read again the recent letter from her cousin Elias Boudinot who was traveling back east with her brother John:

We are telling all who will listen in Washington City of the lawlessness that touches every corner of our Nation, put upon us by the Georgians. The State has usurped the gold mines and taken them under their control. They have run preliminary surveys across the Indian country—ours and the Creeks—and propose to divide all among Georgia's citizens by means of a lottery. Pony clubs run unchecked, intruders and invaders despoil our homes and improvements. Our Lighthorse Guard has no authority. Georgians arrest us and drive us from our homes at bayonet point with no legal process. They whip us; they do unspeakable violence to our women and children. They flood our Nation with barrels of whiskey, and the red soil of the Cherokee Nation reddens with the blood of our people.

We tell these evils to the leaders of the United States, but are they listening?

Some were. In Washington City, Senators Sprague of Maine and Frelinghuysen of New Jersey and Representative Edward Everett of Massachusetts had countered other members of Congress, prime among them Georgia's Representative Wilson Lumpkin. But this past November Lumpkin left Congress to rule as governor of Georgia with the power of President Jackson's Indian Removal Bill in his pocket.

Jackson's bill authorized the exchange of unsettled lands west of the Mississippi for Indian lands within existing state borders. Congress passed the act last year by a small margin, despite Frelinghuysen's three-day speech and Sprague's impassioned plea: "Who can look an Indian in the face and say to him, 'We and our fathers for more than forty years have made to you the most solemn promises; we now violate and trample on them all, but offer you in their stead—another guarantee.'"

Through four years as editor, Elias—though arrested twice by the Georgia Guard on charges of writing libelous articles and once threatened with a flogging—had helped to keep the Cherokee informed of federal and tribal decisions. Of prime importance in this week's edition were reports on the case currently before the United States Supreme Court concerning Georgia's illegal arrest of several Christian missionaries.

A year ago Georgia's legislature passed a law that no white man could remain in the state without taking an oath of allegiance and securing a special permit from the governor. This requirement included missionaries; in fact, Georgia's goal was to end the support and progress of Christian education benefiting Indians.

Last March the Georgia Guard arrested about a dozen ministers and other white men. Serving no warrants, they marched them like captured prisoners—with tunes of fife and cadence of drums—over eighty miles from Head of Coosa near Sarah's home to their headquarters at Lawrenceville. Civil authorities took over there, and the court later released them when their counsels presented writs of habeas corpus showing that in their respective posts, the missionaries served as postmasters: the preachers were considered federal agents.

Many Georgia citizens were sympathetic to the men and their treatment at court was courteous. The good ministers found great relief in their release.

Not so in July when at Governor Lumpkin's request President Jackson had the Postal Department revoke their positions as postmasters. New orders to leave the state were implemented; still, the missionaries defied the order. Arrests were ordered. No fife and drum corps on the Lawrenceville Road this time: the Georgia Guardsmen came equipped with chains taken from horse traces and fastened those chains around the necks of the eleven white men. Mounted guards rode astride with the men chained to their horses' necks or the backs of wagons. Through the forests and trails, they were dragged on bleeding feet; if they fell, cursed and goaded with bayonets.

Several weeks later the Supreme Court of Georgia heard their case at the capital in Milledgeville. The men pled "not guilty" but were convicted. Nine relented and agreed to leave the territory; two did not. Georgia charged Reverend Samuel Worcester and Doctor Elizur Butler,

American Board of Foreign Missions preachers, with violating state law by residing in Cherokee territory without a permit. Failing to swear an oath to the constitution and laws of the State of Georgia, the ministers were sentenced to four years of hard labor in the state penitentiary at Milledgeville.

The Cherokee Nation, though, did not stop there: William Wirt, former Attorney General under presidents Monroe and Adams took on the case. In *Worcester v. Georgia* this year, the Supreme Court was asked to rule if states such as Georgia could diminish the rights of tribes by establishing their own Indian Code. Did the Cherokee Nation constitute a nation holding distinct sovereign powers as granted by Congress and the United States? This ruling would establish the principle of "tribal sovereignty."

Sarah's rage at this unknown answer kept her working at a steady pace until she stepped one last time on the bench, draped the final issue across a rafter. Sunshine poured through the open windows and door of the newspaper office. From her perch on the bench, she saw the lane leading to Reverend Worcester's house. Though he was one of those imprisoned, Worcester's home continued to serve as a church and school among the few houses and commercial establishments so far erected in the capital.

As Sarah watched, Mrs. Worcester led a line of schoolchildren—among them Sarah's young Boudinot cousins and children of friends—down the trail to the creek for their morning recess. Dismissed from line the children ran beneath the trees; the wind carried their laughter, bringing back distant memories of Sarah's times in Springplace.

Leaning with her arms on the windowsill, she rubbed the pocks on her ungloved hands; the scars had smoothed over the years. She smiled at the children's chase games and eager calling, their innocent play overseen by the good minister's grieving wife.

Anger erased her smile as Sarah looked in the direction of the general store; Cornsilk hobbled along a path. A pony club had set a bear trap on the path to his cabin. His screams brought his wife to him, but the teeth of the trap left Cornsilk forever lame.

Over her years home from Salem Sarah had been shocked by scar-ripped faces, missing hands and fingers; she'd seen the cripples, seen the survivors—not of great warrior battles of the Cherokee past, but of the state of Georgia's unbridled brutality.

New Echota moved at a ghostly pace. She remembered council times when meeting grounds were dotted with campsites. She remembered dancing Cherokees celebrating the festivals of her youth. Now she saw drunken farmers leaning against empty buildings that had no use in a Cherokee Nation held captive.

A smattering of people filed in and out of the Supreme Court Building and Council House, general store, and several taverns. Men wore traditional colorful turbans or slouch hats with a feather or squirrel tail dangling. Home-sewn shirts and wool trousers of the locals contrasted with those down from the mountains dressed in traditional garb, decorated hunting coats edged with bright borders, belted with beaded sashes over buckskin leggings. Women wore drab homespun; a few dressed up in bright dresses for a day in town. What would they find when they returned home? Their farms ransacked, their cattle stolen?

"Hallo, Sallie!" came a shout through the open door. Startled, Sarah lost her balance and jumped from the bench. Her boots thumped on the plank floor as she grabbed the tall typesetting stand, steadying herself.

"Lord have mercy!" Harriet Boudinot called as she walked up the steps carrying her baby. "I didn't mean to startle you, dear!"

Sarah laughed. "Well, I should have been straightening up instead of daydreaming."

She waved her hand at the newspapers lying in stacks on tables and drooping from the rafters like leaves in a tobacco-drying shed. "Look, we're through! This issue is finished on time instead of running late like the last two."

"Bless you, dear. You and Stand have done a fine job. Elias is so pleased with the progress of the *Phoenix* while he travels."

Harriet shifted the baby to her hip, picked up a paper, and began to read.

Sarah watched the black-dressed woman as her slender pale hand proudly held the results of her Cherokee husband's dedication to his nation, the man for whom she had steadfastly proven her love for the last eight years. Their marriage in Cornwall had created a scandal similar to John's and Sarah Bird's.

The infant wriggled in her mother's arms, kicking the newspaper; Sarah took the baby. Childbearing had further strained her cousin's wife, always delicate and frail. Add that to Elias's constant harassment by the Georgia Guard, Harriet's health was a constant source of concern to the family.

"Have you heard from Elias?"

"No, I'm hoping for a letter in the next mail pouch. I pray he and John continue to find support with their lectures."

"I hope they tell everyone about the thieves and murderers Governor Lumpkin has turned loose on us!" Sarah said, remembering Cornsilk's limp. The baby started to whimper and she rocked her gently, caressing her soft cheeks.

Harriet visibly cringed at Sarah's words and she immediately regretted her hostility in front of the gentle woman. She changed the subject. "Stand rode over to the Federal Turnpike earlier. He wanted to meet the stage from Fort Augusta. I'm sure he'll have a letter for you."

While Harriet resumed reading the *Phoenix*, Sarah jostled the baby and walked to the typesetting desk; with her free hand, she straightened characters in their compartments while the baby played with her braid.

Harriet glanced up from the paper and then moved quickly to the door. "Sallie! Look yonder."

Throughout the town, people suddenly stopped their bartering and gossiping to watch as Stand Watie, his shirttail flopping loose from his trousers, raced his sorrel down Main Street. Mrs. Worcester left her porch and ran toward the *Phoenix* office, a line of children following her like a covey of quail.

Sarah and Harriet met Stand at the foot of the steps. The stocky man, sweating but smiling, dismounted with a jump, shouting in English, "We did it! We won! The Supreme Court—Chief Justice Marshall—ruled Georgia's Indian Code unconstitutional!"

He took off his hat, his long hair flying, and waved it high. Stand hugged Harriet, then grabbed Sarah and in the process squashed the child between them. The three danced around laughing and skipping to the insistent wails of the disturbed baby.

Harriet calmed the child while Stand called out his news. Men and women who had followed his route crowded around, then stepped aside making way for the missionary's wife to come to the front. Sarah took Mrs. Worcester's arm as Stand moved to the top step of the office. A broad grin covered his round face as he held up the letter, the breeze fluttering its pages.

"In his assenting opinion," he read, "Chief Justice John Marshall writes that the Cherokee Nation is a distinct community occupying its own territory. In our nation, the laws of Georgia have no power. No whites may enter except with the assent and permission of the Cherokee."

His deep voice boomed. "The Indian Code enacted by the State of Georgia is void and Reverend Worcester and Doctor Butler must be released! The Cherokee Nation is a sovereign state!"

Cheers and huzzahs from the English-speaking Cherokees filled the street, quickly followed by a second round as Stand translated into his native tongue.

Mrs. Worcester mounted the steps to a chorus of yelling and joyous laughter. She raised her hands for quiet; her words filled the now-silent street. "My friends, justice has prevailed. Let us thank our Lord Savior with prayer and song."

The wind circled the newspaper office and lifted skyward the woman's words, then caught the tune of glory, "Amazing Grace," in the ancestral tongue praising a Great Spirit with a different name.

> . . . Through many dangers
> Toils and snares
> We have already come
> 'Twas grace hath brought
> Us safe thus far
> And grace will lead us home . . .

As the wind carried away the final notes of the hymn, Harriet leaned close to Sarah. "Praise God that dear Reverend Worcester's name has been cleared. And Doctor Butler with him. Oh, the degradation those poor men have suffered, chained to the tail of a cart. Jailed—"

"Oh, Harriet," Sarah said, hugging her again, but careful not to squeeze the baby, "the missionaries can stay in the nation. Georgia cannot take our land! I must go tell Mother and Father. They'll be so pleased!"

Sarah found Stand and told him with the newspaper printing completed, she was on her way home with the news. Harriet offered to help him fold and ready the pages for dispersal, then the women left the rejoicing crowd and walked the few blocks to the Boudinots' house where Sarah always lodged when she came to town. She scrubbed ink from her face and hands, and exchanged her indigo skirt for a black linen divided one and tall moccasins. She also laid out her leather "possibles" bag containing firing supplies; she pre-loaded powder, patch, and ball down the barrel of the percussion-lock pistol. Its carved hickory hilt with silver inlay gleamed. As she primed the charge with the ramrod, she grinned at the engraving: "To Major Ridge from Gen'l Andrew Jackson."

"We beat you, Ol' Hickory!" she said, carefully placing the long pistol in her saddlebag.

Pulling on doeskin gloves, she walked with Harriet down the front steps as morning shadows dappled the grass under the red oak where Stand held her horse. He took Sarah's saddlebags and tied them on the back of her palomino. Waving to the row of little bright-faced

Boudinots calling *donadagohvi* from the upper gallery, she kissed Harriet's pale cheek. "Thank you for letting me stay."

"Our home is yours anytime. Will we see you soon?"

"In time to help Stand get out the next edition filled with this wonderful news."

A crash of breaking glass interrupted. Three Cherokee men stumbled down the steps of the split-log tavern near the newspaper office. One drunk fell to the ground as the owner came out and looked at his broken window, cursing loudly. Harriet cringed. "May the Lord have mercy on their drunken souls. I'm afraid the celebration has already begun."

Sarah and Stand nodded in agreement, then he hugged his cousin. "Who rides with you?"

"No one. Father was to send Luther to fetch me in a few days, but I want to leave now."

"You can't!" Stand's dark eyes flashed, so like those of her father and her own; one eyebrow shot up in surprise. "It's too dangerous. Just wait. I'll ride with you tomorrow."

"Stand, I'll be fine. I'll be home long before dark."

"You're being bullheaded riding alone." He lowered his voice so Harriet wouldn't hear and worry. His forehead furrowed into a tight pattern of tree rings on the end of a split log. "Keep an eye out for trouble. Governor Lumpkin's cutthroats know nothing of the ruling."

"As if it would matter if they did," Sarah said, arranging her ample divided skirt beneath her legs. She patted the bag behind her. "I've got General Jackson's pistol. And you know I'll use it. Please don't worry." Touching the horse's flank with her heel, she turned and trotted toward home.

Chapter 13

Strangers on the Road

New Echota Road

March 1832

No breeze traveled with Sarah along the New Echota road. The air was still and heavy when she reined in, pausing to loosen the neck of her bodice. She removed her vest, tucking it under a strap on her saddlebag, and pulled her black skirt higher over her tall riding moccasins. She bent low to let the mare have her head.

Such good news she carried! Her people were free to remain on their farms. All the years of losing their land to the white man were over. The highest court in the United States officially ruled that Georgia had no authority to deny the sovereignty of the Cherokee. Now the terrifying lottery—by which Georgia was dividing Sarah's nation into squares on their map, giving farms tilled with the sweat and blood of her people to the holders of the lucky tickets—the lottery was ended!

She beamed, her thoughts swirling with the dust she stirred. No one can bother us anymore. Our dreams have come true! No one can force us to remove to the Arkansaw.

Sarah urged her beloved palomino Dove on at a fast canter. Approaching a bend where the road pulled away from the river, she sensed something . . . what? She stopped.

Distant laughter.

Heading Dove down the steep bank she hid in a grove of willows. The oppressive humidity of her hiding place closed around her throat. She stroked Dove's neck as both took short, fast breaths. Untying the flap on her saddlebag, she took out the long pistol. She pulled back the hammer to its first stop and slipped a copper cap over the nipple, then thumbed the hammer back, cocked and ready to fire.

The mare stood silent. Her mistress waited, listening to hoof beats. It was a pony club! Boldly driving a herd of horses, heading to the Federal Turnpike, taking their booty back into Georgia.

Through the branches around her, Sarah glimpsed a gang of five dirty rogues. These were not sympathizing citizens, but lawless drunken rabble reveling in the blatant go-ahead given them by the state to murder and defile Cherokee families.

"Sure as hell, we gonna make us a bundle on these Injun ponies."

A chorus of affirmative laughter and grunts passed Sarah in her hiding place.

"Oncet I gets my money, I'm gonna buy me some whiskey. Take me a trip back here to Injun country," called a crude, unseen voice. "Find me a lil' squaw. Maybe dig me some gold when I finish up with her."

More laughter. Their words, like icicles, passed through Sarah's sweating body.

The men's vulgar joking died through the trees. Dust settled. Sarah lowered her pistol but left the copper cap over the nipple while gently letting down the hammer, still ready to cock and fire at a moment's need. She slipped it into a deep pocket in the seam of her riding skirt. Fearful, she guided Dove from the bushes and headed south at full gallop. With a pony club on the loose, the road was ripe with danger.

Stand was right, she thought. I shouldn't have ridden alone.

Laying her face close to Dove's neck, she urged her on. She whispered to the mare, an incantation, one invoking protection for the traveler:

Now! In front of you! The dragon will be going, spewing flames.
Now! In front of you! The red mountain lion will be going, his
    head alert.
My name is Sarah Ridge.
My clan is Wild Potato.

Four times she repeated the charm as required, then sang it again. Her body swayed, moving with the palomino's gait and her internal beat of the chant. The sun traveled with her, lower now, filtering through sycamore and pine. Her mind drifted with her words. She pictured the great horned fire-breathing dragon of her ancestors and the mountain lion she often heard screaming in the woods. With her protectors leading her, she rounded a bend.

There, a white man eased his horse from the side of the road, blocking her path.

Sarah looked for a way around him. A cottonwood blocked the left side and the river barred the other. Dove halted a few feet from the rider. With her heart pounding, Sarah eased her hand down her skirt into her pocket; her fingers wrapped around the pistol stock.

"Pardon, ma'am," the man said, tipping his broad-brimmed hat. "Didn't mean to frighten you. I'm looking for the plantation of Major Ridge. Could you be so kind as to tell me how far downriver it is?"

Terror. Fury. Her emotions ran together as she yelled at the stranger, "Who are you? What do you want?"

"Put that down and I'll tell you, ma'am."

Sarah looked at the pistol in her hand. She hadn't realized she was pointing it at the man. She cocked the hammer full back and held it steady. "Who are you? Why are you going to the Ridge plantation? What is your name?"

The man's only movement was a smile crossing his face accompanied by a mischievous flickering in his light-colored eyes. "My, you ask a lot of questions." In his late twenties with tanned, lean features, he sat tall on his dun horse. As she rested the pistol on the pommel, he removed his hat with a flourish

"Samuel Augustus Maverick of Montpelier Plantation, Pendleton, South Carolina. And lately of Lauderdale County in Alabama. Now, if you answer questions as well as ask them, just who do I have the honor of addressing?"

His talk was cultured; his appearance upstanding. Should she engage in conversation? She hesitated, then answered, "Sarah Ridge. Daughter of Susanna and Major Ridge."

The glimmer remained in Maverick's eyes as he studied the woman before him sitting on her pale horse. He observed she was an accomplished rider; she did not sit sidesaddle. Sarah's shining black hair outlined her dark, glistening face; her long braid had edged forward and now fell across her open-necked bodice.

"Then I consider this coincidence another in a long line of good fortune in my travels."

Reading his expression as cordial, Sarah let out her long-held breath. But still needing her questions answered she said, "Why do you wish to see my father?"

"I want to meet with the speaker of the Cherokee Nation to discuss the situation of your people. I mean no harm."

Sarah pointed in the direction she was riding. "Then follow this road."

Maverick turned his horse. "Might I accompany you? Your ride will be much safer if you accept my company. And you won't need that pistol."

She instinctively felt this man a gentleman; his poise, his playful demeanor reminded her of Sam Houston. She lowered the pistol and removed the firing cap, eased down the hammer, and slipped both into her pocket. "Yes, thank you. Do join me. We have not far to travel."

In the remaining hour at a slow walk, Sarah put aside her fear of horse thieves and wayfaring highwaymen as Sam Maverick, small-town lawyer, land speculator, and would-be gold prospector—everything Sarah distrusted rolled into the one man—charmed her with his tales and good humor.

Maverick, the only son of a wealthy businessman and planter, rambled on about his university days at Yale reading law and his scandalous duel over states' rights with Jackson's recently resigned vice-president John Calhoun. Maverick regaled her with his present period of itinerancy through the South in search of a dream: to buy land, to sell land, to make money. In his passionate words, Sarah sensed the thrill of the deal might be a greater reward to the man than the actual profit.

"So," Maverick said as their horses started up a rise, "tell me about Sarah, daughter of Major Ridge."

Seldom needing to explain herself in a country where everyone knew her family, Sarah stammered, "There . . . there is little to tell. I was born here, on this land."

"But you don't speak like—"

"Like you would expect an Indian squaw to speak?" she interrupted with a teasing smile. She didn't wait for Maverick to excuse himself; his sheepish expression showed his regret. "My parents wanted me to have the same education as my brother John. Ever since I was very young, I've been carted to missionary schools at Springplace and Haweis. I've even passed near Pendleton on my way to the Moravian Girls' Academy up in Salem, from which I graduated four years ago."

"Well, that's most, uh, unusual. Are you a schoolteacher?"

"Sometimes I assist Miss Sawyer at her school at Running Waters, but currently I'm helping publish the *Cherokee Phoenix* newspaper in New Echota while the editor, my cousin, is away."

"I'm surprised your family . . . your husband, would let you travel alone, what with the trouble and all." Maverick stared straight ahead.

Sarah glanced sideways at him. "My family has raised me to think for myself. I chose to ride alone today."

He shifted to face her as a soft smile formed on her lips, her eyes wide. "And I'm not married."

Maverick looked across at her. His eyes narrowed to slits as an affable grin eased across his face.

Sarah enjoyed a lively conversation with this charming man and felt regret when the Ridge plantation came into view on its tree-covered bluff above the Oostanaula. The road continued past the whitewashed house and on down to the ferry. From here Sarah always cut across the meadow and let Dove have her head for a run to the stables, but today she followed the road to approach the columned entrance, to bring the guest in through the front door.

During a pause, she wanted an answer to a question, one which she had heard no mention during his stories. "And you, Mr. Maverick? Have you a wife and children?"

"I'm a bachelor, a wanderer. I've decided to see what opportunities lay westward of my childhood home. Your father's reputation as a shrewd but honest businessman is renowned throughout the East by men of power. I've come to see if there's a way I can . . . can help with the results of the lottery now being instituted."

Sarah suddenly surfaced from their pleasant visit, this frivolity that had lowered her guard. Anger whetted a knife edge to her voice. "You mean, you've come to see if you can purchase tracts from the sorry lottery winners for a pittance and turn my people's misfortune into a profit. Well, you're too late, Mr. Maverick. We will run the squatters out. At this very moment *you* are trespassing on sovereign Cherokee land where no white man may enter but with permission!"

He sat straight in his saddle, turning to face her. "Whatever are you talking about?"

"The Supreme Court. I carry home news that Justice Marshall has ruled that Georgia laws are illegal—"

"Oh, that." Maverick's flirting tone turned matter-of-fact. "The Court decided *for* the Cherokee then. But, you don't think that President Jackson is going to enforce Marshall's ruling, do you?"

"Of course, he will! He's the President of the United States. And my father's friend!"

Maverick stared at her. Perhaps the lines in his handsome face exhibited compassion as they eased into a smile, but Sarah read his expression as condescending.

"I'm afraid there's much you don't understand about politics, Miss Ridge. Beware of friendships between politicians."

Sarah jerked Dove's reins. "Good-bye, Mr. Maverick. You have my permission to remain in my nation until you speak with my father. But after you do so, it might be wise for you to ride on." She turned her horse across the meadow toward home. Leaning low in the saddle, she loosened the reins and gave Dove her head.

Maverick watched Sarah ride off at a gallop; the hem of her black skirt whipped against the buff-colored horse. "A fiery, fascinating woman, this Sarah Ridge," he mused, "though today may not be the best time to call upon her father."

Sam Maverick headed for the ferry, adding to no one at all, "But I shall return."

Chapter 14

A Talk in the Parlor

Ridge Plantation

March 1832

"Ain't you back home early, Miss Sallie?" Big Tom asked as Sarah handed him Dove's reins. "Who you done rode with? You ridin' in here like this, by yo'self!"

Beneath the wide brim of the straw hat that shadowed his broad face to an even darker sheen, Big Tom's reprimand came with his responsibilities as overseer of the Ridge plantation. His wife Doll ruled the kitchen and house servants and his son Little Tom ran the ferry. Big Tom had taught Sallie how to catch a horse and how to bridle and saddle, but he knew the roads smoldered with danger.

"I . . . I rode with a traveler, a Mr. Maverick, hoping to see Father," she said. "He's coming later—"

She glanced past the Negro slave who had been in charge of her father's stables as long as she could remember. Through the fence rails, she watched Sam Maverick disappear over the bluff. Evidentially, he had decided not to come to the house. Relief replaced a momentary twinge of regret at the spirited man's departure, but now he would not be bothering her father with talk of the lottery.

Good, she thought. Now I can share my good news!

Pulling her pistol from her pocket, she handed it and the copper cap to Big Tom. "Least ways," he said, "you was ready iffen a pony club rode up. You not see nuttin' on the road?"

Sarah merely shook her head and with a pat to Dove's rump, she ran toward the house. A gust of wind from a cloudbank in the west swirled a tiny dust tornado across the clean-pecked kitchen yard. Chickens and geese scattered, fussing at her as she passed the kitchen cabin where the smell of roasting venison—the special way Doll cooked it with wild onions—filled the air. Noting a gray saddlehorse tied at the front, Sarah hoped the visitor didn't mean trouble as so many did these days.

When the family had moved from Oothcaloga nearly ten years ago and John rebuilt the old cabin on this rise above their ferry and store, he created a landmark. It was the home of a patriarch. Two stories high with whitewashed clapboards; four brick fireplaces and eight rooms with ceilings and walls of paneled hardwoods. Verandas spanned the back and front, with a balcony above the front porch supported by turned columns. A glass-paned front door and three arched windows at the landing of the staircase filled the house with light.

Around the home spread the two hundred and thirty acres used by the family and farmed by black slaves who worked the house and fields, tending orchards and livestock. Near the house stood the kitchen and smokehouse; farther down lay sheds, cribs, and hay mangers for horses, cattle, and hogs, with a cluster of slave cabins.

The ferry Sam Maverick headed for—a flat barge with rawhide ropes tied between trees across the Oostanaula a few miles above its confluence with the Coosa—was a source for currency and barter, as was George Lavender's store and trading post nearby, also owned by Major Ridge. Over the years, Chief John Ross and other leaders had moved to this area known as Head of Coosa.

"Mother! Father!" Sarah called, coming in the side door.

Lettie met her in the hallway that ran the center of the house. The afternoon sun floated through high arched windows and fell to the lower floor, widening Lettie's shadow as she placed both hands on her hips in a posture of displeasure. Her red turban and darker red dress set off her golden eyes and buttery skin. She whispered beneath her breath, her Scots brogue rolling as distant thunder. "Where're yer manners? Must ye yell like a wild Injun? Yer folks are in the parlor with the chief."

Leaving before a second reprimand or barrage of questions as to why she was home a day early, Sarah smiled. Lettie's entitlement came through years of respect and confidence in the women's friendship. As young girls, they played together; as women, they continued to erase dictated boundaries.

Sarah entered the parlor. From a wingchair near the fireplace, her brother raised his large hand and mumbled, "Hallo, Sallie." Watty's customary smile played upon his face, his sweetness consistent with his distracted expression. Above him the paneled mantelpiece—rising to the ceiling—glowed with colors representing the seasons: oak green and goldenrod, red ocher and cornflower blue. Yellow and red wainscoting continued around the room beneath white walls.

Her mother greeted her from the chair beside Watty. Luther, standing, nodded as he waited to translate for her father and the chief. Major Ridge, his eyes flickering with internal flames, seemed to hold back excitement as he called from the settee, "Join us, Sallie, and welcome our friend."

John Ross had risen from his chair near the open window and took Sarah's proffered hand, clasping hers with both of his. A smile lit his pale face as he greeted the daughter of his old friend.

Now in his forties, the chief's eyes, dark brown, deep-set, and keen, always seemed to Sarah to command respect. With but one-eighth Cherokee lineage, he was among mixed-blood leaders who could not speak the language well. His wife was a good friend of Susanna's; Elizabeth Brown—Quatie, she was called—was a full-blood and mother of John Ross's five children, and served as his translator at home. Ross's dark hair showed streaks of gray and rose from his forehead in a pompadour, adding to his six-foot height; short curls edged his temples, trying in vain to offset large ears that transcended all language barriers to hear everything in the nation. His black frock coat and bronze brocade vest, high-collared white shirt, and black cravat contrasted with the casual dress of others in the room.

"How good to see you," Sarah said, speaking in English. Her father had been an ardent supporter of the chief's election and was proud of having helped groom him to lead the Cherokee Nation. Ross's diction, passion and whiteness allowed him to move easily in American circles.

No longer able to contain her excitement, her news burst forth in her native tongue. "Stand received a letter from John! The Supreme Court ruled for our nation! Isn't that wonderful?" She repeated in English for their guest, her words met with smiles.

"Yes," her father said. "We, too, are celebrating! Our chief just learned of our nation's good fortune. John, please, continue. Tell us more."

Sarah took a chair and listened as Luther translated the chief's words for her parents. While John Ross spoke she remembered the dinner at Tennison's Hotel when he gave her President Monroe's Indian peace medal. Then he was a diplomat and negotiator; now he ruled.

"Chief Justice Marshall," Ross said, "has concluded that we have sovereign rights to our land and are in true possession of it. Even though previous treaties signed by our chiefs—many of whom could neither read nor write—included ambiguous phrases that can be interpreted that we have signed away our rights, those agreements do not apply.

"We have placed ourselves under the protection of the United States and as such, Georgia cannot interfere with our affairs. The states control those areas won by war or which we've lost through treaties. We control what remains. Justice Marshall goes on to write that the federal government is supreme over all the states, as well as the domestic dependent Indian nations. The pressures brought by Georgia on the Cherokee are fraudulent."

"So that means," Sarah asked, "that the missionaries will be released?"

"Yes, and soon we shall hope."

Her father added, "Primarily, the Georgians must cease their encroachments. John Ross and I set out tomorrow to ride through the nation to reassure our people that relief is on its way."

"Reassure them," the chief said, "and encourage them to *believe*, to continue planting and tending their crops. We must continue seeking assurance that President Jackson will press our cause with Georgia. Our friends in the North and Washington City have promised to help us."

Ross turned to her father. "I look forward to our travels, my friend. We will pursue our effort because—mark my words—I will never lead my people from their homeland. Never."

Through the open window a breeze entered the parlor; not a cool breeze, yet Sarah felt a shiver as she marked John Ross's final word: "Never."

She pictured the peace medal with the fingers of the hands pointing to the word "Friendship," the memento tucked in a trunk in her room. She remembered John Ross telling her that if you truly believed in something, you must do everything you could to make it happen.

Chapter 15

A Later Talk in the Parlor

Ridge Plantation

May 1832

"I've asked for this private time to tell you that my letters home and reports to others of continued negotiations have been lies." John Ridge's abrupt tone in his native tongue was repeated in his tense stance beside the open window in the parlor. Sarah again sat where several months earlier she heard Chief John Ross vow to never lead his people from their homes. The sun broke through from the west.

Sarah had left Watty in Lettie's care since he might, in his innocence, mention his brother's visit. Father and Mother on the settee were silent. Susanna's gray hair was twisted and tied at the base of her neck, strain tugging at the corners of her lips. Major Ridge's face was devoid of emotion.

On the wall above the mantelpiece hung a portrait of John dressed as a white man, the only feather in the painting the quill he held in his hand, poised over a piece of parchment; the image seemed to be taking notes of the scene in the parlor, secretly recording the confession of its sitter.

John continued. "The good news of the Supreme Court's decision you have heard. The truth you have not. While Elias and I toured the

A LATER TALK IN THE PARLOR

Northern states we received word that the President would not enforce the Court's decision, as did you. We returned to Washington City and immediately secured a meeting with Jackson at the Executive Mansion. I looked him in the eyes and asked if he would honor his Court's decision and use the power of the federal government to override Georgia's laws. He replied that he would not.

"Jackson, in his most direct manner—heedful of his friendship with you, Father, and your history of devotion to the Union—pleaded with me to bring back his words to you. He told Elias and me to go home, to tell our people that our only hope for relief from the Georgians is to abandon our homes and remove west."

The three listeners in the room sat as unmoving as the portrait.

John's voice rose. "I raged at his words. I argued. I renounced his decision as best I could without dishonoring you, Father, and the highest office of the country. I did not crawl away defeated but left his presence embroiled in another plan. Poll the Court itself.

"Elias and I were unable to secure a meeting with Chief Justice Marshall, but Justice John McLean agreed to meet with us. Although appointed by Jackson to the Court, he is long a Monroe man known for his anti-slavery decisions and has remained a friend to Indian causes.

"But I heard only the echo from the Executive Mansion. The Court, McLean said, is powerless against the President's refusal to implement their ruling. There is no remedy which that body can use to force his hand. Justice McLean restated that the cause for the Cherokee to remain in the east is lost."

Sarah saw her mother's hand reach for her father's. Silence.

"John," Sarah said, "We still have the public on our side. You and Elias brought home hundreds of dollars in donations from concerned supporters."

"Yes, but a pittance to keep the *Phoenix* in print. Our national coffers are empty."

Their father still did not comment.

John continued, "I also received a letter from Boston, from the Foreign Missionary Board. They have word from Washington City that it is impossible to protect the Cherokee any longer. All but a few of the Moravians are returning to Salem, anticipating joining us in the west should we move."

John moved to a chair and pulled it close to his parents. "Justice McLean offered to act as our negotiator for a removal treaty on the most liberal of terms."

Major Ridge spoke for the first time. "Is such a treaty drawn?"

"Yes, a beginning. Some of the provisions in it have merit. Elias and I have seen an early draft."

"This cannot be!"

Sarah's head shot up at her father's shout.

"Father, it is," John said, quietly. "An offer of a price for our Eastern lands has not yet been decided, but early drafts give us good lands in the Arkansaw. John Jolly's Western tribe is inviting us to join them. Whites are excluded from the land. The treaty gives us funds for a year's subsistence, funds for transportation, and reimbursement for our farms and improvements. We can select our mode of conveyance whether by river or overland. And much more, Father.

"However, in the document, they write a provision. If any Cherokee is unwilling to remove, those persons will become citizens of the United States and all Indian benefits will come to an end for them."

"When does this removal come to pass?"

Sarah barely recognized her father's trembling voice.

John quietly answered, "We must leave two years from the date of ratification by Congress."

Sounds of the farm drifted through the room: a horse whinny, cattle lowing. A blue jay shrieked from the chestnut tree. A bee buzzed through the open window, then out. For an instant, Sarah visualized the room and its inhabitants as a composition for one of her silk embroidery paintings. Four people posed within a room of great beauty, frozen in time, a picture of home life on the verge of extinction.

Her father stood and spoke, his voice growing stronger with each statement. "This moment we have fought against for so long has arrived. Your news, my son, presses upon my heart and releases my greatest fear. Our Father the President has turned a blind eye. It falls heavily upon my ears.

"During my recent ride with John Ross when we encouraged our people to persevere, I saw fields unturned, crops unplanted, homes raided, and families suffering starvation. I saw only doom for our people.

"I believed the Supreme Court's decision would give us the power to reverse our plight and bring food and goods to the ravaged ones. Now hearing your tale, John, I realize the only way we can continue to live as a people is to negotiate the best terms for removal. The Georgians will kill us all or wear us down in their courts until there is nothing left of the Real People."

The power of her father's words—that inborn talent that had raised him to the position of Speaker of the Council and Counselor to the highest man in the nation—now checked Sarah.

She watched him step to the window next to the mantelpiece, then he turned to face his family. The sun, low from the west, divided his face—half dark, half lit.

"I have met and talked with all the Great Fathers since Thomas Jefferson. I have fought next to my friend Jackson, yet he now strikes us down. The American chiefs have taken our hands in friendship, then taken our land by empty promises. I must conclude our only recourse is to negotiate a treaty that will provide the most money and land in the west."

He turned away, looking out the window toward the river. "To survive, we must leave the home of our ancestors." Susanna bowed her head; John leaned back in his chair.

Never had Sarah heard defeat in her father's voice. With the sinking sun glancing off his face, she saw the trail of a tear drawing a shining path down her father's cheek. She would in the years to come remember that tear slicing her father's face, signifying the end of hope.

Her eyes caught her father's empty place on the settee and again she visualized her imagined embroidery composition. Words came to her from her meeting with Sam Maverick, his ominous warning, a truth now confirmed by her brother. Sarah could picture herself, needle in hand, pulling a thick black thread through the fabric, up and down, letter by letter, upon a blood-red banner: "Beware of Friendships between Politicians."

Chapter 16

Sarah Speaks

My truths.

Allow me to share with you the events that followed that day in May when my brother revealed his conversation with President Jackson, the day I saw the tear run down my father's face. I implore you to remember as I do—always—Sam Maverick warning me to beware of friendships between politicians.

We could not remain.

With no one enforcing the Supreme Court's ruling to override Georgia's laws, in October of 1832 the state spun its big drums. As the barrel ceased to roll, a Land Lottery commissioner reached his hand into the cask and pulled out a numbered chit. Checking his corresponding list, he matched the number to the name of the "fortunate drawer." Some of those Georgians planned to rush into our homeland to collect their "winnin's." Others held their chits high and were rushed by a cadre of speculators, gladly accepting the highest bid for their lucky draw of one hundred sixty acres of Cherokee homeland.

However, within a short time, the sounds of spinning drums and whirling chits fell silent. It seemed one of the Land Lottery commissioners was playing sleight of hand with the wheel of fortune.

Milledgeville Commissioner Shadrach Bogan conceived a scheme. For a selected drawing, he bought friends' lottery chances and pasted *their* names over the true fortunate drawers for the richest prizes drawn that day. He rewarded himself with five fine winnin's, including my brother John's Running Waters plantation.

Commissioner Bogan was arrested, and in an "honest" redraw, John's house and one hundred sixty acres of his land were awarded to a Georgian named Griffith Mathis. My family home on the bluff above the Oostanaula River went to fortunate drawer Rachel Fergason, a Revolutionary War widow.

Mr. Bogan's devious plan disproved the proverb that "there is honor among thieves," but his chicanery was merely one fraud within the greater frauds engaged by Governor Lumpkin and his cronies.

Let me tell you how the lottery worked. Over the past years, Georgia had sent surveyors across their state line into our vast nation, renamed our settlements as counties and divided our farms, forests, and settlements into parcels called "Land Lots." These consisted of one hundred sixty acres or a fraction thereof. For a cost of eighteen dollars, citizens could purchase a draw.

It is said that eighty-five thousand white people competed for the over eighteen thousand lots available that year. Drawers were divided by categories. Say, a bachelor could buy only one draw while a married man with a wife and a son under eighteen or an unmarried daughter of any age could buy two draws. Male or female idiots, insane or lunatics, deaf and dumb or blind over ten years of age were entitled to one draw.

Mrs. Fergason who drew our farm was a Revolutionary War widow and as such was entitled to purchase two draws. I often wondered if she was fortunate enough to gain another Cherokee family's inheritance with her second draw. If not, she still made a substantial profit on her eighteen-dollar investment when she immediately sold our plantation—having not even visited her winnin's—to Judge Augustus N. Verdery, son of a prominent Augusta plantation and formerly a slave owner in Haiti.

Other states that had mapped their lines through our lands—Alabama, Tennessee, and North Carolina—passed laws that would not permit Cherokees to settle within their bounds. They were as anxious as Georgia to be rid of us, but they held back in the courts and let the Georgians do their dirty work for them.

Governor Lumpkin's successful division of our nation still had a major obstruction: our people farmed much of that land, and we lived in those houses and cabins. Stories were told of tall, thin, cadaverous white men, slow talking, slow moving with rifles slung across their shoulders—second or third generation Scotch-Irish mountain men—walking among the vigorous, swarthy Cherokee looking for slashed trees with painted numbers designating their winnin's.

John Ross came home from negotiating with President Jackson to find his ferry and spacious home on the Coosa overrun, his flock of peacocks was scattered. Quatie, his wife, was desperately ill and their children were crowded into just two rooms. He took his family and moved to a simple cabin just over the Tennessee border near Red Clay.

We, the Ridges, and others of the so-called elite were permitted to stay in our homes while negotiations continued with trips to Washington City; the War Department ordered Governor Lumpkin to see that we were not ousted. Anger stirred around us, people saying we received special treatment. We did. Our ferries and pastures were seized, yet we fed the starving from our kitchens.

How did it come to this, you might ask?

It has been said we didn't fight back hard enough against intrusions. Only several decades earlier, our men were powerful warriors! We did resort to violence, at least once.

In January 1830 after investigating intrusions for the War Department, General John Coffee was appalled by Georgia's actions. He advised John Ross that as principal chief, it was his duty to expel the squatters; the General Council authorized Ross to do so and my father was chosen to lead several dozen warriors on a raid.

As in times past the men decorated their horses and themselves with feathers and fringe, and painted their faces. Father resurrected his old headdress of the cape and head of a bull—complete with horns—and led a war party to Cedartown near the Georgia-Alabama line. There they found eighteen families of squatters living in the homes of Cherokee who had already emigrated west.

Our warriors rode as they had as young men. They yelled and terrorized the squatters, rousing them from their beds as had so many Cherokee families been forced into the cold. Father's unit gave the families time to evacuate. As the settlers watched, our warriors burned our stolen cabins and ran off livestock. Then they rode away, killing no one, taking no scalps as in raids of yore.

Father had insisted none in the raiding party should drink spirits, but four warriors found a keg of whiskey in one of the houses. While Father led the men back home, those renegades separated, drinking until they passed out. Of course, the Georgia Guard found them. The men were beaten and tied to their horses to be taken to the Carroll County jail. One kept falling off and after several re-bindings, was discovered to be dead.

My cousin Elias Boudinot and others close to the missionaries had pleaded against such retaliations, warning that the Georgians would use any excuse to justify harsher punishment. Elias was right. It was just what the newspapers wanted: "Wild Indians on the Warpath", headlines read. They wrote of white mothers and children left to freeze in deep snow.

Even Northern supporters admonished our actions, knowing full well how Cherokee women and children were being forced from their farms. A report of Indian mothers and babes forced with bayonets by the Georgia Guard to leave their homes did not warrant a front-page headline; Indians routing whites did.

The time for forceful acts or peaceful negotiations ran out.

Those who believed in a treaty realized that the only way to provide relief for our people was by accepting the best terms to move west. While these leaders conceded that most Cherokee were against removal, they also argued that if only they had the opportunity to present the facts of the situation to those in the mountains, they could convince them of the utter hopelessness of remaining in our homeland. The tribe would then vote in favor of a treaty, thereby accepting that moving was the lesser evil than the extinction of the Cherokee by citizenship and assimilation.

These facts, though, were not passed to the people. John Ross suspended elections in July 1832, which denied my brother the opportunity to run against him. The principal chief appointed Elijah Hicks, his brother-in-law, as editor of the *Phoenix* in place of Elias and forbade publishing any pro-removal views. Ross's men spread rumors calling the Arkansaw a wasteland and a barren desert.

Ross schemed to keep the people from hearing the truth. He made sure his cohorts circulated within any gatherings where removal was discussed and encouraged groups faithful to the chief to withdraw.

Jackson's administration consented to Georgia's demands, both finding ways of manipulating those who now accepted that removal was inevitable against those who continued to believe no one would force us from the land of our forefathers.

As my family and I were embroiled in continual negotiations, I found a place to escape reality: letters came from Sam Maverick describing perilous battles with the Mexican army in Texas, yet interwoven with his adventures were descriptions of pine forests and wide open prairies, faraway places with strange sounding names, places where he wished someday to settle.

In my bed at night as I reread his letters, I traveled with Sam, I rode beside him as we reached a rise and before us spread scenes of great beauty. He reached across and took my hand. "Here we will build our home, Sarah, and raise our children."

In my nights, I escaped the misery surrounding me. Sam would come back and take me away. We would ride free of the pain that enveloped my nation into that strange and wonderful country of Texas.

But as I walked down the stairway each morning, I heard again his words warning of friendships between politicians as our tribe was torn apart.

Divide and conquer. Has that not been found a practical means to overthrow an adversary from Julius Caesar to Napoleon?

We were turned against ourselves, Cherokee versus Cherokee.

Chapter 17
Time Runs Out

The Dwindling Cherokee Nation
Red Clay, Tennessee and New Echota, Georgia
1834 - 1835

The federal government's Cherokee problem meant getting rid of over sixteen thousand souls who had grown to be an irritation for the states that had settled around them.

Most of the people were full-blooded Cherokees, likely to live in the hills, hunt and trap, and raise their crops and livestock following traditional practices in small settlements governed by chiefs and headmen. During the colder months, they retired to their *asis*, huts heated with stones and coals, and existed on stored provisions as had their mothers and fathers before them. Then there were hundreds of mixed-blood families, those whose ancestral mothers had taken as husbands—or *been* taken by—Scots traders and trappers in the late 1700s, and were generally said to be the most "progressive" and "civilized." Black slaves numbered well over a thousand.

Sarah's family and an impassioned group of men, most of them mixed-bloods, believed to save the Cherokee they must secure the maximum money for eastern lands and secure the maximum land in the west.

John Ross held firm for the people remaining on whatever land the Union would allow. As principal chief, he was much loved by those often called the simple people, the full-bloods, the ones who lived in the forests. If their beloved principal chief told them to move to Mexico, most would follow him to Mexico; if he told them to move west, they would move west.

Assimilation into the states would not work, on that issue the Ridges and John Ross factions agreed. In a short time, the money would be spent or swindled by the whites with their whiskey barrels. Cherokee families would be reduced to slaves—lower than Negro slaves, since they had no owners who valued them. Even President Jackson did not want the Cherokees to disappear into the backwoods of the states as citizens; he wanted them to disappear as a tribe into the backwoods beyond the Mississippi.

There were wealthy and educated men, full- and mixed-bloods, who agreed with John Ross. His side, now known as the National Party, had a slew of sophisticated leaders and like-minded men who would do anything to keep their families on the tribal lands. Though his brother Andrew eventually sided with the Treaty Party, another of the Ross brothers, Lewis, would join with John as his loyal right-hand man.

For Major Ridge's reversal to supporting negotiations for a treaty, James Foreman, a Rossman sheriff and relentless agitator for the National Party, ranted against the old leader, saying if not for Ridge the Cherokee would have already received relief from the federal government. Foreman fueled hostility, and proclaimed Major Ridge an enemy of the people. During a council meeting, Foreman turned his rage against the sixty-four-year-old orator and treaty advocates.

During the August council meeting, shouts of "Kill them!" echoed through Red Clay: as Jack Walker, a pro-treaty agitator, left a meeting early he was ambushed by two Rossmen and was shot from his saddle. He died, and later James Foreman and his half-brother Anderson Springston were indicted for Walker's death. The case came to an end, though, when the Tennessee Supreme Court declared their criminal laws did not extend to Cherokee murderers.

Sarah's cousin Elias Boudinot wrote from Washington City that John Ross trembled at the progress of the Treaty delegates' successes. Several of Ross's propositions were rejected, the first to sell the nation for twelve million dollars. However, later Ross signed an obligation to accept the gross amount of money offered by the Senate as sufficient.

The President, Elias wrote after a meeting with Jackson, was willing that Ross's proposal be taken to the people. The *people* should choose, not Ross nor the delegates. Jackson was adamant for a treaty to be decided in the nation, not one signed by representatives in Washington. He told the chief there would be no more changes to the proposed treaty, for him to go home and convince his people to agree to move west, and to not return with another proposal.

John Ross kept his duplicitous dealings in Washington City quiet, never recounting each step in the negotiations to the people back home. As he signed an obligation to accept whatever amount the Senate offered, he wrote Major Ridge and John pleading that partyism be discarded for the good of the nation and people.

Partyism, though, was not discarded; the tribe turned against each other. Factions fought factions.

While Ross stalled, Jackson appointed a duo of commissioners for the Cherokee: former six-term governor of Tennessee William Carroll and a former preacher from Utica, New York, John F. Schermerhorn. The commissioners' orders were to negotiate a treaty with the Cherokee, get it signed in their nation, and to not come back to the capital until they did.

Commissioner Schermerhorn. *Skaynooyahnah*. The Devil's Horn. Large and flamboyant with flying gray hair, he was described as a crafty and subtle man; less flattering, as a man tall on zeal and short on knowledge and discretion.

By the fall of 1835, the powers in Washington City had finally agreed on a treaty for the removal of the Cherokee. The Senate proposed exchanging four million, five hundred thousand dollars, plus thirteen million acres in the west for the eastern lands. The treaty included an additional eight hundred thousand acres—the "Neutral Lands" south of the Kansas Territory for a perpetual outlet to the far west—estimated at five hundred thousand dollars, making the total of the payment five million dollars. Included in this treaty was a perpetual annuity to provide for a school fund, a provision for which the Treaty Party had pressed. This final treaty was approved by congressional consensus. John Ross had previously agreed—if that body so offered—he would honor the offer and present it to his people. This pact promised the tribe sovereignty in their new land.

After several contentious councils over the summer, John Ross called for all the people to attend the annual October council that would be held at Red Clay in Tennessee, since Georgia had outlawed gatherings within the state. Commissioner Schermerhorn planned to read the treaty to the assembled thousands of Cherokees, some of whom had walked over a hundred miles.

The council opened with a prayer by a native preacher. Reverend Schermerhorn waited to read the provisions of the treaty. Ross, the master of delay, called for a conference of representatives of the two factions. John Ridge, Elias Boudinot, Charles Vann, and two others represented the Treaty Party; they met with five others who represented the National Party. After five days of wrangling and divisiveness, the members arrived at a compromise that even John Ridge found favorable. He believed so strongly in the promises from the other side that he felt the parties had finally united.

John Ross then drew up a paper that granted full powers to a delegation of twenty men either to treat with Schermerhorn or to go to Washington City for negotiations. However, Ross added a clause that protested the acceptance of the five million dollars, although that figure had been set by the Senate and earlier the chief agreed to accept whatever amount they offered.

On the last evening of the council, with autumn leaves falling and anxious people listening, Ross had a linkister read his—not the commissioner's—instrument to his followers. Afterward, he called for a vote; the question shouted out across the field in Cherokee was, "Are you willing to take five millions of dollars for your country?"

"No! No!" the people answered from the meadow and forest edge.

Did the words "five millions of dollars" register to the simple people who bartered for deerskins with baskets of corn? What if Ross had said, "Five thousands of dollars"? Or "Twenty millions?"

He then asked the crowd if they were willing to give full power to these twenty delegates to conduct their business. "Yes! Yes!" "*Ve-ve!*" Cheering filled the meadow in waves of huzzahs.

With their assent ringing in his ears Ross dismissed the gathered tribe. They scattered. No deliberation, no questioning. The majority, it was said, believed they had rejected the proposed treaty outright and that they had instructed their delegates to make no treaty. They dispersed into the woods and back to their homes confident they had saved their land.

Ross could now justify any measures he took by acknowledging to all that he acted for "the will of the people." Had he extricated himself from his promise to abide by the Senate's arbitration when he had promised to recommend their offer to his people? Perhaps he felt he nullified his shrouded deal.

Major Ridge and John, Elias, Charles Vann, and John Gunter—others who supported a compromise signed their names to the rejection of Schermerhorn's treaty. They felt that by doing this they were expressing the rule of the majority and assumed a modified treaty would be presented to them; John Ross and a Cherokee delegation left for Washington City in early December.

Schermerhorn, snubbed and insulted—and greatly disappointed—stayed in the country and decisively wrote to Ross that the provisions in the treaty were the final overtures the President would make, and added that the chief and delegation would not be welcomed by the War Department, nor would Jackson meet with them. Schermerhorn's orders remained to get the treaty signed in the native land.

Before the delegates left in early December, Elias decided to remain behind in support of Schermerhorn's determination to hold a General

Council meeting on the third Monday of December at New Echota. A broadside was printed and couriers sent throughout the country warning that all who failed to attend would be considered as giving assent and sanctioning the decisions made by council.

John Ross suggested that Major Ridge replace Elias in the delegation, but the aged orator refused. As a substitute, John Ridge insisted that Elias' brother Stand Watie go instead; Ross agreed. The chief needed to present a semblance of unity when they arrived—John and Stand consented to travel in hope that Ross might yet find it necessary to accept a removal treaty.

When no indication of that transformation occurred at the capital, the cousins left shortly and returned home, finally breaking with Ross only after accepting that a compromise was impossible since he continued evasive and non-committal policies. The government, on their part, refused to negotiate with the principal chief.

Though stories of bribery passed across the land, no one profited personally, not the Ridges, not John Ross. Others, yes; some later manipulated provisions, turned profits for themselves, but the leaders took no bribes, did not receive more than their due.

In the nation, all that remained was for the opposing factions to come together and sign the government's treaty. To ensure that end, Schermerhorn wrote into the treaty Preamble noting John Ross's failure to make good on his commitment to the Senate to abide by their decision of the five-million-dollar amount. The commissioner also recorded Ross's recklessness of proceeding to Washington City and his absence from the homeland: to the Cherokee who chose not to appear at the December council, they were warned that nonattendance would be counted as "assent and sanction."

Whether revered as the good Reverend Schermerhorn or despised as *Skaynooyahnah* the Devil's Horn, President Jackson's Indian commissioner convened a meeting of a General Council at the tribe's former capital of New Echota. The date set was Monday, December 21, 1835.

Chapter 18

Lamentation for a Dying Nation

New Echota Campground

December 1835

"Miss Sarah Ridge, may I present my son John Underwood." Sarah extended her hand to the young white man who she had noticed walking the New Echota grounds for several days, moving through the circles of Cherokee and smattering of whites that milled around the buildings and grounds at the former capital, a witness to the final gasp of her dying nation.

"I'm pleased to meet you, John. Please call me Sallie. We admire your father and depend on his legal services during these days of treaty talks."

"I'm honored to make your acquaintance, Miss Sallie," John replied. "My father has many times mentioned your attendance—and that of your mother's—at this gathering."

A smile broke the young man's smooth cheeks as dark, flyaway eyebrows rose to display intense brown eyes. Though only a shadowy moustache embellished his upper lip, his broad forehead bore creases belying his years. A mere sixteen, some seven years younger than she. As he leaned forward with his hands grasped behind him, ambling among the circled camps of blanket-shrouded Cherokees, Sarah surmised an embryonic lawyer inhaling whiffs of jurisprudence as well as tobacco smoke.

John's father, William H. Underwood of nearby Gainesville, had thrown his proverbial hat into a small ring of Washington City and Georgia attorneys who since the days of *Worcester v. Georgia* four years before, continued to fight for the nation's sovereign rights.

Mr. Underwood and several other white lawyers advised leaders as the final stages of the treaty were prepared while authorities of the state of Georgia oversaw the continual decimation of Cherokee sovereignty.

Sarah asked, "Will you be following in your father's footsteps as a lawyer, John?"

"Yes, ma'am. I'm already reading the law in his office and soon shall study with others at the capital in Milledgeville. Here I'm observing the art of negotiation and am captivated by its intricacies."

Sarah smiled. "And by its perplexing outcomes, no doubt."

Since the sun's height and warmth allowed time for an afternoon stroll, she added, "Would you like to accompany me for a walk around camp?"

Rather than a bonnet, Sarah had chosen a simple knitted caplet as her mother wore; the cap offered wool for warmth and security against the wind whipping through the meadow. Her burgundy wool dress matched her cap, and she clutched a gray shawl tight around her shoulders.

Excusing themselves from the group the two moved among clusters of campfires, the air sweet with uncured pine and popping resin. An eagle shrieked as it left its nest at the top of a distant spruce. An army wood wagon squeaked past with soldiers handing out firewood. While over twelve hundred Cherokees had assembled in previous days, now that Christmas Day had come and gone with no resolution, whispered warnings from the Rossmen had caused the crowd to dwindle to about three hundred hopeful souls.

Pods of elders and women nodded to Sarah, then continued their pipe smoking and grunts in reply to the occasional conversation. She, her mother, and Watty had been sleeping in Elias and Harriet's house; most other visitors were staying in nearby structures or tents and covered wagons. Two small cabins had been built for the commissioners and Major Benjamin Curry, whose officers and soldiers were billeted in a distant cluster of tents that resembled rows of pale haystacks as shadows edged from the woods.

"You missed Christmastime with your family, John," Sarah commented.

"Yes, Miss Sallie. But I prefer escaping the confines of home to mix with the assemblage here. The elders at times welcome me to smoke their pipes, and they share with me their *connahany*. I laugh and chat with the young folks. Though I know little of your language, I listen and watch the seemingly immobile faces. I learn much from what is not said."

"What have you learned?" Sarah smiled. "Other than smoking, silence, and the savory flavor of our corn hominy?"

"If I may speak honestly, I know your family views Chief Ross as the adversary, yet I accompanied my father to the October council. There I learned that President Jackson gave the opinion that Ross only intended delay and that the chief did not intend to make a treaty when he proceeded to Washington City.

"I disagree. I believe John Ross was acting in good faith. He was afraid to make that treaty. He knows the Cherokees are not willing to cede their land, and he knows there is no power under Heaven to make them leave willingly."

Sarah noted a voice already deep, matched to the analytical thinking of an aspiring attorney.

"The chief sought delay," John continued, "but it was only to give the people time to cool. He thought they would see that it was a choice of evils. Give up the lands or face extermination.

"He knows well that the habits and instincts of the simple people cannot bear the contact of a refined civilization."

"You are perceptive, John, for one so young."

"Thank you, Miss Sallie."

As their route brought them close to Elias's house she added, "Yet John Ross has failed to allow the people knowledge of what these years of negotiations have brought. They know only what he chooses to tell them, not the truth that whether now or two years hence they, sadly, will be forced from our mountains and valleys."

A meeting just ending, walking down the steps came Sarah's parents along with John Underwood's father. Elias followed; other members of the committee of twenty paused as Sarah's father spoke.

"We are approaching a conclusion," Major Ridge announced. "We are including the National Party's wishes and stipulations for those heads of families who are averse to removal and wish to remain within the bounds of North Carolina, Tennessee, and Alabama, knowing they will be subjected to the laws of those states as citizens. They are entitled to one hundred and sixty acres of land on which to reside, as well as relocation funds. We have written in those provisions as Article Twelve."

Sarah translated for the group as the members dispersed. Mr. Underwood excused himself, asking John if he would like to join him in their tent.

"I would respectfully ask if Mr. Boudinot could remain, I . . . I would like to engage him in thoughts I have shared with his cousin Sallie."

Elias smiled and nodded in agreement, and as the older ones bid the younger a good evening, Sarah looked up as Harriet opened the front door and called out evening wishes to the departing group. Elias greeted his wife as she walked down the steps.

"Would you care to join us, my dear?" Elias asked. "Young Underwood wishes to join in our ongoing deliberations."

Elias, ten years older than Sarah, was a slight man, a worried man bearing a heavy burden. His ebony pompadour raised his height several inches above his severely coifed wife, and his mixed-blood Cherokee heritage darkened his skin a few shades deeper than Harriet's New England complexion.

Sarah smiled and hugged the frail woman; Harriet pushed an escaping tendril behind her ear and pulled her shawl tight across her thin shoulders.

At Elias's request, Underwood repeated his observations of John Ross that he earlier shared with Sarah.

Elias graciously listened to the younger man and at John's conclusion said, "You are a sharp observer. Allow me to elaborate on our relationship with the principal chief, gained from years of association with him."

Sarah glanced at her new friend, noting a firmness of lips pulled into a slight smile of pride as he heard his opinion acknowledged by the well-known patriot.

"While I and many others have fought against removal," Elias said, "have begged and pleaded with the government to allow us to remain in our nation, it was only through much recognition and prayer that I changed my mind.

"Of late, I have in my writings and speeches publicly advocated for selling our land and removing to the western lands. For this, I am reviled by my people. Ross, conversely, has discreetly negotiated with the War Department and Indian Agents—and President Jackson himself—on the same basis, yet is revered."

Beside her Sarah heard Harriet's sigh. Such grief and persecution this devoted woman has endured through the years of Elias's perils, she thought.

Nodding, Sarah added, "Chief Ross does not fully inform the people of his proposition to the United States, John. He publicly continues to affirm that he will not bend on the Cherokee land rights. His followers think his mission is for a 'better treaty,' one that does not require the Cherokee to leave their eastern lands."

Elias continued. "Ross must explain to the people that the only treaty the United States will find acceptable *is* a treaty of removal. He fails to do that."

In the dusk of this winter day with only his wife, cousin, and a young man listening, Elias's eloquent voice filled with emotion. "Why, I say, why? Why will he not speak candidly to the people and explain to them that *to treat means to sell the land!*

"He feeds them expectations, yet Jackson has told me, told Ross, told the Congress!—that no better treaty will come. It will not! And the people will be totally unprepared to remove when the final gavel falls. If Ross will only tell them of the true nature of his negotiations they will have no choice but to accept the treaty and to prepare for its painful transition."

Elias took a deep breath as he gazed across the meadow, out into the gloaming. Sarah felt he might have been alone, speaking his deepest beliefs to his God above. His voice took on a hymn-like tone.

"John Ross brandishes his sword, saying he is following the 'will of the people.' The people know not what their vote at the October council put in progress. They think they sent their chief to the seat of government to obtain a better covenant, while Jackson has stated to Ross: 'No more.'"

In the stillness that followed Elias's emotional soliloquy, Harriet moved to her husband's side and placed her arm around his waist.

John Underwood raised his head, his shoulders back, chest forward as if standing at attention, having witnessed a truth greater than his own through the words of a Cherokee hero.

To Sarah, Andrew Jackson's statement left her cousin's lips and seemed to reverberate throughout the town that once served as the symbol of Cherokee cultural accomplishments, the dream of a capital city for her nation.

"No more. No more. No more."

Perhaps, she thought, all of us gathered in this meadow hear it.

On Monday, December 28th, the committee of twenty reported to the council that they now recommended the treaty, which was in essence the same as presented by Commissioner Schermerhorn to the October council.

Governor Carroll had sent word from Nashville that he was unable to travel, taken down as he was by a spell of rheumatism. Three hundred hardy Cherokee souls, doubtless many who suffered aches and pains, huddled in the cold New Echota campgrounds, apprehensive always, of personal danger; they listened and smoked and waited.

The Ridges and Waties, with Harriet and John Underwood, stood off to one side of Elias's house. Family members were uncertain of reactions to the speeches they would hear today; young Underwood continued his novice-like enthusiasm as a witness to history.

Sarah watched as her father walked out on the porch. A chair was placed for him to sit, but he stood beside it, merely resting his hand on the high back. Sarah saw in his face a spark and heard power in his words. She squeezed her mother's hand as that sonorous voice filled the meadow.

"I am one of the native sons of these wild woods. I have hunted deer and turkey here for more than fifty years. I have fought your battles. I have defended truth and honesty and fair trading."

The meadow buzzed with *huzzahs*, and then Elias translated his uncle's words into English. Sarah felt as if she were in that distant cave filled with crystals that her father had taken her to as a child—Elias' words resounded as an echo. Sadly, she heard her father's wisdom and pain not once, but twice.

"I have always been the friend of honest white men. The Georgians have shown a grasping spirit lately. They have extended their laws, to which we are unaccustomed, which harass our braves and make the children suffer and cry.

"But I can do them justice in my heart. They think the Great Father the President is bound by the Compact of 1802, to purchase this country for them, and they justify their conduct by the end in view." He paused.

"I know the Indians have an older title than theirs. We obtained the land from the living God above. They got their title from the British."

An eagle swooped and shrieked. The people listened.

"Yet, they are strong and we are weak. We are few, they are many. We cannot remain here in safety and comfort. I know we love the graves of our fathers who have gone before to the happy hunting grounds of the Great Spirit—the eternal land where the deer, the turkey, and the buffalo will never give out.

"We can never forget these homes, I know, but an unbending, iron necessity tells us we must leave them. I would willingly die to preserve them, but any forcible effort to keep them will cost us our lands, our lives, and the lives of our children."

Sarah put her arm across her mother's shoulders. So willowy, so old, she thought. And now Mother must begin a new life.

"There is but one path of safety, one road to future existence as a nation. That path is open before us. Make a treaty of cession. Give up these lands and go over beyond the Great Father of Waters."

Sarah leaned her head against her mother's; her father's eloquent Cherokee words seemed to hover above the campgrounds.

"Give up. Give up. Give up."

Sarah looked across the meadow and felt her father's words now entwined with her memory of Elias repeating President Jackson's statement to John Ross:

"No more. No more. No more."

Elias's translation broke through her reverie.

Not waiting for the English version the crowd began to shuffle. Young people reached down to help the aged rise. Sarah saw faces she had known all her life now streaked with tears.

With Elias at his side, her father walked down the steps and into his waiting people. They grasped his hands and tugged his tunic. Overwhelmed with affection and respect, each greeted their old leader, their friend, then stepped back for the next in line to express their admiration.

As Major Ridge finally returned and stood beside her mother, Sarah realized her parents served as symbols of a nation no more.

Next up on the porch came White Path, the revered old chieftain who during the writing of the constitution in 1827, fought to keep traditional ways. In defiance he had gathered followers to form a council, refusing to agree to accept a list of governing laws in exchange for giving up the ancient ways. The rebellion of these true believers lasted a year until White Path and his warriors returned to New Echota.

Tall—a regal full-blood—dressed in buckskins and beaded feathers, the chieftain spoke from the porch, again with Elias translating. White Path waved his arm and motioned to Major Ridge as he told the people he approved of his friend's words.

Would this old warrior remove? Sarah wondered. Would White Path give up his home, his homeland? He accepts Father's words, but the legendary warrior has forever clung to the ancient ways.

"We do not deny our love of land." White Path's deep voice filled the space between the house and woods. He gestured in the direction of a creek. "But you can sooner turn back the waters of yonder stream and make them seek the springs again, as to lose the hold on the Indian's mind for the home of his birth."

The crowd of watchers and seekers grunted and nodded in approval. The slight breeze that had played among the trees rose to a steady wind.

White Path walked into the crowd and to Sarah, seemed to vanish into an era passed.

Stepping behind her mother, she moved between her parents. She took their hands and placed them within her own. Wisps of smiles crossed their faces. Sarah read in their countenance neither fear nor joy as she again heard her father's words riding on the wind:

"Give up. Give up. Give up."

Chapter 19

The Treaty of New Echota

New Echota Campground

December 29, 1835

"Good morning, Miss Sallie," John Underwood said as he arrived the following day at the table soldiers had assembled for Commissioner Schermerhorn's display. The space before Elias' house was steadily filling with people watching and waiting.

Sarah noticed the young man somewhat disarrayed, his suit jacket askew and his dark hair thatched as if he was unable to tame the vestiges from a night of unrest. "And to you, John, although you seem not at the peak of enthusiasm this morning."

"No, ma'am, I slept but little last night. The sorrows of the poor Indians rang through my brain. Yesterday's speeches sounded to me like the death songs I have read in fiction. I tossed and pondered, and only near morning did sleep come, much to my relief."

"I fear many of us share your distress, dear man," she said. She had arisen early to the rustle of so many sleeping in Elias's house and to endings enveloping her thoughts.

They stepped over near a corner of the porch as the door opened and the commissioner came out wearing a dark parson-like suit. His gray hair and beard—as well as his countenance—seemed subdued for this solemn occasion. The delegates passed by and gathered near the table; Elias remained next to him on the porch.

Schermerhorn's alleged Devil's Horn persona assumed a secondary position to that of heartfelt diplomat as he addressed the general council. He painted in rich tones the land of new homes across the Mississippi River. "Fresh, fertile, free country," he repeated, "where you and your children and your children's children can live unmolested by the Georgians who continue to encroach on your homelands.

"Here you are exposed, insecure, and liable to difficulties with the settlers, but sovereignty awaits you once more."

Elias handed him a large sheet of parchment.

Holding the image high between them, Schermerhorn's finger glided across a map drawn and enhanced by bright-colored patches on one half, austere wilderness on the other. Tracing a path across the states from which his audience was being expelled, his finger paused at the heavy black meandering line in the center of the paper that rose like a tree rooted in the Mississippi Delta, its trunk leading up to leafless branches of thick rivers that fed it. The commissioner followed that naked canopy eastward, calling out names of rivers over which the emigrants would travel: the Tennessee to the Ohio, the Cumberland through Tennessee and Kentucky to meet the Ohio, to float down the Great Father of Waters to that final lower branch, the Arkansaw River. There the lines joined that offshoot to the new Cherokee homeland, theirs for as long as waters flow and grass grows.

Reverend Schermerhorn concluded with the news that the negotiated provisions would be copied onto paper with seals affixed for the twenty delegates to sign. He invited the crowd to join their fellow tribe members at the table where they could see for themselves the picture-map of their new homeland. He thanked the assembly, then entered Elias's house and closed the door behind him.

Sarah and young Underwood edged over the table, conscious of not disrupting the line that was forming.

What do the simple people see, she thought, when they look at the map? Those who can read, have attended mission schools, we have seen maps. If one has never seen a map before, what do the lines and colors represent?

She spotted her mother's friend Flying Bird leaning over the table. Always a part of Sarah's childhood with births and burials but aged now, revered for her wisdom, for healing herbs and soothing ways. Yet unschooled.

Does Flying Bird see the pale green of the state of Georgia and yellow of Tennessee overpainted on our great mountains of smoke? Does she see the vast emptiness of western space? Can she imagine our cabins, pens, and gardens rebuilt in that emptiness?

Can any of us, truly? Sarah shuddered as a wave of fear and dreadful sadness overcame her. Turning away from her friend, she wiped her eyes with her gloved hand.

"Perhaps we should wait to view the map later," she said. "Have you breakfasted, John? George Lavender brought supplies from Father's store last night."

"I'd be honored, Miss Sallie."

That afternoon, Tuesday, December 29, 1835, the committee of twenty met at three o'clock in the Council House to review the pages on which the clerk had written—in his finest script—the final version of provisions offered by the United States of America to the tribe of Indians recognized as the Cherokee. This death knell would forever ring as the Treaty of New Echota.

The first three pages consisted of a Preamble, followed by nineteen Articles covering fourteen pages; the final two sheets with their wax seals awaited the delegation and witnesses to sign their names. Following approval of the document, the council adjourned until six o'clock in Elias's parlor.

The twenty regathered along with Major Currey and a bevy of officers, Mr. Underwood, and two other counsel who would serve as witnesses. Sarah and John Underwood had arranged to meet there. Sarah asked her mother if she wanted to go, but Susanna answered she preferred to stay away and pray.

"May I attend, to be with Father?" Sarah asked.

"Are you sure, Sallie? Elias's house will be tightly guarded by our people as well as the Army, but your father warns of danger."

"I will share his danger."

From the trunk in the covered wagon where the family changed, Sarah pulled on a dark tannin-dyed dress and wrapped her gray wool shawl across her shoulders. Stepping out of the wagon as the sun fell, she saw her mother standing on a nearby rise, looking across the meadow.

"I feel this is my final sunset in our homeland, Sallie. When our men press their pens to that paper, this town, those hills are no longer ours." Sarah hugged her and asked if she could walk her back to the house, upstairs to a bedroom.

"No. I wish to soak up the last rays of this day. Go be with your father."

Sarah turned to leave. "Wait, Sallie!"

Her mother jerked off her shawl. Sarah remembered how years before Susanna spent hours at the loom in a corner of their dining room, snipping, tying the wool weft, and creating rows of green pines onto a red-tan warp. All the hills, valleys, and rivers of her mother's homeland lay in the images woven into her treasured shawl.

Sarah smiled as they exchanged wraps, and hugged her mother.

Reaching Elias's house she caught no glimpse of John waiting for her outside so she assumed the Underwoods were already in the parlor. The grounds, the porch, the hallways were filled with Cherokees and whites, soldiers and . . . and she thought, Rossmen in disguise?

Weaving through the busy house, she moved to a back hall where she knew another door would let her into the parlor. Slipping in, she pressed against the wall.

Rows of beeswax candles lit a table in the center; firelight and another row of candles on the mantel sent a gleam across the crowded room. She saw her father in a chair and that the several dozen signers were here; the usually-spacious parlor appeared ready to burst its walls.

The fire warmed the mass of bodies assembled. Sarah perspired under her mother's shawl but clung to it with love.

After a few minutes, John Underwood eased through the crowd to stand next to her. As the only woman attending, Sarah was relieved to have a friend beside her.

Commissioner Schermerhorn rose. Major Curry motioned to a soldier to quiet the crowd outside. Slowly and emphatically the commissioner read the treaty aloud for a final time to a silent room. The Cherokee delegates nodded and raised their pipes at appropriate times in assent to the words they had struggled to develop over the days.

With the signing pages spread on the table amid candles, ink pots, blotters, and an array of sharpened quills, Commissioner Schermerhorn signed his name on the upper right column next to his seal, leaving space above for Governor Carroll to sign later. He then called for signatures and waited for a committee member to step forward.

No one came.

John touched Sarah's arm and whispered, "They're apprehensive. Some say that to sign the treaty is to sign their own death warrants." Sarah shivered in the heat of the room. Only at this moment did she truly realize the momentous bravery of the delegates.

A log crashed in the fireplace just as the clock on the mantel chimed eleven times.

John Gunter rose and marched forward to the table. Taking a quill, he dipped it into a pot.

"I am not afraid. I sell the whole country of my birth." He scrawled his name in a firm script a bit down on the left column where Schermerhorn pointed.

Next stood Andrew Ross, then John A. Bell; next Sarah's uncle William Lassley, then Elias.

Elias walked back and assisted Major Ridge to the table. Taking the pen, he scrawled his uncle's name, leaving a space between the words. Blotting the ink, Elias dipped the pen and handed it to his uncle who made his mark between Elias's words.

Sarah saw her father's lips move, but could not hear his words. He returned to his seat.

The clerk took over from Elias as several of the delegates who could not write came forward: Caetehee, his mark; Tegaheske, his mark.

Robert Rogers, the husband of a Vann daughter and a young mixed-blood among the grizzled chiefs and headmen, scrawled his name above John Gunter's.

Charles Foreman signed, who unlike his cousin James, upheld removal to save his tribe.

William Rogers, who worked conscientiously in wording Article Twelve, affirming those Cherokees who desired to remain and gain citizenship now scrawled his name.

George W. Adair signed above Elias, then waited and scrawled for his friends James Starr, Archilla Smith and Jesse Halftree as they made their marks.

The clerk rose to assist Tahyeske with his mark, then George Chambers with his; Charles Moore and Tesataesky with their marks; James Foster placed his mark below Sarah's father's.

With all marks and signatures in place—it was done.

A host of white men circled the table, their faces ghostly in the flickering candlelight as they too signed.

From the lawyers in attendance, the honor passed to William Underwood. As she heard his name called, Sarah patted his proud son on his arm.

Then she saw Mr. Underwood waving; she pushed John forward as his father announced, "My son has attended these meetings. I would be honored to have him sign as the final witness."

Watching her friend dip his quill, Sarah heard the melodic chimes from Harriet's treasured ceramic clock that she had carried from her home in Cornwall. Twelve chimes marked not only the ending of her husband's dream of a nation that would serve as a model of native sovereignty within the limits of the United States but as a final dirge to its defeat.

The ceremony was over. The room began to clear. Sarah heard Schermerhorn say he needed a copy of the entire treaty written out immediately, to be sent to Governor Carroll for him to sign. Not finding the clerk, the commissioner asked if another could transcribe the treaty. John Underwood, having written speeches for several delegates during the meetings, raised his hand to undertake the task. A grateful Schermerhorn authorized the disbursing agent to file a warrant for fifty dollars in the name of Sarah's young friend.

Taking her father's arm, she led him from the parlor. The hallway remained filled with soldiers and hangers-on, the meadow with anxious Cherokee acknowledging an ending to their way of life. She walked with her father out the rear door and down the stairs, taking their first steps onto the soil of the homeland that was no longer theirs.

Susanna emerged from the side of Elias's house. A sliver of waning moon failed to light the frigid night. Handing her father's arm to her mother Sarah turned back, allowing her parents this momentous evening to speak of sunsets and dying ways. Perhaps they would speak of a new home in a new land.

Or, perhaps, her father would tell her mother the words he spoke as he marked the treaty: "I have signed my death warrant."

Pulling her mother's shawl tight around her own trembling shoulders, Sarah left her parents knowing she would never learn the words they shared on the night the land of their ancestors passed into the hands of the United States of America.

Chapter 20

Ashes

Ridge Plantation

November 1836

A streak of early sunshine edged its way through the golden canopy of the chestnut tree and cut a line across Sarah's bed. In moving her hand to brush light from her eyes, she also brushed away the veil of sleep protecting her from reality.

Eyes closed. Familiar autumn sounds triggered images of the plantation at work. Memories: Novembers … first frost … hiding in the busy lard-making kitchen, out of the way, waiting for a taste of crisp cracklings. Hams to smoke, bacon to cure. Doll calling her children, Little Tom and Milly, to bring more buckets from the well. Lettie ladling salt into the big water crocks, stirring with the paddle. Watching Lucinda drop in an egg to see if it would float, signaling the perfect brine.

Long ago sights and sounds, vanishing with the candle glow in Elias' parlor as she watched the treaty papers fill with names, almost a year now.

These months of watching, like Lucinda, to see if the removal egg would sink or float. Never did it float, never did the perfect mix of human compassion and laws combine to keep the Cherokee people from sinking into the choking brine. The last of the hogs. The last crops of sweet potatoes and turnips. Final rides through forest trails. An ending of life in their homeland.

Sarah stretched and rested her arm across her eyes, blocking the sun.

A good harvest. So very needed. Displaced Cherokees milled around Lavender's Store waiting to be fed. Everyone who still farmed shared their crops with others and found places for family and friends to camp.

From the dining room below she heard her mother giving packing directions to Milly and Lettie of what to take and what to leave, dividing family possessions between those being sold off and items crated for the trip to what some called the Promised Land. Or a forsaken people left to wander in the wilderness.

Must get up, she told herself.

Her hand dropped from her face and glided across her blankets. Amid the folds, the crackle of paper brought her fully awake. She sank back in her covers.

Four years. Four visits. Four letters.

Last night at supper a traveler friend of her father's told news of Texas.

"Davy Crockett of Tennessee died in San Antonio, one of a great number of men, 'bout two hundred. Jim Bowie from Kentucky. One of the Travis boys, William from over in Alabama—well, they fought the Mexicans to the last man in that mission called the Alamo. After that front failed for the Texicans, General Sam Houston and his Texas Army retreated to a river called San Jacinto. But ol' Sam surprised the Mexicans during their siesta. Captured that General Santa Anna. Now The Raven's president of the Republic of Texas! And he's given Cherokees right good land to live on in the eastern part of the new republic. Tall pines, good hunting.

"Go to Texas," the traveler said, "we have friends there. Houston will help us. Sam Maverick from over in Lauderdale County, he fought in the Siege of Béxar. Told me a while back he'd be taking his new wife to Texas."

Major Ridge shook his head, "No, we will go to the Arkansaw."

Sarah, choking on a piece of venison took a sip of water, politely excused herself from the table and came to her room. Later when her mother looked in the door, Sarah waved her away.

Sam. Married.

That day on the road ... four years ago in a world so different from now. Three times Sam Maverick again passed through, stopping to see her. Four visits and four letters, brief, all. Yes, she knew he speculated buying lottery winnings, turning a profit on sliced-up farms and plantations won by fortunate drawers for cash. As she grew to know him, Sarah felt there was an element of Sam she could never completely admire. But within this man of multiple slices, she sensed another surface, one of self-assurance, visualizing what *could* be. Qualities she wished for herself. Her perception of him—that the thrill of the deal was more exciting than ownership—was not unlike her distant dreams when she returned from Salem School.

Now, *if* there had been a future, that door was closed.

On his last trip through, Sam took her hand as they walked down the bluff. A stolen kiss behind a willow, shielded from view by his dun horse. "I'm going to Texas, but I'll be back."

Hearing his words, Sarah built a wall of self-protection around her, a shield from the immediacy of daily pain she saw in the faces of family and friends as each week brought more new indignities, more strife between the Ridges and John Ross. She avoided local men who might have wanted to marry the aging daughter—at twenty-four—of a respectable Cherokee planter. She foolishly imagined a romance with Sam. In her dreams, she escaped the dismal endings of her world. She rode with him, free in Texas.

She never wrote him, he the wanderer, yet letters came with far-away names: Colbert's Reserve in Alabama; New Orleans; San Felipe de Austin; San Antonio de Béxar. Brief scribblings, excited expectations, the colors of vast grasslands and endless skies that Sarah turned into pictures to replace the destruction around her. She loved—*if* she loved—the myth of Maverick more than the man. And now that myth had no place in her reality.

"Sallie?" Lettie stood in the open doorway. The goldenrod walls of the room glowed in the morning light as if to refute the occupant's misery. "Aire ye ready to get up? I need to go through yer trunk to see what ye want to take on th' journey."

The journey. As if the preparations for an exciting visit to Salem or Washington City. Trips like those would be no more.

"I'm awake. Come on in."

Lettie opened the trunk with a loud *bang* against the yellow wall. "I dinnae care if I scratch up these fine walls since that white trash what won our place dinnae know any difference anyhow. All they aire used to is sleepin' in dirt-floor shacks with th' dogs an' pigs an' chickens."

When Sarah didn't comment, Lettie paused from pulling a linen bedgown from the trunk. Then she dropped the lid with a *clunk*. The women's mutual anger at the removal was matched.

Holding the gown, Lettie walked to the side of the bed and stared at Sam's letters, then looked directly into Sarah's teary eyes. Lettie's long, tapered fingers ran nervously across the linen as she made little creases. Dropping her argumentative tone, she replaced it with one of care and concern. "I could be outta place, but I need to speak me piece, I do."

Sarah looked up and mumbled between tightened lips, "Yes."

"Miz Susanna says ye got a mess a' bad news last night at supper, but dinnae be pretendin' that way down deep inside that ye didn't have an inklin' that man was not gonna come back for ye. I told ye from the first time I saw him that the likes of him was not gonna marry a' Injun girl. Even a rich, schooled girl like yerself."

Sarah turned her head. Chestnut leaves scratched at the window.

"He set his mind too high. He desires to be a rich man in Texas. Even if that's a different country, no white man like him was gonna to take an Injun girl there, set her up as th' lady of his house. Now I'm sorry ye aire going through this hurtin', but quit yer mopin' and get on with what ye has to do."

Sarah closed her eyes. Lettie's footsteps told her she'd retreated to give her friend the solitude needed to allow her words to glide down and settle as were the leaves outside the windows.

Images bright as the spring day in Sam's arms ran through her head, then darkened to a gray bleakness as Lettie's words took hold. Yes, Sarah *had* always known—somewhere deep down in a secret place where she kept the truth hidden—she'd known there would be no future with Sam. But the dream was easier than facing the reality of moving west. Easier to imagine riding off with Sam to a far-away country than accepting she would join her family in the humiliating removal.

She beat her hands against the quilt as sadness changed to anger. Whatever dream she had was over. No dream could save her from being herded like an animal to the Arkansaw. She would be moving west and her family needed her.

It hurt. The knowledge hurt so much. But now she must do what the rest of her family had done. Accept that the removal was happening. Accept it and get on with preparations with the same dignity as her mother and father.

Sarah rolled to the side of the bed and stood. Removing her blanket, she pulled on a housedress. She gathered Sam's letters from her bed and crushed them to her breast. Standing at the window for a moment, she looked across the meadow at the willow beneath the bluff. Then barefoot she walked down the stairs and into the empty parlor.

A fire broke the chill of the room. The hearth warmed her feet as she silently dropped the letters, one by one, onto a smoldering log and watched Sam Maverick's words and her dreams curl to ash.

Chapter 21

What Is Happening to Us?

Ridge Plantation

November 1836

"No, Sallie, you may not ride alone," Susanna said as the two women stood in the almost-empty dining room.

"But Mother, I've ridden to Running Waters a hundred times. Everyone here's too busy packing. I'll be home long before dark." John's farm was only six miles up the New Echota Road from their plantation.

"No. You may not go unless you take someone with you."

Sarah clenched her teeth, then walked out on the front porch. She pulled her wool shawl tighter around her blue dress. Last week's cold snap continued as had her resolve to face the removal and accept the death of her dream of Sam. The reason for her trip was to tell Sophie Sawyer, the missionary who taught John's children at Running Waters, that she'd decided she would take Sophie up on her offer to help set up a school in the new Indian Territory.

A black squirrel circled the broad trunk of the chestnut and skittered around several times. For a moment it stopped, took the nut from its mouth, chattered at Sarah, and then replaced it. The squirrel's coat gleamed in the sun and contrasted with patches of ocher and vermilion lichen clinging to the gray bark. Spreading its back legs, the squirrel arched its tail and surveyed the area. Sarah watched, unmoving.

Scrambling to the foot of the tree the squirrel hopped across the canyon-like base onto brittle, fallen leaves. Working with mysterious instinct, it ran from spot to spot, stopping, looking, sniffing, its body stretching, compressing as it searched for the perfect place to bury the chestnut.

A place near the corner of the porch was the right one. Sarah barely breathed as the squirrel moved a layer of leaves, then began to dig, its front legs vibrating with action. Body and rump hammered the nut into the soft soil with a rapid, age-old rhythm. It patted the soil and rearranged the blanket of leaves, then ran back up the tree, circled one last time, and disappeared with a series of jumps and leaps through the soaring limbs.

It was a mystery she'd always pondered, how squirrels remembered where they'd buried their cache when the hard winter months came. Those nuts they didn't find grew into trees, the Great Spirit's way of letting the workers of the woods replant the forests. But if the squirrel forgot where it planted this chestnut, she'd never know it. She wouldn't be here to see a sapling sprout.

But more pressing matters flooded her brain now. "So how am I going to get over to see Sophie if I can't ride by myself?" she said out loud.

A deep voice answered from behind the tree. "Watty . . . go with . . . Sallie." Lettie had been teaching him to speak in English and now Watty's simple thoughts emerged.

Startled, she watched as her brother leaned out from behind the tree, his adoring smile beaming, his thatch of hair not unlike the squirrel. Dear Watty, she thought, that squirrel ran all around you. You're a friend even to the creatures of the woods.

Jumping from the porch she joined him on the far side of the tree and sat on a big root. "That might work, Watty. I'm sure Mother would let you go with me. I only need to tell Sophie I'll teach with her. We can take the little buggy."

"Look." Watty pointed to a space in front of his crossed legs where he'd cleared leaves, leaving a rectangle of red soil. His face metamorphosed into a mask of sadness. Within a border of small pebbles lay a childlike picture created in river pebbles, moss, and twigs. On the left of the picture, a large stick figure of a man stood next to an outlined house. A trail of rough garnets meandered its way across to a tiny stick figure surrounded by a forest of twigs and moss.

"Watty 'fraid to go west. 'Fraid he get lost." He twisted his fingers, nervously winding the strings of the old beaded doeskin pouch his mother had sewn for his garnet collection. Watty liked to chip and file the gray quartz rocks people brought him to uncover the deep red garnets.

Sarah took his huge paw-like hand in hers. "Poor Watty. You'll be safe with the family. We'll build another house and you'll live there."

"A house like here?" he asked.

Sarah looked up at the graceful porch posts, glass panes, and shutters. She knew the massive timbers that formed the original cabin could never be duplicated. "Yes. Watty's new house will be big and strong like this one. And you'll have a nice new room. I will, too."

A smile lit up his face. "Sallie take care of Watty?"

"Yes," she said, hugging him. "I'll always take care of you."

Sarah's mind wandered on the return trip from Running Waters. She let Watty drive. He loved holding the reins and the old mare *Dilasgesgi*—Stamper—was the gentlest of the stable and wanted nothing more than to follow the road home.

Sophie was delighted with Sarah's decision. The missionary teacher filled Sarah's head with plans for a school in the new land. For the first time Sarah felt encouraged about the move. She would help Sophie teach Cherokee children to make the best of their new lives.

Sarah had cringed, though, when she saw John's plantation. The large white frame house and outbuildings were no longer a working farm, but a distribution point for food for starving Cherokees. John and

Sarah Bird had already moved their family to New Echota, living in the Boudinot house with Elias and his children. This past August, Harriet's physical weakness had defeated her powerful spirit: Elias buried her in the capital city of the disenfranchised nation she loved.

A shroud of sorrow covered the land as those who accepted the inevitable began enrolling at New Echota for the removal and worried about how the children and old ones would endure the trip.

A sound mingled with Sarah's thoughts and the repetitive *clip-clop* of Stamper's hooves. Chestnuts popping in a fire . . . No! Gunfire!

She grabbed the reins from Watty's hands. "Hold on!" she yelled, slapping the leather strips and urging Stamper to a gallop. Unable to tell where the shots were coming from, she raced toward home and safety.

At a trail leading to the cabin of Climbing Bear and Amoneeta, a couple John's age, a mesh of fresh hoof prints patterned the loam. Riders—a pony club?—had recently raced from the path and turned onto the empty road ahead. Above the woods, more smoke than usual rose from Climbing Bear's chimney.

Sarah grabbed the tomahawk from the floor of the buggy. Watty clung to the seat; fear froze his face. "Watty," Sarah said, "we're going to see if our friends are safe. Now you must do everything I tell you."

He nodded and she handed him the tomahawk. "Hold this and don't put it down. Give it to me when I ask." Then she took out the primed pistol from the bag she'd brought, placed a cap on the nipple, and eased down the hammer. She guided the buggy along the wooded path, a path she'd traveled many times to her friends' farm. Leaving the shelter of the trees the trail opened. She saw the cabin ablaze. No riders were in sight. A red-shirted figure lay in the yard.

Reining in, she jumped from the buggy. "Stay with me, Watty." He followed her clutching the tomahawk.

Climbing Bear lay face down. Her heart racing, Sarah put the pistol down and carefully rolled him over. His dark face was a battered pulp of flesh; blood streamed from a gunshot wound in his shoulder.

Sarah stroked his forehead. His eyes opened. "Amoneeta. Find her," he mumbled.

"Stay with Climbing Bear!" Sarah yelled to Watty as she grabbed the pistol and ran toward the cabin.

Flames edged the front window. She ran around the side, pistol cocked, ready to fire. Stock pens stood empty. Amoneeta was nowhere in sight.

Sarah ran back to the open front door of the cabin. She released the hammer on the pistol, laid it down, and took a deep breath. Covering her nose with her arm, she ran through the door. Flames raged in the chimney end; logs pulled out and scattered. Across the room, she saw Amoneeta lying next to an overturned table. Her iron cooking kettle lay next to her, empty. Corn mush covered her face and neck like a lumpy death mask. The banditti had poured corn mush on her head! Grabbing a quilt from the bed, Sarah draped it over the woman.

With a strength she didn't know existed, she lifted her friend. Clutching the limp woman to her chest, she carried her into the yard. Climbing Bear, now standing, leaned against Watty for support.

Tears from the smoke and horror rolled down Sarah's cheeks as she knelt and placed Amoneeta on the ground in front of the two men. Climbing Bear fell, kneeling, sobbing wretched wails. Lifting the quilt, he touched his wife's shoulders, tentatively, terrified. Reaching for her face, he began to scrape the heavy mush, pulling away layers of skin.

"Wait!" Sarah yelled. She ran to the well. She lowered the bucket, then pulled up the rope, hand over hand. Running back, she set the bucket beside Amoneeta. Sarah ripped off her petticoat, soaked the muslin, and gently dribbled water over Amoneeta's face and neck to dissolve the pasty mixture.

As the corn mush slipped away, the words of Flying Bird came to Sarah, an incantation for burns: "*Water is cold, ice is cold, snow is cold, frost is cold. Relief, I say!*" Repeating the lines in her mind, seeing the revered woman of her childhood performing the ritual, Sarah cupped her hands in the bucket, filled her mouth with the cool water, and blew a spray over Amoneeta's face, over and over, slowly revealing the seeping, bleeding face of the once-beautiful woman.

Throughout the ordeal Watty stood still, silently staring, obediently clutching the tomahawk as his sister had told him. When Amoneeta's face appeared and her bloody lips moved with a groan of untold agony, Watty dropped to his knees. Breaking Sallie's rule he laid the hatchet beside him. Pressing his hands together, he bowed his head as the missionaries had taught him to do whenever he wanted to ask God to help a friend.

"You must do something!" Sarah's rage filled her voice. Flames leapt high in the parlor fireplace and she saw again the burning cabin, saw Climbing Bear battered and bleeding. A picture of Amoneeta's ravaged face flashed through her mind and with it the memory of Watty's terror. Even now, three days later, he was so frightened he wouldn't leave his room.

When Sarah had returned with the buggy—she astride Stamper while Watty supported Amoneeta and Climbing Bear—Susanna had clung to her children as in times past, her arms shielding them, protecting them. Amoneeta slept upstairs now in Sarah's room, her blistered face soothed with a salve of aloe vera balm and turmeric. Climbing Bear, his shoulder wound cleaned, bandaged and healing, kept watch. Lettie had burned Sarah's blood-stained dress, and as she sat next to her mother in a parlor devoid of decoration she wore black crepe, mourning this latest tragedy.

General John E. Wool, along with two of his officers stood next to Major Ridge, whose drawn lips and piercing eyes defined his somber mood. Luther translated from the corner. The sharp blue uniforms of the United States Army contrasted with the old patriarch's faded one and lent an official tone to the emotional meeting.

"I cannot express enough, Miss Ridge, the sympathies from the Federal government and men under my command," the general replied. "I have marshaled all resources available. I've ordered my men to attend sales to identify the stolen horses. This band of ruffians has not left an easy trail to follow." He shifted his sword and stepped toward her. "And I can't begin to tell you how I regret that a young lady such as yourself had to witness such a—"

Sarah raised her hands and concluded his sentence: "Such a maiming of an innocent man. Such a brutal violation and disfigurement of an innocent woman. Those animals threw a pot of boiling corn mush in her face! Whites call Cherokees savages? The savages are these Georgians free to ravage our nation!"

Her mother patted Sarah's leg. She clenched her fists; beneath her gloves, her fingernails bit into the palms of her hand making obscure new moons in her skin as she willed her tears not to come.

Susanna took Sarah's tight-fisted hands into hers. "General Wool is a friend. He's truly doing everything within his means," she whispered.

Sarah lifted her head and faced her father and the officers. "What is happening to us? Why can nothing be done to protect us? We, the Real People, are no longer a people at all! The Congress promised us if we signed the treaty we would move west where we could continue to live as a nation. But there will be none left to move!"

A lieutenant stepped forward. "General Wool, sir? Might I interject?"

"Yes." The general gestured with his hand, "My aide-de-camp, Lieutenant George Paschal."

"Madam. Major Ridge. Miss Ridge," the young man addressed them, his demeanor serious and his voice bold and gallant, a contrast to his slight stature. "Your Treaty Party is the forerunner of an enlightened faction of your nation. It is through you and your compatriots that your people can be saved. As a native of Georgia—I come from near Athens—and having as a lawyer traveled this area for some years, I have developed an understanding of the situation."

The officer cleared his throat with a slight growl, proceeding as if presenting a case before a sympathetic jury. "As you know, the tragedy you witnessed is but an ongoing plot to rid the state of your people. Chief John Ross hampers the removal effort, giving false hope to the simple folk such as your friends, hope of retaining their hereditary lands."

He rested one hand across his waist and the other on the hilt of his sword in a military manner. "It is of utmost importance that all your people realize there is but one road to safety, and that road leads west."

The lieutenant pivoted on his heels, facing Sarah. His voice softened. "And you, Miss Ridge, you must be very watchful for your safety."

Sarah met his gaze, this man of dynamic posture, short and wiry, his complexion russet, his uniform well-tailored—this George Paschal. What message was he sending in those dark, inscrutable eyes? She had been introduced to him several times before on General Wool's visits and thought him a bit presumptuous. He was about her age and on his last visit he'd given her a book of poetry; when she read the love poems she thought of Sam.

She looked away and covered her mother's hands with her own, then addressed the group. "My life has been indelibly changed by this tragedy. A woman cannot witness such an atrocity as I did without it affecting her. As to what I'm going to do in the future with these new emotions, I do not yet know. But I will not live in fear as a helpless victim."

To Sarah's surprise, Lieutenant Paschal bowed slightly to her, speaking as if there were no others in the room. "You, Miss Ridge, are a brave woman and it is an honor for me to be in your presence." She met his gaze and nodded, unwilling to match the smile on his lips.

General Wool ended the intimate moment obvious to all. "Lieutenant Paschal speaks for those under my command. I will do what I can to protect the interest of your nation. But I can only emphasize that a speedy removal to the Indian Territory is all that can save your people."

"That is our cause now, General," Major Ridge said, "but the simple folk do not prepare. They do not go to New Echota for enrollment. When you allowed the council to convene at Red Clay this fall, John Ross sent word into the forests and hills telling all Cherokee they need not leave for the west."

"I allowed the council to proceed, but I told the principal chief that he holds the future of his people in his hands. He has the power to lead them. He can do them much good—or much evil."

"He does them evil," Major Ridge said. "We who leave now will join those who have gone before and unite with the Western Cherokee government. John Ross, when he finally leads the remaining people west—and they *must* leave or disappear into the hills—he will find us established. I know him well. He will then want to be the leader in the west. I fear when our deluded tribal members arrive, there will be more bloodshed."

"You may be right," General Wool said, "but I can only prevent bloodshed here. I wish you and your family a safe trip west."

As the officers took their leave, Sarah followed her father onto the porch. An icy wind whipped the folds in her skirt, rustling the crepe. Lieutenant Paschal paused at the end of the porch, then took a step forward. She walked to him as her father returned to the hall.

"Miss Ridge? Have you had an opportunity to read the book of poetry I gave you?"

Sarah remembered a verse about peering into the light-colored eyes of a lover, lines that sang to her of Sam not the dark brown eyes of the man before her. "Yes, I have. Thank you."

"Might I speak to you again? Perhaps this coming Sunday?"

Something about this George Paschal—his passion, his sincerity—lit a spark in Sarah's mind like flint against iron. Perhaps, she thought, at this juncture of my life this officer might carry a ring of keys to future doors.

The wind whistled and her skirt whispered as Sarah replied. "Yes, if you wish. Come late afternoon, come for supper."

Chapter 22

A Multitude of Decisions

Ridge Plantation

November 1836

Miscellaneous chairs and a rough table were all that remained in the dining room on Sunday. The buffet and its contents of English china and French crystal were long since packed and crated. The utensils were odds and ends; the plates and cups were simple crockery; a basket of pinecones and nuts was the only decoration on the table. Sarah had requested Doll's roasted venison and onions, turnip soup, and potatoes boiled with mustard greens. Three family members and George Paschal gathered, her father at the head of the long table, her mother to his right, George and Sarah to his left. Watty refused to join them and had eaten earlier in the kitchen. He was growing more and more reclusive, his smile supplanted by a far-away stare.

As Lettie removed the plates and dish of baked apples Major Ridge spoke to Lieutenant Paschal. Sarah translated. "You're a lawyer, is that not true?"

"Yes, sir," he replied, "I studied Greek and Latin at the state academy in Athens and read law in Lexington, where I received adequate instruction to pass the bar examinations and receive my license. I later practiced law in Auraria. My mother owns a hotel there and I assisted her in that endeavor, also."

"And your father?" Susanna asked.

"A hero of the Revolutionary War for Independence, madam. He died some years ago. My dear mother, through her devoted efforts, continues to manage her establishment."

As Sarah translated she appreciated her parents drawing answers from their visitor, ones which she also had wondered about.

"General Wool tells me your law practice involved pursuing gold claims for the lottery winners," her father said.

Paschal hesitated, then proceeded as if expecting this probing. "Yes, sir, but I deeply regret that unfortunate enterprise. I feel now that during that feverish era, I and other Georgians hurried your nation's decline. Restitution for my actions is part of my reason for joining the Army and assisting General Wool.

"I am," he continued, "a believer in the fair treatment of all races. My mother raised me so. She teaches Negro slaves to read. Surreptitiously of course. I apologize to you, sir, for any untoward distress I caused your people by entering your nation at that time."

"Unfortunately, it is too late for anything to change. But Lieutenant Paschal, we appreciate your concern and accept your apology." Major Ridge rose, his chair scraping across the floor. Reaching for Susanna's chair, he shifted it out for her and helped her rise.

They look so very old, Sarah thought. More than that they look tired, tired of climbing a mountain of broken promises.

George Paschal stood and thanked them for supper. Her parents smiled. Did Sarah notice—or only imagine—a look of approval in her mother's eyes? Major Ridge offered his hand and the young man shook it. Sarah noticed his glance linger on the scars tracking the back of her father's hand, trails of parallel lines etched beneath his shirt cuff.

Choosing to stay in the dining room instead of retiring to the dismal, cold parlor across the hallway, Sarah indicated her father's chair at the fireplace end of the table, then angled her chair toward Paschal.

A moment of awkward silence. Should I, Sarah thought, explain Father's scars to this white man who wishes to court me? Will this realization of my father's past scare him off? He's only seen what we have become in the past decades. Well, if he can't accept my heritage perhaps this is the time for him to turn and run.

"You noticed the scars on my father's hands," she said. He nodded, his expression a mixture of curiosity and embarrassment.

"The taking of European names does not erase our pasts. My father Kahnungdatlageh was a warrior in his youth. The Man Who Walks on the Mountaintop—The Ridge—he is called. When he fought the Seminole at Horseshoe Bend General Jackson bestowed him the rank of major.

"But long before to attain manhood and warrior names, all young braves faced a tribal ceremony, the *asga siti*. It means 'to be made dreadful,' to receive a strong heart needed to face danger and terrorize the enemy."

Involuntarily Sarah rubbed the back of one gloved hand, remembering the scars that traversed her father's arms and body. Paschal leaned forward in his chair listening as she painted a legend.

"In the long ago on a dark night, the chief gathered the young men while warriors danced and sang, invoking the Great Spirit to fill the naked boys' hearts with courage and strength. The warriors wore moccasins and deerskin breechclouts, their heads shaved but for scalp locks wrapped in beads with eagle feathers. They painted their faces in red, white, and yellow patterns.

"The young men, coached by the medicine men had prepared for this night. As each stepped forward the chief pressed duel sharp points carved from the bone of a wolf into the boys' bodies, scratching bloody trails across their arms and chest, across their backs from hand to hand, from their feet up across their chests and shoulders, down their backs. The boys stood unflinching as their blood spilled, as they would one day spill the blood of those they fought."

Paschal said nothing, mesmerized by Sarah's images.

"My father as a young warrior indeed spilled the blood of his enemies. He earned his place as a chieftain leader not only from his oratory skills but with bravery."

Sarah looked away from Paschal, out through the window at the dying day.

"In a time different from now my father fought the Shawnee, the Creek, the French, the English, and the Americans. He rode his pony along the valleys and ridges into Tennessee and Kentucky following the Great War Path. He raided white invaders' trading posts and farms, stole horses, took scalps."

Sarah let out her breath adding, "Now you see an aged planter and diplomat, a warrior tired of fighting."

Paschal found his voice. "But many of your people, your family especially, have realized that ancient times are behind them and the future lies in the acceptance of modern ways. You speak your native language, yet also English flawlessly."

She inwardly cringed at this man's flowery speech.

"Yours is a wealthy people, wealthy in land and customs. Educated and enlightened whites, such as myself, wish to see you continue as so in the west, even help you through the turbulent times ahead . . ."

Paschal cleared his throat with its accompanying growl. Then in a higher, unsteady tone, he said, "Miss Ridge, I am a man who—"

Lettie stepped in from the hallway. "Miss Sallie? Aire ye be needin' anything other?"

Sarah looked up and smiled at Lettie's question. Her friend had been stationed in the hall, timing her entrance to allow Sarah to escape from her visitor. This morning when Lettie selected the violet gown that now brought out Sarah's rich complexion, Sarah told her she felt Lieutenant Paschal would ask to court her and she was not certain what her answer would be.

Lettie, having overheard the lieutenant's conversations at his previous visits had scoffed. "He makes me think a' Rabbit, from th' old Cherokee tales Doll tells. Rabbit trickin' Otter, trickin' Possum. The man might help ye, being white an' all, an' ye might be all right. But ye should keep a look-out fer Rabbit."

Heeding her friend's words, Sarah had promised she would be wary. But now she wanted to hear what George Paschal had to say. "Thank you, no." Only Sarah saw the teasing smile on Lettie's face as she departed.

Sarah smoothed the ribbons at her waist. "Please continue."

He took a deep breath, his voice now firm. "Miss Ridge, pardon my directness, but I am a man who knows his feelings, and I see no need to delay any longer in telling you what I wish you to know."

He stood and began pacing, his hands clasped behind him, periodically flipping the hem of his coat as he flexed and folded his fingers. A fleeting image of a bantam rooster with rustling tail feathers—rather than Rabbit—flashed through Sarah's mind. The sincere tone of George Paschal's words immediately erased the image.

"I admire your family and can appreciate your situation as the daughter of an elder statesman. I see a place for me in the future of the Cherokees, as a lawyer, as a defender of your people."

He stopped and stood behind her father's chair, his hands gripping the back, "I confess to being taken by you, by your demeanor and your strength, and I feel a strong affection toward you."

Paschal walked around the chair. Lowering himself to one knee, he took Sarah's hands in his. "I realize you've been under a great deal of strain recently. You are facing a multitude of decisions and now I'm asking you to make one more. Will you marry me?"

His eyes met hers, unflinching.

Sarah blinked. This was not the question she'd expected. Courting? Yes, she was prepared to know this man better. But marry him?

She took a deep breath as his last words echoed in her mind. They were the words she'd dreamed of hearing for years from Sam and now she was hearing them from George Paschal.

Her hands felt sheltered in his. Then in a gesture that gave no hint of her position, she pulled away and stood. He rose and stepped back.

She faced him in the silent room. Although a bit taller than he, his grit and determination made him appear larger. She smiled. "Thank you, Lieutenant Paschal, for your kind words. I will speak to my parents."

His smile was pure pleasure.

"If you would like to return tomorrow, I will have my answer for you."

"Yes. Yes. I would be honored to ask your father for your hand."

"That is the proper European manner and after I talk with my parents you may. But it is my mother who would give approval."

They walked to the hall tree near the front entry where Paschal took down his sword and fastened it around his waist, then retrieved his hat. He opened the door as a rush of cold wind blew down the Oostanaula. Taking her arm, he ushered her out to the hitching post. Standing next to his horse he lifted her hand to his lips, then quickly mounted. "Until tomorrow." With a tip of his hat, he smiled.

Sarah answered his smile with her own and waved as he turned and trotted away into the night.

George Paschal was correct, she thought. She *had* had to face many decisions recently. Now this one that could change her life forever. She needed to think, to relive her past, to chart her future. She pulled her shawl tighter and shivered in the chill of the evening.

Picking up her sewing box and embroidery ring from the parlor, Sarah walked down the hall and out the back door to the kitchen cabin, the only place she knew that would be warm and empty this time of day. Sunday was the servants' time with their families. Coals were banked in the kitchen fireplace; a log smoldered.

Scents of onions lingered; through the louvers of the pie safe she could see baked apples waiting should the family feel an evening hunger. Sarah removed her gloves, pulled Doll's rocker near the hearth, and lit the candle on its swing-out arm. Arranging her embroidery ring, she slipped her needle from its anchor and looked at her sampler.

She knew the classical principles taught her by the lady at Tennison's Hotel and at Salem School. But when she'd sketched her design for this one she'd released herself from rules. She created her version of a mourning sampler: a classic urn stood to the right, but she included no traditional figures, no line of mourners, no funereal crypt. Only her home. In her smoothest capturing stitch, the walls of the house on the Oostanaula emerged in silk thread. She ran white satin ribbon in a twisted chain for porch posts, and decorated flowers with a variety of bright colors in French-rose stitches.

Where the chestnut tree stood, she substituted—emblematic of a mourning piece—a haunting, green-black willow, draping and sad. To balance the urn, on the opposite side of her composition, she embroidered a light-colored horse drinking from the watering trough. Upon the urn where the name of the deceased should read, Sarah had embroidered in her tightest backstitch a single word in black: "Home."

She worked now on a jade border, random undulating stitches requiring little thought, allowing her freedom to visualize her potential role as the wife of George Paschal. Before she could ask her mother, she must ask herself. Sarah's mind focused on images from her life:

Picture: As she had watched George, his staccato movements, his odd and nervous mannerisms, she had thought of Sam, his complexion fair, his long stride ambling, confident. Two men, opposites in appearances and temperament, yet . . .

Fact: Sam had married another woman and moved to Texas.

Picture: Her parents were old. John had Sarah Bird and their children to care for. Watty had only his sister, and her parents remained with her. She, the child, had become the parent.

Fact: George said he could help her family and as a white man, she knew he could open doors for them. But he must remove west with her family; she would not remain with him in Georgia.

Picture: The lawyers and well-meaning supporters of the Cherokee had failed in Washington City. But legal actions would not end here.

Fact: As a lawyer George's counsel could help her family and the Treaty Party. How had he worded it? "A defender of your people."

Picture: He said he felt affection for her. But could he be certain until he had come to know her? And what did she feel for him? How would she feel in his arms, in his bed? Would she ever feel for him what she had imagined with Sam? Could she ever love George Paschal? Did love matter?

She anchored her needle and traced her fingers across the raised threads of her sampler outlining the urn and its embroidered, "Home."

Fact: For the first time, she saw a glimpse of her future.

Sarah stood before the dining room fireplace. Lettie had unpacked a dress from a trunk and ironed it, a blue calico edged with white lace with matching gloves. Sarah wrapped a darker blue shawl around her shoulders; her hair was pulled up and twisted in a loose bun. Sapphire earbobs dangled and a matching lavalier rested between her breasts.

She heard the horse whinny as Lieutenant Paschal tied it at the water trough. She heard his footsteps on the porch, the jangle of his spurs, his sword slapping against his boots. She heard his knock and Lettie's greeting.

Paschal stepped into the room, removed his hat and gloves, and set them on the table. Walking toward her, he greeted her and bowed slightly. Boldly taking her hand, he kissed it and asked, "You have your answer for me, Miss Ridge?"

Her words flowed as she'd rehearsed them. She had answered all her questions in the time since last she saw him. "Yes. I will marry you, George Paschal."

Confidence turned to elation in his face. "Thank you. Thank you."

She smiled, but she still needed to complete her script. "I have made my decision and received my mother's approval, but I would like to add some thoughts."

She saw a furrow darkening between his eyebrows. "Yes. Please go on."

"I will marry you, but I see no need for us to pretend that we are young lovers blinded by desire. I feel warmly toward you and look forward to sharing an intimacy with you. But for now, my heart is my own. I hope this will change in time as I grow to know you."

A MULTITUDE OF DECISIONS

His expression didn't vary. She took a breath and continued. "As my husband, as the husband of the daughter of Susanna and Major Ridge, you would of necessity remove to the western lands with my family. I have promised to teach in Miss Sawyer's school there and would want to do so."

He slowly began to nod.

"If you wish to marry me under these conditions, and if you will use your talents as a lawyer—more so, your status as a white man—to help my people, then I will accept your proposal. But you must respect my standing in the nation and do not ever, *ever* hold me up to ridicule." Her words were soft but firm.

With no hesitation, George answered, "Yes. Yes, Miss Ridge. I will respect and take care of you. I'll protect you and your family. I will do all you request and more—"

He stepped forward and pulled her tightly to him, his arms encircling her, pressing her waist and shoulders. She felt the brass buttons on his uniform nudging her breasts, the hilt of his sword brushing her hip. His breath was briefly aromatic. His lips touched hers, gently at first, and then a power seemed to come from within him.

Sarah's emotions changed from surprise to fear to an unknown response that Sam's brief kiss had never aroused. She let her lips relax and sensed a warmth in the chilly room, a warmth that permeated her body. She felt the power of George's arms.

Responding, she lifted her hands to encircle him and felt the strength and tightness of his shoulders. Their kiss intensified. She relaxed in his arms, her body molded to his. In this moment Sarah's entire being told her that her decision was the right one. In George Paschal's embrace, she felt safe.

Chapter 23

Questions & Sealing Wax

New Echota Campground

February 1837

Sarah walked to the covered wagon parked beside Elias' house and unlocked her trunk. Her rosewood letterbox was the last item she packed so it would always be within easy reach. Her keys still out of her pocket—she'd asked Lucinda to sew large pockets into the seams of her skirts for this journey—Sarah unlocked the box and checked for blotters and sharp quills. She was relieved no ink had spilled; she'd made sure to screw the silver lids tight on the bottles. Rolled sheets of paper rested in their slot, but there was no stick of sealing wax in its bin. She tucked the box under her shawl and went in search of a quiet place to answer Hester's letter, her school friend's words now rustling in her skirt pocket.

But where? The former capital was now the point of embarkation. On this clear winter day, people milled around or stood in lines as directed by the troops under the charge of Major Currey. They came from every part of the nation, some in aristocratic carriages, others in wagons or carts; they came horse- or muleback, but most walked. Some accepted their fate with anticipation: they were moving to a new homeland to join family members and friends already settled. Most, though, were confused and fearful of retribution by Rossmen.

At night sounds of howling and yelling ricocheted across the meadow, anger fueled by whiskey. Lieutenant Paschal had helped Stand run off two white Georgians—scavengers who fed on the melancholy of the people by hauling barrels through the woods, planning to fill their pockets with transportation funds paid the enrollees. Barrels were not hard to spot, but jugs slipped through easily. Most emigrants stayed away from the whiskey sellers; they sat and waited for someone in authority to tell them what to do, where to go.

In December Sarah's family left the plantation—a sad caravan of wagons loaded with trunks and crates, carriages crowded with family and slaves. Following them, a small herd of cattle, oxen and horses. The old folks had moved into Elias's house, and Susanna helped Aunt Susie and Uncle David Watie care for Harriet's motherless children.

Sarah and Watty, along with their Watie cousins slept in tents nearby. The slaves, too, waited to be processed and certified by the government for enrollment in the overland trip west. When the time for removal grew near, Susanna—who always referred to Lettie and Robinson as "our foundlings"—asked Lettie if was there any place she would want to take her nineteen-year-old brother to start a new life. In the end there was nowhere to go, so it was decided to register them with other Ridge slaves, since freedmen—emancipated slaves—could not go west with the Cherokee.

John, Elias, and Stand were working with the Indian Agents sent to administer enrollment under direction of the two former governors, William Carroll of Tennessee and the now-replaced Wilson Lumpkin of Georgia. President Jackson personally appointed Lumpkin to oversee the removal saying that after all, this predicament was the result of the State of Georgia so Lumpkin had better deal with it!

Lumpkin continued to hound the Cherokee. He accused John and others who had negotiated with the Union of arrogance, saying that because they had observed for so long the dealings in Washington City, they thought too highly of themselves! Here they were not statesmen, not solons but clerks!

Sarah remembered with a smile last evening grouped around a campfire behind Elias's house when the cousins told the family about Lumpkin's reprimand.

John held a printed copy of the treaty from which he wanted to transcribe information.

Catching the firelight he read: "Article Seven. The Cherokee nation having already made great progress in civilization . . ."

"Yes, we have!" Elias commented, gesturing to the masses huddled about the faded buildings of the nation's dream of a capital. "Look at our great progress toward civilization!"

Sarah noted sarcasm in her usually-pious cousin's voice.

John chuckled and continued. As he read, his inflections mimicked Elias's tone.

And deeming it important that every proper and laudable inducement should be offered to their people to improve their condition as well as to guard and secure in the most effectual manner the rights guaranteed to them in this treaty, and with a view to illustrate the liberal and enlarged policy of the Government of the United States towards the Indians in their removal beyond the territorial limits of the States . . .

Stand guffawed. "*If* we ever get there!"

Others joined in muted *huzzahs* as John continued. " . . . it is stipulated that they shall be entitled to a delegate in the House of Representatives of the United States whenever Congress shall make provision for the same."

"I'll show Lumpkin!" Elias said. "*I'll* be the delegate in the House of Representatives!"

John gently shoved him, arguing as they had in childhood play. "No! *I'll* be the delegate to go to Washington City! *I'll* be the solon!"

In the firelight Waties and Ridges laughed. Beneath their bittersweet banter, though, lay the recognition that the road to the new territory and establishing a new nation was fraught with uncertainties.

When Congress ratified the treaty last May, the singular major change they voted to strike from the agreement was Article Twelve. Those carefully negotiated paragraphs allowing Cherokees who chose to remain in states bordering Georgia to receive land and annuities—to enjoy citizenship in the United States—were not an option Andrew Jackson and Congress accepted. All must go.

Walking to the corner of the old print shop, Sarah stopped where a nailed paper fluttered in the breeze. It was the article John had copied last night. She read her brother's handwriting in two columns; one Cherokee, one English:

> To the Emigrants. The Treaty of New Echota.
> Signed December 29, 1835. Ratified by U.S. Congress May 1, 1836
> To wit:
> ARTICLE 8. The United States also agree and stipulate to remove the Cherokees to their new homes and to subsist them one year after their arrival there and that a sufficient number of steamboats and baggage-wagons shall be furnished to remove them comfortably, and so as not to endanger their health, and that a physician well supplied with medicines shall accompany each detachment of emigrants removed by the Government. Such persons and families as in the opinion of the emigrating agent are capable of subsisting and removing themselves shall be permitted to do so; and they shall be allowed in full for all claims for <u>the same twenty dollars</u> for each member of their family; and in lieu of their one year's rations they shall be paid <u>the sum of thirty-three dollars and thirty-three cents</u> if they prefer it.

A shadow swooped across the old newspaper shop. Sarah and others looked up at the wide-spread wings of an eagle. *Uwohali.* The sacred bird of the Real People. She remembered feeling the gold-threaded embroidery of the eagle on the crimson sofa where little Sallie sat in the Elliptical Saloon after meeting President Monroe. The eagle with its olive branch and clutched arrows. Now the arrows were pointed at the Cherokee. She watched the bird as it circled and landed a distance away at the top of the massive spruce.

Sarah continued her search for a private perch of her own.

Leaving the newspaper office where the line of emigrants ran long out the door, she acknowledged the mockery of her brother and cousins working inside the building—writing out removal enrollments—the same room where they once proudly wrote columns for the enlightened nation.

The *Cherokee Phoenix* was a memory now, the print shop merely a room, the rafters naked of drying sheets. The press was long gone, stolen years before by the Georgia Guard. Sequoyah's treasured typeface had been tossed down a well.

Sarah clutched her letterbox and spun around. Nowhere to sit. Nowhere to write, nowhere to be alone. Then she noticed her father's big coach parked behind Elias's house.

Walking to the backyard, Sarah avoided the windows out of which little Boudinots might be peering. Big Tom was tending the tethered horses and guarding family supplies. When he turned to greet her she held up her hand in silence, then whispered to him to unlock the carriage door for her. He did. She ducked low and snuck in.

Taking a deep breath, Sarah closed her eyes and relaxed for the first time in so long she couldn't remember when. The drawn curtains let in just enough midday light. She rested her letterbox on her lap, unfolded the leaves to its desk configuration, and set out her instruments and paper.

She pulled Hester's letter from her pocket and unfolded the brief sheet. It was dated December and addressed to Lavenders Store, but the letter had found Sarah only yesterday. She caressed the creased note, her one remaining keepsake of correspondence with her dear Salem School sister. Sarah had treasured Hester's stacks of letters tied with ribbons, words read and re-read of girlish affection, courting and lovers, slavery and escape, and the horrid split over the treaty—nearly a decade of friendship. But Sarah had burned them all, watching words and wads of sealing wax melt until nothing was left. She didn't know where the removal would take her, but Hester's abolitionist stories of helping slaves to freedom, her guidance for Sarah in the tribal split . . . well, should the letters fall into the wrong hands . . .

December 15, 1836
New Bedford, Massachusetts
My dearest Sarah,
 How can Jackson's men live with themselves? Newspapers here in the Northeast are filled with letters of support for the Cherokee, yet the Congress votes to send you away! Your reports of the plight of your people bring tears to my eyes. The obstinate methods of the vile John Ross fill me with rage. Why can't he see that if all are against your Nation, then the Treaty your family signed gives your people an outlet for survival? The Georgians brutalize you, as they brutalize their slaves. They will not change. If only the disconsolate Negroes could be offered wagons and flatboats to leave their pitiless masters, to settle in a land where they can be free of subjugation. My home now is a stopping point on a railroad of which you may have heard rumored. I and my parents are well. I pray for your safety and that of your beloved family. Write and tell me where you are—and of your affectionate Lieutenant you described in your letter arriving yesterday. Are you yet married?
Devotedly, Hester

Sarah smoothed her curled writing paper, passing her hands across the blank sheet as she pondered which of her friend's questions to address first.

She, of course, had no answer to how untrustworthy politicians lived with their abhorrent decisions. Politics: the art of the inexplicable.

Well-meaning writers of letters and memorials to Congress, those of whom Hester spoke, presented words—often backed by donations—but no assembly had risen to take on Indian causes. Black slaves had strong abolitionist friends and a rumored route of known homes and helpers willing to risk arrest for aiding slaves to freedom, Hester's home one on a list that circulated by tune and tale.

Yet no faction demanded the Cherokee remain.

The difference? Black slaves did not own land.

Indians possess land that white people want. Whites possess the power. It could not be clearer.

Why can't John Ross see? Another treaty will not be negotiated. Never will there be a good time to leave, but the longer he waits the worse it will get. The remaining Cherokee will listen to him. He holds their lives in his hands.

She dipped her quill into ink and poised the point over the sheet. She would write these thoughts to her friend, but first, she would answer Hester's last question, one which continually wore on her mind:

New Echota, 1837, early February (I know not the date—)
My dearest friend,

    No, I am not yet married. I am torn between accompanying my old and weak parents and my loving brother to the West—and remaining here until George Paschal resigns his Army commission, which is taking unexpected time. He wants me to wait here with him, of course, but says if I choose to go he will join me later. But can he? How will he travel? He can enroll in the removal as my husband, but otherwise he would have to pay his own expenses. And a white man traveling alone would not be welcome in the new land. I wish I could await your loving advice, but if I am to go with my family, we leave soon. I must shortly make my decision to marry—or not.

She filled the remaining sheet with answers to Hester's other questions and promised to write upon her arrival west, signing with affection.

In the seclusion of the coach, Sarah creased her letter and addressed the front. As she waited for the ink to dry, she thought how George

QUESTIONS & SEALING WAX   157

spent as much time as he could away from his duties with her and her family. Her affection for him grew with these visits.

Shifting her focus back to the present, she wondered if there was sealing wax somewhere in her shattered capital. Surely John and Elias must be melting drops onto enrollment documents and stamping official seals.

She closed her writing desk, left the secluded coach, and went in search of a stick of wax.

Chapter 24

The River of the Cherokee

Ross's Landing on the Tennessee River

February 1837

"Mother, what must I do? And please, don't ask me to pray..."

"Then, my daughter, you must ask the Great Spirit."

"The Great Spirit tells me to take care of you and Father and Watty."

"Then you must."

"And leave George here?"

"You are hearing the Great Spirit, Sallie, but listening with separate ears. You must balance your ears. Consider *Selu*, our ancestral mother. She gave us corn, she balanced our women who farmed with our men who hunted. Just as winter balances summer, planting balances animals. As women we provided, we lived our own lives. Men did not dominate. But that is no more.

"You have waited long to select a husband. I believe George Paschal to be a good man. If you choose to marry him and bring him west with you, in that manner you take care of your brother and father and me. We need our strong daughter. With George as your husband, a white man, and a lawyer, you can continue to help us in many ways.

"You will be his wife, and there is much you must give up. The time of balance for the Cherokee is no more. The government now controls our lives. *Selu* cries as we cry and depart our land.

"Your father and I are old. If we do not survive this journey, it is how it should be. We hope to live long lives in the west, but neither my God nor the Great Spirit can promise that."

A dreadful weakness set over Major Ridge. He was too ill to embark on the long overland route: a three-month drive over rough roads—or no roads at all—up through Nashville, across the southwestern tip of Kentucky to cross the Ohio River at Golconda in Illinois. Then crossing the Mississippi at Cape Girardeau, driving or walking across southern Missouri, fording the headwaters of the Black River to Springfield, and down to the land the Cherokee still called the Arkansaw, but now known as Indian Territory.

Susanna decided to send the Ridge family wagons and carriages from New Echota west in the care of the slaves with Big Tom overseeing, Doll in charge of providing meals and Little Tom and others herding the horses and cattle. Lettie stayed with Sarah, but both women cried as Robinson climbed into the driver's seat of a wagon.

They left with other emigrants of the Treaty Party who went on without the Ridges and Waties. Stand would manage the journey on the Tennessee River route. So the family packed their belongings and walked or rode almost sixty miles to Ross's Landing, a former trading post established decades before by John Ross's father. George secured army tents for the old folks, but Sarah and Watty slept in their blankets under a tree.

On Monday, February 27, the family crossed the river and walked three miles into the Tennessee woods to the Brainerd Mission for Sarah and George's marriage ceremony. Standing in the old log mission from her childhood, Sarah felt that today was a gathering at home. But it wasn't home. She remembered dreaming of her marriage ceremony as a girl, stepping down the staircase in a silk gown, joining her parents, walking between them into the parlor to take the hand of a faceless young man.

For her marriage at Brainerd, she wore a simple muslin dress, blue and unadorned. Brother Butrick read the ceremony and George, handsome in his uniform and joyous in his manner, made the moment cheerful for all. Sarah, too, smiled and accepted the family's congratulations, but the pall of imminent separation weighed heavily upon her; Sam stayed where she had willed him in his now-sealed closet of her mind.

The couple lived separately for the next four days; George had arranged to have himself assigned to assist with the departure, but then he was to return to New Echota until he could resign his commission under General Wool's command. Sarah would again stay at Elias's house and see that George was enrolled to emigrate with her as soon as they could join a removal party.

John and Elias planned to move west in the fall, also overland. It was up to Stand now to take the old and weak on the river route, the Tennessee River, the River of the Cherokee.

Since the beginning of time—when Buzzard flew over the earth while it was still soft and he grew tired, letting his wings dip low, gouging out valleys and raising hills—the Cherokee had fished and trapped and paddled their dugout canoes on rivers and streams. The Real People built their towns along the waterways, made war on them, and bathed their children in them. A river is an Old Man, they believed, whose head rested in the mountains, his feet in the sea.

But the Tennessee, unlike other grand rivers, didn't flow into a great lake or sea. The river twisted and bent from sources somewhere in the Appalachians, gathered streams, and wove generally south—sometimes looping north—in a series of long pools, slanting and snaking down slopes. The pools were navigable, but at the entrance and exit of each lay piles of rock where sand and gravel congregated, blocking and damming the flow.

On down in Alabama at the shallow shoals where forever Creek and Cherokee had gathered mussels and trapped fish, the Old Man flattened to a mile-and-a-half wide, falling eighty-five feet in fifteen miles, his waters spread across near-impassable flint shelves. There in a great reversing bend, he turned and flowed north. He gave up his name when he joined the Ohio River near Paducah, Kentucky, some miles after the Ohio's confluence with the Cumberland. He was no longer. Still, his blended waters continued, merging with the Mississippi at Cairo, Illinois, to eventually find their way through the Delta and into the Gulf of Mexico.

Now the Old Man, the River of the Cherokee, served as the outlet that would carry his people from their homeland.

On Friday morning, March 3rd, the day of departure for her mother and father, Sarah stood on the bank near the landing holding Watty's hand and watched as Stand and George found places in the boats for her parents and her Uncle David Watie and Aunt Susie. George had spoken with Dr. Lillybridge who assured him he would attend his wife's family and see to their comfort. As Sarah watched, Susanna stepped on the boarding plank and stumbled. George steadied her and she continued. Watty clutched Sarah's hand and began to cry.

She led him to a spot under a canoewood tree, near a flowering dogwood covered in white blooms. He kneeled next to her, watching intently as she cleared space in the soft gravel and broke sticks. Sarah laid out a roof shape and with a twig, etched a curling swirl of smoke rising from a chimney. Below, she lined sticks in a row, a pebble for each head.

"Watty's new home in the Arkansaw," she said. She named each figure and pointed out the tallest. "Watty safe under the new roof."

He took a pointer stick, touching each person, and repeating each name. Then he looked at his sister, his lips quivering. "No Sallie. Sallie say always take care of Watty."

It was all she could do to keep from sobbing, but that would only upset him more. Taking the stick again, she drew two more figures on a large flatboat rectangle. "Sallie and George. Come to Watty's house on next boat."

"Next boat. Soon?"

"Yes," she answered and hoped that once again she didn't lie.

She dried Watty's tears and led him down the bluff and onto the flatboat. Stand tried to make room for him in the cabin, but Watty was the last one boarding. The best Stand could do was find a crate of bacon and seat him at Susanna's feet. The old folks, also, were in the open.

"Stand!" Sarah called. He edged his way to her. "Can't Mother and Father be out of the weather?"

"I tried, but there are so many children, Sallie. They're scared. We had to crowd them into the cabin." He shook his head in disgust. "Lucinda and Luther will be with them. Pray for good weather."

Sarah knew the river route would be shorter and less physically demanding on the old ones, and on Watty. Overall, 466 people—half of them children—boarded eleven flatboats. The educated and ignorant, substantial and poor, sober and drunk; all looked for the last time at the hills of their ancestors.

Dr. Clark Lillybridge, the physician hired by the government to tend to the Cherokees on this trip, moved through the crowd administering cathartic and sudorific—sweat-inducing—herbs to those suffering ague and diarrhea. Soldiers piled on. The boatmen, rough-talking mountain men, raised their oars amid a chorus of curses. The eleven flatboats making up four flotillas, poled and rowed their way into the current to drift at the mercy of the Tennessee. A tall, white thunderhead poked above Lookout Mountain and it, too, drifted, toward the river.

George carried Sarah above the muddy bank as she exited the flatboat, her arms imprinted from her mother's final hug, her hands chilled by her father's parting grasp, her cheek wet with Watty's resurfaced tears. As the couple climbed the bluff, George removed his coat and placed it across her shoulders to ward off the chilly outliers from the approaching storm. Wrapped in her husband's arms, Sarah watched the boats until the green of the river replaced their charcoal shapes.

"You've done well, Sarah. Now they are in God's hands."

"Thank you, George. And thank you for your help."

"I vowed I would care for you, my dear, and now I continue along that vein. I regret I cannot offer you a Grand Tour of Europe for our marriage holiday," he added, chuckling, "but I've arranged for our united lives as Lieutenant and Mrs. George Washington Paschal to commence. First I shall take you on a carriage ride."

She paused, looking one last time at the river. Her mother had told her she must now look forward, not back. "When we leave you, your new life begins with your husband. Our future now depends on your fulfillment in your marriage." Cherishing those words, Sarah turned and took George's arm.

He led her up the bluff to a stand of hickories where a carriage waited, a blanket folded on the leather bench, their valises tucked behind in the rumble seat. One of John's servants stood by guarding, then left.

"Are we going to Elias's now?"

"Soon, my dear. But today and tomorrow are ours."

They drove two miles along the trampled path where from throughout the nation, emigrants had merged for their walk to Ross's Landing. At Citico Creek, George veered the horses onto a newly cleared road.

"The Army is building a small camp in preparation for upcoming removals," he commented.

Sarah cringed. An entire force of Army personnel to remove her people!

As they emerged from the trail Sarah saw a long agency barracks with a cluster of tents and new cabins scattered around. Several soldiers with axes and shovels worked near the main structure.

A sergeant called out a greeting. "Lieutenant Paschal!" He was a young man with shaggy ginger-red hair falling beneath his cap, and he ran to meet them.

George introduced Sarah to his friend Sergeant Tynor Newsom. He saluted George, then removed his cap with a flourish and bowed.

"Missus Paschal, ma'am. An honor to meet you. Everything is ready, Lieutenant Paschal, and I shall see to your horse. May I add my hearty congratulations on your marriage."

George thanked him profusely and headed toward a cabin nestled at the end of the trail. Square and small, swirls of bark still dangled from its notched corners; welcoming smoke drifted from the rock chimney.

Pulling up, he turned to Sarah. "Our regiment will begin occupying the camp shortly, but I've arranged for us to spend the next two days here before I return to duty. Your marriage lodgings, my dear."

George's smile of delight that Sarah remembered from Monday's ceremony lit his face as he took her hand and helped her step from the carriage. The new-hewn scent of pine reached her as they crossed the porch of the house. George opened the door and she stepped in. Following her mother's wish, she did not look back.

Amber. Sarah's eyes filled with amber. She was surrounded by the color: fresh-stripped yellow pine walls chinked with red clay; plank floors planed smooth; red cedar shakes woven in the pitched roof. Amber flames burned in the river rock fireplace. Several thick beeswax candles stood on the mantelpiece waiting to light the coming night. A room warm with color, warm with heat.

Next to a three-legged stool stood a water crock. On the stool a basket held loaves of bread and small cakes; another flat basket of food crocks, plates, and cups sat on the floor. In a corner, a familiar sheet draped over a trimmed limb was positioned to cordon off a chamber pot and dressing area where a copper washtub peeked out. In the center near the hearth lay a thick pine straw pallet, neatly spread with blankets and fine linens Sarah remembered from home. Smoothed across the pallet, a bedgown Susanna had stitched for her daughter years before fanned out.

Sarah brought her hands to her face. Only a few hours before her heart was breaking and now it filled with wonder. She turned to George, speechless.

"Lettie," he said, smiling. "I requested she assemble what she could since you and I would be assisting your family."

So ... George and Lettie ... and her mother ... they planned this time for her. She now accepted their gifts and trusted George's assurance that her departed family was in God's—and the Great Spirit's—hands.

While a cold, wet wind followed the flotilla down the River of the Cherokee, roaring down hills and through the woods, for two precious days in the cabin Sarah's body learned, expressed, and rejoiced in a wife's passion for her husband. George's experienced hands, mouth, and lithe body drew from her sensations of response she had not known until he loved her. She possessed in her emotional history only motherly instruction from Susanna, giggles and fantasies she'd shared with Hester, and titillations from her Jane Austen books. George, with no confession, obviously was experienced to lead and teach.

Before the hearth, a candle perched on the little stool, they lay. Patterns of firelight moved across their bodies, one light, one dark. Her love for George appeared as she had hoped as he released from within her sensations that swelled and waned and swelled again. They rested wrapped in soft quilts, shared bites of smoked ham, dried venison, and nibbled berry-smeared bread. Then his touch on her thigh, a brush of her breast sparked simmering embers within them, and they crawled again beneath the blankets nibbling instead on an ear, a finger, a nipple. They existed but for each other's pleasure.

When their time in the woods came to an end, they boarded the carriage and drove away to begin their life together. Sarah kept the memories of their amber cabin within her heart and often allowed intimate moments to revisit her body, inducing the slightest of smiles.

Chapter 25
My Dearest Mother

Ross's Landing

February - June 1837

The same gusts that blew over Sarah's amber cabin chilled and soaked the old folks and Watty as they huddled on the keelboat through treacherous canyons. Sarah later learned that eighty miles downriver, at Gunter's Landing in Alabama, the family obtained a cabin in the steamer that took over towing the flatboats. Her aged father was given preferential treatment while Rossmen continued to spread hateful rumors.

When their steamboat reached Decatur, the river was too low; the emigrants were put on open railroad cars to Tuscumbia, bypassing miles of shoals where mussels clung. From there they were put aboard the steamer *Newark* that towed two long keelboats up to the Ohio, and on to its confluence with the Mississippi, then south. Turning northwest into the Arkansas River, they steamed upstream past Little Rock, and finally arrived at Fort Smith at the end of March. Friends met them at the dock and they began their long wagon ride up the Line Road to what would soon be home on Honey Creek. No one knew that once the State of Arkansas surveyed its boundaries, the Ridge farm and trading post would lie within state lines.

None of the emigrants under Dr. Lillybridge's care died on that trip, a record that would remain unchallenged on any future removal. Susanna and Major Ridge had fallen ill, and the doctor treated their severe coughs with his camphorated tincture of opium, an elixir he prepared by steeping opium in alcohol, honey, and camphor. His magic potion worked. The dedicated doctor toiled day and night with no medical assistant, going from boat to boat making sure all under his responsibility received his best care. All—young and old—survived the ordeal.

Weeks later a rumor spread east that Major Ridge had died shortly after arriving at Honey Creek. Sarah grieved and John began making preparations to go west immediately. Then a letter arrived from Stand denying the rumor, reassuring her that all were in good health and that her father was busy organizing the building of his new store. Stand added that Susanna was strong and that she was pleased with the new landscape, all abloom upon their arrival. He made no mention of Watty.

March turned into April, April to May. Sarah helped John's family, and General Wool accepted George's resignation from the Army. John enrolled Sarah and George to emigrate on the next river removal. The sheriff of Cass County, though, had other plans for George: he arrested him.

A whiskey peddler pressed charges against George for destroying his kegs of whiskey. Under General Wool's orders, George had led a group of soldiers that hacked open the barrels. Although selling whiskey to Indians was against federal law, the sheriff and the Georgia court held George personally responsible. Sarah sent word to George Lavender at her father's store and he posted George's $300 bail and paid his fine. He was free to go west.

Now Sarah and George sat on the bluff above Ross's Landing in a tent he had borrowed from his former unit. "My love," George said as they breakfasted on a tin of army rations. "Do you still have your letter-box in your possession?"

"No, dear. I sent it on in Robinson's wagon."

"Yes, then will you be remaining in the tent? I'll leave my valise here and ride over to the post to see if General Wool can spare quill and paper for his old aide-de-camp. I wish to write my mother before we proceed westward. I'll return as soon as possible."

"Certainly. I'll stay here." Oh, yes, she'd be gratefully alone! Lettie was gathering the final river-washed clothes she'd hung on limbs farther up the bluff.

Sarah propped her back against George's valise, for comfort more than to secure the valuable contents.

Yesterday John had ridden to the landing carrying a box of provisions for Sarah's journey, purportedly for one last brotherly farewell and gift of additional supplies. Sarah knew what to expect; George did not. Since Mother and Father had not been well enough to travel overland, the family arranged for Sarah and George to transport their cache of script and specie, notes, and gold nuggets.

John stashed food and medicines from the box in Sarah's bags; the treasure he placed in George's valise. This sign of trust by the family pleased George no end, and Sarah perceived in her relationship a deeper connection from her husband when in the early morning hours, he came to her with a sense of passion reminiscent of their times in the little cabin.

Finally, tomorrow, she was carrying out her promise to Watty. Blessed with late May rains and a rushing river, she and George would embark in the morning and follow her parents down the River of the Cherokee.

Now tired and dirty, she fell asleep.

Thursday, June 1, 1837
Ross's Landing, in the former Cherokee Nation
My dearest Mother,

Oh, whatever have I done? This marriage, this voyage? I liken my role to Hercules, although in modesty, mine is a somewhat lesser goal than making the world safe for Mankind. Perhaps more accurately, I am helping these sad, unfortunate people, <u>and</u> making the Cherokee cause beneficial to myself at the same time. I view me as a champion, a modern-day warrior, though I fill my quiver not with arrows, but with words. I lack, however, Hercules' lion skin and club. During the past six months since I've asked for my Sarah's hand in marriage, there were times, dear Mother, that I have needed to wield my own version of such a club.

The dastardly high sheriff of Cass County. Arresting me for axing whiskey barrels! Such a turn of events. My actions, though, truly were more altruistically motivated than merely obeying General Wool's orders. You and my honorable late father instilled in me the evils alcohol can bring, dear one, and I confess that I attacked the barrels with relish, knowing that any devil's brew that soaked into the red clay would keep many a'pitiful red man sober a few days longer.

I must admit to you, though, that had I <u>not</u> been married to the daughter of the much-maligned Major Ridge—had I been an independent temperance man or missionary destroying the kegs—I feel certain that the Georgia authorities would <u>not</u> have come down so hard on me. I see now, first hand, the prejudices directed at even prestigious Cherokees. And the magistrate accorded inappropriate inferences concerning my union with the daughter of a Chieftain.

It became necessary to use all my influence as a white man and an attorney. I berated the sheriff for arresting me—George W. Paschal, Esq., the colleague of the brothers Lumpkin—Colonel Joseph Henry Lumpkin <u>and</u> Governor Wilson Lumpkin—and the distinguished Senator John C. Calhoun! My prestigious connections fell less on the magistrate's ear than, fortunately, Sarah's family funds funneled into his pocket, which finally freed me.

George lifted his ink bottle and tilted it. Enough ink to last, he thought, grateful for General Wool's permission and the use of a table at the post.

Lorenzo Columbus George Washington Paschal considered himself a fortunate man. His father, a respected schoolteacher and persistent entrepreneur, suffered recurrent financial setbacks during George's childhood, but because of his father's guidance and his beloved mother's love of books, George excelled in learning and reading law. Through Agnes Brewer Paschal's benevolent and unselfish nature—even teaching slaves to read and spell, and helping the community with her spiritual and healing powers—he had acquired his belief to minister to those less fortunate, as well as self-determination and a strong resolution not to fail. As the fifth of Agnes' ten children and her final son, leaving his mother had been a hard row to hoe. And, unfortunately, he left her in trying circumstances when his course led westward.

Four years ago George had hung his new law license on the wall of his new office in the new town of Auraria—poetically "the city of gold" in Latin. As the county seat of newly-designated Lumpkin County, Auraria was located about sixty miles east of his future bride's plantation and six miles south of Dahlonega, the site of a recent gold discovery. Well, recent for white Georgians; the Cherokee had been picking up nuggets in those hills forever.

When the state added the Gold Lottery to the already divisive Land Lottery, the spinning drums enticed numerous gold companies to seek deals with the fortunate drawers, all of whom required legal assistance for filing deeds; then they needed lawyers to pursue broken contracts and file suits over land titles.

George's practice flourished; with his father's death, he encouraged his mother to sell the farm near Oglethorpe and move to Auraria where he purchased a hotel for her to manage. Agnes served as a lively and gracious hostess and the mother of a successful son. Life was good.

Yet as so often with the fickle wheel of fortune, or in this case the fickle lottery, Auraria's bustling courthouse turned out to be situated on a lot not owned by Lumpkin County, but that of a fortunate drawer. Which, when claimed, forced the court to move to Dahlonega along with the majority of George's clients and his mother's boarders, resulting in his first investment failure. He struggled, helping his mother as best he could, but finally, he joined the Army. He would, he promised Agnes, make his way in the world, pursue a route to success, and find means to support her.

As I have written earlier, in joining the Army my dearest Mother, I ingratiated myself to General Wool, who found me worthy. And through him, I encountered the Ridge dynasty, my new family—while retaining my same familial love for you, dear one. They are well appointed and I am on the cusp of westward movement, the geographical direction I wish to pursue. Though my original dream was Texas, the Arkansas Territory is now a state—a new and burgeoning Western state—and will suffice for now.

The extended Ridge family is of substantial circumstances—and then there is the gold Major Ridge is said to have found in a cave, back when only Cherokees knew the source of nuggets.

Within the valise I will now carry with me at all times, even to use as a pillow at night, rests a great amount in gold entrusted me by my father-in-law, plus a tidy sum of script and specie delegated by my brother-in-law to purchase improved land for his family, since he will be unable to leave until autumn. We all surmise land values will increase when the remainder of Cherokees pour into the new territory. Another source of bounty for me, my dear Mother, in carrying the paper on land notes.

As the newest white member of the Ridge family, I recognize my standing in the western state will be assured. As an accomplished lawyer, I acknowledge my abilities will be needed.

And then there is my bride; I am truly fond of her, I must confess. Sarah is a good woman, a helpmate, an honest woman—handsome and intelligent. You know how I have always appreciated the coquettish girls in school, and later as a successful attorney? Yes, I enjoyed flirting and the resulting opening of romantic doors that my adept advances previously unlocked. Forsooth, my fortunate and opportune choice of Sarah as a loving wife slams shut those doors.

Universal events are moving fast, as fast as the fabled hind that could outrun the flight of an arrow, my dear Mother. But given my wits and prowess, I will rise to the occasion and address any adversaries that might come my way.

The universal events to which George referred was The Panic. New President Van Buren, acknowledged as Jackson's puppet, had barely taken office when the bubble burst. Every bank stopped payments in specie: gold and silver were replaced by paper script. Shops issued their own barter tickets, such as the baker printing "Good for a loaf of bread" and the barber "Good for a shave." When you went out to trade, the trader looked over your tickets and selected the ones he could use to his best advantage.

George, Jacksonian to the core, blamed the greedy banks and speculators, not the former President. Westward expansion meant a thriving nation! Settlers poured into the West and Eastern speculators, smelling money, took advantage of the situation. Government money received for lands was deposited in banks, credited to the government and then loaned out to speculators. That gave the government more credit in banks than the amount of its capital, ending up with assets consisting almost entirely of the notes of speculators.

Jackson had no way to staunch the flow than to issue an order that only gold and silver should be received for the public lands. But banks didn't have specie available to redeem their bills and states, counties, and cities paid their debts in warrants. Cotton fell from fourteen cents to five cents a pound; flour rose from five dollars a barrel to twelve dollars. In the Panic that followed, nine out of ten men in business would go bankrupt.

The new President could do nothing to stop it; George helped vote him in and felt if anything could be done, Van Buren would. But for now, gold was what counted.

Worry not for me, my dearest Mother. I am a welcomed and trusted member of a strong though ostracized faction of the Cherokee tribe. On the morrow, I and my bride board a riverboat to the West.

Your loving son, George W. Paschal

Chapter 26

The Suck, the Boiling Pot, the Skillet, & the Frying Pan

Leaving Ross's Landing

June 2, 1837

Terrified, Sarah clung to George's promise of protection when he had asked for her hand. If ever she feared for her life, it was now as she clung to the side of the boat.

"Hold on, my dear!" he yelled clutching her shoulder, pressing her to him as the waters of the Tennessee raged and splashed over the gunwale. Late May rains were no asset in the raging torrent.

They sat on a low crate in the open front of a hewn-plank flatboat. Gray and weathered, the boat was fifteen feet wide by sixty feet long and manned by five foul-speaking boatmen. The head boatmen, the pilot, steered the boxlike craft from the stern, standing on the top of the wide cabin with a long rudder pole. Two pairs of men stood on either side of the cabin paddling long oars to steady the barge through the current, sweeping them back and forth, then lifting them as the current took control.

This morning as a bright sun blessed the day, the boats followed Sarah's parents' route, casting off from Ross's Landing along with the shallow-draft steamboat *Guide*. Over three hundred emigrants, rural people accustomed to walking and horseback, were crammed into the convoy of flatboats along with their possessions, plus boxes and barrels of supplies to last three weeks. Several smaller flatboats were lashed to each side of the steamer to avoid them drifting into the churning paddlewheel at the stern; the boats heaved and bumped into each other with the ebb and flow of the current despite desperate contortions and curses from the boatmen.

About eight miles downriver from Ross's Landing, Sarah and George's flotilla encountered Tumbling Shoals, a stretch of deep water with huge boulders strewn amid the swift current. The boats bumped and twisted with the rushing current as they entered the Narrows, where for centuries warriors stood on the cliffs above with bows and arrows, and picked off invading tribes in their canoes—and later white men.

Throughout this winding of the Upper Tennessee, early European boatmen had bestowed names to treacherous pools and rapids where the River of the Cherokee denied them a smooth run. Collectively, the thirty-mile stretch of obstructions was known as the Narrows; individually, the Suck, the Boiling Pot, and the Skillet. And just when the exhausted boatmen came out of the Skillet, they had to run the Frying Pan.

The boats wove through the shoals above where Suck Creek poured in. Aboard, Cherokee who knew ancient stories knew this series of pools as the *Ufitiguhi*, the Pot in the Water—the haunted whirlpools—and they froze in fear. Sarah had heard tales of how throughout generations these whirlpools grabbed and dragged canoes into their depths, swallowing warriors.

The *Guide's* captain slowed and yelled orders to the side flatboats to unlash and reposition. Now in pairs, each packed with fifty or more emigrants and several soldiers, the boats were released a set at a time with the steamboat to follow; on the open bow deck of one of the first pair, George held Sarah close as they raced into the Suck.

Here The River narrowed and channeled all his water into a ribbon 150 feet wide, moving fast as he prepared to reverse his path with a switchback to the south, swirling, whirling, sucking beneath his surface anything he chose: drifting logs, boats, or people.

Sarah raised her head and looked at the wall of stone in front of them. How wide was the hairpin curve? They were heading straight toward a wall edged with its jumble of fallen rocks. Afraid to see, she buried her head in George's chest, but she couldn't cover her ears, couldn't block the fierce roar of The River, block Lettie's screams and the boatmen's curses as they pumped and pushed with their oars.

Sarah felt the boats turn and squirm. They now rotated in the Boiling Pot's broad and deadly whirlpool. The boatmen paddled hard, urging the boats to face downstream. But the circling current grabbed and held them. With mad paddling and poling, they reached the edge of the pool where they entered the southbound flow. Weaving and wallowing as the current caught them again, they headed into the Skillet.

The boatmen made for a channel. If Sarah leaned a bit she could have reached out to touch the chiseled face of a jagged pillar as they sped by. She felt a bump, heard the splintering of wood and a boatman's curse as he pulled up his broken oar. Soldiers unlashed a spare from the cabin roof. Relieved that the boat wasn't breaking apart, Sarah took a deep breath as they entered a fast-moving pool.

She could see the Frying Pan with its wide expanse of projecting, ragged rocks. The boats shot through sideways. The boatmen cheered while horrified Cherokees heaved great sighs of relief as the boats wallowed their way to a sandy bank; grounded, they awaited whoever came through next.

"We made it, my dear. We made it." George wrapped her in his arms and she clung to him, her body shaking. She felt his chest tremble as he hugged her.

The people began to clamber over the beached prows of the boats. "Halt!" shouted a sergeant. The boatmen joined in, yelling, cursing. The soldiers called the people to get back in the boats, shouting that they couldn't get off without permission of the colonel, who was on the *Guide*.

"Oh, George!" Sarah said, "The soldiers think they're running away! But they just need a necessary house!"

George climbed onto the roof of the cabin and stumbled to where several soldiers stood nearby the pilot. He motioned to the sergeant;

THE SUCK, THE BOILING POT, THE SKILLET . . .   177

George wore his military uniform, insignia and all, although the sergeant knew he had resigned his commission. "These poor people only need to relieve themselves. Let them exit the boat to do so!"

"Hit ain't a'lowed, Mister Paschal. I got my orders not to let 'em escape."

"They have no intention of escaping! This is *not* a prison ship! These people have paid or requested voluntary emigration to the Indian Territory. Please, some compassion! They will return."

The early "escapees" came walking back from a canebreak along the sandy river edge as more climbed over the side.

"Let 'em go!" the sergeant yelled. "They'll come back. Looks like we got us a lieutenant *and* a Injun expert here to take care of 'em."

"Ignorant uncouth animal!" George mumbled as he sat back on the crate.

Sarah smiled. "You're so gallant!" She started to pat his leg, but quickly slapped her own hand. Wincing, she said, "Deer flies! Oh, no. What's next?"

George laughed his laugh Sarah loved to hear, like a pleasant rushing brook running across rocks . . . not those they just passed through! He lifted her hand from where it rested on his trousers and gently rubbed the red welt rising near the edge of her glove.

"Determined endurance, my dear. Just a few weeks more and we'll arrive at your family's home at Honey Creek. Better yet, I'm sure there's a fine hotel established in the new town of Van Buren, and we'll repose there before continuing our journey to your parents' headland. Perhaps return there. I'll open a law office and build you a new home."

"Yes, dear. How lovely that will be." Optimism was a trait new to her, living so long under a canopy of endings. Since George had come into her life, he had eased a portion of that pain.

"But in our current circumstances now, Mrs. Paschal," he said smiling as he rolled a blanket and tucked it under his arm, "might I accompany you in finding a pastoral necessary house of your own choosing?"

She took his hand, laughing. "Yes, thank you, George."

From her perch on a crate, Sarah looked down at her husband as he napped, rolled in his blanket, his valise a pillow against the rough deck, his face relaxed now. The sun beat down on her drying, filthy dress—after two days stained, muddy, and damp.

Lettie sat beside her, dozing. Her head leaned against Sarah's shoulder as the rhythm of the waters rocked the occupants to sleep. The meager provisions that were offered to the emigrants failed to fill their bellies; a shroud of silence covered those who sat and watched the hills recede.

The steamer again towed the flotilla; the rumble and splash of the paddlewheel filled the calm afternoon as they plied through a long stretch of uninterrupted water. All the boats, save one, had arrived through the Narrows safely—a flatboat smashed against the wall of the Suck. Climbing Bear and Amoneeta's boat. Climbing Bear was thrown overboard, but managed to swim out of the whirling turbulence and was rescued by the steamboat as it plowed through afterward; the flatboat made it to a sandbar.

When the damaged craft caught up with Sarah's, she sat with Amoneeta to comfort her, the woman's ravaged face contorted by fear that her husband had perished. What a relief when the steamer shot through the Frying Pan and the couple reunited.

Now with her love for George, Sarah empathized with Amoneeta on a level never before experienced. In her girlish fantasies, Sarah had not understood the all-encompassing bond with a husband, companion, and lover. Her uncertain future loomed as treacherous as the rapids through which she recently traveled, but her affection for George provided a lifeline.

Chapter 27

Twice-dead

An Island in the Tennessee River

Near Decatur, Alabama

June 1837

"Miss Sallie!" Lettie motioned and called in a heavy whisper from the other side of the flatboat. Lifting the hem of her grimy skirt, Sarah stepped around heaps of emigrants and made her way to where Lettie sat next to Amoneeta. Several days earlier below the Frying Pan Sarah had received permission to have her friends and their belongings transferred to her flatboat. Climbing Bear leaned against the gunwale, asleep near his wife.

"Amoneeta's 'bout burnin' up with fever."

The woman's scarred eyelids lay closed. Sarah rested her fingers on Amoneeta's forehead, then pulled back as if touching hot coals. She took a handkerchief from her pocket and gave it to Lettie to dip in the river. Tenderly, Sarah wiped her friend's face, cringing, remembering similar motions the day in front of the burning cabin. Among the pockmarked scars left by the boiling corn mush, Amoneeta had received an oozing cut when her boat crashed into the rocks at the Suck. Sarah followed the red line to the edge of Amoneeta's hair and down her neck. "Try to keep her cool, Lettie. I'll tell George."

Struggling back to George, Sarah whispered. "A dreadful red streak in her neck. I fear the poison from her wound is traveling through her."

"She needs treatment. When we dock at Decatur, I'll locate Dr. Gray."

Through the late afternoon light, they could see houses and frame buildings approaching in the distance. The *Guide* puffed and paddled its flotilla toward the Alabama town, then turned toward a low cane-covered island dotted with pine saplings. The boatmen untied the flats and rowed and poled onto the sandbank, beaching the boats. Soldiers jumped to shore.

"George? What's going on?" Sarah asked. "Why aren't we docking at the wharf?"

"I'll ask what's happening," he said.

Crawling across the cabin roof he approached the pilot. Tobacco juice ran down the man's gray-streaked beard. His mane-like hair framed his face. He reeked of an odor far older than this trip.

"Why are we stopping at the island? Why aren't we docking in town?"

The man spat over the side, then swallowed. A brown line of spittle trickled into his matted beard. George winced.

"Orders. Sarge says the Injun Agent says keep 'em on the island. Keep 'em away from the whiskey. An' I'm following orders."

It was no use to argue—even to comment. George shook his head, then headed back to Sarah. "He says they have orders to land on the island."

"But why? Surely there's a building in Decatur where we can stay? We have sick people on board!"

"There's whiskey in town."

"Ah, yes. We must keep the red man sober."

"Sarah, dear, you know it's true. Look what happened before we left. Without doubt, there are people in this town who would delight in selling whiskey to the emigrants." As they watched, the steamer finished unloading supplies and people and pulled away from the shore. Soldiers began handing out provisions.

"You're right. We'll just have to spend the night on the island. It will be safer in the long run. But I worry about Amoneeta. I need to find my herb basket."

"I should get the doctor for her. Let's get you off and situated first."

The Cherokees coughed and stumbled their way through clouds of mosquitoes and deer flies that buzzed and whirred about the island. Lettie and George carried their bags and set them in a mid-way clearing. George cut an armful of cane and spread it on the sand, and Sarah covered the rough boughs with blankets for a bed. Climbing Bear carried Amoneeta and gently laid her down. Collapsing next to his wife, he removed his slouch hat and turned away to cough. Sarah watched him shudder, followed by a deep rattle.

Sarah found her herb basket, woven of strips of rivercane and edged with deep indigo patterns. For as long as Sarah could remember, her mother had stored medicinal herbs in a hamper similar to this. When Sarah married, Susanna presented her with this basket that she'd been weaving for days at Elias's house. "The medicines of the white doctors can be good," she told her daughter, "but never forget the ways Flying Bird and I taught you."

Sarah's fingers moved between the small crocks, tiny baskets, and yarn-tied clusters of leaves. Lettie brought a kettle filled with river water and set it in the fire. Pouring boiling water into a small bowl, Sarah stirred in hemlock leaves and several spoons of precious sugar, then urged Amoneeta and Climbing Bear to drink the strained liquid.

Lettie tossed in wild onions to boil while Sarah pulverized more hemlock leaves on a flat rock. She mixed hot water with a spoon of flour and stirred the gooey mixture, smoothing it over Amoneeta's wound. Lettie pounded the boiled onions while Sarah removed the couple's shoes and the women spread the onion poultice over the soles of their feet.

"Rest. Don't move. Sleep and get better," Sarah told the feverish pair.

Lettie whispered to her as they stood at the edge of the cane break. "Och, Sallie. Ah dinnae reckon that travelin' to the Promised Land was gonna be like wanderin' forty years in th' wilderness. All these po' folks an' lads an' lasses."

"We'll make it, Lettie. Somehow." But was this statement, like her promises to Watty, another lie?

George came through the thicket of cane. "I don't see the doctor. I'm going to find him now. You and Lettie watch over my valise."

As her husband made his way between clusters of crying children, collapsed grandparents, the sick and the supporting, the sun sank behind the tall pines of Decatur. Weak cookfires flickered amid the rivercane.

George crisscrossed the island going from group to group in a fruitless search for Dr. Gray. He found Homer Anthony, the removal agent, near the beached flatboats. The plump man's circular face was flushed with worry. His white hair flying, he shook his head to requests as his wards begged him for remedies and better places to sleep.

"Where's Dr. Gray?"

"He stayed on the steamer over to town."

"What for? Look at these people. We need him here!" George swept his arm to encircle the entire island.

"We do, yes. But he's going to see 'bout requisitioning more medical supplies there. Says he's running low."

"Well, Mrs. Paschal believes we have two in our party with raging infections."

Anthony's face turned moon-like. "Gol' darn. Devil's sending everything he's got to wipe out these poor folks. I'll send one of my boatmen for the doc."

"I would feel better going myself, Mr. Anthony. The way your boatmen feel about Cherokees, suffice it to say, procuring assistance from a doctor is not a top consideration."

"Well, uh, my instructions are for no enrollees to go ashore, and, well, you're on the manifest—"

George cut him off. "In other words, Mr. Anthony, you fear that as the husband of an Indian, I will get drunk if I go ashore?" he countered.

The man stuttered, embarrassed. "Uh, well, guess you'd be all right. Take one of those canoes the steamer left for us. Tell Dr. Gray it's my order for him to return immediately."

By the time George and Gray returned an hour later the other canoes were missing, and the noise of drunken carousing drifted across the channel from a brightly lit shack on the bank. George grabbed a lantern and held it high to light the way through the restless camp to where Amoneeta lay sleeping in Sarah's arms. The doctor, an older man in military uniform was respectful when Sarah told him the curative herbs she had administered.

The physician kneeled and put his ear to Amoneeta's chest. "I fear the infection has gone to her heart," he murmured. George held the lantern as Dr. Gray brought out a supply of calf's foot jelly and swabbed the woman's throat, then her husband's. Climbing Bear, less feverish, held his wife while the doctor sliced into her arm and bled her. Sarah turned away, unable to watch the blood pour from her friend's body. Then the doctor dribbled a small dose of chlorate of potassium through her scarred lips, followed by a little brandy. Amoneeta resisted, coughing and retching.

George passed the lantern to Dr. Gray as he and Sarah accompanied the man for a short distance. He gestured to people calling for help. "I think she'll pull through, her husband, too," he said. "I must go."

George led Sarah to the river's edge. They walked for a bit, not talking, not touching, sharing this opportunity to be together. As they neared their campsite, George put his arm around her shoulders in a brief hug. "She'll make it, dear. She's had proper treatment now."

Despite George's optimism when they reached their little fire, Amoneeta lay dead in her husband's arms.

Lettie clutched a blanket with which to shroud the woman should her husband release her. "She started breathin' real hard," she whispered. "Then all of a' sudden she went still. She jes gave up th' ghost."

Climbing Bear looked up at Sarah. His voice cracked, echoing a pain beyond her comprehension. "Her spirit long ago flew away. She once told me she died in the fire . . . and she's been dying since."

As word passed, stillness enveloped the island. Sarah, her eyes filled with starlight, lay next to her silent husband. As dawn erased those stars, she cried. George enlisted several soldiers to dig a shallow grave near a small pine. Sarah alerted others and each gathered to mumble their chants or prayers.

A silence passed over the mourners; Lettie stepped back. She started humming a song many would know.

As her voice grew stronger, Lettie's melodic Scottish lilt surrounded the bowed heads.

On that cane-covered island, the sun golden and foretelling a new day of unknown perils, she sang for Climbing Bear and the travelers:

Swing low, sweet chariot
Coming for to carry me home
Swing low, sweet chariot
Coming for to carry me home

I looked over Jordan, and what did I see
Coming for to carry me home?
A band of angels coming after me
Coming for to carry me home.

Lettie allowed the word "home" to drift through the early light. The circle of friends and strangers turned away giving Climbing Bear silent time to say his final farewell to his twice-dead wife.

Chapter 28

The Promised Land

Decatur, Alabama

June 1837

Huge raindrops pounded Sarah as she and George lifted their belongings onto the railroad flatcar. She had left Lettie on the covered side porch of the station; a deep cough had settled in overnight.

Mr. Anthony ran back and forth like a mother hen, egging on his bedraggled flock through the rain as evening approached. Soldiers pushed and prodded; some helped lift baskets onto the splintered wood floors of the cars.

Here at Decatur the Old Man of the River complicated his big bend with a series of near-impassible shoals, shoals where since time began he gave his people food, fresh-water pearls, and shell ornaments from the mussels that clung to the rocks. Here the River of the Cherokee became the river of the Creek, the Chickasaw, and the Choctaw.

Between Decatur and Tuscumbia, for more than thirty miles the flow spread wide and treacherous across a flinty rock bed and denied steamboat traffic except at flood time. Flats and keels navigated downstream by shooting the rapids. If boatmen from below were determined to go upstream, they could muscle through by poling shoal after shoal.

The River failed to give his permission to the ever-growing population that required transportation of cotton for exchange of money and materials—and to westward-bound white settlers. Left to find a better solution, Man took over and built his iron river: the Tuscumbia, Courtland, and Decatur Rail Road.

None of the emigrants—Sarah and George included—had ever seen a railroad before, although they knew of the developing lines that ran in Northern states. John and Elias had warned them of the fear the mountain people might encounter at Decatur. The very act of climbing onto iron-wheeled platforms defied any experience the emigrants had known.

George handed his valise to Sarah for safekeeping and left in search of the agent. Sarah walked among the confused crowd, explaining in Cherokee about the row of cars before them. "The *atsila nvnohi* will take us across the hills. Now we ride and do not have to walk or be spilled into the river."

Few were comforted; the words themselves meant "fire road." As she tried explaining by pointing to a parked locomotive sitting nearby on a siding, her images conjured up a fierce fire-breathing apparition.

George approached the harried removal agent. "Why is that locomotive languishing here, unprepared and unstoked?" he shouted through the downpour.

Homer Anthony shook his head as he looked at the vacant space in front of the line of cars where neither locomotive nor firewood tender stood ready to take the party around the shoals. Water poured off George's broad army hat as he followed Mr. Anthony to where the stationmaster stood on the covered platform, protected from rain. A lantern hanging on a post cast a yellow glow across the deck.

The tall, gray-clothed man belched loudly. His face was a long line of bones that ended in a dark goatee; bleary red-rimmed eyes testified to what George assumed was last night's drinking bout. He answered in a bored drawl and pointed to the engine and tender on the siding. "*Comet's* done blew a cylinder. She's here but can't run. They're bringing over *Triumph* from Tuscumbia."

The rain, the waiting, and the disorganization edged Anthony's voice. "Well, *when* will it be here? Many of these people are sick! They're getting soaked!"

"I know, I know. *Triumph* was s'posed to be here already. But it ain't."

"I need it now!"

"It ain't here. It'll be here when you see smoke over there." He pointed to a distant hill barely visible through the rain. "What with the storm an' it gettin' late, Tuscumbia might not a' sent it at all."

"These people must have a place to bed!" Anthony's red face seemed nearing explosion.

The stationmaster's insolent drawl was barely audible above the din of the falling rain. "I thought Injuns liked sleepin' out under the stars."

"You'd count yourself lucky to have a roof over your head half as grand as the homes and cabins these people left behind! I demand humane treatment of them!" Anthony slammed one fist into his other hand. "Starting now! With a place for the night out of the rain!"

The stationmaster glared at him. "Now where's that gonna be, mister? I don't have no order for overnightin' these Injuns. They's s'posed to be able to camp out when these things happen."

"*These things* are happening all too often! I want to know what's available in Decatur that I can commandeer for the night."

The lines of the stationmaster's face formed a skeletal mask of light and shadow. "Well, there's the Methodist church ... it ain't big enough though, I reckon. The schoolhouse neither. Now down by the wharf, there's Mr. Patton's warehouse where they keep cotton bales. It ought to be empty this time a' year, but you'll have to pay him."

Anthony wheeled, furious and dangerously red in his face. "Come on, Lieutenant Paschal. We'll look it over." George turned up the collar on his uniform; the three men left the platform and headed toward the river while Sarah waited under the roof.

With permission received and payment made, the chilled, soaked Cherokees settled for the night as best they could in the relative dryness of the warehouse. They draped wet blankets and clothing on pegs and over boxes of supplies. Sarah went back with a dry blanket and brought Lettie to the warehouse.

Dr. Gray moved among his wards; soldiers passed out smoked ham and dried venison. Halos of light surrounded candles and dotted small spaces as the healthy tended the ill.

While George and Climbing Bear slept fitfully, Sarah went over to a cookstove in the corner of the building that someone had fired up. Along with potatoes, she boiled a few onions she'd found in a crate and applied the smelly poultice to Lettie's chest and feet; her friend's cough that had begun after leaving the island had intensified in the rain, and her fever spiked. As morning approached, Lettie rallied.

The chill, though, received by others who had sat for hours on the flatcars took its toll. A child, the son of a farmer from Haweis, and a woman, the mother of a ferry owner on the Coosa, both died.

As the first light of dawn pushed through the overcast sky, two caravans of mourners moved past Sarah, the dead wrapped in wet blankets. George left to help with the burials while she continued to repack their belongings. When he returned—his jacket smeared with mud—his expression spoke more anger than grief. "The stationmaster said the cemetery was for whites only. We had to bury them on the side of a road."

Sarah gasped. "But they're Christians, George!"

"It makes no difference, dear."

She stood beside Lettie's pallet where she'd gathered their valises and supplies. Reaching for George's hand, she felt a need to tell him she didn't know the trip would be this bad, to apologize for the treatment he was enduring because he married her. "George, I'm so sorry you . . . " Her voice trembled.

He took her hand. "Sarah, dear, it's all right. I knew events such as this would occur. I know how Indians are treated. Don't you remember? I rode with General Wool in search of Amoneeta's attackers."

"But it wasn't happening to *you* then. Now it is."

"It's happening to *us*, my dear. And as long as we are emigrants, it will continue. But when we arrive in Indian Territory, the Cherokee will again have an autonomous government and live in peace. They will prosper, as before."

"Do you really believe that?" She wanted so much to trust his words.

"Yes. I'll work to make it happen." Despite the public arena in which they stood, he put his arm around her shoulders and pulled her to him. "Your family is powerful. They will lead their people in forming a strong government."

She leaned against him. His tense muscles relaxed for a moment and she longed to lie next to him as she had in their amber cabin. She longed for his touch, his strength, his sheltering arms encircling her body.

He patted her hand and smiled a comforting smile. "Only a few more weeks, my love, and we'll begin our lives anew. I miss my dear wife—"

Suddenly the stationmaster ran down the road, shouting. "*Triumph's* coming! Move 'em along! Get 'em on the cars!"

Mr. Anthony stepped out on the porch as Sarah and George hurried in to gather their gear. Lettie and Climbing Bear assisted each other; both were feeling physically better, though weak in spirit. The agent bustled around, encouraging the emigrants to hurry.

The rising sun could not find enough holes in the dark clouds to light the morning. Through a dreary mist the Cherokee clung to their wet belongings. A tired trail of soggy exiles shuffled toward the track, filling the muddy area in front of the station. The soldiers herded them onto the cars just as the locomotive topped the hill. At that moment, a shaft of sunlight lit up the smoking, belching rolling apparition.

The people nearest the cars stopped abruptly as the charging monster rumbled toward them. The rumble changed to a roar; a burst of black smoke rose from the stack. Churning wheels, metal on metal, screeched to a halt.

Near the front of the group, Sarah held Lettie's arm as George and Climbing Bear carried their bags. Before them, the line disintegrated as terrified families fell to their knees or ran to the safety of trees and buildings. Children clung to their parents' tunics; old people cowered.

Prayers to the Heavenly Father mixed with pleas to the Great Spirit as the Cherokees invoked spiritual intervention to save them from *atsila nvnohi*, the fire on the road.

An old medicine man, dressed in a deerskin tunic and leggings as had his ancestors, pulled out his buckskin pouch of *tsolagayvli*, the sacred tobacco. He walked toward the locomotive as it headed into the wye, the turnout to reverse its direction, and backed with the tender toward the line of waiting cars.

People gathered, watching as the medicine man produced his ceremonial bow and quiver of arrows. He circled the slow-moving, belching engine. The stationmaster stood waiting to connect the tender to the lead car. He looked at the approaching man waving his arrows, then ran for the safety of the station.

The tender hit the car with a *clunk!* as the jolt rippled down each car in succession. People screamed and stumbled; some fell from the cars.

The medicine man lit his twist of tobacco and blew smoke, dancing, chanting. The man intoned an ancient ritual to destroy the nightwalker that molested his people. His magic smoke surrounded and entrapped this fire-breathing demon, altered now into the shape of an iron dragon. Ancient chanting mixed with modern mechanical sounds.

With the nightwalker contained, several groups again crawled onto the cars just as the engineer shifted forward, setting off another chain reaction, another violent lurch of terror. On the flatcars, people tumbled; those hanging on the sides fell to the muddy ground. A mother pulled her screaming child from the rolling path of the wheels. The medicine man shook his arrows at the fiery engine and continued to chant and blow his sacred smoke.

The stationmaster, bold now, yelled from the safety of the platform. "Get 'em loaded on the cars! We're pulling out! Now!"

The more sophisticated helped lift the mountain people back onto the cars. Lettie and Climbing Bear managed to climb on board. Leaning against George, Sarah watched the horror of Decatur recede from view as the locomotive huffed and puffed up the hill toward its destination at Tuscumbia.

A memory came to her, one of her youth listening to Brother Butrick preach in the Brainerd mission of his belief that the Cherokee were one of the Ten Lost Tribes of Israel. Lettie calls this a trip to the Promised Land, she thought. But is it?

Her only answer was the clatter of the wheels and the cries of tired, terrified people huddled together on the shuddering railroad cars heading toward an unknown fate.

Two weeks later, a steamboat towing a flotilla of keelboats approached the new wharf at Van Buren where willows hung as green draperies beneath a high bluff. While the boats had chugged slowly up the Arkansas River, passing through Little Rock and beside grassy prairie and tree-covered hills, the emigrants' spirits lifted. The new homeland resembled the old in many ways.

"Look!" Sarah called out. "There's Stand! And Little Tom!"

"Lord have mercy, Sallie," Lettie replied. "We made it. An' it's a bonnie land. It sure does look like a bit a' home!"

The days following their transfer from railroad to a side-paddle steamer that towed larger and more commodious keelboats—the long journey up the Lower Tennessee, down the Ohio, and on down the Mississippi to where the Arkansas River poured in—seemed to Sarah like waking from a sad dream. Now her eyes filled with family.

Sarah and George disembarked with Lettie, after saying a sad *donadagohvi* to Climbing Bear. He stayed on the boat to meet relations at Fort Gibson, deeper in the heart of the Indian Territory.

At the foot of the gangplank, Sarah watched with pride as George took charge. She and Lettie had washed and brushed his dirty military uniform as best they could. Sarah's hair shone blue-black in the sunlight from a good soaping last night; her calico dress, though as clean as she could get it in a river washing, was snagged and stained.

Van Buren lay as a cluster of buildings and frame houses; there was no fine hotel yet completed, but it wouldn't have mattered. All Sarah wanted to do was to get their belongings loaded onto the wagons that Stand and Little Tom had brought, drive as fast as they could to Honey Creek, and fall into the sheltering arms of her mother.

She peppered her cousin and servant with questions as they loaded baskets and bags. To her great relief, her parents were healthy, and Watty was happy helping to build the new house. Stand and Tom assured Lettie that Robinson thrived, having grown into a fine man on the overland trip.

The women's joy shattered to sorrow, though, as Stand told the travelers of Tom's father, Doll's husband, killed when a wagon overturned. Sarah closed her eyes, fighting back tears and memories of Big Tom. He had always been a part of her life.

As she told them of Amoneeta's passing and Climbing Bear's illness, Lettie stepped away. Sarah let her tears flow as Lettie's quivering voice lifted in song.

> Swing low, sweet chariot
> Coming for to carry me home
> Swing low, sweet chariot
> Coming for to carry me home.

Lettie's words drifted across the bluff toward a weary family struggling up the trail, walking slowly to a waiting buckboard. The horse shuffled. The grieving father placed a small blanket-wrapped body on the planks. The wagon drew away, followed by a line of emigrants searching for a burial place in the Promised Land.

ILLUSTRATIONS

President James Monroe Indian Peace Medal 1817

Major Ridge (circa 1820s)

John Ross (circa 1820s)

John Ridge (1825)

Elias Boudinot (circa 1830s)

ILLUSTRATIONS

Stand Watie (circa 1840s)

Sarah Ridge 1826

Sarah Ridge Paschal (from original painting, circa 1842)

Susan Agnes (Soonie) Paschal 1846

ILLUSTRATIONS 203

George W. Paschal (circa 1850s)

Major Ridge Plantation House, Chieftains Museum,
Rome, Georgia, National Historic Landmark

Part Two
Arkansas
1837 - 1848

[Sarah Paschal is] considerably colored by nature with an aboriginal tint, is plainly of a strong masculine spirit. Speaks English very well, quite naturally as if she had no other language.... She has very black eyes. Several, two at least, children.

Lt. Col. Ethan Allen Hitchcock writing in his diary, March 13, 1842, after his visit to Sarah's home in Van Buren.
A Traveler in Indian Territory - The Journal of Ethan Allen Hitchcock
By Grant Foreman

Chapter 29

Sarah Speaks

You see how treacherous was our removal? But compared with the plight of those from our homeland who would eventually follow, our strife was minimal, so very minimal.

Much depended upon who oversaw each company of emigrants: Dr. Lillybridge on my parents' journey lost none under his care; our Dr. Gray had not the same skills. Mr. Anthony, our removal agent, made demands and compassionate soldiers often helped us. Later parties were led by agents who lacked sympathy, companies moved along the trail with no doctors or worse, quacks who collected government revenue to fill their pockets. By then most of our United States supporters had abandoned us.

Most importantly, though, we did not wait until the removal deadline passed. We knew our Cherokee home had been usurped, and nothing would change to allow us to remain.

In the summer of 1837 we metamorphosed from "emigrants" leaving our beloved nation to "immigrants" arriving in a new one. When I stepped off Stand's wagon into my mother's waiting arms, I did so with a dream of a future. I stowed my memories of Amoneeta and the horrific endings I witnessed into that place in our souls where we honor and release profound pain.

Mother, trim, robust; Father, rotund, animated; both rejuvenated with preparations for a new beginning. And Watty, dear Watty. My big bear of a brother clung to me with patting paws, his face lit with smiles.

Our eighty-mile journey north straight up the Line Road from Van Buren was rough. Stand, having made the trip several times now, successfully forded streams and navigated the stumps of razed woodlands. This northwestern strip of Arkansas was a rugged country infested with desperadoes and squatters who camped in derelict cabins, sold whiskey, and hid in creek beds waiting in ambush to rob new immigrants of relocation funds. Stand and Tom kept their rifles ready, but we encountered no marauders.

Although not the mountainous wilderness of our ancient people, the natural state of the new land where my family settled was not dissimilar to the Oostanaula. Here more prairie spread, trimmed with creeks and hills, dotted with groves of cottonwood and ash, hickory and persimmon. In the bottomland sycamore, pecan and willow marked stream beds, same as home.

Father and Stand had selected property on Honey Creek, rich fertile acreage in what was thought to be in the northeast corner of Indian Territory. Father settled on the south side of the creek; members of the Fields and Lassley families, Mother's relations, built on the north side.

However, there was something we didn't know. Arkansas, in its admission to the Union a year before, had established its state border with Indian Territory a few miles west of us. With no obvious survey markers, our farms and the new store, located some miles south of the Missouri borderline, fell within the boundaries of Benton County.

You see, it was not as if we were arriving on virgin soil graciously given us by the United States in return for our massive hereditary lands.

Just as we over the past decades had ceded our eastern nation to a fraction of what we once held, boundary and ownership lines here, too, shifted: President Jefferson purchased this vast western area in 1803 from the French who had bought it from the Spanish who had usurped the land from Indian bands through murder, disease, and slavery. Native tribes had forever roamed this area between the Arkansas and White Rivers and on down into Texas. The Western Cherokee, Eastern

Cherokee, and other Southern tribes now all had to fit somewhere in the designated "Indian Territory."

The federal government would only quit altering their boundary markers when at last they drew the final lines around their states for admission to their Union.

So here we were—we, I mean my family as leaders in the Treaty Party—relocated to the territory that had been given in treaties to the faction known as the Western Cherokee. Those of our fragmented tribe were led until recently by Father's old friend Chief John Jolly and consisted of about a third of all remaining Cherokee.

Most of our Treaty Party arrived in 1836-37; soon to come were the remaining twelve thousand Eastern Cherokee, the bulk of the people led by John Ross that would be named the "Late Immigrants."

And don't forget the whites. The new states of Missouri and Arkansas were not partitioned for Indian settlement. Everything Congress gave us, they eventually took back.

That summer and fall of our arrival my family busied ourselves building our futures. Mother, Father, and Stand oversaw our slaves and hired workers as houses and outbuildings rose on the prairie. George found good acreage for John a few miles west on Honey Creek just inside the Territory and purchased land with improvements from a Western Cherokee for one hundred twenty-five dollars. John's concerns of speculation proved right: prices for similar plots later soared to five hundred dollars or even more.

We were fortunate. We had money. Most of the signers of the treaty were successful farmers or businessmen in the homeland. The government had valued our home and the ferry at about twenty-five thousand dollars, making Father the third richest in the Cherokee Nation, following John Ross' brother Lewis Ross, richest, and "Rich Joe" Vann. My brother John's home at Running Waters with remuneration for his ferry in Alabama was appraised at twenty thousand dollars. John Ross, who had moved some years past from Head of Coosa to Tennessee, fell in line below Father in the top five on the wealthy list, receiving just under twenty-four thousand dollars for the home and peacocks the Georgians seized, as well as forty acres under cultivation at his old cabin across the border at Red Clay.

With each removal detachment arriving west, came the poor and starving families. Living off government subsidies while they scratched out meager livings on the prairies, farmers who once provided for their families now hunted dwindling deer herds or raided beaver colonies for pelts. They needed trading posts to sell skins for flour, sugar, and dry goods. The Ridge's store at Honey Creek offered it all. George helped Father stock the general store with merchandise ordered from New York and bought locally from farmers: corn by the bushels, hogs and beef to slaughter and smoke.

John and Sarah Bird arrived safely in the fall with their children. Elias, along with his children and new wife, Delight Sargeant, and our Lassley cousins in the large overland caravan, came in late November. Elias traveled on south to Park Hill on the Illinois River to build near Reverend Worcester and continue their translation of the Bible into Cherokee.

By that time my menses had ceased. I delighted in my growing belly as John and Sarah Bird built their home. Nearby, a schoolhouse rose where Sophie Sawyer came to teach. I fulfilled my promise to help her teach until Emily Oolootsie blessed us with her birth on May 18, 1838.

With Mother, Lettie, and my aunts surrounding me, Emily joined us with a loud squeal in the bedroom of my family home that George and I shared. On those spring nights when I had rubbed my rounded belly I never visualized within a chubby, blond baby girl. George was delighted. He called Emily his "Baby Brewer," saying she resembled his mother's family.

Emily became part of my new life and routine. I could enjoy motherhood and still help Sophie teach several hours a day while our servant Milly cared for Emily. George was an attentive father who played with the baby each evening when he came home from clerking at Father's store. I knew, though, that he was eager to return to his practice of the law, fearing he might remain in obscurity during these productive years of his life.

George found several clients for collections and litigation in the new Washington County seat, Fayetteville, not far southeast of Honey Creek. I encouraged him to open an office there where we could be close to family, but in winter he decided to ride the eighty miles down to Van Buren, where he felt steamboat trade would thrive. Wharves knifed the riverside; whistle-blasts announced steam packets; construction soon began on a courthouse that would dominate the town with a clock tower. He wrote with pride of his friendship with Colonel John Drennen, the founder of the town who also served at Fort Smith across the river.

There he lived and worked out of a small log cabin with a young Cherokee apprentice, William Mosley, and contracted for lots for a new brick office on Main Street, diagonally across from the courthouse, and a new house where Emily and I could join him. I was overjoyed.

Since the duties of a frontier lawyer served as a collecting business for local and Eastern merchants, George—ever the writer and detailer—meticulously accounted for money he collected for his clients. There were times, though, when George felt he should give vent to a cause. Shortly before I moved to Van Buren, he wrote an anonymous letter to the Little Rock *Arkansas Gazette* condemning a local family for witchcraft!

When he later confessed to us that he was the author of the letter, Mother and I decided it was time for me to move to Van Buren. Though George's behavior seemed odd at times, he had supported me wholeheartedly throughout our removal journey and spent a year helping establish our family's homes and store. I soon arrived with Emily and a contingent of help. With the aid of Lettie and Robinson, I oversaw the completion of the new Paschal residence on Thompson Street. Mother sent along Milly to care for the baby, and Milly's husband, Isaac, to handle outside duties, the pens, and the animals. George moved from the cabin and went daily to his office on Main Street, and we established our new home life.

Robinson learned skills of town farming and care of the house gardens. After time for frost passed, I planned to plant flower beds along the front porch, peonies, and chrysanthemums from seeds George had requested at Drennen's Mercantile.

With so many upheavals since our marriage at Brainerd Mission, we would start anew. I desired to be George's helpmate, his wife, and his lover. Now was the time for George to reap the rewards of his pursuit of the law.

But a smooth transition was not to be.

My people, the Treaty Party who had removed early, now confronted the bitter consequences of those who believed John Ross's promises, those who remained.

Chapter 30

Letter to Hester

Van Buren, Arkansas

January 15, 1839

My dearest friend Hester,

 When last I wrote, George Paschal and I had safely arrived in Indian Territory and to my great relief found my family well. I am now mother to a beautiful blond baby girl some eight months past named Emily Oolootsie. As happy as she makes me, I write you now not of the joys of motherhood, but of sadness for my people. Bear with me as I ramble on to you—my only remaining friend in the East—concerning reports of which you may have read in newspapers. What or whose versions you have read, I know not. I now tell you truths. You may pass on my news to your abolitionist friends as you see fit.

 This past summer, fall, and now winter—into this pot we have been poured that simmers with other Indian bands, Arkansas Statehood, Western Cherokee, and our Treaty Party—came the survivors of the abominable removal across the western wilderness.

 Almost a year ago Principal Chief John Ross submitted another plea to Congress reiterating that the Treaty my family and others had signed—and which that body enforced—was illegal and not supported by his people.

Ross's request to Congress went unacknowledged, but in it, he asked if the Cherokees were—like deer and bear—to be hunted down throughout the hills? Marched from their homes at bayonet-point? Shipped to a foreign land like chattel?

The unspoken answer was "Yes."

Last May Gen'l Winfield Scott, to whom President Jackson had assigned the malevolent task of ridding the state of Georgia of its nuisance, announced that the two-year period for voluntary removal had expired.

Here I write the words I find myself saying so often, <u>If only.</u> If only John Ross, under whose leadership we achieved such greatness, had encouraged the people to put their affairs in order so much pain could have been avoided—

Our people waited in filthy stockades in a forty-square mile area around Ross's Landing, and farther south on the Tennessee River at Gunter's Landing. As drought ensued, the dreaded sicknesses—measles, whooping cough, bilious fever, dysentery—ravaged the crowded camps. Army doctors dispensed medications, treating symptoms as best they could. Or not.

Greedy whites floated downriver in trading boats, hoping to relieve the captives of their removal funds, selling pies and cakes, and of course, whiskey. A thousand Cherokee escaped into the Smoky Mountains to hide in deep forests, ravines, and caves. They resisted removal.

The final forced emigrations happened thusly: Gen'l Scott planned to schedule removal parties of about a thousand exiles leaving every three days. On the 6th of June, the first of three parties departed in flatboats down the Tennessee, as had George and I, to be picked up by steamers and keelboats below the shoals at Decatur.

But by the time the third group was herded onto the boats, waters ceased to flow. Streams, wells, and springs dried up. Several leaders convinced Gen'l Scott to suspend the emigration until Fall.

He set the 1st of September to resume. As people languished in camps, epidemics spread and whiskey peddlers loitered.

John Ross returned in July from Washington City where he had at least successfully negotiated an increase in the final treaty payment to $6,600,000 from five million, though far less than the twenty million he proposed years before. He requested that he be appointed as Superintendent of Removal and Subsistence, saying he would serve without salary, leaving his brother Lewis to contract transportation and supplies.

When Fall came, Gen'l Scott finally ordered his soldiers to stand down. Perhaps, then, the Great Spirit stepped up. Clouds opened, the drought retreated and the final long marches began.

The rest, as would an army, left overland in regiments of a thousand every few days. Miles and miles of handcarts and covered wagons snaked across the route. Horses, cattle, and oxen; men, women, children; the remaining missionaries. The aged, the infirm. There could be no waiting, no rest, no turning back.

They crossed the riverways of their ancestors. They passed through Nashville where Andrew Jackson, old and withered, sat in his lovely plantation, the Hermitage. Could he—as were some of his former battle warriors passing nearby—have walked the miles that lay before them? They passed over lands once theirs. Often white settlers felt pity and fed the emigrants while others demanded fees at tollgates and ferries.

Winter turned: Snow. Ice. Howling winds. At Cape Girardeau, the Mississippi River would neither freeze firm nor flow, allowing emigrants neither to pass in wagons nor flatboats. They huddled on the eastern bank in blankets, under canvas, or merely in thin clothing, leaning against their fallen horses and entrenched wagons. Their fires blew out; they ate dried provisions or nothing at all. The blood of their shoeless feet dotted the snow. If the strong were able, they buried their loved ones in shallow graves. If not, they blessed them and walked on.

Over four thousand, it is said, dear Hester, died in the camps and on the removals. John Ross's wife, accompanying him in the final river passage, was among those who perished. The last party left Tennessee on January 4 and is yet to arrive.

Does this story not remind you of the Jews forced out of Egypt? Remember the tales I told you at our Salem School, of Brother Butrick and his belief that the Cherokee are one of the Ten Lost Tribes of Israel? Cherokees believed in John Ross and he believed the President and Congress, believed that these leaders would never treat a people as their own ancestors had been treated, persecuted, and tortured, the Puritans forced to remove across the waters to attain their freedom of faith. The American leaders—many of whom are descendants of those persecuted—approved laws to repeat those inequities from which their ancestors escaped!

Is it any wonder the Late Immigrants need to lay blame for their loss, their pain, their dead? I fear that blame will fall on the Treaty Party, on my family.

I shall have a difficult time folding these many pages, my dear friend. I will tie them tight in a bundle, press my seal, and pray for a safe arrival. My husband, daughter, and I are somewhat settled in our new home in the town of Van Buren in the State of Arkansas, where you may reply to this sad missive. Please tell me good news of your New England family, of your life and loves.

Until then, I remain your friend,
Sarah

Chapter 31

This Good Life of Mine

The Paschal Home on Thompson Street

Van Buren, Arkansas

May 18, 1839

"Emily Oolootsie thanks her family for celebrating with her father and me the anniversary of her birth. Now my baby begs her leave for bed."

Rising from her chair at the foot of the dining table, Sarah caressed the squirming child in her arms. In saying those words, "my baby," a warm rush flushed her spine. All around her, everything within her immediate universe followed that tiny word: my family, my husband, my home. Sarah absorbed the affection and admiration radiating from faces directed toward her and was in this moment the reflection in their eyes: a confident, poised mother, wife, daughter, sister, cousin. From this knowledge emanated a sense of decorum, of propriety; the rustle of her burgundy silk gown affirmed her notions.

Through open porch windows floated melodies from Robinson's guitar, where he'd asked if he could play and sing during Sarah's festivities. Holding her baby and basking in her happiness, Sarah caught soft lyrics of a song Robinson had recently picked up from a traveling troubadour named Luke:

Spring winds a' blowin' and the garden's in the ground
Our love is safe and growin' while the world turns 'round
May days come like whispers and years step just behind
Let warm rain fall, darlin', on this good life of mine.

Yes, Sarah thought, this good life of mine.

John rose to pull his sister's chair from the end of the table. Sarah paused between her parents who chucked the baby's chin and stroked her blond curls. At the hallway door she handed Emily over to Milly's care, then returned to her seat.

From the head of the table, George smiled and added, "I only wish my mother could be here to celebrate her mirror-image granddaughter's anniversary."

As Lettie brought in the coffee service, followed by others with bowls of strawberry pudding, Susanna asked, "How is your mother's health, George?"

"She's well, thank you, as she apprised me in a recent letter. I would like to travel to Georgia for a visit, but the responsibilities of my practice require my presence here."

"You've done well in establishing your business, George, and this house," Major Ridge commented, leaning back in his chair while Lettie moved around the table.

Though work on the house and outbuildings was not yet complete, Sarah wanted her Honey Creek family to celebrate her new life in Van Buren; a fortuitous visit by Elias added to her pleasure.

Susanna had given her a set of her own Welsh bone china, copper lusterware with red feathers centered in cobalt medallions and edged in gold. Sarah kept the dinner service and crystal stemware in the new walnut buffet George had ordered, centered between two bookcases. Items from the plantation had been dispersed among the family; furnishings embellished freshly plastered walls and polished oak floors, accented with loomed rugs. The glass sheets covering several of Sarah's framed embroideries had not endured the overland trip west; those she had ordered from New Orleans with the window panes and fanlight over the front door. From the dining room wall, her gold-framed mourning sampler of the old homeplace twinkled in candlelight from wall sconces and the large candelabra centering the table.

"Thank you, sir," George replied to his father-in-law. "I believe each of your family has done well in re-establishing your dynasty here in the west."

"By the will of God," Elias added, nodding appreciation to Sarah as he took a bite of strawberry pudding.

"How goes your collaboration with Reverend Worcester in translating the books of the Holy Bible into native syllabary, Elias?" George asked. He had mentioned earlier to Sarah that her pious cousin seemed more relaxed than he'd seen him in a long time.

"The translation of St. John is tedious, but we persevere," Elias replied, gesturing toward the bookcases. "The *Old Messenger's Christian Almanac* we completed sits on the bookshelves in many homes, including yours, I see."

Elias, as an assistant missionary to Worcester—who was known affectionately as the Old Messenger—worked on the new press the preacher brought west last year, purchased with Northern donations and funds from the American Board of Missions. In establishing the mission at Park Hill, the growing area attracted brothers John and Lewis Ross as well as other Ross Party leaders who bought plantations and improvements from the Western Cherokee, whom some now called the "Old Settlers."

Elias added, "In our travels, we've noted newcomers who formerly were opposed to removal now showing no disposition to quarrel. Perhaps peace can finally be attained."

"We now live under our Western brothers' laws," Major Ridge said. "I feel as much at home here as the Old Settlers themselves."

"But the Late Immigrants have brought their own constitution and laws," John commented, resting his cup in the saucer with a slight clatter. "John Ross will not rest until he again crowns himself principal chief of all the Cherokee."

George sipped his coffee. "I hear he's called a council meeting for next month at Takatoka."

"Will you attend, Father?" Sarah asked.

"Yes. All three of us, plus Stand, are invited."

Elias added, "Stand and I have talked. We disdain, all of us around this table and my brother, from again entering into the political fray. But I feel we should attend the gathering and watch the proceedings. Not speak, though. The Rossmen might consider any discussion a threat."

"I overheard," George said, leaning back in his chair, "a conversation in Drennen's Mercantile a few days past. The speaker, a white, suggested that any Treaty Party members might be removed from the upcoming council."

"Rumors, dear," Sarah interrupted, "we cannot not believe all we hear."

"We go as observers only," Major Ridge said, "as do many of the Western Cherokee. With John Jolly having relinquished his chieftain position, Chief John Brown's guidance will allow election of representatives to seats on the council."

John shook his head. "Perhaps, though I suspect John Ross will fill those seats with men who will vote him in as principal chief. He has a way of insuring himself, as we know, the highest post." His bitter tone filled the room; John's lost opportunity for principal chief those many years past when John Ross suspended elections still stung.

Susanna nodded. "The Late Immigrants outnumber the Old Settlers and our party two to one. They worship John Ross. I hear of much anger." Her spoon clanked as she stirred her coffee, her irritation obvious to all.

Mother's strain and shortness of temper show, Sarah thought. Susanna's gray hair escaped her braid and flew around her lined face, accentuating her sixty-five years of change. Sarah resolved to speak with her mother about her distress before she left.

John leaned forward, "I fear Ross's power. I fear he will alter the laws now established here. I fear—" he paused. "We've all heard rumors he will enact the Blood Law from the Old Nation."

"But that law does not exist under Western Cherokee laws, so he cannot," Elias said.

Sarah looked at each around the table. "Surely John Ross will accept the overtures from those who came before? The Rossmen will be prevented from ferreting out Treaty signers now living peacefully under Western Cherokee laws?"

All were silent until Elias answered, "We can only pray so."

Lettie came in quietly and whispered in Sarah's ear. At the next pause in the conversation, Sarah announced that the guests' beds and pallets were prepared. With well-wishes for pleasant nights, the family separated for the evening. Sarah stepped out the front door and thanked Robinson for sharing his music, reminding him Lettie had saved a bowl of strawberry pudding for his dessert.

The following morning, Susanna, Major Ridge, and John climbed into their coach for the drive to Honey Creek. Elias mounted his horse for his return to Park Hill.

Sarah's peonies at the edge of the porch were in full crimson bloom. The bricks of her home shone a soft sunny sandstone as she stood on her porch beside her husband. Her baby in her arms, she waved and called, "*Donadagohvi!*"—for the final time—to three of her family.

Chapter 32

A Stained Slouch Hat

Takatoka, Indian Territory

June 1839

The council to unite the Western Cherokee and Late Immigrants was convened on the 3rd of June by John Ross at Takatoka. Within a week, six thousand Cherokee arrived. On June 14, the Ridges, along with Elias, Stand, and others of the Treaty Party joined the gathering; they left the same day after hearing anger among the Late Immigrants. Ross did not accept Western Cherokee Chief John Brown's joyful welcome to the new country nor his wishes for peace among the factions.

Instead, Ross disapproved the Western Cherokee codes and government. After two weeks of frustration, Brown dissolved the council on June 19th and set another council date for October. The Western Cherokee leaders and Treaty Party members returned to their farms. The Late Immigrants stayed until John Ross dismissed them, angry that the convention had not gone their way.

But some did not leave. A half-full moon shone through the cottonwoods that covered the campground. Moonlight illuminated tailored shirts contrasting with beaded buckskin; rifles and pistols contrasted with tomahawks and knives as a group of Rossmen headed for a secret meeting in a torch-lit cabin near the council grounds. Several dozen warriors gathered. "Traitors!" "Liars!" rumbled within.

"Thousands have died!"

"My wife and son froze to death!"

"I saw the Ridges talking with the Western chiefs in private."

"They influenced John Brown to break up this council so we go unheard!"

"Read the Blood Law!"

"That law does not apply here in the West, though."

"We have not accepted the new government. The Blood Law still stands!"

"Invoke it for their deaths!"

The leader's hand crashed on the table. "Silence!" He lifted a paper. "'Whereas the Blood Law has been in existence for many years . . . that if any citizen of this Nation should treat and dispose of any lands belonging to this Nation without special permission from the National authorities, he shall suffer death.'"

The air filled with war whoops, echoing through the night as down through the centuries.

The leader continued: "'Be it further resolved, that any persons who violate the provisions of the Act . . . any citizens of this Nation may kill them in any manner most convenient, within the limits of this Nation, and shall *not* be held accountable.'"

"John Ridge's own words!"

The leader silenced them with a wave of his hand. "Our court is here! Now!"

A man in a dark shirt stepped forward. "No! We must tell John Ross. It is he, as principal chief who should decide."

"No. He knows the Blood Law will be upheld, but he can't know of this meeting. It's too dangerous. This council must proceed without his knowledge. We must bear responsibility."

"Read the list of traitors!"

"Major Ridge, John Ridge, Elias Boudinot, Stand Watie, John Bell, James Starr, George Adair. We know who they are! We vote by clans!"

Three Deer clansmen yelled, "Invoke! Invoke the Blood Law to Major Ridge!"

"We of the Wild Potato Clan of his mother, John Ridge must pay!"

Other clansmen stepped forward and pronounced death sentences for Elias and Stand, followed by churning anger from other clans.

The leader lifted a stained slouch hat off the head of a man near him. A squirrel tail dangled from the beaded band. The leader dropped in strips of paper and stirred them.

"In this hat are numbers, one for each of you present. You will all draw. Those who pull numbers marked with X, those leaders will gather parties of executioners to kill the traitors to our Nation!"

A line formed. One by one the men stepped into the circle of light, each plucking slips of paper from the hat. A warrior pulled a "six" marked with an *X* and let out a *whoop!* Another drew a plain "fifteen" and wiped his forehead, relieved to be a follower, not a leader.

A middle-aged man, Bird Doublehead, pulled out a plain number. "No!" he shouted. "I will help lead the execution of Major Ridge! Thirty years ago he used the Blood Law to slaughter my father. Now he dies under his law!"

The leader and others near him nodded in agreement.

A young man edged forward and reached for the hat. The leader pulled it away. "No, Allen Ross. We have another job for you. You must go to your father's house and stay with him until the executions are over. He will be the first the authorities question. John Ross must be free to say he did not know our plan."

Allen Ross stepped back. The line continued moving until the last man.

"We ride Saturday morning, three days hence." The leader tossed the empty slouch hat into the air. The squirrel tail circled in the torchlight.

"Go! Each of you. Let the executions begin!"

On Saturday morning, in his home at Honey Creek John Ridge sleeps. The pink flush of dawn lights the bed as his wife, Sarah Bird Northrup, once the pride of Cornwall, slumbers beside him. In a room nearby sleeps his mother, Susanna, visiting since her husband has ridden south to tend to a sick slave hired out at John Latta's farm near Evansville. In other rooms, John's seven young children dream the dreams of the innocent.

About twenty-five mounted men surround the Ridge home. Some older warriors have fought and killed in this manner, but most have not. Some draw their rifles from their saddle scabbards. Others hold ready pistols or knives. Three dismount. With stealth, they walk on moccasined feet up the front steps, across the porch. They open the front door and pad noiselessly up the stairs to John's bedroom. One knows the house: John Ridge fed and clothed him and his family when they arrived hungry and ill from the old nation.

The executioners enter the room where John and Sarah Bird sleep. The leader walks to the bed. He places his pistol at John's head and pulls the trigger. *Snap!* Misfire.

John wakes to the pistol at his face. He lunges. Sarah Bird startles, fully awake, screaming as the three men grab her husband and pull him from the bed. John fights with all the strength in his slight body. The executioners drag him across the room, down the stairs and into the yard. He fights as Honey Creek absorbs his screams and those of his wailing wife, mother, and children who rush out on the porch. Warriors fill the yard.

The women and servants shield the eyes of the young ones, but cannot avert their own from the scene before them. Two men hold John by his arms; others grab his body, his legs. Whoops and yells drown out his beseeching cries for the murderers were instructed not to listen to John Ridge, to his fine oratory, not to be persuaded by his pleas.

One man plunges his knife into John's chest. Others join him. Two dozen times the men's knives men rip his body. Blood gushes from a final swipe across John's neck, shooting out and soaking his nightshirt.

The women beg the men to stop. John is still alive. Five grab him by his arms and legs and throw him into the air. Each of the assassins delivers John Ridge one final indignity, marching across him, kicking him, stomping his silent form.

As the men mount and gallop away Sarah Bird rushes to her husband. Susanna, her loose white hair wet with the tears of her grandchildren gathers the little ones, crushing them to her. Sophie Sawyer runs from her cabin near the schoolhouse, calling in the name of the Lord. The servants gather in terrified clusters.

John tries to push himself up on an elbow. Sarah Bird cradles his ravaged body in her arms and looks into his dimming gray eyes. Words gurgle from his mouth. He tries to speak, then falls back. It is over.

Far south, thirty men arrive at Park Hill in the same dawn glow. They hide in a grove of sycamores a short distance from Reverend Worcester's mission where Elias Boudinot and his wife Delight are staying while their house is being built a quarter mile away. The designated assassins calm their horses as they wait for Elias to leave the preacher's house.

Near nine o'clock, Elias walks toward his house to inspect the progress of the workers as they fit new windows. The morning resonates with drumbeat sounds of hammers drifting across the prairie.

Four executioners dismount and walk toward Elias. "Elias! We need supplies from the public medicines! White Deer is sick!"

The ruse works. Elias beckons and turns, heading back to Worcester's. "Yes! I heard he was ill. I'll get what you need at the mission. Come with me."

Two men walk with him toward the mission. It's so simple, so easy. One man drops back and plunges his Bowie knife into Elias's back. The other man grabs his tomahawk from under his shirt, and splits open Elias's skull.

The assassins run to their horses. The band rides off. The carpenters, at the sound of Elias's death cry, climb down their ladders yelling for help. Delight hears the ruckus and races from the Worcester's home; the elderly preacher follows. Beside her blood-soaked husband, she kneels, screaming.

Elias's dark eyes are open. Is his last image on earth the face of his wife? Or the eyes of his assassins? The gentle editor and pacifist missionary lies dead on the mission grounds.

The Old Messenger falls to Delight's side. He whispers, "I have lost my right arm."

About ten o'clock, a group of executioners led by James Foreman wait near the Line Road, about a mile within the Arkansas border at White Rock Creek: brothers Anderson and Isaac Springston; James and Jefferson Hair. Bird Doublehead, twelve years old when Alexander Saunders and Major Ridge executed the Blood Law on his chieftain father, has waited for this very moment.

It is a small group, not like the two groups of twenty-five and thirty who at dawn rode to kill John and Elias. After all, how many hearty warriors does it take to hide and shoot a seventy-year-old man?

They've been looking for him, knowing he left his home on Honey Creek several days earlier on his way to Evansville to see to a sick slave working at John Latta's plantation—the Lord's Vineyard—down on the Line Road. Perhaps he'll ride on to Van Buren and visit Sarah.

Seeking the best location to waylay their prey, the men spied on him as the old patriarch and his young servant boy spent last night at the farm of his friend Ambrose Harnage near the settlement of Cincinnati.

The warriors have ridden ahead to conceal themselves in a thicket of trees and scrub brush where the Line Road crosses the creek. Major Ridge is nearing his destination; this ambush may be their last chance. They know the traveler's horses will need to drink. The day is hot. Major Ridge will stop for a while, perhaps dismount. Or merely rest in his saddle with the reins slack as his horse lowers its head and drinks. Getting on and off a horse for an old man may be more an effort than just relaxing in his saddle.

The executioners spy the two riders approaching the creek and draw their rifles. The riders stop where wagon wheels have etched furrows in the limestone. Clear, shallow waters rush across flat outcroppings of rock. The boy's horse pauses at the bank. Major Ridge's fine-bred roan mare edges into the flow, her shoed hooves finding solid footing. She drinks.

Does her rider notice the absence of singing birds as he relaxes? Has he at dawn and later, felt two twinges in his heart as the spirits of his son and his brother's son left their bodies? He has long known he signed his death warrant as he signed the fateful treaty.

Shots shatter the silence. The old man jerks as five well-aimed bullets pierce his body. He slumps forward in his saddle. His horse rears; hooves scratch the creek bed. Major Ridge lies in the stream. The boy panics at the first shots and races toward the nearby settlement of Dutchtown. He looks back at his fallen master before entering a thicket.

The Cherokee warriors ride over to the body, their rifles still drawn. One dismounts and kicks the old man to verify he is dead. Doublehead's death is avenged. The Blood Law is enforced.

The leader tosses his slouch hat in the air. The squirrel tail circles. War whoops rise then settle in the creek bed.

Retribution has been served.

CHAPTER 33

Peonies, Chrysanthemums, & Poor Joes

The Paschal Home

Monday, June 24, 1839

As George and Stand talked in the dim-lit parlor, Sarah opened the front door and slipped out.

She sat down on the porch, moon-shadowed by the roof, shielded from the eyes of Stand's small army of protectors hiding in the brushy lot across Thompson Street. Arranging her black muslin skirt she crossed her legs beneath her as dark visions hovered around. She floated back in time. Amoneeta's twice-dead burial. Nancy's distant funeral. Sitting for days on the porch of her childhood home. But this time she suppressed the wailing rising within; her expression of sorrow would unsettle her white neighbors.

Dead. They're all dead. Murdered.

Her life changed in an instant today when George walked home from his office. He called to her to give Emily to Milly and come into the dining room. He sat Sarah at the table, leaned across, and grasped her hands in his. He told her impossible stories, rumors he'd heard yesterday yet kept secret during the night. Rumors that turned real today.

229

She denied them. Once before rumors of her father's death . . . now again! John, Elias—No! Lies! Lies!

Rocking back and forth on the porch, silent sobs cascaded through her body. George's stories were true. Stand verified them just now in the parlor and told details.

Her shoulders heaved as waves of anguish poured from her soul. Tears streaked her face and trailed onto her dress.

She'd insisted Stand tell her everything he knew. She needed confirmation of the patchwork George had so reluctantly stitched together for her as yesterday's simmering stories ignited into today's truths.

Her dear cousin had ridden in an hour ago, taking a chance stopping to see her on his ride to join a group of soldiers sent to Fort Smith. Stand's small band of braves—most of whom now waited across her street—were already planning reprisals for the killings, though outnumbered by the five hundred warriors assembled at Park Hill to protect John Ross. General Arbuckle had arranged asylum at Fort Gibson for the survivors of the assassins' list: Stand, John Bell, James Starr, and George Adair. They rode soon to meet their protectors.

In her parlor earlier George leaned against the mantelpiece while Stand paced. Lettie sat next to her on the settee. Sarah heard her cousin's words, but stared not at his trembling lips or his tensed body, coiled as if to spring. She focused not on his round face so resembling her father's, but on his moccasins as each footstep covered the bold flower patterns in her looped wool rug, each step seeming to erase from Sarah's life all that was beautiful and good.

Contingents of Rossmen, Stand said, had been assigned to execute seven Treaty Party leaders. Four groups failed their tasks when he and others were warned; three succeeded. Stand related, as gently as possible, the chronology he had pieced together:

Sarah's hand within Lettie's drew into a fist.

All were killed within a few hours of each other . . ." Stand's words stopped coming.

George shook his head. "All but you, Stand. Thank God."

As if telling a new story Stand began again. "Aunt Susanna sent riders to Park Hill and the Lord's Vineyard warning Elias and your father, Sallie. The distance was too far. They arrived too late.

"Rufus McWilliams rode Reverend Worcester's horse from Park Hill to warn me at your father's store. He raced over the miles to deter another band of patrolling murderers, though already Rossmen were watching me. Two sat on the porch."

Back and forth, back and forth, Stand paced.

"I noticed Rufus dismount Comet, Worcester's fast horse. Seeing the horse had been ridden hard, when the Rufus called me to a sugar barrel and haggled loud over the price, I listened between his rough words to his whispered warning. I sacked the sugar, told him I'd tie it to his horse, then mounted the tired animal and rode him hard back to Park Hill. I saw my brother—"

Stand paused his words, ceased his movements. He stood at the center of the rug over the flower-filled cornucopia, his feet erasing a crimson peony and a purple chrysanthemum.

"Delight and Mrs. Worcester were praying in the mission. I walked into the preacher's house. Even within the throng of mourners and curiosity seekers stood Rossmen, spies pretending to pay their respects. Elias was laid out in the parlor. I pulled back the sheet covering my brother—"

Stand resumed his pacing. The peony and chrysanthemum reappeared, but Sarah visualized colorless impressions where Stand had stood, moccasin-shaped ecru footprints. The absence of color blended with the blackness filling a hole in her soul. Stand said he had offered ten thousand dollars to any man who would give him the name of the murderers who had done this thing! No one spoke out.

Cowards. Murderers all. Sarah sat on the darkened porch. Her father's body tossed into an unmarked grave.

And John.

The light in the parlor went out. Behind her, the door opened and the two men stepped onto the porch. Stand squatted beside her, his arm across her shoulders. "George says you ride to Honey Creek in the morning."

"Yes. I must be with Mother, with Watty. With Sarah Bird, the children . . ." Her words floated off in the dark.

"Good. We need you there. To take care of the family and manage the store and farm. Do what you can."

Sarah's words returned in a burst of anger. "But John Ross, Stand. He must pay!"

"I don't have the forces to kill him now. He surrounds himself with henchmen. I must ride, Cousin. I'll send messages as I can—"

Sarah felt his hand lift from her shoulder. "I'll help you, Stand. We will avenge our family's murders." The bitterness in her voice surprised even her.

George waited beside her as Stand ran across the street and disappeared into the woods. "Come to bed, dear. You must rest. We leave at sunrise."

"Not yet, George. You go in. I need this night to grieve."

He knelt and wrapped her in his arms. She shivered in the warm evening. As he left she resumed her rocking.

Returning, George draped a shawl across her shoulders. "Lettie asked if you want her with you?"

Sarah hesitated. "No. Please tell her I need to be alone."

She sat. She rocked. Moonlight edged toward the west; its swath crawled onto her skirt. A bright gleam fell on a crimson peony near the steps, its head bowed. Blood red. The red of the bleeding hole in the Jesus of her youth. The blood that poured out of Nancy, blood the doctor drained from Amoneeta. Now from her family.

She forced an end to her bloody scenes and replaced them with pictures of her father teaching her to ride, letting her break with proper European tradition, allowing her to ride astride in her little saddle. Oh, he loved her. Loved her spirit.

John, dear John, weak in body, but so strong, believing he could light the way for a blinded people.

Elias. Never had he distrusted God. And now his God had taken him from his earthly mission.

Watty. Who told Watty?

"Mother. I'm coming," she whispered.

Rising, her legs unsteady Sarah opened her front door and stepped inside. Moonlight entered a window and fell on the rug. The peonies, the chrysanthemums, the bordering garlands of yellow primroses and bright blue morning glories seemed to glow, restored from their paleness while Stand paced and told his story.

Sarah wanted no representations of happiness, no beauty, no pretensions of joy.

Death. Only the reality of death like the blackness in her soul. She must preserve her anger and keep it in her heart. She walked to the fireplace and from her embroidery basket removed her scissors.

The first light of dawn spread through the parlor as Lettie stepped in from the hallway. Sarah lay on the rug curled like an infant, a black-swaddled mound.

"Sallie! Sallie!" Lettie grabbed Sarah's limp body, shaking her, looking around the room. "Have ye gone crazy?"

Sarah, rousing, pushed up. Lettie knelt and held her, trembling, crying as Sarah saw the ravaged rug. Each flower in the cornucopia, the peonies, the chrysanthemums, lay scattered across the room. Colorless holes remained.

Honey Creek, summer low, gurgled and burbled, annoyed and bothered to let its waters reflect a pleasant pink from the angry red sunset. Dusty willows along the bank drooped gray in mourning. Crowds of weeds huddled: stinkweed stinking; feverfew toothy and bitter with quinine; prairie gayfeather ashamed of its happy name.

Sarah picked a cluster of pale poor joes, then crushed the fuzzy petals in her fist and tossed them aside as she cleared space in the sandy soil. Watty sat next to her with his legs crossed, his black hair hanging long. He fingered his untied moccasin strings, slowly rocking as he watched his sister explain the tragedy.

Placing sticks and stones she named each: a big stick Watty; their stick parents; John and Sarah Bird and seven pebble children; Elias and Delight and his little pebbles; Sallie and George and little pebble Emily. She drew a line at the base of the picture. First, she removed their father, then John and Elias, covering the sticks with a dusting of sand.

"They're all in holes in the ground, Watty, but their spirits have gone to heaven to live with the Great Spirit of the Cherokee, with Jesus and God of the white man." Speaking in native tongue, the final word, *yonega*, drifted across the creek.

Watty quit his rocking and stared at the little mounds, then back to Sarah, his black eyes brimming. "All . . . gone to heaven?"

She nodded, then sat still. A killdeer wading in the shallows peeped its repetitious call. A hidden blue jay shrieked, refusing to abide the solemn moment.

Sarah pushed her bonnet back and let the black grosgrain ties dangle. She straightened her backbone, easing her strained muscles. They had ridden hard to get here. She planned to attend to as much of the family business as possible here, then return to the safety of Van Buren with her brother and mother—if Susanna would come.

In the four days since the murders, the countryside simmered with rumors of reprisals, of full-out civil war. The bodies of the murdered were buried fast: her father with no ceremony in that shallow grave at the Piney cemetery not far from the Line Road; Elias, with Reverend Worcester's trembling blessings, at Park Hill; John in a clearing near his home farther down Honey Creek. The surviving Treaty signers scattered.

Susanna, stoic and strong, had stayed at John's farm helping her daughter-in-law and Sophie Sawyer pack to leave for the safety of Fayetteville. Hysterical, John's widow feared for her children to walk on the raw ground where their father's blood had been scraped away. Watty, at the homeplace, lived in a world of confusion. Aunt Bessie Lassley and other keepers tried their best to comfort him, but the words they gave—*shot, knifed, tomahawked*—only created more fearful pictures in his puzzled head.

Watty now stared at the sticks and pebbles. His fingers began to flutter bird-like. He looked up at the sky. Leaning back he reached under his tunic and untied his doeskin bag from his breeches. From the sack, worn and stained, he emptied his treasured childhood collection of garnets into his hand, then dribbled the faceted stones in a circle above the row of sticks and pebbles. He bent forward and blew dust from the three sticks. Slowly, one by one, his father first, then the John and Elias sticks, he wove them through the air, then stuck each upright within the jeweled circle. "Fly away to heaven."

"Yes," Sarah said, hugging him, fighting back tears. "They flew away to heaven."

His head fell to his chest, his hair fanned across his shoulders. The two sat for a while not speaking. Birdsongs, stream splash, a distant disgruntled pig: the sounds of the house pasture. Sarah waited for Watty to absorb the reality. He lifted his head, his eyes moist. "Watty go to heaven, too?"

She forced a smile. "No. See?" She took the biggest stick and the Susanna stick, moving them between her own and George's. "Watty and Etsi. They come to live with Sallie and George."

Her brother took a deep breath. A smile brightened his face, then slipped away. "Live in town?" He tilted his head, peering at her. "Watty not like town. People laugh at him."

Sarah shook her head. "No. I will take care of you. No one will laugh at you."

He picked up the Watty and Sallie sticks. He squeezed them tight, his smile tenuous. "Watty go to Sallie's house. Not to heaven."

With his other hand, he reached beside him and stripped snow-white blossoms from a cluster of poor joes. Slowly he let the star-shaped petals sprinkle down within his heavenly red circle over the three sticks of those who had flown.

CHAPTER 34

The Daughter, the Sister, the Cousin

The Paschal Home

December 1839

During the summer and fall of 1839, a civil war embroiled the Cherokee Nation. Shortly after the murders, councils were convened of all three factions: Rossmen and Late Immigrants, now calling themselves Nationalists, Western Cherokee, and a smattering of Treaty Party. Attended by many or few, the latter two meetings were quickly dismissed for fear of reprisals.

In July, a month after the murders, John Ross read a proclamation of amnesty and full pardon to the murderers at the Nationalist convention, stating publicly that they could not be punished on any account. He gave amnesty to all Cherokee for crimes committed since the arrival of the Late Immigrants. He specifically pardoned the assassins of the Ridges and Boudinot. Since in the eyes of many they were not murdered, merely executed in compliance with the Blood Law, the measure was readily approved.

Stand vowed to anyone who cared to ask that he would personally kill John Ross if he found the opportunity—and the killers of his brother, uncle, and cousin should they cross his path.

The Secretary of War in Washington viewed the Treaty Party executions as murders, and the Commissioner of Indian Affairs ordered General Arbuckle at Fort Gibson to arrest and punish the killers of the Ridges and Boudinot, along with John Ross as an accessory. The citizens of Arkansas wanted the assassins of Major Ridge to be tried in state court since the act was committed on Arkansas soil. Companies of dragoons scoured the hillsides, but the murderers disappeared within the nation.

The soil of the new homeland soaked up the blood of fallen Cherokee. Rossmen retaliated in the name of the Blood Law; Ridge followers killed Rossmen with no pretense of law, only revenge. Sarah's grief and anger grew entwined like a blood-watered bramble. She brought Susanna and Watty to live with her.

"Look at this," George said before leaving for morning court. He greeted Susanna and handed his wife the newspaper, pointing to a headlined column on page one.

Sarah anchored her needle in the button she was replacing and lifted the paper to catch light. She noted yesterday's date of December 16, read a few lines, then translated to her mother, "The *Times and Advocate* out of Little Rock, Etsi. Lies written by John Ross's nephew."

Directing toward George as he warmed himself beside the fireplace, she read aloud in English, "An erroneous impression has gone abroad, much to the prejudice of the Ross party."

She silently read on.

"Lies!" she shouted. "This is not worthy of printing! Who will believe these lies?"

"Those who wish to believe will," George answered.

She skimmed the column. "This is so truly contemptible that it barely deserves an answer. But someone must refute it!"

"You," he said. "You tell *your* point of view."

"Surely the editor of the *Times and Advocate* wouldn't print what I wrote in defense!"

"Probably not. But write you must. I'll post your words to Little Rock, to the editor of the *Arkansas Gazette*. As my colleague, I'm certain he'll publish a letter written by my wife."

Sarah translated the gist of their conversation to Susanna. The lines in her mother's thin face drew to a serene smile as Lettie came into the room.

"Is it good with ye and Miss Susanna if Robinson walks Mister Watty down to th' riverbank for fishing? He'll stay right with him. Me brither thinks there's likely some bluegills lying 'bout this sunshiny day."

Sarah asked Susanna, then replied to Lettie. "Yes, Watty would like that. Just remind Robinson if he sees any of the town boys to rush Watty back home. We don't want any teasing and upset."

"He'll make sure to steer clear a' that rubbish. Robinson dinnae like them, no."

During the day Sarah read and re-read the Ross letter in the Little Rock *Times and Advocate*. At supper, she kept the conversation pleasant, laughing at Emily's squash-orange face and at Watty's tales of catching perch and compliments for the trout Lettie fried for all to enjoy. He and Robinson had stayed until a bank of clouds rolled in with no one bothering them; Watty's stories brought laughter to the table.

Between smiles, though, Sarah composed lines for her letter to repudiate the lies that had permeated her mind all day.

With the family bedded for the night—her mother and Watty sharing Emily's room, the baby in with her and George—Sarah returned to the dining table and lit the candelabra.

She brought Mr. Webster's dictionary from the bookcase; spelling was not her strong suit, if she stumbled in letters to family or friends, she worried little. But this letter must be perfect.

From a drawer in the buffet, she retrieved the *Times and Advocate* and several sheets of stained newsprint George kept on hand to jot notes of his thoughts. She set out her treasured pencil and metal-nibbed pen set he'd given her when Emily was born. The fluted lines in the silver tubes ran to embossed forget-me-not wafers on the ends, which she used for stamping sealing wax on her letters. She had a pair of tiny boxes, each holding graphite and extra nibs; she set them next to her inkpot and sanding block. Extending the telescoping end of the pencil, she twisted out the collar, inserted a new graphite stick, and then twisted the barrel tight. She would begin with a draft of her thoughts.

"For the <u>Arkansas Gazette</u>," she wrote.

"The Editor of <u>The Times and Advocate</u>, in an article found in his paper of the 16th ultimate, seems to me to have been most egregiously misled by that ambitious and artful agitator John Ross."

She opened her dictionary, found "egregiously" and verified its spelling. Then she struck through "agitator," and replaced it with "demagogue."

She continued:

I deemed the communication signed by Mr. Ross' nephew unworthy of rebuke. But when the editor of a newspaper suffers himself so far misled by the partial statement of a man, whose interest and policy it is to deceive, it is time the public should be advised that their organ has been deceived.

Sarah looked again at the *Times and Advocate* article. Where was the quote she wanted to use?

That Editor seems to take the responsibility of assuming that "an erroneous impression has gone abroad, much to the prejudice of the Ross party." Like many other logicians who rush to conclusions because they are told that the majority are of the same opinion, he assumes it as certain, that the Ross party compose the greatest number of the Cherokee people. Now granting that this is true, does it follow that they have a right to annihilate the government of the Old Settlers, and stealthily and in the most cowardly manner to assassinate the leaders of the immigrants who entertain different views to themselves?

Yes, most believe everything John Ross utters, she admitted, but her side must be heard.

Men, too, whose whole lives had been devoted to the work of the civilizations and elevation of the Cherokee people. For, without disparagement to others, no impartial person at all acquainted with the history of this unfortunate people can deny that the slain were the most devoted friends of civilization, and the promulgation of the Christian religion, that the Cherokee people ever had.

"Elias," Sarah whispered.

At the time of the bloody tragedy, one of their number was engaged in the translation of the scriptures, and was the only man in the nation who united the ability, and the religious zeal necessary to the successful prosecution of the benevolent undertaking. He was a devout Christian, educated in the higher schools of the United States, and perfectly acquainted with the tongue. For many years he was known as the enlightened editor of the Cherokee Phoenix, and had perhaps effected more in a short life towards the moral improvement of his people, than the whole of the Ross party combined.

She reread her last sentence, then scribbled over "enlightened" with "accomplished." She checked several spellings in her dictionary, then looked again at the newspaper as she sanded a point to her lead.

I know not by what process of reasoning Mr. Ross brought the Editor of the Times to the conclusion that the Ridges and Boudinot "had forfeited their lives, by the murder of Doublehead, and by betraying the nation of the emigration treaty." Surely Mr. Ross did not inform the editor that Doublehead was killed . . .

When was he killed? Before she was born. 1810? No. She'd heard discussion recently—1807. Yes. On a corner of her paper, she subtracted 1807 from 1839.

. . . upwards of thirty years ago, and while John Ridge and Elias Boudinot were yet infants, and when the Cherokee people were in a state of savage darkness, without either laws or constitution, and with no other rule of government than the immediate decree of their council, the faithful execution of which ofttimes depended upon the bravery and determination of their young men as executioners . . .

That was the way then, yes. Not now. The Blood Law.

But the reputed executioners of Doublehead may be said to have outlived the generation which saw his fall. The Cherokee people afterwards rose from their hunter state to a nation of civilized men, who claimed "that they would lose nothing by comparison with the neighbors in the surrounding states . . ."

She put down her pencil and rubbed the imprints in her fingers where the fluted barrel pressed, then re-read her last sentences.

Yes, the promise of acceptance if we took on the ways of the white man.

"John believed," she said aloud, replying to her unspoken statement.

. . . the son of one of these executioners had risen to be the brightest ornament of his people, and had passed the meridian of life; the Cherokees had for years enjoyed the benefit of a "prescribed rule of civil conduct," with John Ross as principal chief, and Major Ridge as his chief counselor, and yet no complaint was ever made that

Doublehead was wrongfully slain, or that his executioners should be brought to punishment. The killing of Doublehead was a matter of history, and yet no one ever thought this retribution a matter of deserving legal investigation.

The Blood Law. "Father," she whispered.

After the transfer of the residue of the people with their sham chief, one of the reputed executioners of Doublehead is found within the limits of the United States and within the jurisdiction of a sovereign state, where the Editor of the Times and Advocate has assumed the high station of a faithful sentinel . . .

Published in Little Rock. The capitol of the State of Arkansas where father was murdered. Father's killers *must* be tried in the state courts!

She picked up the newspaper and reread the lies. In the flickering candlelight, Sarah wrote words from her soul. She wrote that John Ross deluded the Cherokee people that they could remain east, that the western land offered them was a barren desert and a certain graveyard; she wrote how twenty thousand white Georgians invaded her country and overwhelmed the Cherokee, forcing them to bargain for the best provisions to move west. She compared Ross's arrival west to an imagined event: what if the young Queen Victoria of England crossed the Atlantic with the remaining Anglo-Saxon race and planted her red lion flag in the United States, bringing laws to prostrate the Americans? Sarah wrote of the injustices to the Treaty Party and of Ross's amnesty of their murderers. She rhetorically asked if he was so innocent, why hide behind his banditti guard? Who truly believes that *he* does not know the names of the murderers?

Leaning back, Sarah rubbed her neck and rubbed her cramping hand. Careful not to make a sound, she pushed back her chair. The ceramic clock on the buffet read two o'clock. Walking into the parlor she stood beside the mantelpiece, warming herself by dying embers while letting her fiery words expire as well.

Gazing at the bare planks, she remembered how on that June morning after Stand related the bloody details, she and Lettie had collected the desecrated crimson peonies and purple chrysanthemums scattered around the room and placed them on top of the rug. Rolling it, they carried the rug out to the backyard washpot fire where they held hands as Sarah's colorful flowers faded to gray ash, symbolic of the passing of her good life.

Exhausted now, Sarah gathered her papers and instruments, placed them in the buffet, and snuffed out the candles. In her bedroom, she checked on her sleeping daughter, then quietly removed her clothing and slipped into bed. George shifted at her movements. She ran her hand across his back, tracing the curve of his waist and across his hips. He rolled toward her. She embraced him, pressing his body to hers. In the darkness of their room, Sarah released her remaining fire.

Over the following days, Sarah carried her words in her mind as she went about her daily life and tasks. On the night of December 21, she slipped out of bed, and in the candlelight of the dining room, reread her letter, marking, scratching, checking words in her dictionary, then painstakingly copied her draft to the *Arkansas Gazette* onto George's finest paper with her silver pen.

All was written but her closing paragraph. She paused, reviewing, remembering, reliving; she paced the parlor, her moccasins treading in ghostly silence across the flowerless floor.

Returning she wrote:

In writing this article, I have no disposition to elicit a controversy with Mr. Ross, or any of his cohorts. Experience has too woefully taught me that they do not defend their principles with paper or argument. The knife, the ambush, and the bullet are their means of disposing of their enemies. But if they desire to know who it is that dares expose their principles and atrocities, let them be answered that she is the daughter of him whom a dozen of their young men shot from a lofty precipice, the sister of the man who was awakened from his slumber by twenty-five ghastly wounds and the cousin of him whom they slaughtered with a tomahawk and Bowie-knife, just as he was answering their petition for charity.

In a voice breaking with tears, she whispered, "The daughter. The sister. The cousin."

Dipping her pen into the inkpot, her hand sure and strong, she signed her letter: *Sarah Ridge Paschal.*

Chapter 35

Answers Great & Small

The Paschal Home

March 1840

In the months following the publication of her letter, as Sarah awoke each dawn next to her sleeping husband she lay unmoving, her breath shallow, her heart pounding to the beat of rageful images she confronted in her malevolent dreams.

Except for friends and family, she received no response to her letter from the reading public. If George heard negative comments, he kept them from her.

She listened to morning sounds, willing her rage to lie still. Susanna and Watty rustled in Emily's room. The baby, now almost two years old, slept with Lettie in the back room. Milly came in from the cabin where she and Isaac lived. Lettie would hand over Emily to Milly's care and tiptoe out the squeaky door, down the steps out to the kitchen cabin where Robinson stayed. He would kindle the kitchen fire before he and Isaac checked the horses and cow. Then Isaac left for his work at Mr. Lansford's tin shop.

Robinson went about his chores, feeding chickens, shoveling the pens, and tending the gardens before he left for hired work. Sarah took over Emily's care while Milly helped Lettie prepare breakfast. One of them would fire up the washpot, or if it was a hired day for Lettie, she'd walk over to John Bostick's Mansion House where she washed and ironed for the hotelkeeper.

With money so short, the bartering notes and coins the servants brought back helped cover the costs of feeding and caring for a household of nine. Or ten, rather. William Mosley, George's assistant, slept in the back room of his office but often took meals with the family.

As morning sounds retreated, Sarah relived her nighttime images before they faded, vague and terrifying scenes where she tortured and killed her family's phantom murderers. Most often the apparitions wore the face of John Ross. In one recurring vision, Sarah watched Ross as he reviewed her letter in the *Arkansas Gazette*. She saw her adversary reading her words, heard him cackle, saw him toss the newspaper onto a roaring bonfire. And there at the apex of the flames rose her father's face, serene and peaceful.

Emily's whimpering always erased Sarah's nighttime terrors and brought her fully awake. Her mother's presence and her chubby, babbling daughter afforded Sarah her only moments of true happiness. She dressed and forced herself to present a strong face to her household.

Her body felt weighted with bones made of stones. That misery combined with an ache in her mind caused her to scold and shout at the servants. Each time she regretted her words and promised herself she would rein in her actions, but she had little patience with those around her.

Even with George as he darted around the house rushing to his office or to a church meeting, all in his impetuous manner. "Always scurrying from pillar to post," as Susanna had termed her son-in-law. Busy George. Sending William off with a collection note; writing Stand's petition to the Secretary of War. Letters to creditors—his own and others for the family widows. Notes to church supporters eliciting donations for a new chapel in Van Buren. Innumerable letters to the editors. And any path, no matter how serpentine, that might lead to money.

One of those money trails led to Washington City: on a sunny afternoon in March 1840, George prepared to board the waiting steamboat along with Stand and other Treaty Party members to meet with the Secretary of War. The other trail remained in Van Buren: George, regretting he had not yet formed a partnership to handle his office affairs, reluctantly instructed Sarah to supervise William and the collections business.

George bussed Emily's cheek beneath her bonnet and twirled a ringlet through his fingers. Dressed in his new traveling suit, puffed up with importance on his first trip as counsel to the seat of the federal government, George stepped into a piloted pirogue for the short paddle beyond the sandbank where the anchored steamer puffed its cloud of dark smoke.

As the little boat pulled away from the dock, Sarah waved Emily's little arm to her departing father and sighed.

All I needed was more responsibility, she thought.

Walking back down the dock, Sarah made her way across Water Street and a few blocks west to Main. Chalky dust from the dry, rutted street clung to the hem of her black dress. At the foot of Main, she crossed over to avoid passing Armstrong's Saloon and Eatery where Mr. Armstrong's often-rowdy clientele seemed to enjoy his advertised specialties of a dish of tripe or baked 'possum along with their copious tankards of beer. When Sarah reached the boardwalk, she set Emily down to let her toddle along the planks in her soft moccasins.

As they approached Drennen's Mercantile, Mrs. John Ogden stepped out and greeted Sarah, who lifted the baby so the lady could see her. Chucking Emily's chubby chin, Mrs. Ogden commented gaily on the baby's blue eyelet dress with matching pantaloons and fingered her blond curls.

"Now Mrs. Paschal," she said, "please feel free to contact Mr. Ogden with any questions you have during Mr. Paschal's absence." The older woman then touched Sarah's gloved hand. "Or myself, if you have any, shall we say domestic problem, what with the Indian troubles and all." Then she added with a sincere smile, "I found your piece in the *Gazette* most enlightening."

George had told Sarah to seek John Ogden's counsel, a friend and fellow lawyer, for any legal problems. Thanking the woman for her kind words, Sarah turned onto Thompson Street for the last few blocks to her home.

As she walked, she remembered the conversation on her porch last night.

She and Stand had little time yesterday when he arrived on the steamboat from Fort Gibson, and this morning he and the other travelers had met in George's office to review his claims proposals and drafts of petitions. But last night after supper with George completing preparations for his morning meeting, Stand carried two rockers to the front porch and lit his pipe.

They had not been together since that fateful night almost a year ago following the assassinations. They now exchanged family news, speaking in Cherokee lest any passers-by should overhear.

"You made my heart surge with pride when I read your letter in the *Gazette*. Any repercussions?"

"Thank you," she said. "No, some compliments. If any controversy, George failed to share it. As I wrote in my letter the enemy defends their positions with knives and rifles. But you know Stand, I feel . . . well, I feel I can do more than write a letter."

He stopped rocking. "What do you mean?"

"I'm not certain how to put it into words, but my thoughts, my dreams recently, have been of revenge. But more than revenge, more of a . . . a restoration of our family name."

"Tell me more."

"I've come to realize I would die for the treaty that our family believed so deeply, gave their lives for."

A coyote howled on the bluff above, beyond the Drennen's house.

"No, Sallie! We've seen too many of our family fall—"

"Let me continue. Father believed Jackson was his friend. But Mother told me that in his heart, Father knew Jackson did not have the power nor the will to negate forces long set in place, even before Jackson's time."

"Yes, we all believed until—" Stand looked off into the night.

"Yes. Until," Sarah said.

Visualizing the reverse side of the Indian peace medal given her by John Ross in Washington City—the two hands with fingers pointing at the word "Friendship"—now each sentence came as her proclamation: "From the days of George Washington those treaties were mere strips of hide tied above the already-severed Indian hand to staunch the flow. Jefferson traded our land to Georgia, loosening the ties. Those Presidents following down to Jackson, let it bleed until drained. President Van Buren merely tossed out the body.

"But it is John Ross—by his arrogance, by his refusal to sign, by his failure to deliver his people from evil—who is to blame for the deaths in the stockades and across the wretched plains. If the Ridges are guilty by signing, he is guiltier by not signing. But —"

"Continue."

"The Rossmen were sent to kill those whom they hold responsible for the deaths of so many of our people. I say they missed the one most guilty. They missed their leader. And I will help you complete their job."

She stopped rocking; the coyote resumed its yapping wail.

"Those are powerful words, Cousin. I respect them and will take them to heart."

Stand's final words from last night came back to Sarah as she set her squirming daughter on the lower step and let Emily climb to the porch and waddle around the vacant chairs. Somewhere, sometime, Sarah knew she and Stand had a mission to complete.

But right now almost a dozen people looked to her for answers great and small. She had decisions to make, bills to pay, and a dwindling supply of income with which to support her household.

Chapter 36

Poultices & Notes Payable

The Paschal Home

May 1840

No, this can't be.

Sarah shifted in her bed. Every part of her body ached. She felt as if her skin was pulling away from her bones. Drums pounded in her head. Wet with sweat, she threw off her bedsheet under which earlier she huddled for warmth.

"I don't have time to be ill," she whispered to her empty room. She had been fighting a lethargy all week, dragging herself from home to George's office. Milly picked purple coneflowers from the herb garden and prepared the roots. Sarah drank the tea and chewed the leaves and seed heads. Last night she left her supper untouched, asking Milly to put Emily to bed.

Susanna and Watty had stayed until last week. The women celebrated Emily's second anniversary of her birth as best they could, yet memories of their good lives the year before—the final gathering of their loved ones—shrouded the festivities. With a tearful *donadagohvi*, Sarah promised her mother and Watty a Christmastime in her home.

Now she could barely move. Across the hall, Emily's whimpers escalated to a full scream.

POULTICES & NOTES PAYABLE

Sarah heard Milly enter the room, consoling the baby in a mixture of English and Cherokee endearments. Morning sounds: Milly chattering, removing Emily's nightdress, setting her on her little chamber pot, the gentle trickle, Emily's giggle as Milly washed her bottom. Dressing sounds, baby babble, and then the two appeared at Sarah's door. Sarah tried to rise but fell back on her pillow.

"Etsi! Etsi!" her baby called, laughing.

"Etsi can't hold you, baby. Etsi doesn't feel well." Sarah shook her head. "Milly. I hurt all over. Chills, fever."

Milly opened the windows and a breeze wafted through, fluttering the tie of her green turban. "Get some air in this sickroom! Don't you worry none. I'll take th' baby today."

"Can Lettie help you?"

"Mr. Bostick's done sent for her. Washin's piled up at th' hotel."

"You let our ironing go, then. You've got too much to do. But can you send Robinson to Drennen's for the mail?" She turned her head as a coughing spasm racked her chest.

"Looks like you needs a' onion poultice. I'll cook one up."

"Oh, Milly. I'll smell so bad! I need to go to the office and check on the notes William collected yesterday."

"You ain't goin' nowheres. Robinson can tell William to bring his papers over to here."

Sarah's room reeked of boiled onions. She had slept all day after rousing earlier while Milly—ten years younger than Sarah but always in charge—made her stand and take off her nightdress while she covered the sheets with an old blanket. Milly spread her poultice and draped a sheet across Sarah's naked body. The hot, slimy onions, encasing her chest and feet, soothed her to a coma-like state, then dried to a healing cast-like cocoon. Sarah couldn't move.

Helpless, she felt tears well up in her eyes. She worked her hand out from under the sheet and wiped the stream pouring from her eyelids.

Her tears stung. She looked at her hand; a smear of onion pulp was stuck to her finger. Whimpering through her pain and misery, Sarah drifted again to a feverish sleep.

Milly peeked in the door, then walked over and set her candle on the side table. She lowered the windows for the night as Sarah opened her eyes. She imagined they looked as red as they felt. Milly picked up the candle and peered at her, grinning. "Looks like you been poulticin' your eyeballs!"

Sarah found the strength to laugh, which brought on a coughing spell. Taking a deep breath, she blew her nose on a rag and said, "My fever's down. I'm feeling better. Thanks to you."

"Good. Emily's been a good girl. Lettie put her down, sleepin' tight, now. But that Mr. Hanger stopped by askin' when he could 'spect his money for them letterbooks he ordered for Mr. Paschal. Said it's been a while."

Money, Sarah thought. A groan slipped out.

"An' William brought by th' papers. I had him leave 'em on the table with th' mail. Oh, he said he needed some money, so I give him a dollar outta the buffet tin. An' he tol' Robinson, Mr. Paschal's horse done come up lame."

Money. Mail. Horses.

"Ol' Cat's down?" Last year her dear father had given Sarah one of his older carriage mares for George and William to use on collection trips. "Is Dove all right? Has Robinson mucked the pen recently?"

"Dove's fine. Pen's good and dry."

Then what could it be? Sarah thought. No matter. "Well, if Robinson can't see a cut or thorn, he'd better get Youngdeer to stop by after he gets off at Mr. Moore's to check Ol' Cat." The young Cherokee man who worked with the blacksmith as a farrier had a special way with horses. "You can pay him out of the tin."

"I will. But right now, I'm gonna bring you some fresh water an' a cup of marrow soup. Build your blood right up. Then we'll get a fresh poultice on you. Come mornin', you'll be good as new."

Milly's magic worked. Sarah's body aches diminished, though her cough was a nerve-wracking rumble. She had no choice, though; she had to tend to the papers and mail. After Milly washed her and put her in a fresh bedgown, Sarah sorted smaller stacks of newspapers, mail, and accounting sheets. She looked at the sheet headed "Notes Receivable" that William had written out in his bold, clear penmanship. She had asked him to reconcile everything he could find in George's letterbooks and invoices. A long list of individuals' names and titles of businesses showed collections due and George's commissions. If only she could get these people to pay, the income should be sizeable:

> Slocomb Richards & Co: commission owed on a $300 collection.
> Henderson & Gaines: two months behind on payments for legal services.
> John McNair: the man owes George a sizeable amount for collections.

She shook her head, then picked up the sheet titled "Notes Payable." Taxes on the office building, bills from mercantiles, farrier, butcher; blacksmith repair on a buggy wheel. On and on and on.

She pulled some letters over and first broke the seal on one addressed to George from Chilton, Alabama. From his cousin, W. W. Paschal.

> April 26, 1840
> Dear Cousin George,
> It is with great concern that I write you again requesting you to assist me during my unfortunate financial downturn. The South's bumper crop of several years back, as you know, brought me a price of sixteen cents per pound, rebounding from the Panic year of 1837, but resulting in a glut on the mills of the North and those of the markets in England. This past year I was able to cover my costs with the harvest sold at twelve cents, and in anticipation of a rise in the price this year, have planted my acres widely. However, so have planters throughout the South, and a buyer recently passing through the Chilton area spoke of a possible decline to five cents come this picking

time. If that price should prove to be true, I will find myself in dire straits.

So he wants George to loan him money? Sarah thought.

As you advised, in anticipation of future positive returns, I have increased my slave population to a dozen field hands, with the profits accrued last fall. Yet I do not know how I will find funds to support them if the doom of the projected collapse in the market should occur. Perhaps I will consider selling my plantation here, or should the worst predictions come to fruition, pack my belongings—leaving my land to my creditors—and remove my slaves and myself and go to Texas, where I hear your brothers Isaiah and Franklin Paschal are reaping great successes in the western town of San Antonio. I hear land is a pittance and plantations can be had. But such a removal would bear heavily upon my wife and small children. Perhaps I should apprentice myself to the study of law, but such an indenture would cause continued poverty upon my family. I am, Cousin, distraught in my situation.

Oh, poor man.

I have heard from my Paschal cousins in Georgia and your esteemed Mother, of your success in your legal endeavors in your new practice in Arkansas. In her last letter to me, she wrote of the inheritance you anticipate from the unfortunate demise of your wife's father . . .

Inheritance?

. . . and I pray the wealth she mentioned has come into your hands. Perhaps you can assist me in my situation?
    I remain your devoted but desperate cousin.
    W. W. Paschal

Into George's hands?

Sarah leaned back on her pillows and took a deep breath that brought on another coughing spell. She closed her eyes, panting in a shallow rhythm, absorbing this revelation of her husband's life. A horse whinnied and Emily babbled. Robinson laughed.

She sighed. We owe Father's estate thirteen hundred dollars, plus the five hundred Mother gave us to build the house last year.

What to do now? Write George? Write his cousin, telling him we don't have the money?

Yes. She would write a short note and be gentle with this poor cousin in his distress, sympathetic to his position, but firm that no money would be forthcoming until George returned from Washington City. Then, if Stand was successful in getting the government to pay the estates for claims, perhaps George could send him a small amount.

She lifted the "Notes Receivable" sheet again.

How many outstanding debts aren't listed? she wondered. Oh, George!

Sarah let out a deep sigh that brought about a coughing spasm. Shaking her head in dismay, she picked up several letters, turning over each to see if it carried the name of the sender.

She had letters to read, letters to write, collections to chase, and a household to maintain. Exhausted, angry, and sad, Sarah covered the papers with her pillow and fell into a deep healing sleep.

Chapter 37

Holy Bible, Holy Moccasins

The Paschal Home

December 24, 1840

"Help! Come quick! It's Mista Watty!" Robinson charged up the bluff from the river, shouting. As Lettie stepped out of the kitchen cabin, he spun around and headed back. Yelling for Sarah, Lettie quickly covered the distance to the house, banged on the back door, then ran after her brother.

Sarah opened the door. Lettie called back, "Somethin' bad with Watty!"

Crossing the yard Sarah ran down Lafayette Street toward its ending at the river, her shawl streaming. As she ran she could hear popping sounds coming from nearby. Gunfire!

"Watty!" she yelled.

Robinson reached an old shack in the ravine. Lettie was almost there—screaming that she was coming—when three white boys ran around the edge of the shack and took off up Water Street toward Main.

Sarah saw Lettie disappear into the shed. As she approached, she could see Lettie's red dress through the slats as she bent over. Is he shot? Dead?

"It's the poppers!" Robinson yelled to her as she rounded the corner post.

Watty lay curled in the corner, his hands pressing his face, his knees pulled to his chest. Lettie knelt next to him stroking his arms, patting his knee, and murmuring, "Och, now. Och, now."

"It's the poppers, Miss Sallie, the Christmas poppers," Robinson continued, "Those town boys scared him 'most to death! They've been throwin' and throwin' 'em. I couldn't make 'em stop! Firecrackers don't scare me, but Mista Watty just ran and the more he ran, the more they tossed.

"I hit one of 'em. Then two jumped me."

Sarah saw blood above his eyebrow.

Lettie eased back and Sarah took her place, crooning and rocking her terrified brother until his tears ran out. She blamed herself. She feared something like this would happen. Hoped it wouldn't, hoped she could surround Watty with a protective net, but her innate knowledge of the vile deeds humans do to each other had once again been verified. The town boys, a younger, milder version of the Pony Clubs that once rode through her nation had reached her brother here in her town. As she held him close she knew the only way to protect him was to get him back to Honey Creek.

Susanna met them on the street. Watty left his sister's sheltering arms and ran to his mother.

Christmas Eve dinner was served late, but the afternoon sun still filled the dining room as Susanna returned. "He's sleeping," she said. Watty cheered a bit during the meal but had taken leave after the apple cobbler.

With the upset of the day winding down, the two women sat with remnants of dinner scattered across the table. George had walked up the hill to Colonel Drennen's house and Milly was putting Emily to bed.

Susanna asked, "Do you remember our Christmastimes at Springplace? The one just after I was baptized?"

"Susanna Catherina," Sarah said smiling.

"Yes," her mother said, "that dear name Mother and Father Gambold bestowed on me."

"I remember the cold mostly. That was the winter of the deep snow . . . I was, what? Seven, eight years old? John was in his second year at Cornwall."

"Yes. And your dear father, knowing how I wanted to be with the Gambolds for Christmas, bundled you and Watty in the wagon and we drove from Oothcaloga to Springplace."

"There were so many others who came!"

"Over sixty, I believe, came to the love feast. The outpouring from the snow-covered hills to join in fellowship with those dear missionaries for their celebration of the Savior's birth. Those were loving times, with loving friends."

Sarah smiled. Her mother's recollection of details never ceased to impress her. "I remember holding my taper while the missionaries sang hymns in German. The gifts they gave! That little doll with cross-stitched eyes and a gingham dress. My first doll that was not made from corn shucks!" Sarah also remembered the bloody painting of Jesus, but quickly blinked, refusing to let the image materialize.

The women sat quietly lost in the past.

"I miss my good Moravian fellowship," Susanna said.

"I know you do, Mother. Up north you have the New Springplace missionaries. I'm glad so many of our Treaty Party have remained with the faith."

"I stayed with Brother Schmidt at Barren Fork on Spring Creek for a few days. It's lovely there. His support has helped me retain my faith over these months."

"George is working so hard to build the Presbyterian church here, but I care so little for their society."

"Why is that? It concerns me that you have no congregation with which share your faith."

"All my years of instruction, at Springplace, at Salem, I . . . I felt the missionaries, the church, and the Bible readings, demanded me to believe in something to which I cannot relate. I know you do and I do not wish to counter your beliefs, Etsi.

"I *do* feel a spirit, call it the voice of God or the Great Spirit, when I'm alone or need consolation. When I used to ride Dove through the woods, and now when I walk to the river or tend my flower beds. That is my time to commune, not sitting on a hard pew while a man reads stories about people long past."

Susanna tilted her head and pursed her lips. She said nothing.

"Churches demand so much time and devotion. For George, a congregation fills his needs. I respect his faith as I respect yours. He is devoted to his church, but his dedication takes away from his time to attend his legal business."

Susanna nodded. "All those gatherings and pleas for donations he organizes with the locals."

"Yes. I don't know what we're going to do. For income, that is. People not paying. And now . . ." She ran her hand over her rounded belly and saw how her mother's eyes brightened with joy. "I think March. Too long for you to stay here."

"I can return. Or you and Emily can come with us now. Be in Honey Creek for our next blessed birth?"

"Thank you, but I feel I should be at home. I have Lettie and Milly, and Flying Bird's daughter Flying Pheasant is close by." She smiled and patted her belly again. "I think he's a healthy boy in here."

Susanna rested her hand above the folds of Sarah's skirt. "A blessing on my grandson."

Sarah continued. "I'll encourage George with his collections. We still owe you and Father—you, so very much for the house and furniture. With money so hard to come by all over the country, well, I just don't know."

Susanna brushed cobbler crumbs from the tablecloth. "There's Stand's claim in the family's name against the government for the deaths. Unpaid emigration expenses. Don't fret. Money will come.

"Though, Sallie, dear, I think I need to get back to oversee the store. Watty needs the country. Others are helping, but I need to be there. No more traveling. Begin life . . . after your father."

"I know. Especially now that Watty's been attacked. I feel so awful."

"You need not. You've given me time to heal, to restore my strength. Watty has been beside you, the person he trusts most. I was planning to wait until after the servants had their holiday, but I mentioned leaving sooner to Tom today. He would like to get home as soon as he can so I'm thinking we should prepare the carriage and pack tomorrow, leave the next."

"I agree. But before you go, there is something I've been wanting to do, just haven't had the strength."

"What can I help you with, Sallie?"

"I want to write in the family Bible. Remember the lovely one Elias and Delight gave George and me when Emily Oolootsie was born? I've not written any entries on the pages, our marriage, her birth. Or the deaths. I'd like to enter those, and Father and John."

Sarah moved dessert plates and crystal from the end of the table, then folded back the runner. She brought her fluted pen and a bottle of ink. From a bookcase, she took the large leather-bound Bible. Her mother pulled over her chair. Sarah opened the thick pages to "Marriages." To her surprise the first line of the list was filled in—filled in with the most beautiful script she'd ever seen!

"*Geo. W. Paschal* and *Sarah Ridge* were married at *E. Brainerd in Tennessee* on the *27th* day of *February* A.D. *1837*."

"Oh, I do remember that blessed day, Sallie. It seems a lifetime away."

"It was, Etsi—but who wrote this entry in my Bible? Who?" The women stared at the list.

"Oh, yes. You just said you hadn't made entries. Did George?"

Sarah turned the page. Births. Same script. And not in George's scribbles.

Aloud she read: "*Emily Anderson Paschal* was born at *Honey Creek, Cherokee Nation* on the *18th* day of *May* A.D. *1838*."

"Anderson?" Susanna repeated the name. She leaned in.

Sarah pointed to the script. "Mother? Someone has written 'Emily Oolootsie' as 'Emily Anderson'!"

"How can that be?" Susanna said.

Hearing George's footsteps on the porch, Susanna rose and slipped into the hallway, leaving her daughter to discover the answer.

Sarah flipped the table runner over the Bible. Walking into the parlor she opened the door and smiled at her husband.

"Did you enjoy your visit with the Drennens?"

"Decidedly so, my dear."

"A soiree? Or just family?"

"A small gathering of townsfolk. Mr. Bostick and his wife. The hotel is bustling, each steamer lets off a new influx. Peter Hanger with his wife and daughter, and his new bookkeeper Miss Anderson who entertained with minuets from the pianoforte. And Reverend Willard with his wife—"

"Anderson? Who is this Miss Anderson?"

"She's . . . she's a friend of the Hanger's daughter, come from New York seeking a frontier life—"

"She plays the piano? And has a lovely handwriting?"

Silence. Sarah walked through the parlor into the dining room. She motioned to her husband to follow.

"George?" At the table she uncovered the Bible.

He looked at the book, then back to Sarah. "Oh, yes. Lovely handwriting. I asked her to fill in—" George stopped.

Sarah took a deep breath. "That woman has been in my house?"

"Oh, no. No," George stammered. "I . . . I took the Bible to my office. She used my writing instruments there. I thought it gracious of her—"

"So gracious that you let her fill in her *own* name rather than Emily *Oolootsie*? Our child's birth name?"

"Well, well she had difficulty in spelling 'Oolootsie' . . ."

"That makes no sense, George!" Sarah forced her voice to not fill the entire house.

"Well, last August . . . when you were in Honey Creek . . . you'd been so distraught, so angry, since the assassinations. And you were always upset with me. The money I'd spent on the furniture. Everything. Then you took Emily and left for your mother's.

"It was wrong I know, but when I met Miss Anderson at the mercantile, well, she was friendly, flattered me so, and I—"

"Did you fall in love with her, George?"

"No! Oh, no, Sarah! She was sweet on me. I . . . I returned her affection, briefly. Several times she came to my office while William was away on collections. But then I left to visit you and Emily in Honey Creek."

Sarah looked away, remembering. George's trip to visit her had lifted her spirits and helped to bring her back from that dark place. He doted on her and took her on walks. When they made love beside the creek she felt as if her amber cabin had been transported west. She touched her belly; the child within was a result.

Yes, she *had* left George. She justified her need to be with her mother and Watty, but in truth, she was fed up with him, fed up with his half-truths about his debts and business.

"But still, George, that doesn't explain *her* name where our daughter's name should be!"

"Oh, my dear one, I was so weak! When she so beautifully wrote our marriage in, she said she wished it had been *her* name next to mine. So when she couldn't spell 'Oolootsie,' I said for her to write her name there. Yes, I know it was foolish, but at the time—"

He reached out, his hand covering the entry.

"Please, let's mark through it, Sarah. Correct the entry. Or I can purchase us a new family Bible. I have ended all affection for her. Any communication, as was tonight, is purely genial."

Yes, remove the intruder, Sarah thought. Her hand moved to her pen, then stopped.

"No, I won't defile Elias's Bible, our history. I will accept your moment of weakness, George, when you broke your vow to me, your promise that you would not hold me up to ridicule."

She looked up. George's shoulders slumped and his proud stance sagged. "Because I, too, broke my vow to you to honor you. In my grief, I lost faith in you, in your abilities, in your help and concern for my people." She picked up the Bible, walked to the bookcase, and returned the book to its place.

"Let this remain a memento to our marriage, as a reminder of our need for compassion for each other."

George stepped forward and took her in his arms. The child in her belly bridged the pain each had caused. Sarah felt George heave a deep sigh of relief.

In February more crates arrived from George's trip to Washington City and a buying trip with Stand to New York for merchandise for Ridge's Store. His selections, his taste in the purchases were, of course, impeccable: a pair of marble-topped lamp stands, walnut with the latest Empire spirals, and a silk tapestried shawl fringed in tiny tassels he lovingly presented to her. She'd accepted them, though still worried about the money he'd spent.

Her baby, now only a month from birth and active within, seemed to appreciate a stroll to rock him back to sleep. On a warm day, Sarah walked to Drennen's Mercantile to refill her tin of baking soda. Enjoying her walk, she stopped in at George's office and greeted his young Cherokee assistant, William Moseley.

"Mr. Paschal's over at Mr. Ogden's office, Missus Paschal," William said from the table where he was wrapping a package for mailing. A pair of beaded moccasins lay nearby; the pale deer hide, sueded and supple, was decorated with intricate beaded patterns of blue and green and red. Deer forms represented her father's clan, the trees reminiscent of her family's departed homeland. Sarah remembered her mother long ago sitting next to the parlor fireplace sewing beads into the deerskin for a gift to John in distant Cornwall.

Puzzled, she looked at William and said, "Whatever are you doing with my brother's moccasins?"

The young man lifted the shoes from the table. "Mr. Paschal asked me to post them to New York."

"To whom? Who is he sending them to?" Her voice began to quiver.

William indicated a letter on the table. Sarah set down her soda tin. As she read George's script, her hands started shaking. Addressed to a

Mr. Greenfield at Van Pelt's Mercantile, George thanked the man for helping him select his recent purchases.

"These fine beaded moccasins," Sarah read out loud, "were cut out for my wife's much-lamented brother."

Sarah continued reading, barely able to comprehend George's words. Her voice rose.

"She and I believe that you will appreciate them more highly than any other among his numerous friends, for your past and ongoing assistance in provisioning my late brother-in-law's store, and that of my esteemed mother-in-law's present establishment."

She threw the letter on the floor.

"I did *not* give my husband John's moccasins!" Sarah yelled at William. He stepped back from the table, his expression a shock of terror.

Picking up the letter she wadded it and threw it on the table, then grabbed the shoes from the startled young man's hands.

"Missus Paschal! I'm sorry! I was just doing what Mr. Paschal told me to do!" Fear filled his eyes as he faced the raging woman.

Calming, Sarah said, "It's not your fault, William." She shook her head so hard her bonnet bobbled. "I apologize for my tone. Please have Mr. Paschal come to the house the minute he returns." Clutching the moccasins to her breast, she turned and walked out the door.

A half-hour later, she awkwardly pushed herself up from the front porch steps where she'd sat waiting. Holding the moccasins, she walked to meet George at the corner of Lafayette Street. She didn't want anyone in the house to hear what she planned to say.

George paused meekly in the road, clutching Sarah's forgotten tin of baking soda like a peace offering. She approached him without a greeting and said, her voice devoid of emotion, "Let's walk to the river."

They passed a few townsfolk, then entered the ravine. When they reached the water's edge she turned to George, the moccasins in her outstretched hands, and asked, "Why? Why would you think I would ever part with John's moccasins?"

It was evident that George realized the magnitude of his mistake. As if addressing a judge, he pleaded his case. "I was wrong, dear. I apologize for my error in judgment. Mr. Greenfield has been generous in our dealings, had provisioned your father's and John's store, and mentioned how intrigued he was with indigenous beaded craft skills. I failed to appreciate the sentimental attachment you hold for the shoes."

Sarah stomped her foot. "*Sacred attachment* would be more appropriate!" George allowed her family Bible to be desecrated by that woman and now this! His insensitivity left her cold.

Sarah glared at her husband. While waiting on the porch she had determined to listen to his explanation, to hear his justification of his callous action before she made her final decision.

Her conclusion resolved, grit chilled her words as she said, "George, I no longer chose to be your helpmate. You've broken the bond of respect that you promised me. Twice now you have put your need to please strangers and associates above my cherished family possessions.

"Your actions tell me that you have a greater desire to help others—outsiders—than love and respect of family."

"Sarah—"

She held up her hand. "Let me finish. You pursue government claims for my family and I appreciate your doggedness. I know you have a strong passion to make a name for yourself, in a wider range than here in Van Buren and the Cherokee Nation. You trifle with strangers, you pander to people who you think can help you advance in your social and legal pursuits. So do it. Move to Little Rock to pursue those fields. I will keep our home here, we will continue as a family. Stay until the baby comes, if you wish. We will act the roles of husband and wife for the prying eyes of Van Buren and Little Rock, but the love I have felt for you since our marriage, I no longer feel.

"My family needs me and I need them. In the future, I will make my own decisions and act accordingly."

Not waiting for George's reply Sarah turned and walked toward the house. He stepped to follow her, then stopped. A steamboat whistle screamed from the docks. A wagon rattled its way up Lafayette Street. George looked at the soda tin in his hand, drew back, and threw it as far as he could across the ravine.

At the sound of a *clunk!* Sarah glanced back in time to see the box explode as it hit a tree.

Back in his empty office, George shuffled through papers: a letter from young lawyer Andrew Campbell suggested a partnership here in Van Buren; a clipping he'd saved from the Little Rock *Democrat* listed qualifications for Arkansas Supreme Court justices; an offer invited him to join the Antiquarian and Natural History Society in Little Rock.

"If only I resided in Little Rock," he said aloud

Chapter 38

Rumors

The Paschal Home
November 1841

A year later George returned home from his office in Little Rock. Throughout Arkansas and the Indian Territory, he and others were hearing rumors that President John Tyler would be sending an Army officer to investigate the fraud conducted by agents and contractors involved with provisioning the Cherokees and other Eastern tribes who had been forced to remove over the years.

The man selected was reputed to be many things: a West Point graduate, a shrewd investigator, a learned and honest man well-connected in Whig circles, and a critic of the government's broken treaties and specious Indian policies. Major Ethan Allen Hitchcock, soon to be promoted to Lieutenant Colonel, tall with noble features and penetrating eyes—became the talk of the territory, a celebrity of sorts.

Hitchcock proposed to tour Indian Territory, planning to meet at Fort Gibson with General Arbuckle and Colonel Mason. He would also meet with John Ross and attend a Nationalist council meeting.

All of this made it imperative for Stand and Sarah to have Hitchcock's ear as well. No group knew the history of the Treaty Party and John Ross as well as the cousins. They had their truth to tell, and they knew Hitchcock's steamer would stop off at Van Buren before he began his investigation journey to Fort Gibson.

Stand arrived at Sarah's in anticipation of a meeting. Although George spent the afternoon with Col. Drennen at the horse races where Hitchcock was expected to be in attendance, the investigator failed to show. No meeting was arranged.

Stand left, but told Sarah and George to stay alert to Hitchcock's next trip to the area. For now, all they could do was wait.

During his time examining fraud in Indian Territory, Lt. Col. Hitchcock traveled on his own schedule by horseback and steamboat throughout the land. He filled his journals with injustices done not only to the Cherokee but to the Creek and Chickasaw, Choctaw and Seminole. He met with representatives of earlier migrations: Osage, Delaware, Biloxy, Kickapoo, and down near the border with Texas, the wild Comanche. He entered into his diaries huge sums for rations and annuities—paid and unpaid—for grafts and bribes.

He learned of an Indian agent who arrived poor but now had money enough for a plantation valued at $17,500, with many slaves. He met Army officers who by marriage into the tribes now operated profitable stores. He learned that bacon provided by the government was taken by contractors, and then resold. Beeves driven from Missouri were too poor to eat, but when turned out the cattle wandered and returned, then were driven to another agency and resold again. He was told that dried beef packed in barrels was often teeming with maggots.

Hitchcock rode untold miles on horseback over trails. He ate the meals offered him, cornbread, bacon, and fried eggs off a hewn log for a table. Conversely, he celebrated the arrival of the New Year of 1842 with fine courses and rich desserts on the mahogany dining suite at Lewis Ross's mansion at Park Hill.

Along the way, the Choctaw told Hitchcock sad stories of their trail where they cried, and how of the 15,000 who removed west, 2,500 died along the way.

The Creek told him of their trails where they cried, where 11,000 souls came west and 3,500 died. And how with the Creek, when a debt is paid by death the case is closed because it went against their blood laws to keep anger and hatred alive.

The different factions of the Real People told Hitchcock their versions of the trail where the Cherokee cried, how of those final 16,000 people who stayed behind waiting for John Ross to lead them west, 4,000 perished. Each faction told how the Blood Law John Ross brought with him had torn apart the nation, and how the case would never be closed.

At Fort Gibson, General Arbuckle and Colonel Mason told Hitchcock of Cherokee schemes, of murders, of the Ridges and Boudinot assassinations, of civil upheaval. Agent Butler shared his thoughts on Ross's power over the Old Settlers and Treaty Party.

Lt. Col. Hitchcock met with Chief John Ross, attended his address at the council in Tahlequah, and overnighted in his home. Hitchcock wrote in his diary that he admired Ross's leadership. But he also wrote of hearing that if so many Cherokee were not afraid to cast their votes, Ross would lose his power.

As the investigator concluded his four months in the west, Agent Butler arranged for Hitchcock to meet with Stand and Sarah at the Paschal home on Thompson Street.

On Saturday evening, March 12, 1842, George basked in the glow of the candelabra that lit the parlor and the settee and chairs the Ridges had brought west along with his New York selections. The dining table laid with Sarah's ivory-handled silverware sparkled with crystal and her family's English china. George did, of course, have cause for self-satisfaction; his connections in Little Rock were paying off in contacts and contracts; his partnership here of Paschal & Campbell thrived.

"Lieutenant Colonel Hitchcock will see that the Paschal residence can rival that of Lewis Ross, except in scale that is."

Sarah passed him across the replacement diamond-patterned carpet where once peonies and chrysanthemums bloomed. At the mantelpiece, she lit the sconces beside two portraits of herself, the romanticized painting done in Salem at sixteen and one completed last month. A girl with dreams wearing her father's gift of the red shawl across her green gown; the other a black tucked bodice with pagoda sleeves over a white waist with lace collar. The dress she now wore. Mourning black. The serious recent painting seemed a sad memorial to the carefree younger Sarah.

Then and now, she thought. Did the smiling girl at Salem School ever imagine she would live anywhere but her family home on the Oostanaula? Did she imagine motherhood to a vibrant three-year-old daughter and a nine-month-old boy, her precious George Walter? The young girl's portrait seemed to shake her head.

From the settee, Sarah Bird Northrup Ridge said, "I'm so glad you have had your portrait painted, Sallie. I long for a recent one of our dear John."

Sarah smiled. Her sister-in-law had often mentioned in her grief that the only painting she had of John was the one from long ago, of him holding the quill, recording the demise of his nation. She said she longed for a visual memory of him happy in the new land, looking forward to living where broken promises had forced him to reestablish with his family. Taking those words to heart, Sarah made sure the same wish should not befall her loved ones.

John's widow, along with Stand and John Watie who rode as a guard for his brother, had been in continual contact for the past week since word came that Hitchcock had ended his tour of tribes and was again across the river at Fort Smith. They arrived yesterday; Sarah had stood ready to entertain at a moment's notice. Agent Butler made good on his promise to get Hitchcock to come, but she was distressed that the traveler had waited until the day before his departure back East. He sent a note this morning from the fort that he would arrive at six o'clock, at least giving her time to have supper prepared. This was their only chance.

Hitchcock entered alone, with no aide and no Colonel Drennen. Introductions made, they moved to the dining room where Lettie and

Robinson placed bowls of boiled squash and sweet potato pudding, and two baskets of fresh-baked flour bread on the white linen tablecloth; at each place setting tiny butter plates held fat pats. Robinson, especially dressed in a black vest and white shirt, brought out the large roasted turkey. As George stood to carve, Sarah noticed the officer fingering her silver knives and forks; he seemed to savor her dining accoutrements. A chunk of treasured ice—the last for the season from Cragg's Ice House—melted in each crystal water glass. Word had come that Hitchcock was a teetotaler; George raised his glass in toast of their guest, and began the conversation, of course, with an anecdote about himself.

"I have had the recent honor of induction into the Little Rock Chapter of the Antiquarian Society. Are you, by chance, also a member of that organization?"

"I'm familiar with the society. I appreciate their mission, but have not yet been settled in one place to join any sort of association."

"As a scholar and man of literary tastes, I'm certain when you do settle you will find pleasure in the like-minded men associated with the society."

To change the subject, Sarah said, "Colonel, I understand your given names are 'Ethan Allen.'"

"You are correct, Mrs. Paschal."

"Are you related to the revered Revolutionary War hero," she asked, "or to the gunsmith?"

"The former, madam. My family hails from Vermont, the gunsmith from Massachusetts. And although I'm greatly impressed by Allen's invention of the rolling-tumbler repeating pistol, I see no place for it in a military setting. His so-called pepperbox seems to be accurate at close distances only. More likely a weapon for blackguards or gamblers sitting around gaming tables. Are you familiar with such a firearm, a lady such as yourself?"

"No. No, not at all." She immediately regretted her casual question. "I saw an advertisement in one of my husband's newspapers showing the patent diagram. I noted the inventor's name, similar to yours . . ."

Seeing Stand's scowl and George's expression of confusion, Sarah determined not to attempt further conversation.

Stand addressed the evening's subject. "I hope you have learned of the plight of the Cherokee in your interviews while here, Colonel."

"Yes, on many fronts." Addressing Sarah Bird he added, "Let me extend my sincere condolences to you, Mrs. Ridge, on your personal tragedy. And to all family members here on the loss of your loved ones." He nodded all around. In the hush that followed, George began offering turkey for each plate.

Stand continued. "Thank you, Colonel. Yet the instigator survives. He grips the reins of our nation in his iron fists."

"If you refer to Principal Chief John Ross, we have met. I attended council in Tahlequah and have visited in his home."

"If I may, I will address several issues here, Colonel," Stand replied. "One, that of Ross and his henchmen planned the executions of our family based on our signing the Treaty of New Echota in December 1835. Yet, some ten months *prior* to the signing, John Ross agreed to the allowance fixed by the Senate, a sum not exceeding five million dollars be paid to the Cherokee Indians for all their lands and possessions east of the Mississippi river."

Stand paused. "Allow me to relate to you what truly happened. Ross agreed that a treaty should be referred to the nation, but he sent out word to the people not to attend the council at Red Clay in October. In truth, sir, the treaty was read to only the few Cherokee who attended. Yet it *could* have been read to all. John Ross kept the people away and then he ran away to Washington rather than bring the Nation together. The President and Congress had made their decisions, the removal amount agreed upon, and those of us who signed did so to save our people."

"I have not heard of these particular details," Hitchcock said as he cut his slice of turkey.

"John Ross," Stand said, "held our tribe back with promises that they would not need to remove, although he knew President Van Buren would not reverse Jackson's decision. When the people were dragged from their homes and placed in the wretched stockades, *then* he made a deal brokered by General Scott for additional money. Ross secured our remaining people as hostages, then moved them throughout the hell of winter."

Hitchcock laid his knife across his plate. "Strong words. Yet I can see how you might choose to view Chief Ross's actions in that manner."

"Have you requisitioned an accounting from Ross for all the monies he received from General Scott," George asked, "and from the government? Has the amount he recently received been paid from the Cherokee fund? As Counsel for the Treaty Party, I have petitioned money be paid to the Nation."

"An accounting is in progress," Hitchcock replied.

John Watie turned to the colonel. "Perhaps someone has informed you that my brother cannot ride to any place without me and others armed to protect him. Rossmen roam, seeking out signers."

"As well," George added, "reparations for the Treaty Party are being held. After we dine, I have documents I'd like to show you."

As the conversation continued, Lettie and Robinson removed the plates, then brought out bowls of preserved peaches topped with fresh cream Milly had whipped with sugar.

Supper concluded, Hitchcock thanked his hosts for their delicious meal. Sarah nodded and murmured, "You are welcome," in reply to his gracious comments. While others moved into the parlor, George ushered the guest near the buffet light where he showed him copies of letters he'd written to the Secretary of War and Agent Butler requesting unpaid removal claims and reparations.

Upon returning to the parlor, Colonel Hitchcock offered his thanks and polite good-byes. As the door shut, the men settled to review the recent conversation, Sarah Bird retired to her bed, and Sarah, though weary with planning and worry, oversaw the evening's endings, having sent Milly to bring in the children from her cabin where they had stayed during supper.

As she helped carry dishes out to the kitchen, though, she could not shake the disturbing feeling that perhaps she had entertained a spy.

Lt. Col. Hitchcock returned to his cabin on the steamboat *Effort* to record in his diary details of his evening in the Paschals' home.

He would enter his personal opinions, one being of him meeting John's widow, Sarah Bird Northrup Ridge, formerly the pride of Cornwall, Connecticut: "Mrs. Ridge looked dull and subdued and did not make much impression. I confess I do not like to see white women marrying Indians or half-breeds, though I have not the least objection to white men marrying half-breeds."

He would write in his diary information that he had not shared with the group, knowledge he held back:

> I had no other purpose than to keep things quiet in the country. Paschal spoke of the treaty of 1835 and denied the right of the Government to pay the expenses of the Ross party, over and above $20.00 a head, in their emigration, from the fund provided in the treaty. This I think correct myself, but I did not tell an important fact in this business, that Congress by special appropriation added over a million to the treaty fund, not called for by the treaty, a sum more than sufficient, I think to cover all extra expenses under General Scott's arrangement with Mr. Ross.

Hitchcock went on: "Agent Butler had told me of Stanwatie and that he had threatened the life of John Ross; that he is of a cool determined character and that Ross will not be allowed to pass out of the Nation to Washington if he meets with Stanwatie."

Here Hitchcock would be right.

He would describe George:

> Paschal is a young man, that is, for meddling in national matters; is a lawyer in Van Buren and a sort of editor, writing considerably for the paper published in Van Buren especially on Indian and frontier affairs. He has the reputation of considerable talent; I do not

perceive much depth in him or much information. He is sprightly and writes editorially so to say, filling his sheet with adjectives and aims at poetic personifications, covering over the real subject matter with words. His mind is bent all to one side which he admitted to me was likely to be the case.

And here he would again be right.
Hitchcock would describe Sarah:

He [Paschal] married the sister of Ridge who was murdered, and his wife, considerably colored by nature with an aboriginal tint, is plainly of a strong masculine spirit. Speaks English very well, quite naturally as if she had no other language. She said but little, but what she did say was uttered with a peculiar firmness of muscle about the mouth, a kind of tension, the result of strong feeling.

Again, he would be right.
Lt. Col. Ethan Allen Hitchcock would write further to comment on a rumor he'd heard from Agent Butler concerning Sarah: ". . . that Mrs. Paschal had a man's dress and intended to disguise herself with it, and kill Ross herself if an opportunity offers. I place no great reliance upon this story . . . ."
But here he would be wrong.

CHAPTER 39

Thornes of Revenge

The Paschal Home

April 1842

For a week now Robinson made his daily visit to Mr. Moore's blacksmith shop as an unpaid apprentice at the forge and anvil to learn the farrier trade, striking, tapping, and bending horseshoes. He was also there for lessons in the spirit ways, to learn from Youngdeer how he listened and spoke to horses. The young Cherokee farrier, known throughout the territory for healing even the most lame and ill horses, instructed Robinson under the guise of training.

Last night, though, a strange horse was left in Sarah's stable. Today at noon Robinson came home with a message: "Youngdeer says to say 'hello' to you, Miss Sallie, an' for me to pass on to you that Sallisaw Creek is real pretty this time a' year."

Those words commenced the plan that Sarah, Stand, and Youngdeer had devised. Upon hearing this message, Sarah knew to go to a certain bend of the creek to meet up with the farrier. The two would ride all night under the waning full moon and arrive at Park Hill before sunrise.

Stand knew they had a compatriot in Youngdeer, raised by his Cherokee aunt who had nursed him through a smallpox outbreak that took his parents. She loved him as her own and he planned to care for her when she finally arrived west. When the removals had begun Youngdeer sent word to his aunt, begging her to enroll, come live with him in Van Buren. She wrote back that messengers roamed the hills warning not to believe the traitorous signers of the treaty, that the chief would find a way for them to stay in their homes or lead the people to a land beyond the territories that he would buy to be theirs forever.

Youngdeer's aunt was one of many left on the winter trail, blanketed in ice where she huddled against a broken wagon as a blizzard raged. Wounds, long festering, consumed the young farrier's mind.

A Treaty Party spy had spread the word around Park Hill about the wisdom and magic of Youngdeer for curing horses. When John Ross's favorite horse Wind Feather went lame, word was sent for Youngdeer to come.

Robinson didn't know the plot, but Lettie did. As soon as her brother delivered the message she had him saddle the mysterious horse. Lettie brought the children to Sarah for her to hug, perhaps for her last time, and then Sarah released them and the household to Lettie. Milly would stay at all times with the children; Eliza, brought here on Susanna's last visit, would help with cooking; Isaac was to continue his hired work. Robinson would remain on the Thompson Street property until Lettie told him otherwise. George was in Little Rock, out of Sarah's way.

Lettie retrieved a bag of clothing and items from its hiding place in the attic. She and her mistress closed the door to Sarah's bedroom; several hours later a black man emerged draped in Sarah's hooded cloak. Lettie escorted him to the stables. Unseen, he mounted the horse and headed for Sallisaw Creek.

Late afternoon sun threw long shadows as Sarah dismounted at the creek. She stuffed her cloak deep in a boulder crevasse, then led the horse to drink. Larkspur and pinkladies mixed with the cascading cane along the sandy banks.

She looked at the beauty around her, then suddenly started shaking. What was she doing?

Had she kissed Emily's blond curls for the final time? Held George Walter to her breast for the final time? George, his shock . . . he would be left with her orphans. Lettie, Milly, Watty—he would have to add another stick to his heavenly circle. And Mother. Susanna wanted revenge, wanted John Ross dead, but not at the loss of her daughter!

Sarah widened her eyes, blinking; tears might streak her stained cheeks.

But Ross must die. Stand had begged her not to take on this mission. She countered. Who else could do what she and Youngdeer must do? Do what Stand himself desired, more than his own life?

If she failed, she might come back to this place and ride home to her children. If her plan succeeded, she likely would not return.

She startled at the sound of hoof beats. Her instinct was to hide in the rocks, but why? If it was a stranger, a Rossman, even an acquaintance, who was she but an old black slave man watering his horse?

Youngdeer rode near, then pulled up short. Trim and handsome in a tunic and beaded belt, fringed deerskin leggings, and moccasins, he leaned down. His gray eyes narrowed.

She walked to him and held up her hand for shaking. "Louis LaBranche," she said. In a deep Creole dialect, the name sounded "Loo-ee La Bronsh."

"Come from down Louisiana way. I's run away from the LaBranche plantation house in Sain' Rose Parrish. Been a long way comin'. Been hirin' myself out in Van Buren for a while now. Good with horses, for sure. Mista Moore lets me sleep in the blacksmith shed, help out with stokin' and all."

Youngdeer leaned down. "Missus Paschal? Is that you?"

She took off her stained slouch hat. "Yes."

Youngdeer shook his head. "Even knowing, I don't recognize you. You're a man! Your hair! John Ross will never recognize you!"

Sarah and Stand had planned for that event, and now she touched the tiny pocket she had sewn into her right-hand sleeve cuff, reassuring herself of her calling card.

Lettie had concocted a disguise as ingenious and devious as, she had said, Mr. Defoe would for Robinson Crusoe. Even Sarah could not reconcile her image to that person appearing earlier in the wardrobe mirror after Lettie cut off her braid and finished snipping the ragged ends of what remained. Lettie rubbed her hands in lard, dipped them in a bowl of ash, and then trailed and twisted strands until Sarah's head looked like a burned-out haystack. Lettie reminded her not to touch her hair; with the job Sarah had to do, she didn't want greasy hands.

Lettie then dipped a finger into a bowl of boiled-down black walnut husks. She massaged the stain around Sarah's eyes, across her nose, and far down her neck, blending it in with her deep brown skin. Sarah's hands—always gloved—needed extra darkening.

The winding sheet around her breasts was the worst part. Following Hitchcock's visit a month ago, Sarah had weaned George Walter; at a year old he did well with mashed squash and beans, but he had to get accustomed to spoons of sweetened cow's milk. Her breasts were naturally large; the pressure intense, but at least no milk expressed onto the bindings. Lettie inserted a tightly-rolled cloth between Sarah's breasts and that spacer seemed to help the pressure. She would have to find excuses in the company of men when she needed to relieve herself, but those occasions would be contingent on events.

Sarah's total transformation continued with rough boots and worn breeches showing a few patches, a frayed calico shirt, and an old canvas vest; under the brim of the hat Sarah completely disappeared.

"Well, Youngdeer, *allons-y, bon ami*!"

"What's that mean, Missus . . . I mean, Louie?"

"Let's go, my friend!"

The blood-red dawn spread across the prairie at Park Hill highlighting John Ross's plantation. Reverend Worcester's home, the mission, the print shop—and Elias's house—lay only a mile farther. Sarah sat on her horse a short distance behind Youngdeer and listened as the gate guards questioned him.

Yes, he was Youngdeer the farrier from Moore's Blacksmith shop.

Yes, he had ridden all night from Van Buren to heal the horse Wind Feather.

No, he carried no weapons. He dismounted so the two men could search him. They had him unbuckle his saddlebag tool kit and unroll the leather sheets that wrapped his tools; they inspected everything, his rasp and pincers and hammer. His hoof knife; the tall guard hefted it.

"In case the pain is caused by a hoof that needs trimming," Youngdeer said.

"Whitetree will watch him," the taller guard said. "Who rides with you?"

Youngdeer knelt and calmly rolled up his tools. "Moore's slave. Name's Louie."

"You! Slave. Get down," he called to Sarah.

Lettie had practiced a search in Sarah's bedroom yesterday. But Lettie knew what she was looking for.

Sarah, dismounting, stood by the horse's neck and held the reins in her left hand while she stroked the horse's head and scratched him under his chin, keeping her right arm active. The guard walked up to her; she recognized him. A nephew of James Martin who had once threatened her brother's life. He looked hard into her eyes, jerked off her hat, then plopped it back on crooked. He ran his hands across her shoulders, lifted the back of her vest, slapped her waist and on down her hips and legs, down to her boots.

"Nothing!" he shouted.

The guards walked to the gate and spoke in low voices. The tall one told Youngdeer to mount, then opened the gate. The Martin nephew straddled his horse to lead them through. Sarah mounted, then slowly released the breath she'd held for minutes. Rivulets of sweat trickled from her hair, around her ears, down her neck; she blotted her skin with her shirt but dared not touch her hair and get oil on her hands.

They followed the wagon trail around the house toward the barn. Stand's spy had drawn a layout of the large, several-storied log house, adjacent barn, and kitchen cabin, all secured behind a split-rail fence.

Immediately after the murders, a hundred Rossmen had fortified the property. When civil war with Treaty Party survivors and Old Settler sympathizers seemed imminent, Ross had refused General Arbuckle's offer of protection at Fort Gibson, preferring his own army to the government's.

That was three years ago. Now on this early morning, there were only two guards at the gate. Other riders were posted around the perimeter surveying the endless prairie. The spy had told Stand how Ross enjoyed his tea on the porch, watching the sunrise from behind a trellis screen of deep red rose vines. Sarah caught sight of a figure there now.

Youngdeer dismounted at the barn and called for Louie to bring his tools from his saddle. Sarah unbuckled the box and followed the barn guard Whitetree to the lame horse's stall. The guard who brought them tied his horse at the corral and walked to the kitchen cabin behind the main house.

Youngdeer immediately put the plan in motion. He called to the guard in Cherokee to hold Wind Feather's hoof, then in English, he ordered Louie to go get water from the well in the center of the property.

Sarah grabbed a bucket from a peg and walked toward the well, then veered off. Without changing pace, near the corner of the house she set down the bucket and reached for the loaded pepperbox pistol now tucked between her breasts.

She walked along the side of the house to the porch where John Ross sat in a bent-cane chair drinking his morning tea. The chief glanced up as Sarah's boot hit the bottom step. He glared at this strange black man with a gun in his hand. From the cuff of her right sleeve, Sarah tore President Monroe's Indian peace medal and slapped it on the table.

"I want you to know who killed you, John Ross. I, Sallie Ridge," she said, pulling off her hat.

He picked up the peace medal without taking his eyes off her.

"Sallie? Can this be you?"

"Yes. I've come to avenge my family. To avenge the deaths in the stockades and on your wretched trail. Killed by your arrogance! You say the Treaty Party is guilty by signing! I say you are guiltier by *not* signing!"

She stretched out her arm and aimed at John Ross's heart. She pulled the trigger.

The hammer hit the cap with a flash and fizzle. Misfire.

Before she could fire again, Ross grabbed the pistol, twisting Sarah's arm hard, forcing her down in the chair next to him, the action shielded by rose vines.

In a hushed voice, he said, "You, Sallie, least of all would I expect to assassinate me! Your cousin yes, but you?"

"Stand and I share blood. I avenge Elias as well as my father and John." Her strength faded; her voice trembled. "How could you murder them?"

Ross leaned in close. "Sallie, Sallie, no. I didn't."

"But you knew. You could have stopped it. And you can heal the nation now with just a word of compromise!"

Ross shoved the pistol into his coat pocket, then reached across the table and picked up the medal. The powerful voice that Sarah had heard so many times fell to an intimate whisper.

"I gave you this medal in Washington City. I told you then that if you truly believe in something you must do everything you can to make it happen.

"I believed I could alter the government's path, save our land. I hated your family for giving up, for causing the fracture of our people."

Sarah's voice quivered in anger. "The Treaty Party accepted that *nothing* could save our land. Only removal would save our people! Why could you not see that?"

"They turned against me, against the laws."

"Bringing the Blood Law west was merely your excuse to kill my father."

"Your father knew he would be killed long before he signed the treaty against my will. When the immigrants arrived they needed someone to blame for their despair."

She looked him hard in the eyes, but no words came.

"Sallie, you must go before someone sees you." He reached to hand her the medal.

"I want nothing of yours. Neither your talisman nor your twisted truth!"

Standing, she grabbed a rose vine and ran her hand down the vicious thorns. Like knives, the barbs ripped her fingers and palm. She stepped toward John Ross and wiped her hand across his face.

"Now you wear the blood of the Ridges and all who died for your arrogance!"

He drew back. The peace medal fell to the floor.

She grabbed her hat. Walking down the steps, she steeled herself for the chief's yell, alerting his guards. Ready to run for her horse, she forced herself to walk at an even pace. She heard only silence as she picked up the bucket; bypassing the well she walked into the barn.

Youngdeer turned at her entrance. He had been primed to act at the sound of Sarah's shot. He would slash the guard's neck with the hoof knife, mount his horse, lead Sarah's to her, and together ride to safety—or more likely, into gunfire and death.

But now he said, "It was a deep thorn, Louie. Look! I've put salve on the horse's foot. We can go now."

Youngdeer handed the thorn to the guard. "Tell the chief, no charge!"

The thorn was easy to find, cruel though it was of the spy to stick it in the horse's foot so deep that only someone knowing where to look could spot it.

Youngdeer tied his tools on his horse and Sarah quickly mounted. The barn man ran for the kitchen to summon the gate guard to lead them out.

Sarah looked where John Ross stood behind the trellis. He could still alert his men. His words in this very moment could end her life just as his silence ended her family's.

She and Youngdeer trotted down the path toward the gate. She pictured John Ross wiping her blood from his face, but it didn't matter: the stain remained. Revenge was hers. Perhaps better than she had hoped.

The sweat of her breasts had moistened the gunpowder. Her children still had their mother, alive, not shot or arrested. She had avenged her family and her people with words as well as with action.

As she passed, the chief walked across the porch and entered his front door allowing Sarah to ride home a free woman.

Chapter 40

Sarah Speaks

Pause with me now, if you will, and let us consider the great mystery of why events occur as they do.

You've read thus far the reasons why I was filled with bile and rage with a gnawing need to avenge my family's murders. And you've read in Colonel Hitchcock's diary entries that he disbelieved the rumor that I would dress as a man and attempt to take John Ross's life.

Yet, I did.

That day in Park Hill as our nemesis—still alive—entered his house, I followed Youngdeer, my perceived master, toward the gate. I pulled a kerchief from my vest pocket and wrapped it around my bloody hand. The guards took no notice. We trotted southeast through the early morning, heading back to Sallisaw Creek where we would part. The farther we rode from Park Hill, the fewer Rossmen we saw still surveying the horizon for Stand's armed raiders.

At some point, I unwrapped my bandage and looked with pain and pride at the blood seeping from my hand while other emotions buzzed around me like hornets.

Several times over the past weeks I'd driven the buggy from home to a secluded ravine to practice loading and firing the small pepperbox pistol Stand had provided. I practiced to familiarize myself with the weapon, but more so to test my grit. The pistol was a six-shooter with revolving barrels, each requiring powder, patch and ball, and copper firing caps, so this process required precision and focus of mind.

When Stand gave me the pepperbox the day of our meeting with Hitchcock, he warned that the small lead ball—a point-thirty-two caliber—might not penetrate a man's head even at close range. To guarantee instant death he advised at least two quick pulls of the trigger as I aimed at Ross's heart.

It was one thing to practice successive pulls of the trigger, yet very much another to visualize pointing the gun at the villain's black heart.

I carried in the buggy a jute bag that Lettie had stuffed with hay and was the size of a man's chest. I placed the headless effigy on the side of the ravine, standing close as I fired in quick succession. I watched the bullets enter the upper left of Ross's chest, saw him fall back, and saw his blood pouring out the hole like the bleeding wound of Jesus' side in the Moravian paintings of my childhood.

In my mind those images—one of the Savior and one of the Murderer—fused, creating in me the spirit of a woman who must do what only *I* could do: sacrifice my life to kill John Ross.

In the ravine, I was that determined woman, but in my bed in the dark of night, my motives blurred. The daughter, the sister, the cousin could be sacrificed. But what of the mother? My children's loss—and for *my* mother another death of a child.

Youngdeer and I rode back in silence. We forded the Illinois River and on the other side when we dismounted to let our horses drink, he broke that silence.

"Why didn't you kill him?" He glared at me, his words bitter, his expression twisted in confusion. The smallpox that brought him to his aunt had pitted his handsome face; his hatred for John Ross pitted his heart.

Moving in front of my compatriot, I showed him how close the pistol was to Ross's chest when I pulled the trigger. The misfire, and that from the chair where he'd shoved me I'd said he had the power with just one word to end the killings now.

Showing Youngdeer the still-seeping wounds in my hand, I told him how I'd ripped my hand through the roses and wiped my blood across the chief's face. How I said to John Ross he now wore the blood of the Ridges and all who died for his arrogance!

"Still, he lives!"

"He does, yes. But now he is stained by the blood of our people."

Youngdeer looked away. I remember the sadness in his words: "He always was."

I explained how Ross said he hated my family for giving up, for splitting our people, and when the immigrants arrived they needed someone to blame for their misery.

Mellowing, Youngdeer took my wounded hand in his. Then he peered across the river: "But why did he not call out for help? Or turn the gun on you? Why let us ride away?"

"Guilt? Pity for me who he'd known as a child? To arrest me, to have me shot, well . . ."

I, too, had pondered the chief's inaction on the trail back. Was it the notoriety he would bring to his party if Major Ridge's daughter lay dead on the porch of Rose Cottage?

Youngdeer shook his head, his voice sad. "It was a personal conquest for you, but what change will come for the nation? He still rules with his eye on his army and retains the ear of the government!"

He was right. What had altered, but my insult to him? And what would be the consequences?

A misfire had saved not only John Ross's life but Youngdeer's and mine. Would my words and actions help our nation?

Only five would know of our failed plot. Youngdeer and I would relate the story to Stand and he to his spy. These three men—plus Lettie and me—would take our brave plan to our graves.

And, of course, John Ross knew.

His next movements would tell us his reaction.

Would he regret his years of hatred and animosity—acknowledged by my blood on his face—and reconsider the division in our Cherokee nation? Call together leaders to begin talks to heal our rift?

Would he consider stepping down, perhaps choosing a pastoral existence for himself over this life of warring factions?

Or would my blood on his face enrage him even more? Knowing he could not kill a woman, would he put out the word to kill Stand? Have Youngdeer quietly knifed?

And what would I do with my failure? I had not killed him, yet I survived. I must live with that regret inside me, return to my responsibilities as wife and mother, daughter and sister, and conceal my emotions as I must conceal my missing hair.

Yes, it is a great mystery why events unfold as they do.

Chapter 41

It's All About Hair

The Paschal Home

May 1842

Emily screamed and ran from her mother's bedroom.

"Milly!" Sarah yelled. "Catch Emily!"

Sarah quickly closed the door. Covering her face in her hands, she pressed hard against her eyes, suppressing tears within the blackness.

She had tried to be so careful not to let her daughter see her without her bonnet or turban. Now as Sarah stood before the wardrobe in her chemise the four-year-old skipped into the bedroom, blond curls bouncing, happy and grinning, holding a handful of flowers she'd gathered in the garden. Sarah had no time to cover her head. Emily's eyes grew big as she stared at this strange creature with wild short hair. She turned and fled.

Two weeks earlier, when Sarah had ridden home under the cover of darkness from Sallisaw Creek, Lettie began reversing their transformation, changing the old slave man back to a lady of the town. But now Sarah was a lady with a lowly condition: she and Lettie concocted a tale of how Sarah had been walking near the river when a mangy dog wandered near her. He was drooling. Fearful of hydrophobia, she pushed him away with her parasol and accidentally touched his scabby back! Her bonnet fell off! When she replaced it, she must have touched her head with the mangy itch on her glove!

To justify her shearing, the women decided that an application of foul-smelling sulfur powder would complete the ruse. Better the embarrassment of mange than speculation of any other reason.

In a few days, the odor of rotting eggs faded, but Sarah knew it would be years until her hair grew back. When she committed to the cause—accepting that she could leave her children orphaned—the worry of cutting her braid was her second hardest decision: only lunatic women in asylums or those diseased cropped their hair. She chose the latter, but at times felt she fit the former category. Her relentless despondency hovered like a dark cloud.

At least millinery fashions were in her favor with snug bonnets trimmed in voile and netting. At the time of shearing Lettie left the front of Sarah's hair long enough for tendrils slicked back behind her ears; her braid they twisted into a netted bun. At home, hiding her short hair was hard, but so far servants and visitors hadn't questioned her wearing a traditional turban.

Emily's innocent entrance was the first failure of Sarah's drama of deceit. George's return from Little Rock today would be her next test.

Over the past year, the Paschals had gone their separate ways. George had taken the very able Andrew Campbell as a partner to run the legal and collection business in Van Buren, then established an office in Little Rock to attract new clients and politick for a seat on the Supreme Court. With elections six months away, George let his desire for the judgeship be known, but the pay was a pittance.

Buoyed by Colonel Hitchcock's visit, when George returned to Little Rock he continued pursuing claims for the Ridge family and followed up with letters to the Secretary of War and Commissioner of Indian Affairs, though with little consequence. Money was still owed to the family and the nation; public funds, when they came, ended up in John Ross's coffers. George now came home to write more letters, perhaps to wrangle a meeting with Agent Butler of the Indian Agency should he come to Fort Smith. George, as a Ridge family member, would not be welcomed within the boundaries of Indian Territory.

Sarah heard blasts from the *Rialto*'s whistle announcing the steamship docking. She visualized George disembarking with his valise, chatting with friends and acquaintances on Main Street, stopping in to speak with Andrew and William Mosely; the young Cherokee assistant who had been with George all these years had stayed on to help Andrew. Sarah had an hour, maybe more.

She called Lettie to come lace her white bodice over a brown skirt, then continued dressing, finishing off with the shawl woven with crimson peonies that George bought her in New York. Sarah slicked back the front of her hair, tied on her netted bun and centered her tan bonnet; a jaunty bow knotted off-center under her chin belied her despondency. She picked up her hand mirror and walked into the living room.

Out the window she saw a normal afternoon in early May: Colonel Drennen trotted by on his favorite strawberry roan; little George Walter laughed as Robinson let him dip the ladle into the bucket and dribble water over the porch blooms. Emily stood quietly holding her bouquet of wilted flowers. Sarah felt the urge to kneel beside the sad child and draw in the sand—as she had so many times with Watty—drawing a happy little Emily and a mother with long hair, then with short hair, a picture of the same loving mother.

Sarah sighed. I've been distracted for so long. I must find time to spend with my daughter. But not today.

Sarah moved to the mantelpiece and stood before her portrait. She lifted the hand mirror and compared the two faces. Already in just these months since her portrait sittings, the face in the mirror revealed furrows of worry unseen by the painter on Main Street. Sarah had forced herself to display her feelings of love for her children as the painter stood at his easel. If Sarah had been successful in her murder attempt, this portrait would be all that her children would have of their mother.

The lips in the mirror moved to whisper, "It changed nothing."

No news had reached her of a proposed peace for the nation, but then neither had word of an assassination attempt on the chief's life.

She shook her head. It's too soon to know.

Her worry now focused on today. She felt if she could gain George's acceptance of her hair she could move forward, move out of this pretense of her own making, regain for herself a sense of . . . of *worth*.

Back in her bedroom, Sarah faced her difficult role as she pictured George lying beside her in bed tonight. Since their estrangement she'd been tepid toward him when he came home; of course, accepting her duty as wife, she'd acquiesced to his physical desire while silently fulfilling her own needs. Tonight, though, she wanted him to hold her, to feel his fingers stroking her short hair, to again feel safe within his arms, sheltered from her failed deed of which he knew nothing.

What would she tell her husband when she removed her bonnet? What answer would she give George when he gasped, "Sarah, whatever have you done to your hair?"

What answer would she give? Mange—or murder?

"Mange," Lettie answered as they set the dining table. Sarah had begged help in composing her reply for her imagined scene. "I shall tell him. Nastiest itch I ever saw! Dousin' ye with sulfur th' first time dinnae peg it, so I shorn ye meself an' doused ye again! Iffen ye tell him 'bout th' chief's murder ploy, he'll raise a mess a' trouble with Mister Stand, with Youngdeer. Especially with ye. Forever."

Sarah took a deep breath. "But I'll look like this for years! What can we do?"

"Ye must keep yer head covered 'til th' right time." Lettie paused. "Och! Th' box a' lacy linens Miss Susanna an' th' aunts sewed for ye! For yer wedding night. There's a sleepin' cap in there, a right pretty one."

Sarah nodded. Their amber cabin . . . George and the scent of fresh pine, the glow of the fire. Yes, she recollected stepping from behind the privacy sheet hung in the corner, her muslin bedgown stitched with gentle rows of lace, her hair long and loose. The cap. George had untied the strings and twirled her hair, caressed her shoulders, his hands moving with affection and tenderness she again needed to feel.

Sarah climbed the back stairs to the attic room. She opened the trunk; her wedding attire folded and wrapped in muslin had survived the trip west. As she lifted the lid, lingering traces of pine-covered hills drifted to her nose. She took a deep breath, closed her eyes, and for a moment was transported to the Oostanaula. Then she unfolded the cap and removed her bedgown.

The evening drama progressed perfectly, from George's entrance at the front door to his compliment on her new bonnet to playtime in the parlor: George Walter's gift of a carved steamboat and Emily's fancy-dress doll with painted blond curls. Emily barely left her father's side all evening and cuddled her doll during the meal while George entertained with stories of Little Rock. Sarah replied to his questions about home with the ease of rehearsed dialogue. After dinner, George joined Milly in putting the children to bed with the promise of a story from the *Sabbath School Advocate* children's magazine he had brought back from a Methodist church service.

Sarah found no lines or verse as she lit the bedside lamp and removed her bonnet. Lettie tapped on the door and came in to untie her lacings, reporting that George was reading to the children. While Lettie folded Sarah's clothing, she slipped into her wedding bedgown.

"At least it still fits," she mumbled, smoothing lace and ribbons.

"Looks fine. Now pull yer hair in front a' yer ears," Lettie said, placing the cap.

As Lettie started to tie the cap strings, Sarah, her voice dull and lifeless said, "Leave them loose. It will come off soon enough."

"Now ye tell him to come an' talk to me if he's upset with th' cuttin'. I'll set him straight."

"Thank you, I will."

Lettie put her arm around Sarah's shoulder and squeezed, then walked out the door and shut it.

What now? Sarah thought. Get in bed, under the covers? Sit in the rocker? Pose on the edge of the bed?

She chose to stand near the wardrobe. As George entered he shut the door, glanced at her, then walked to the rocker and hung his waistcoat over the back. He sat and untied his shoelaces, not saying a word. He unbuttoned his shirt and loosened it from his trousers, then stepped to her.

He lifted the cap from Sarah's head. He held her at arm's length, blinked several times, and grabbed her to him. "Oh, my poor darling! Emily said you were frightening to see and you were so ill-tempered toward her!"

Sarah drew away. "George? What?"

She stared at him, startled to see in his face such warmth and compassion; his eyes welled.

"I was reading a story to the children," he blurted out, "the one of Sampson and Delilah. When I got to the part where Delilah cuts Sampson's hair and he loses his strength, well, Emily started crying! 'Did Mother lose her strength?' she asked.

"I had no idea what she meant! Then in her own little trembling words, she told me about the sick dog down by the river."

Sarah held her breath.

"Oh, my poor, poor dear wife! You must have been terrified! Fighting off a dog with hydrophobia! And mange! You must be devastated, humiliated! And yet your disguise is without fault! I did not in any manner see other than a new lovely bonnet covering your stately netted bun."

Sarah stuttered, searching for words. "Oh, George. Thank you. Thank you for your understanding. I've . . . I've been so nervous. What you would think? So unworthy . . ." She covered her face with her hands, but this time she let her tears fall, tears of release, tears that washed away these past weeks of fear and failure and farce.

He let her cap fall to the floor. He smoothed her hair, ran his fingers down the center, and swept the tendrils behind her ears.

He smiled. She smiled.

When he took her in his arms and as they held each other in bed, memories of the amber cabin crept into Sarah's mind and her husband's affection crept into her heart, crowding out his failings.

CHAPTER 42

From Mud Pies to Blood Ties

The Paschal Home

May 18, 1842

Over the past week, Sarah and George attained a level of routine in their marriage that events had never allowed to blossom in their five years together. Sitting now on the porch with her gloves in her basket and a sampler in her lap, she felt a sense of harmony as she fanned herself while the children played in an elm shadow.

With a new baby in the household—Milly and Isaac's son, Andy—the young slave Eliza cared for the children. At twelve years of age, Eliza provided an imaginative maternal touch to her wards. Now they were making mud pies and laughing.

Sarah loosened her turban a bit and pushed back an errant lock. Following George's return from Little Rock she had spent the day with Emily, letting her comb her hair any way she wanted. Dressing in fancy town dresses they strolled to Drennen's Store for a chocolate of Emily's choice, her distress forgotten.

Sarah's crushing distress also faded; her moment on John Ross's porch seemed more like a dramatic scene from a novel. Now Sarah wanted only to be a patient wife to her husband and mother to her children. She was hopeful another child might come from her renewed closeness to George, but yesterday her "time of month" arrived.

Perhaps next month I'll conceive, Sarah thought as she knotted off a finished leaf design on her sampler. Reaching into her basket for her scissors, she snipped the thread and glanced up to see George walking swiftly up Thompson Street.

Why? she wondered. Wednesdays were his deacons' midday meeting. She had nothing prepared for a meal now, since this evening she planned a celebration for Emily's birthday.

George walked toward the backyard. Milly came through the house and whispered that Mr. Paschal wished to speak to her.

She quickly folded her needlework and called to Emily to help Eliza with the little ones. When she stepped into the parlor George met her with a full embrace.

"What?" she said, stepping back in panic. "Is something the matter? Mother? Watty?"

"Oh, no, my dear. No. I don't mean to frighten you, but I didn't want to interrupt Emily's play. I do have grievous news, though. I just received word that four days ago, James Foreman baited Stand into a fight up north at England's Grocery. Stand killed him!"

"Is Stand all right?"

"Yes, he writes us of the event. I have been hearing rumors but shielded you until the time I could share the entire story."

He pulled the letter from his pocket and ushered her to the settee. "He writes on this recent Sunday," George read.

Honey Creek
May 15, 1842
Dear Cousin & George,
    I write hastily since you will hear rumors of yesterday's events at England's. I am well. James Foreman is dead. Details will come out, but all in our Nation know Foreman has bragged of killing your father & threatened me many times over. My brother John & I, back from Missouri, proposed to go by for groceries

at Baltz's, but James Miller a white man who had joined us suggested England's where the liquor is better. When we walked in, at the bar stood a row of planners & participants in John Ross's day of slaughter—Foremen & Isaac Springston & Alexander Dromgoole. Springston shortly left. We now know Foreman sent him to his house for his guns.

George cleared his throat and continued. Sarah shook her head as gruesome images returned.

Our supplies gathered, England poured whiskey for John & Miller & me. From the end of the bar Foreman lifted his own glass & said, "Stand Watie, here is wishing you may live forever." I lifted my glass, saying, "I can drink with you, Jim. But I understand a few days hence you were saying you were going to kill me." He replied, "Say yourself!" & straightened up, bullwhip in hand. I threw the glass. Fists, whip, my knife, & out the door we fell, he hit me with a board—all so fast. I cut Foreman & as I mounted he called from some 20 paces, "You haven't done me yet." I fired my pistol from my horse. He stumbled, ran, crawled. John & I rode off just as Springston returned with guns. Foreman I was told was still alive, but died shortly.

Retribution, a small portion, is made for our family, Sallie. George, I will need you to prepare for an eventual trial in Little Rock as England's is within Arkansas.

I fear what comes next. 80 armed Rossman arrived Maysville some days back seeking me, I hear. It seems John Ross prefers not to cease our Nation's divide. I gather warriors now.

Sarah closed her eyes. Ross's blood-streaked face returned, wavering, ghost-like.

Good, she thought. James Foreman is dead. She saw him crawling, slithering like the snake he was. He rode with the Rossmen cowards and shot an old man off his horse.

Her mind raced as she thought: after Ross let her walk away, did he pause to consider between a pastoral life or continued warring? If he did, he chose the latter. And Stand's name headed his list.

Could hers be next? No. He passed over his opportunity to have her killed. Youngdeer. Surely he is safe. No one knows but for Stand and the spy. And Ross. She resolved to send Robinson to check on the farrier.

She moaned, grabbed her head, and squeezed her turban hard. Her head now ached as if it would explode.

As she turned over her ungloved hand, she saw in her palm the recent scars from the rose thorns. She had tried, but the remaining Wild Potato Clan daughter failed in invoking the Blood Law, to take an eye for so many of her family whose eyes are closed by death.

The killings continued.

Chapter 43

Lilacs for the Dead

The Paschal Home

March 1843

Sarah closed the front door and stood on the dark porch. She unwound her turban and draped it across her shoulders; her almost-year of hair growth made concealing less troublesome. The evening was cool as she moved to the edge of the porch for a view of the western sky.

Above the bluff on the dark horizon, the comet glowed as a pallid emerald dot followed by a blue-white tail of great length.

For several nights clouds concealed the mystical streak the newspapers were calling "The Great Comet." Reported sightings excited readers; the comet with its lavish tail was seen by some as the forerunner of the Second Advent of Christ. Sarah had little time to worry about the end of the world. But there *had* been her worry of earthquakes. Susanna long ago told little Sallie the story of how she was born during the time of the great earthquakes; in January the Thompson Street house shook and windowpanes rattled.

Another *gado alitelvhvsgv*, a small earthshaking, had frightened citizens of Van Buren two days following the birth of Susan Agnes on February 20th.

Disbelieving these omens Sarah reveled in her beautiful daughter she called Soonie, so much a Ridge with her dark hair and dark eyes. An easy birthing with Lettie, Milly, and Flying Pheasant attending. Sarah would take little Soonie to her breast after this respite on the porch while Eliza watched over Emily and George Walter.

Sarah hoped tonight George had a clear view of the comet in Little Rock where he had lived since the second week in January, having been admitted as a Justice to the Supreme Court.

The new father replied to Sarah's letter of Susan Agnes' birth with delight, hoping to see his daughter as soon as his judicial duties allowed. Ever the businessman, George had established a retail business in Van Buren before he moved. Having invested in fabrics and items from Van Pelt's in New York, he currently offered staple and fancy goods as well as boots and shoes on consignment with his friend Samuel Griffith's shop next door to George's law office on Main Street.

When accepting the Supreme Court judgeship, George and his partner of several years, Andrew Campbell, dissolved their formal partnership here. Sarah was sad to lose that connection; Andrew had become like a member of her family and she continued to include him for suppers in her home. In final disposition, Campbell had arranged to send $2,100 back east for collections and payments. William Mosely, George's long-time Cherokee assistant, continued to handle day-to-day clerical duties for Andrew in the brick building on Main Street.

Alfred W. Arrington, Esq., joined Campbell who continued the collections side; Arrington took on litigation, and would lead Stand's defense though George was unofficially overseeing preparations for the trial, soon to begin in Bentonville.

Sarah, realizing she had stared too long at the comet's green glow, closed her eyes; crimson dots dappled the blackness behind her eyelids. She watched the images fade, then opened her eyes to the night sky.

Oh, she thought, if only this cosmic phenomenon could predict the end of the Cherokee's world of war. But nothing could stop it. Like the comet's trailing tail, blood follows blood.

John Ross continued to deny any knowledge of the Ridges and Boudinot murderers; General Arbuckle continued to inform the Secretary of War of the contentious and violent positions of the three warring parties and requested President Tyler not to allow an audience with the Cherokee delegation now in Washington—if Ross was included.

President Tyler eventually addressed the situation with a letter to Congress acknowledging and deploring how the Cherokee relocation had been handled by the Federal government. He said he'd read various treaties that promised friendship, as well as protection and guardianship. He then promised a new treaty.

Congress, though, was dealing with more pressing issues: the war that the Republic of Texas was fighting for independence from Mexico. And farther north hundreds of wagon trains filled with thousands of people were assembling in the town of Independence, Missouri, to set off for Oregon Territory, still under dispute with Great Britain.

The Treasury was more concerned with expenditures for wars and international treaties than in a new structure of funding for one of many tribes of Indians. In Indian Territory, many Cherokee lived off provisions provided by the government. Families starved, some died.

Not only the Cherokee suffered. Lawlessness prevailed throughout the territory.

The world did not end that March as predicted. But on a Sunday in May came a worse calamity for the Paschal family. Their friend Andrew Campbell's life ended abruptly.

Three days later Andrew's funeral procession assembled on Washington Street in front of the Union Church. The popular young lawyer's tragic death brought out Van Buren's mourners who lined up in an ordained cortège order: the Episcopal priest led; the wheeled bier holding Andrew's shattered body in a pine coffin followed, pushed by

LILACS FOR THE DEAD 301

pallbearers consisting of friends and associates of the deceased. The third group, the Judiciary, came next, that being Supreme Court Judge George Paschal and the Seventh Circuit Judge; members of the Bar and officers of the courts came next, followed by the ladies and husbands of the Van Buren Temperance Society, of which Andrew had been a fervent member. The sixth group was designated "Strangers present, and Citizens generally."

Sarah, dressed in black crepe and veiled bonnet, joined William Mosley in the last group. She could have walked with George, but as soon as the procession reached Main Street, he and Mr. Arrington were going to politely step out from the Judiciary and Bar groups. Saddled horses were hitched to the post in front of George's office. They needed to ride to Bentonville where Stand's trial began in a few days.

Having left the Supreme Court sessions in Little Rock to come upriver Wednesday morning after Sarah sent word by steamer of Andrew's death, George attended necessary details and grieved his friend after talking to the county prosecutor who had headed the inquest: a rifle shot to Andrew's back, vicious stab wounds over his body and arms, his skull battered and broken by a stone weighing, so it was said in the coroner committee's report, three or four pounds.

The sun refused to shine as Sarah reached for William's arm and mouthed a silent "thank you" to a woman who moved aside to make room at the front of the Strangers and Citizens' group. William, by rights should have been a pallbearer, or even walked with the fourth order next to Mr. Arrington, since everyone in the courts had worked with him. William, though, was an Indian.

Sarah wished to the depths of her heart that Lettie could also walk next to them, but the presence of a slave in cortège was prohibited.

It was a touching moment now when George, after stepping out of line, removed his hat and laid his hand on the bier. Lettie and Robinson waited on the boardwalk at the corner; the young man came down the steps and handed something to George. As the procession turned the corner, George motioned to Sarah and William to come over. He handed William the wooden cross Robinson had constructed with Andrew's name and a red-stained winding rose carved in the crosspiece.

Sarah's tears welled; she squeezed George's hand. While he and Arrington mounted their horses, she and William caught up to the rear of the procession as shopkeepers and bar patrons lined the boardwalks. William held the cross high. Lettie maneuvered behind the watchers and kept pace with the procession. Robinson slipped back into George's office and with a tow sack in hand, followed his sister.

Boardwalks and town slipped behind the cortège at the dog-leg bend up to the town burial ground on the bluff; the marching mourners thinned. As the bier rolled into the grounds, Sarah blinked back her tears until the pallbearers slipped the ropes from under the coffin and the first hands-full of clods rumbled onto the box. Mourners gathered in little clusters, then dispersed in the still-gray morning. Sarah now waited with William beside a lilac bush while the black grave diggers finished their jobs.

Another waste of a wonderful life, she thought. Over the several years since Andrew moved to Van Buren when George took him into his office, Sarah had always enjoyed the younger man's company at suppers, his Scotchman's brogue, and his attention to the children. Lettie and Andrew could speak a streak of Scots Gaelic that only the two understood. From Robinson's mandolin came Robbie Burns' melody "My Love is Like a Red, Red Rose" and the two would dance around the parlor. Andrew was one of Sarah's family, a kindly uncle who let the little ones tousle his ginger hair and beard.

A bachelor with no nearby family, as far as anyone knew Andrew had no enemies. Why, then, such a vicious murder? A simple theft of his collections from his saddlebags could have been accomplished with the first rifle shot. Why the stabbing and battering? And why leave his silver engraved watch, his treasured Highlander dirk, his gold breastpin, and his purse with change in it? Why remove his saddle and bridle and let the horse run free?

That was the first clue that something had happened to Andrew, when his horse arrived at a farm near Lee's Creek on Sunday evening.

The farmer sent Andrew's horse to town Monday with the mail rider. Since Andrew was not in his office—ending speculation that his horse had escaped the stables—several townspeople rode out early Tuesday to find him. A neighbor in the area of Lee's Creek and his family had already formed their own search. With others scouting the rough terrain, on Tuesday evening they found Andrew's body. The coroner committee's inquest followed on Wednesday at the site, twelve miles north of town at Lee's Creek where the assailants had dragged Andrew some distance from the road.

People remembered that when Andrew returned to the office from a collections trip last week, he found the door latch broken. He and William found nothing disturbed, so the unknown intruder was not pursued. Was that forced entry a prelude to the attack? Did the assassin—or assassins—scheme and wait?

Sarah had heard that Andrew's final blows with the rock had occurred at the creek. Oh, had the dear man survived the shot that went through his body? Then the slashing? The dragging? Finally, his skull crushed.

She dabbed her tears. The burial ground, far above town was silent but for the scraping of shovels. William stood at her side clutching the cross, lost in his memories.

Andrew's death will change everything, Sarah thought. Van Buren townsfolk were in an uproar, forming vigilante parties. George said he would return after Stand's trial to investigate. But what about continuing as a judge on the Supreme Court? The pay was minimal and his rooming and office in Little Rock were costly.

Letters in the newspapers, Sarah knew, held up the Supreme Court to ridicule for its low pay and poor counsel; one writer in particular noted George's youth and lack of experience. With Andrew gone, he needed to take over the Van Buren office. He and Mr. Arrington would at some point be paid for handling Stand's defense, but when?

A breeze rustled her crepe. As she straightened her skirt she noticed the stems of lilacs fanning out in their green-and-purple glory. Sarah broke a long stalk and continued her musing.

Her mother still oversaw the reserve of nuggets and gold coins her father buried and slipped an occasional coin to her whenever they visited. But Susanna, too, waited for federal claims George and Stand had filed on Major Ridge, as did John's and Elias's heirs. If only the government would pay them for their land, the removal, their dead. Until funds came, though, George would have to provide.

The sound of the gravediggers patting the mound with their shovels brought Sarah back to the moment. "We're done, Missus Paschal," one called.

Sarah pulled coins from her purse and thanked the workers. William clutched the cross as they stood at the head of Andrew's grave and watched the men until they passed from sight back down the bluff. The crosses and headstones of past and newly-buried dead stood at attention, awaiting Andrew's final good-bye.

As arranged, Lettie and Robinson slipped from behind an abandoned shed and walked hand in hand to Andrew's gravesite.

Lettie fell into Sarah's waiting arms. Her tears held so long from public eyes poured down her face, her sobbing unconstrained.

Robinson knew. William knew. Now the three stepped back behind the lilac bush to allow Lettie her final moments with the man she loved.

For more than a year Sarah had seen the two speaking their own language, heard casual chatting turn soft at times, saw occasional touches and special Scotch recipes Lettie prepared for additions to family meals. She knew the servant and George's partner's friendship had evolved to affection.

When Lettie confessed her love for Andrew and told Sarah that he responded in kind, so began what the lovers called the "Grand Ruse." Lettie and Sarah would head off in the buggy to a secret ravine where she would then wander to give the couple privacy when Andrew met them on horseback. Sometimes William joined the ruse, if Andrew required additional justification to escape questions from Mr. Arrington.

Secrecy. Hiding. Concealing. Lying. A mulatto slave and a respectable white lawyer. A futile romance.

In desperation, Sarah devised a plan. She wrote to her Salem School friend Hester explaining Lettie's situation and asked for advice. Could Lettie somehow reach a line of the fabled underground railway to which Hester indirectly referred? Could Lettie wind her way to New England and find safety in Hester's New Bedford coastal hometown? And Andrew join her there?

Hester replied asking if Sarah could have her mother draw up papers of freedom for Lettie. Once in conversation, Sarah casually mentioned to George her consideration of giving Lettie and Robinson their freedom. He immediately answered, "No." A magistrate—*if* one would agree to hear the petition—would have to decide the validity of ownership. Susanna's acknowledgement of having found the children and not having returned them to their rightful owners would be perceived as perpetuating a fraud against the government for the expenditure of removal funds for two Negroes within her and Major Ridge's oversight. Lettie and Robinson were family property and lived under George's roof. Period.

Hester also wrote that although her abolitionist cohorts encouraged black slaves to escape the bonds of southern plantation owners, once they arrived in the North the attitude of the majority of whites did not include equality. Free to be not owned, yes, but many whites feared that if all Southern slaves came North, their communities would be overwhelmed. Freedmen lived separately on shared-crop farms or in towns, often in poverty. Sadly, a white lawyer with a Southern half-Negro wife would not easily gain social acceptance. So the sneaking, the Grand Ruse, continued until Andrew was ripped from Lettie's heart.

Lettie stood at her lover's graveside. A gentle wind rustled the lilacs. Behind the bush, Robinson pulled his mandolin from the tow sack. One last time Lettie danced with Andrew's spirit to their cherished melody as the brother sang for his grieving sister:

> Oh, my love is like a red, red rose
> That's newly sprung in June:
> Oh, my love is like the melody
> That's sweetly played in tune.

As fair art thou, my bonnie lass,
So deep in love am I;
And I will love thee still, my dear,
Till all the seas gang dry.

Till all the seas gang dry, my dear,
And the rocks melt with the sun;
And I will love thee still, my dear,
While the sands of life shall run.

And fare thee well, my only love,
Oh, fare thee well a while,
And I will come again, my love,
Though 'twere ten thousand mile.

Lettie laid a rose stem on the mound that she had cut from a bush at home, the bud not in full blossom, a memento of the couples' unfinished love.

The three returned to Lettie's side.

They bowed their heads in personal prayers as William said, "*Donadagohvi*, our friend." With a hammer from the tow sack, he reverently pounded Robinson's wooden cross with its incised rose vine into the rich loam where the marker, like Andrew's body, would degrade and decay over the years.

As would the vibrant clusters of lilac blooms Sarah stooped to lay across the grave near Lettie's rosebud.

Chapter 44

Sarah Speaks

Along the paths of our lives, we leave symbols to acknowledge the deaths of those close to us. Those simple memorials turn to dust and diminish, and stone monuments gather moss as testimonials to loss.

Of my many losses of those dear to me, I hold all close. But one broke me, and within hours shattered me again.

November 1844. In Little Rock there were no blooms. On a cold, raining morning some eighteen months after Andrew's internment, I stood under my parasol and visualized the burst of purple and tight red rose on his grave. Today I stood at my precious Emily's mound.

George waited at the cemetery gate talking with the preacher and a friend, Mr. Underhill who graciously had offered his plot for our Emily. George's heart certainly was broken—his dearest "Baby Brewer" who was so much the image of his mother was gone. But George presented his grief to the world in a manner much different than I: he spoke of case law and temperance meetings. I refused to leave my firstborn alone on this burial slope at the Arkansas riverside.

I could not take a step.

Few in this town attended. Acquaintances of George's: Mr. and Mrs. Pendleton, proprietors of our boarding house; Mr. Borden, editor of the *Arkansas Gazette*; several of George's judicial and Temperance Society associates. They murmured condolences and tipped their hats to me as they left.

Milly remained at the Franklin House with George Walter and little Soonie. I wanted not to risk the health of my two remaining children to the cold and damp. I shivered in my drenched gray dress and wool cloak; I had no mourning crepe.

I tell you now, I could not move from my Emily's graveside. I could not leave her alone. She who was always the center of attention, my firstborn, my precocious treasure. I stared as rain hit the fresh soil above where she lay in a hastily-made pine box. At one point I found myself counting the drops as if I could count them all, as if raindrops made a difference in anything relating to my reality.

Mother would receive my hurried note in a few days, but I begged her not to come. Watty, dear man, would sprinkle his garnets and within another dusty picture draw another cross, this time a small one beneath the line. Lettie would weep—my dearest friend and cohort—but whom I insisted she not come either, she who by then hated George Paschal so passionately.

Three months before when I agreed to leave Mother's home at Honey Creek and come to Little Rock to nurse George, I arranged to bring Milly with me. We all thought it best to let Lettie remain and care for Milly's little Andy, Lettie's sisterly heart broken by George's cruelty, of which I shall tell you shortly. Added to her loss of Andrew, her pain knew no end.

I, too, would still have been at Honey Creek with my children—not residing in a public boarding house where travelers leave poison—but for the boiler of the *Marietta* exploding as it passed Pine Bluffs with George on board returning from the East where he had visited with his mother in Georgia, then traveled to Washington City and on to New York City. Of the sixty or so passengers, he and a dozen others were burned and scalded by steam. He had been taken to the Franklin House in Little Rock under a physician's care where I and the children joined him. But he was now healed.

We lately took over adjacent upstairs rooms when they became available by the vacancy of a pair of wealthy invalids who had steamed upriver from New Orleans to bathe in the Hot Springs some fifty miles west.

Of course, the room was cleaned and the bedclothes changed, but the maid overlooked the medicinal packet secreted in a corner, a packet that held deadly grains extracted from opium. Yesterday while I went out into the hallway in reply to a question from Milly, Emily found the hidden paper, unfolded it and touched her tongue to it.

The doctor who came assured me my daughter would have known no pain when in her curiosity she ingested the morphine grains. The poison would have rushed through her little body and seized her tiny heart before she crumpled to the floor where I found her, a surprised, yet sleepy expression on her perfect face surrounded by blond curls.

As I stroked Emily I knew not what the paper contained, but I knew it was poison. I covered the packet with a pillow wanting no one near to it. I shoved George Walter into the hallway, terrifying him even more as I screamed down the stairs for Mr. Pendleton to run for a doctor.

Oh, on that hillside I wished only for the cold wind to blow away my grief.

When word reached George at the circuit courtroom, he rushed back. At the end of that tragic day, we held each other in bed, our tears and bodies merging into shared sorrow for our loss.

We resolved there was no blame to be placed, neither on the traveling invalids, Mr. Pendleton, or the maid. Nor on George for living here, nor me for bringing the children. Nor the God whom George holds more highly than I. There was no clan from which I could invoke Blood Law retribution.

George found solace knowing Emily Anderson Paschal rested in Heaven.

I found no peace knowing Emily Oolootsie Paschal lay in the cold ground before which I stood that day.

I had only regret. In last week's *Gazette,* I noticed that a portrait painter had set up a studio. I chose not to spend money on portraits of my children. And now I was left with only my memories.

So many regrets washed over me from when I left Van Buren more than a year ago for Honey Creek shortly after Andrew died to my standing on that hillside beside my daughter's grave.

Permit me to return to the past, to the months following Andrew's murder.

George accompanied us as we moved to Honey Creek, then he returned. I allowed his brother Augustus B. Paschal who had traveled from Georgia some time before to move into our Thompson Street house. Leaving Robinson, Isaac, and Eliza, I took Lettie and Milly with her child and my little ones to Mother's, arriving late May. There she could mourn Andrew with no questioning eyes upon her.

Van Buren citizens had formed a committee to investigate the circumstances before and after Andrew's assassination. They scoured the countryside, talked to all living on nearby farms.

Then there was the discovery that the twelve-hundred-dollar payment Andrew sent earlier—in United States Treasury notes—never reached the merchant George contacted in New York, instigating a filing by the federal government, leading to a search tracing the missing bills. It was discovered that the trail of the mailbag in which the bills were posted in Van Buren seemed to end at Fayetteville. Finding a postmaster involved, a case evolved to a court trial in Washington, resulting in his and a New York accomplice's convictions, and the postmaster at Fayetteville dismissed.

I stopped reading newspapers following Stand's trial, where my cousin had been exonerated of all charges in James Foreman's death with a ruling of self-defense.

George wrote a pamphlet detailing—editorializing—the events of the trial. That pamphlet, slanted toward the Treaty Party, caused a backlash against George as a Supreme Court Justice. More newspaper articles in Little Rock and elsewhere were published, condemning an unnamed justice for allowing his name to be associated with prejudice against John Ross, much less printing booklets and selling them for profit. One questioned George's impartiality since he was married to a daughter of the Ridge family.

Oh, the power of pressmen! Newspaper owners controlled what citizens learned—and believed—whether true or not! They acted as a public conduit for, yes, legitimate local news and goings-on, but they also printed slander, caused small talk and suspicion, creating divisiveness with innuendo and outright lies. Editors regularly concealed their sources and published letters signed "An Interested Citizen" or "A Devoted Democrat." And the ever-popular "Anonymous."

One September day Lettie walked into Mother's parlor carrying an issue of the Van Buren *Intelligencer*. She handed me the broadsheets, folded lengthwise to page three, to the advertisements.

She said nothing. She stood before Mother and me, tense and fragile as if she might shatter.

The first headline I saw was at the top, a $1,250 reward offered for the murderers of the vicious Rossman, Isaac Bushyhead. "Someone finally killed Bushyhead," I commented to Mother in Cherokee.

"Good. He deserved killing," she replied.

"Och, no! There!" Lettie said, leaning forward to run her finger down the column.

I saw first the bolded words in all-capital typeface: "NEGRO MAN."

Then my eyes moved up taking in the entire announcement. I read aloud for Mother to hear. "Auction. I will offer for sale, in the town of Van Buren, on Tuesday the 26th of this month—"

"That is today!" Lettie said, her voice quivering.

I looked at her face shining with tears. I continued, " . . . a well selected stock of Dry Goods, Hardware, Cutlery, Boots, Shoes, Clothing, and so forth. And in addition, one Riding Horse, one likely NEGRO MAN . . ."

"Go on!"

" . . . aged 25 years . . ."

I heard her groan.

" . . . one fine Gold Lever Action Watch with extra jewels and independent second hand—town lots in Van Buren . . ." I skipped the locations on Main Street. I knew which lots they were, also the listed "valuable tract of Land . . . 160 acres . . . northeast of town . . ."

My eyes froze on the signatures: SAM'L L. GRIFFITH, AGENT, FOR GEO. W. PASCHAL.

"That's me Robinson!" Lettie yelled. "There! For sale! Right between th' ridin' horse and th' pocket watch!"

"No!" I denied. "George wouldn't sell Robinson! He's family! It must be one of his brother's slaves, the ones he brought from Georgia. George wouldn't sell Robinson or Isaac! He can't, anyway. He has no legal right! Mother, you gave them to me!"

Lettie yelled, "But that reads a man twenty-five years ol'! Robinson's age! Isaac's some younger!"

Mother stood; she wrapped Lettie in her arms and held her while she sobbed.

I rushed to the barn and told Luther to saddle the fastest horse, that he must ride to Van Buren. I told him why, then returned to write a letter to George.

When Luther rode in three days later he verified that yes, George had sold Lettie's brother. That when Luther handed George my letter, he read it, then said for him to tell Mrs. Paschal that as head of the household, all slaves given her by her mother were his property to do with as he saw fit. Then George turned and walked away.

Luther added when he asked other slaves in town, they told him that Mister Paschal had been hiring out Robinson to sing and play his guitar at various saloons. George was offered a sum for Robinson, but knowing Robinson's talents, instead decided to sell him to the highest bidder. A gambler from New Orleans bought Robinson, then left downriver on the *Marietta* the next morning.

Mother that day yelled louder than Lettie. "I have *not* given Lettie and Robinson to George! Or Milly, Isaac, Eliza, anyone! How dare George!"

Time. Distance. They worked against us. Robinson was gone to New Orleans or who knew where.

Time and distance worked, also, on me. A year aged my outrage and distance faded my desire to address my anger to George. He I would not see until I came to Little Rock these three months back to help him recover from his burns.

I had yet to confront him over his act of selling Robinson.

Sometime after the auction George left Van Buren—blood money filling his pocket—and spent the next six months traveling, first to Georgia where he visited his mother. Then on to Washington, serving as a witness in the Treasury theft case of Andrew's deposit and working with Stand on negotiating a new treaty.

When he returned to Little Rock, before he could disembark the *Marietta* took her revenge for having carried Robinson downriver.

I have digressed as I shared with you these memories of events that returned to me graveside as I grieved my Emily. My grief coalesced with Lettie's for the loss of her brother, yet she had a focus for her anger; I had but Fate to blame for my dead daughter.

My sorrow overwhelmed me.

I finally glanced up to see George motioning from the street, the carriage ready, he inside it.

Removing my right glove I pressed my handprint into the fresh soil, knowing my imprint would be splashed from sight by drops and rivulets before I gained the carriage.

"I have no flowers for your grave, my love," I said.

CHAPTER 45

Snakeskins

The Franklin House

November 16, 1844

George glanced up from his writing at the sound of Sarah's sigh at the doorway. This room on the lower floor, the one in which he had recuperated, now served as his office. Mr. Pendleton had retired to his home; the house sat empty, but for Milly consoling the two remaining Paschal children.

Still chilled from the cemetery though now in a brown housedress, Sarah shivered. Her answers to George Walter's questions about Emily pulled at her heart as she tucked the three-year-old and baby Soonie into their bed. Two little ones cuddled where three had slept; she could not bear seeing Emily's empty pillow and clutched it now.

Lantern glow haloed George, his pen poised on paper.

"Are you writing Emily's obituary for the newspapers?" she asked gently, caressing the muslin where once her daughter's curls rested. "Please state that she died of . . . of chills and fever. Yes, that will suffice . . ."

She watched as a shadow darkened the furrow between her husband's brows.

"No . . . no," he stammered. "But I shall, I should be. I will stop what I'm writing and, yes, mention chills and fever—"

Stepping into the room Sarah's voice shifted from caring to caustic. "Well, then, George? Whatever are you writing? What can be more important than our daughter's obituary?"

Setting his pen in the staff, he stood and moved from behind the desk; the lampshade wobbled. The room was small, the bed on which she had nursed him back to health was stacked with papers and pushed to the corner to accommodate this makeshift office.

"Uh ... Mr. Williams and Mr. Dodge today ... knowing of my—our bereavement. They asked me, though, if I would present a speech at the Temperance Society ... on this Tuesday ..."

"Three days from your daughter's burial? Four days from her death? How dare they? How dare you, George? Where is your sense of decency?" Sarah's volume grew with each question until the word "decency" reverberated throughout the hotel.

George stepped forward. She raised Emily's pillow and hit him in the face. He grabbed it as Sarah moved around the desk and lifted the sheet of paper. George moved to the door, grasping the pillow like a shield. Sarah leaned into the lamplight and read aloud:

Mr. President and my respected Temperance Society auditory:

The severe providential dispensation which has, within the last few days, bereaved one of a fond and cherished hope, has completely disqualified me for any labored mental effort. Had time been allotted me I could not have made any studied preparation. Nevertheless, I have not felt entirely at liberty to decline the call of the Society, to lend my feeble aid in the cause of temperance. The pledge I took in early life, was not only one of <u>total abstinence</u> on my own part, but that, on all proper occasions, I would lend my influence for the benefit of others. The undertaking, therefore, is with me, this evening, a matter of duty paramount to inclination—

Sarah's voice trailed off. She looked up from the sheet. Her questions quivered with disbelief. "What does this mean, George? That you are going to give a speech as your daughter molders in a hole on the hillside?"

"Well, I said . . . I explained my reluctance—"

"No! You never said, 'My precious, innocent daughter died from taking poison!' You call Emily 'a fond and cherished hope'! You never write what you mean, George. You couch your meanings in pompous words. You are the biggest hypocrite ever!"

She shook the paper at him. Then she read again from it: "'. . . on all proper occasions, I would lend my influence for the benefit of others.' Benefit of others! Your daughter just died!"

"Sarah! Lower your voice!"

"No! I want the world to know who you are! I wish I could walk down the street yelling instead of to this empty house."

She grasped the edge of the desk.

"The only honest phrase in this speech, George, is that you do not drink whiskey! You are a man of multiple truths. You change them as does the rattlesnake as he grows and sheds his skin. But that does not make him a new snake. He is the same snake but with a new skin.

"You pander to those you think can be of use to you. You hold yourself higher than anyone. You ferret around, getting money wherever you can. You chase my Cherokee cause for the almighty dollar. You insist on the title of 'Judge', but they ran you off the court because you were only there for perceived prestige. The *Honorable* Judge Paschal! You have no honor!"

She took a breath, providing power to the words she'd held back for so long.

"You are a fraud and a fake, George. You dishonored my family Bible and my dead brother's moccasins. You show no dignity for our daughter's death. You hold yourself out to be against slavery in the Union, yet you have taken ownership of my servants. And *you sold Robinson!*"

Sarah slapped the paper onto the desk. "I hate you, George. Almost as much as Lettie does. You sold her brother to get money to go East, to play the successful lawyer, the important witness quoted in New York newspapers, the legal counsel to the Treaty cause in Washington City!

"I know you to be the fraud you are. Others do also, but they need you. They overlook your deceptions. I, too, am guilty of my own deceptions as your 'respectable wife'. My snakeskin, too, is ever-changing, because I keep secrets about you, about myself. My truths I deal with continually, but not when it comes to my child!

"Tomorrow I will take Milly and my surviving children home to Van Buren. Your brother can continue to live in my house because I need protection with the Treaty Party being hunted down.

"You can do what you want here in Little Rock. I know I will have to see you again, but do not approach me in any manner."

She grabbed Emily's pillow from George and slammed the door on her way out.

Because of her vow to avoid newspapers, Sarah did not read the short paragraph in the local newspaper on Emily's passing due to chills and fever. Nor did she read in the Little Rock *Gazette* the verbatim text of George's speech where Mr. Borden—perhaps because he'd attended Emily's internment—inserted an asterisk at the end of the first sentence. The editor noted at the bottom of the column, translated into normal words for the benefit of his readers: "Judge Paschal's interesting little daughter, six years old, had died only five days before the meeting, and before he was spoken to, to address the society."

Sarah would not return to Little Rock for several years, but on her brief visit in March 1846 when her steamboat docked at the wharf, she climbed the hill alone. The mound had flattened, her handprint merely a memory.

George had told her he'd selected a gravestone, granite, topped by a book since he had so loved reading to Emily. He told her the stonemason inscribed *Daughter of G. W. and Sarah Paschal*, with the dates, *Born May 18, 1838* and *Died Nov 15, 1844*.

What she did not know until that moment was that those truths were chiseled beneath a lie: *Emily Anderson*.

Chapter 46

Go or No

The Paschal Home

November 1845

There was something else Sarah did not know that night she yelled at George in the hotel, shouting how she hated him. Sarah had no notion that as she and George in their grief clung to each other in bed, tears mingling, their intimacy produced a connectivity that would shortly re-bind them. Sarah conceived the evening Emily died and in July 1845, her son was born. Sarah considered the baby entirely hers except for his last name: Ridge Watie Paschal.

Pushing her foot gently against the floor, Sarah rocked and absently caressed Ridge's dark hair while he nursed her breast at his mid-morning feeding. So like John, she thought, though with Father's dark eyes.

As the baby had grown in her belly she could not help but picture a visual replacement of her oldest child, imagining her daughter's spirit having re-entered her body since Emily had been taken only hours before. Now she was grateful that Ridge came to her as his own person.

He as well as his older brother would memorialize the line of family men now gone.

A leafless elm branch rubbed against the parlor window in the November wind. She made a mental note to ask Robinson to trim it. Then with a deep, arresting gasp causing Ridge to gurgle and lose hold of her nipple, she remembered Robinson was no longer here.

Now a year after returning from Little Rock to Thompson Street, Sarah still misjudged moments for memories. She still saw Emily sitting on Andrew Campbell's lap as he jangled his gold watch fob for her to bat and saw Robinson digging, letting Emily press seeds and covering them in the garden.

All gone now. Two by death; Robinson's fate unknown. And to the household, a fate worse than death.

Lettie and Sarah had talked and cried for Robinson and Andrew. Lettie's innate strength allowed Sarah to accept Emily's missing place in the family, but no words nor untold tears could wash away Lettie's pain. Her rage at George simmered always. Through an unspoken pact, George seldom addressed any of the servants; if he had a request, he told Sarah and she delivered his requests.

After George's move home when Ridge was born, Lettie no longer addressed him by name. If she must speak to him directly, she said, "You." To Sarah and the household, Lettie referred to George as *Him*. Though she omitted his name from her tongue, she held his cruel deed in her heart.

George, upon hearing his name eliminated as Lettie served supper his first evening back, mentioned it later to Sarah. "Your act of selling Robinson was abominable," she answered, "as well as illegal. If you wish to pursue this conversation further, perhaps we should include Mother." Thereafter, whenever Lettie shunned him he would look away in bitter silence.

The first months when Lettie returned from Honey Creek she would walk the wharves, meeting steamboats docking from New Orleans, pleading with debarking slaves if they knew anything of Robinson. And when she came home, Sarah could see from her red-rimmed, sunset-colored eyes that her quest had proved fruitless.

"Why doesn't Robinson write us?" Sarah asked on a day as Lettie grieved. "He is so very fluent in his penmanship, even helping George Walter with his characters."

"Ye cannae know, Sallie," Lettie replied, shaking her head. "For a slave to admit to knowin' that he writes is dangerous. For Robinson to gain access to paper and pen, he might have to steal from his master. An' who might post it for him? He cannae walk into a mail post."

And yet, somehow, Robinson overcame those barriers.

On a blustery day when George picked up the mail at Drennen's, he was handed a letter postmarked Mobile, Alabama, addressed to "Lady's Maid Lettie" in care of Mrs. Paschal. George shoved it into his pocket. Stepping aside to an alleyway on his way back to his office, he read Robinson's precise script. Robinson wrote that after leaving Van Buren, he had arrived in New Orleans with the gambler who had bought him. The man was not a bad man and hired him out for playing music in saloons. When the man won a large pot, he took Robinson to Mobile and bought a gaming house.

"I play my guitar and mandolin and sing in the saloon, dear Sister. I work in the establishment cleaning and cooking and am well cared for. I suffer only my distance from you and Mrs. Paschal's family. With this letter, I wish to tell you this so you will not worry."

Burning, as always, from Lettie's shunning, George returned to his office where John Ogden and William were working. He seldom acknowledged regret, but he did admit that in selling Robinson he had misjudged the intensity of the family uproar his deed precipitated. Placing the other letters and parcels on his desk, George walked to the stove. Pulling open the door, he tossed Robinson's letter into the flames.

"Let sleeping dogs lie," he said aloud to the busy men. No one paid him any attention.

With no word, nothing could curb Lettie's yearning for news of her brother. Walking back one day from the wharves as she passed through an alley behind a saloon, a melody resonated; words and tune brought her to a stop. Listening, she was filled with joyful memories.

> Spring winds a' blowin' and the garden's in the ground
> Our love is safe and growin' while the world turns 'round
> May days come like whispers and years step just behind
> Let warm rain fall, darlin', on this good life of mine.

Robinson's song!

Lettie moved to the open back door. Breaking the rules of decorum, she walked up the steps and entered a storeroom. Edging closer to the public area, she stood at the doorway behind the bar.

It was then she caught the eye of the barkeeper.

"What you doing here, girl? You pickin' up a keg a' brew for your master?"

"No, sir. Meself is Lettie, Mrs. Paschal's lady's maid. That troubadour, playin' that song. May I beg yer pardon to speak to him? He may know of me missin' brither."

The mention of Sarah's name held the key.

"Wait out back. I'll send him out when he's through playing this round."

She listened to the end of Robinson's song, then another her brother played so often on summer evenings while she and Andrew danced:

> O ye'll take the high road, and I'll take the low road,
> And I'll be in Scotland a'fore ye,
> But me and my true love will never meet again,
> On the bonnie, bonnie banks o' Loch Lomond.

The music ended. Lettie waited, hoping for news of Robinson while fighting back tears of memories of Andrew.

A well-dressed white man with deep brown eyes, a trimmed beard, and over-long brown hair dusted gray stepped out the back door. "You wish to speak to me, ma'am?"

"Yes, sir." Composed now, she introduced herself as she had with the barkeeper, then asked, "Aire ye Mister Luke? Walking by, hearing yer songs, meself wishes to know if ye remember me brither, Robinson? Those songs aire ones he used to sing for me. Do ye remember teachin' them to him, at an earlier time here in th' town?"

"Robinson? Yes! A young man of such fine talent. How is the boy?"

Overpouring with words, Lettie told Luke how Robinson had been sold downriver last year. Had he seen him in New Orleans? Heard anything of him?

The man's voice filled with compassion, but all answers were no.

"I will be returning to New Orleans soon. I pledge to you, I will keep an ear out for him. Should I hear of him, I shall write you here."

Lettie told him Sarah's name and to address any letter to Mrs. Paschal. With thanks and a fond farewell, she took her leave. Buoyed by the personal contact, she walked home.

Though as months passed with no letter, with no arriving slaves having word of Robinson, the grieving sister stopped meeting steamers; her sorrow she buttoned up within, her anger she wore like a veil.

With George's return, Sarah resolved once again to manage her home and marriage patiently. In their intimate times, she chose the memory of their amber cabin; those occasions proved few since her household now included not only her three children and six servants, but George's brother A.B., shortened from the family custom for multiple forenames, Augustus Burrell Julius Nichols Paschal.

A.B., the oldest Paschal son at age forty-two, was the only member of George's family whom Sarah had met. The second oldest, Isaiah Addison Sanders Goode Paschal, had also studied law in Georgia and recently I.A. joined his more adventuresome younger brother Franklin Lafayette Warren Greene Paschal in San Antonio. Franklin arrived in Texas in 1836, the year of the Battle of the Alamo. After serving in the Republic of Texas Army and later the Texas Rangers, he was elected

GO OR NO

the first sheriff of Bexar County, a title he would long use even when representing San Antonio in the state legislature.

A.B., though, was the true merchant, the buyer and seller of all forms of merchandise, human and otherwise, necessary for customers' homes, farms, and enterprises. A temperance man as was his brother, A.B. spent his days in town or overseeing his dozen or so workers at local farms. Although he was personable—Sarah enjoyed her brother-in-law's company—his enterprises meant that except for supper and Sunday dinners, her home was generally void of the Paschal brothers.

George, too, had business reasons to stay away: earlier in the year, he and John Ogden had joined in a legal partnership. Between the two lawyers with William as chief clerk, business boomed with locals selling lots and carrying financial notes for Easterners who poured into Arkansas or merely stopped off before heading north to Missouri to meet up with the Oregon Trail, or south to Texas, hoping to get there while the land was cheap, before the Republic would finally attain statehood.

"Miss Sallie?"

Sarah startled awake in her rocker, Ridge asleep at her breast.

Milly smiled. "Lordy, looks like you two can sleep anywheres! Want me to put Ridge in his basket now?"

"Yes . . . please." Still groggy, Sarah kissed Ridge's cheek as she handed him to Milly. "I don't know what I'd do without you to care for him, and Soonie and George Walter."

"Well, they's as much mine, I do believe, as my Andy. Him an' Soonie be two peas in a pod." Milly often carried the two-year-olds, one under each arm; she still grieved for Emily but seldom mentioned the dear one's loss.

"They are, Milly, they are."

Cradling Ridge, Milly added, "William done come from the office to say Mista' Paschal's comin' home for dinner soon. Lettie and Eliza are fixin' to set the table. William said to tell you Mista' Paschal ask iffen you could eat with him."

Pondering George's request, Sarah looked at her milk-stained dress. "Yes, but I must change. Thank you."

A half-hour later, adjusting her fresh white bodice, Sarah pulled out her chair next to George's vacant one at the head of the table. "I do so hope something dire hasn't happened to one of the family," she told Lettie as she set out bowls. "Good news comes so seldom."

"Want meself to bide in th' hallway?" Lettie asked. "In case ye need me to come to ye?"

Sarah nodded; with settings and food placed, Lettie stepped into the hallway just as a burst of mid-day wind announced George as he opened the front door. He walked swiftly to the table.

Out of character, he bent and bussed Sarah's cheek before sitting down. With no reaction or comment, she reached for the squash dish as George raised his hand. "Wait, dear. I have news. Not good news, I fear. I received this from a rider sent by your cousin." He handed her Stand's letter.

She held it to get light from the windows. Stand's hurried handwriting was hard for her to see; as well, she wanted Lettie to hear. "Read it to me."

"He wrote Thursday last. Steel yourself, dear," he patted her hand. "'Thomas Watie has been murdered by John Ross's thugs—'"

"No! Not Thomas!" Sarah covered her face with her hands. Her cousin. Another of Stand's brothers. Dead.

Looking up, she saw Lettie peering from the doorway. Sarah shook her head. "Read on," she said.

> Our ride for capture fruitless, I and about 60 men are now camped within the picketing of old Ft Wayne here on the line. Treaty men as well as Old Settlers have assembled. We are surrounded by 200 Rossmen. A fight is certain within days. The Arkansas militia at Maysville, 2 miles hence, has yet to come. Dragoons billeted in Benton County consist of 1 scanty company and are of no use as

they have few horses. Families of the hunted flee across the line into Arkansas and Missouri in fear. I have requested the military provision them, yet they starve. General Arbuckle at Ft Gibson supports us. But he is yet to send troops.

"George! This is war!"

"Yes, it seems the division has been laid." He paused. "I will inform Governor Drew that things cannot long remain in their present position without endangering the peace of the frontier."

"Back to Stand's letter. Mother?"

"Of course. He says to tell you your mother and brother are with his Sarah, safe at his home. Well protected."

"We should somehow get them here. Tom and Luther can bring them down."

"Travel could be hazardous, dear."

"I suppose." Sarah took a sip of water. "Go on."

"Stand informs me that a delegation of Western Cherokee led by Ezekiel Starr is soon to return from an exploring party, investigating land perhaps obtainable in Northwest Texas, that strip bordering the Colorado Territory. They are in hopes of presenting President Polk with a new option to gain that land for the Cherokees, where the factions can find peace, away from this land stolen by John Ross and his marauders."

"Oh, George! A split of the nation?"

"That seems a viable conclusion. The parties have been warring here these seven years." He reached for her hand. "I know this news distresses you greatly. Let us partake of our dinner now. I must return to my office to write Governor Drew."

Sarah handed him the squash bowl and took a spoonful for herself as she heard Lettie retreat from the hall. She would pass the word on to the other servants who would murmur prayers and remember Thomas from visits past.

Sarah, though, merely moved her squash and ham around her plate, taking few bites. Word of war and that of another beloved cousin killed by John Ross's murderers left her with no appetite.

By the end of the year, President Polk offered invitations to the three factions—Nationalists, Treaty Party, and Western Cherokee—to meet with him in Washington City next March. Stand would lead their party and appointed George as counsel.

At supper on a night before Christmas, after A.B. offered his thanks for the meal and retired to his room, George invited Sarah to join him in the parlor. He led her to the settee and sat beside her.

"This meeting with President Polk is what we've been waiting for. His orders for Congress to divide the country or accord us a new treaty will be partial justification of the cause for which your father, brother, and cousins died."

He took her hand. "I want you to come to Washington City with me."

"George? The children—"

"They can stay here with Milly and Lettie. We'll take Eliza as your maid. Your presence will be an acknowledgment of Cherokee strife. The President will be impressed meeting the orphan, the sister, and cousin of the Ridge and Watie families."

"I don't know what to say, George."

"Say, yes. Please, Sarah. For your family's legacy. For those who have died for your Cherokee Nation."

She just looked at him, then down to her lap and said nothing. After he went to bed and Sarah said good-night to her children, in the dining room she took her pencil and paper from the buffet.

Lighting a single candlestick, she placed it on the table. She drew a line down the center of the sheet, making two columns. One she titled "No" for reasons to stay in Van Buren. The other she headed "Go".

Stay with children, she wrote first on the left side. *Long trip. Hard trip. Costly.* She marked through the last word since George had told her the government would reimburse their expenses. Still, there would be costs. She would need city dresses, not her simple home attire. And the trip would be long; six months, maybe more.

She rested her chin in her hands, then wrote: *Mother and Watty*, although they were protected by Stand. But . . . he would be leaving as head of the Treaty delegation. Still, he would keep them safe at Honey Creek with his family.

Oh, so many tugs to say, "No".

She shifted the paper and moved the "Go" column into candlelight. George had said she could be an asset to the delegation. *Meet President Polk.* She smiled, remembering the colorful gowns of the ladies surrounding President Monroe, his daughter in the receiving line, the crimson drapes, the embossed eagles stitched in the settee fabric.

This time, though, she thought, I know the perils of politics.

Might she not in some way be able to influence a congressman through some manner or action? Perhaps. She wrote *Influence*. She knew Cherokee politics better than most men. She knew the lies, the murders. And her own attempted murder.

Father, she wrote. *John. Elias.*

Then her pencil raced down the page: *Thomas Watie. John Fields. Ellis Suel Rider. Archilla Smith. Joseph Swimmer. Millboy.*

James Starr, who signed with Father. His young son *Buck* was shot with him on the porch and watched his father die. *Crawfish. Black Fox.*

Jacob West and his sons, *George and John West*. These patriots had beaten and then killed the Rossman Isaac Bushyhead. George West supposedly dealt the final blow that killed Bushyhead. Jacob took the blame, was tried in a Nationalist court, and then hanged. John West received a hundred willow lashes and banishment from Indian Territory; George disappeared.

Andrew Campbell. Lettie had told her last year that she had overheard some Rossmen talking on Main Street, saying that Andrew's murdering scoundrels were a band of quarter-breeds, the Starr boys. Said how they had waylaid the lawyer, not knowing that he was a friend of the Ridges, only he was said to be carrying money. Sarah supposed it could be true. Within the Treaty party, surely some were thieves. But why his violent death, if all they wanted was money? Why not rob him of his watch and dirk? Surely, she would never know.

War raged within her nation. All these years and all these deaths.

Her candle burned low as Sarah stared at her list. Perhaps her presence could be of influence. She decided to accompany George to Washington City.

"Go," she said to the empty room.

Silently, she resolved to take her older children. And Lettie would go with her.

CHAPTER 47

An "Eat-crow" Face

The Paschal Home

January 1846

As murders raged so came death by a different manner: smallpox. Smallpox deaths were horrific. People who stayed in a steamboat stateroom or the same hotel or house as an infected victim could be overcome by a high fever interspersed with wretched chills days or weeks later.

For some death came quickly. Within a few days, blood would pour from mouths and ears. They bled to death sometimes before they experienced the agony of pustules. The route of smallpox had paralleled the trails of broken treaties. Now white, black, and red travelers carrying smallpox debarked in Van Buren on steamboats from New Orleans where the disease raged.

In January 1846 while George met with Stand's men and Western Cherokee in the compound near Honey Creek, Sarah and Lettie carried the children to Dr. Frank's medical office. George Walter bravely withstood the pain of scraping, though little Susan cried throughout the vaccination process. Ridge at six months was too young. Sarah saw to the servants who had not been vaccinated, engaging Dr. Frank to come and perform inoculations in the backyard.

When George returned from old Fort Wayne, he opened the door to his son and daughter proudly showing off their vaccinations. His six-year-old rolled up his sleeve to show off his bandage. Little George's shock of chestnut hair bounced; his eyes, the dark brown of his father's, danced with excitement.

"Father! Mother says because I'm old enough not to scratch the scab, I have only Dr. Frank's bandage!" The white linen wrap lay perfectly tied in place around his upper arm. "But look at Soonie!"

Soonie waved her hands. Sarah had knitted a red mitten for her right hand, and a matching long sleeve for her left arm with ties around her neck. Dr. Frank instructed Sarah to change each bandage daily and to not let either child get the area wet.

"Yes," George said. "You children must not scratch your arms. Be brave!"

"But in ten days the scab will fall off. I'll have a bumpy scar, Dr. Frank said. Do you have a scar, Father? Mother showed us hers!"

George removed his suit coat and rolled his sleeve high. He kneeled so the children could see the circular scar. "I was vaccinated in the Army. George Walter, when you go on to school and should you join the Army, your scar will serve as proof. It will allow you to go places other children and soldiers cannot go. Your scar is a badge of honor."

"And me?" Soonie asked. "Can I go anywhere I want, Father?"

"Yes, you can, Susan. You can go anywhere your mother thinks is a good place for you."

Little did George know how timely was his comment. At supper that evening, after reporting on the Honey Creek family and regaling Sarah and A.B. of his week writing declarations with Stand, he told them of an early February departure for the federal capital.

With supper over, A.B. and the children left the table. Sarah remained to listen and comment as George shared issues decided upon by the delegations. Then while George finished his pecan pie, she proposed her own decisions she'd recently resolved.

"I've requested A.B. have a vaccination, but he is reluctant. I'm unclear on his reservations. Perhaps you can encourage him, George?"

"Of course. I shall."

"However, I have a second request," she continued. "I feel my presence can benefit you and Stand in Washington City. Perhaps I can help in some yet-unknown way. I do not, though, want to leave George Walter and Soonie for such an extended time. Six months away, not knowing what is going on in this town, the epidemic and all, will be a constant worry and distraction for me."

"Well, I suppose George Walter is of an age where he can absorb the excitement of the governmental process. I shall find time to show him the Capitol, a learning adventure. Susan, though, will require Eliza's constant care."

Sarah shifted to face him. "I want Lettie to accompany us."

George stopped mid-bite. "No!"

"I've spoken with her. She will address you appropriately. She is the best servant to care for the children in the city."

"No," he repeated, slamming his fork on his plate.

"Yes. She can navigate the city and adapt to boardinghouse living better than Eliza. Milly can care for Ridge here at home with Eliza to help her run the household for your brother. For me to be at liberty to help you and the nation, I need Lettie with me."

"Sarah. You know how I feel over Lettie's insolence toward me. I—"

"Wait, George," she turned, then called, "Lettie? Can you please join us?"

Lettie entered wearing a deep green dress that set off her golden eyes. Her hair, usually wild and mane-like, was slicked back and captured with a green bow. Sarah looked at her with pride as she spoke, knowing Lettie's inward pain would survive; only her outward anger would be revised.

"Mister Paschal, sir. In times past, meself has not exhibited proper terms an' demeanor while addressin' ye. Miss Sallie has spake of her desire to include meself in yer Washington City journey. I want ye to know I shall act as is proper for ye servant of yer household."

George glared at Sarah, then took a sip of his coffee. He looked away. Sarah had seen that distant stare when so many times in their past George seemed to be writing notes in his internal letterbook for a presentation to an audience.

He heaved a great sigh. "Then so be it. I shall expect no further insubordination from you, Lettie."

Only Sarah saw Lettie's sly grin—the expression the women would forever refer to as Lettie's "eat-crow" face—as she answered in her most servile tone. "Yes, Mister Paschal, sir. Thank ye for yer permission to serve yer family."

As Lettie left the room Sarah added, "Thank you, George." She reached to pat his hand, but he pulled away.

The confrontational scene, though, caused both to forget to again ask A.B. to secure a smallpox vaccination.

CHAPTER 48

Portraits & a Word-Picture

Washington City

March 1846

"Sit still, Soonie. Mr. Young will be done soon," Sarah said, stepping away from the tufted chair where Susan wriggled. The portrait painter sketched her three-year-old's face onto a large sheet. George Walter, awaiting his turn, sat next to Lettie behind a screen shielding artist and subject from the waiting area of the small studio.

Asking around, an acquaintance of George's had recommended a friend, LaSalle Young on G Street. Having viewed his sample portraits of children, Sarah determined him to be adequate and had pointed to those more outstanding works on display that she wanted her children's representations to resemble.

Soonie held her favorite stuffed calico doll; Mr. Young did a quick sketch of the doll on the bottom of the sheet to copy into Soonie's lap for the final version. He jotted notes of her cornflower bonnet with a matching short cape and suggested a pale canary yellow for her white dress skirt to offset the blue of her other garments. He told Sarah he would paint the tufted chair a deep sapphire. She agreed, hoping the final portrait captured her daughter's beauty and energy.

Thinking perhaps her presence was distracting Soonie, she excused herself and joined Lettie and George Walter in the sitting area. Mr. Young babbled to his tiny subject; all seemed well.

She raised her finger to her lips with a gentle *shush* as George Walter started to say something. What a fine boy he had proven to be on the long journey. He sat straight and still now, dressed in short trousers, hosiery, and brown shoes, a short tweed jacket similar to his father's suits. Sarah leaned back in her chair. In the silence of the studio, she let the past month flow by.

John Bell and George Adair formed a portion of the Treaty Party delegation, traveling with George as counsel. Stand would follow later; war persisted in the territory. Accompanying the Treaty men was Ezekiel Starr of the Western Cherokee, just returned from the exploring party. Ezekiel, suffering from erysipelas, braved the pain of red patches staining his body. The respected leader insisted on making the trip to report to President Polk who shared his enthusiasm for splitting the tribe by removing the two smaller factions to the Northwest Texas territory, leaving John Ross unfettered to rule his domain on land once accorded the Western Cherokee.

The group secured comfortable steamboat cabins from Van Buren down the Arkansas River, though the turn upstream at the confluence with the fast-flowing Mississippi River was treacherous. At Memphis, they debarked and hired two stagecoaches to connect with the Natchez Trace to Nashville for the long overland trip east toward Washington City.

The experience Sarah treasured most dearly came when the party overnighted in Knoxville. After settling the children in their room for the afternoon, Sarah hired a maid to watch her little ones while she walked with Lettie along the bank of the Tennessee River.

The women came to a warehouse, dilapidated with age but seared into Lettie's mind. They stopped as she described clinging to her mother's dress, the shouting auctioneer as he called for bids.

"Pull ye purses out!" Lettie remembered. "Bid up this fine piece of property." Her voice quivered as she told Sarah how the man urged the crowd of slave traders, landowners, and tradesmen. "Here for ye purchase an asset to any establishment or plantation! House servant or field hand! Ye see in her arms an' standin' beside her proof! Good breeder! She comes with girl child an' boy babe to grow up into valuable hands!"

As wagons rumbled over cobblestones Sarah ignored dictated decorum and held her friend as she cried, painting a word picture of a terrified ten-year-old.

Looking across at Lettie, back-lit now by tall windows and transoms that let light fill the portrait studio, Sarah could barely reconcile that image with the thirty-eight-year-old woman who smiled back at her.

Lettie's loss of lover and brother had driven her to a dark place of grief. But in leaving the town that held manifold memories, Lettie seemed to blossom upon arrival at the capital, where Negroes were allowed more freedoms than even in the women's hometown. Though not permitted into dining rooms and such, Lettie accompanied Sarah to Center Market and mercantiles, dressmakers, and outings such as this. With Sarah's deep color offsetting Lettie's lighter complexion, the women often caught the eye of shopkeepers but none refused admittance. Upon hearing each speak, who was mistress and who was lady's maid?

On walks through this cosmopolitan city, Sarah overheard conversations in French and German and unrecognizable languages; well-dressed foreigners, liveried servants, and ladies with their maids all went about their touring, occupations, and selections of purchases. Passing on the boardwalks were coloreds who lived and worked in the city. Black slaves brought to erect government buildings had stayed on in swampy shantytowns, often in extreme poverty. Most still served their owners, but a large number of freedmen worked as tradesmen or owned businesses on the east side of the Anacostia River.

The long journey ended last week with the Paschals arriving at their reserved two bedrooms in the boardinghouse owned by Mrs. Terry on Eighth Street near E Street. The petite widow whose Unitarian broad-mindedness welcomed a white lawyer with a Cherokee wife insisted, however, on a separate attic room for Lettie, although she spent nights in the children's room.

Ezekiel Starr with others moved into Mrs. Eliza Schuyler Hamilton's home on the south side of Pennsylvania Avenue. She was the revered widow of statesman and writer, Alexander Hamilton. Ninety years old now, Mrs. Hamilton had fallen on hard times and was renting rooms to congressmen and delegates. Mrs. Hamilton's house sat adjacent to Coleman's National Hotel on Pennsylvania at Sixth Street where political figures gathered in the popular dining room only a block from the Capitol building. John Ross with his delegates, Sarah heard, were rooming at Brown's Indian Queen Hotel across from Center Market on Pennsylvania Avenue.

"Mrs. Paschal? Miss Susan has completed her sitting. Please bring the young gentleman." Sarah returned from her reverie and led George Walter around the screen. She picked up her happy daughter as the painter removed Soonie's chair from in front of the gray screen. The three-quarter standing portrait Sarah had selected for her son would include a simple pastoral background.

"Do you ride, Master George?" Young asked as he set up another large sheet on his easel. "Would you like to hold a riding crop?"

"No, sir," George Walter answered. Looking around, he spied a rack of military embellishments. "But I will join the Army someday. May I hold the sword?"

Mr. Young smiled and said, "That is admirable, George. But I fear the sword's length will cause my rendering of you to be off-scale. Are you a reader?" He reached for a book.

"Yes, sir, I am. My father is a famous lawyer. Do you have a law book?"

"I can paint in any title you request. What shall it be?"

"It's an old book Father admires. 'The Attorney's *Vade Mecum*'," he said, pronouncing the two foreign words in his best Latin as his father had when he had let George Walter look at the book at his office.

"I know not that title. Can you spell the two last words for me, please?"

"Capital V-a-d-e, Capital M-e-c-u-m. Father's has a red leather cover."

The artist scribbled a note. "Then red it shall be! Now, you hold the book this way." He positioned it in the boy's hands, shifted his shoulders a slight angle, and turned his chin forward. "Pretend you're a soldier in the Army as well as a great legal mind following in the footsteps of your father." George stood straight and smiled.

As Mr. Young began his sketch of her proud son's face, Sarah returned to her seat near the window with all misgivings about the portrait painter resolved.

CHAPTER 49

A Friend Appears

Washington City

March 1846

When President Polk convened the First Session of the 29th Congress on December 2, 1845, of primary consideration were the impending annexation of Texas to the Union and the consideration of a treaty with Great Britain over the Oregon Territory.

In his letter to Congress, the President also mentioned tariffs, imports, and the "serious difficulties of long standing that continued to distract the several parties into which the Cherokees are unhappily divided." He would be submitting to Congress measures "to put an end, if possible, to the dissensions which have long prevailed and still prevail among them." In March, upon the arrival of those "unhappily divided parties," there was much politicking to be accomplished.

The reception held on Thursday afternoon, March 26, for those divided parties was not—to Sarah's dismay—in the Elliptical Saloon of the Executive Mansion, which was now known as the White House. When Martin Van Buren refurbished the house at government expense, the oval State Receiving Room, the red room of her youth where she met President Monroe was over-painted blue, the crimson drapes replaced to match; the suite of fifty red chairs and settees with their golden-thread eagles were reupholstered in blue and silver damask bearing a wreath surrounding an eagle and its dreaded arrows. Kings and heads of state were received in the Blue Room, not Indians who had been swept from the path of western-bound Manifest Destiny. Sarah would not be revisiting the red room of her memories.

Cherokee delegates of the warring tribunal now congregated in a bland receiving room in the War Department. This building of Sarah's memory still faced H Street immediately west of the White House. The Cherokees were dressed in "sadly needed" new clothing, as a newspaper article had mentioned, purchased with funds allocated by the Commissioner of Indian Affairs William Medill.

Sarah, the only wife in attendance, wore a day gown she had engaged a local dressmaker to sew using the budget George was allowed for new clothing. She selected a sedate dark brown herringbone twill with black piping, though she did spend a trifle extra for black kid gloves. Lettie had tacked a twist of claret-colored silk roses to a black bonnet brought from home.

The *Daily Union* newspaper had mentioned earlier that the "delegation is accompanied by George W. Paschall, esq., of Van Buren, Arkansas, as attorney. Judge Paschall is accompanied by his lady, who is the daughter of the late Major Ridge, the lamented Cherokee chief, who lost his life *for signing a treaty under the direction of the President of the United States*." Although George agonized over the misspelling of his name, Sarah was pleased her presence was noted.

President Polk had been apprised of her attendance today. Accompanied by the Secretary of War and Commissioner Medill, they wove their way through the assembly and paused at the Treaty Party retinue. The President, taking Sarah's proffered hand in his, extended his condolences to her for the sorrow her family had suffered with the unfortunate deaths of her father, brother, and several cousins.

"Thank you, sir," she answered, her eyes meeting his. "I hope you will provide a conclusion to what your predecessors began these many years ago so that Cherokee who believed in President Jackson's treaty will not have died in vain."

The gray eyes of President Polk's Scotch-Irish heritage were the color of her mother's. He nodded with a compassionate tightening of his lips but said nothing, merely patting her gloved hand. His recognition of her nation's plight was enough for Sarah who knew a confrontation was not her place; Polk's sympathies ran toward the Treaty Party and Old Settlers. The President and his entourage moved on to another group.

Sarah watched as the delegates mingled. Her gaze hesitated at the entryway where to her surprise, Senator Sam Houston handed his broad hat to an officer. The tall man, dwarfing spectators in height as well as legend, surveyed the room. Houston caught her eye. After a brief handshake with the President, although hailed by others The Raven moved directly toward her. She heard him call responses to questions of his arrival from Texas: just this day, weary of travel, residing in the National Hotel.

"Why, Miss Sallie," Houston said, after greeting those around her. Taking her hand, he shifted to Cherokee, "I read in a *Daily Union* delivered me on my coach journey that you accompanied your husband. Learning of this reception, I determined to seek you out should you be in attendance. I'm pleased my intuition proved accurate."

"I'm honored, Colonneh," using his tribal name. The Raven before her was not the turbaned, clean-faced rake who had visited her father on the Oostanaula, nor the gallant congressman who retrieved her dropped glove at the reception at President Monroe's soiree. Now in his early fifties, he was a tired, mustachioed statesman. But Sam Houston still expressed his renowned individuality with a shawl of Cherokee weave draped across his shoulders and carried a gold-tipped cane.

George fretted beside her, clearing his throat, anxious to draw the senator's attention; Houston touched Sarah's elbow, guiding her a few steps away from the surrounding crowd.

They spoke of times past, how their paths had not crossed since the removal, though George had often apprised of Sarah the celebrated man's triumphs and defeats.

A FRIEND APPEARS

"You have achieved so many titles," Sarah said. "Congressman and Governor from Tennessee, General and President of the Texas Republic, now Senator. I know not how to address you, my friend."

Houston laughed. "Colonneh, my dear. And always, your friend. I grieved upon learning of the loss of your father and brother. How goes your life as the wife of the counsel?"

"I accompanied my husband hoping to be of influence on the part of Father's Treaty Party. May I ask your position on the President's view of splitting the nation?"

Houston lowered his voice in the room speckled with Cherokee speakers. "I can say in all honesty to you privately, the new State of Texas has no desire to cede a portion of our uppermost strip of land to benefit the Cherokee. Our statehood is contentious with Northern states who oppose our inclusion as a slave state. Time will come when Texas will re-draw our boundaries.

"Heed me, daughter of my old friend, no territory or state in the Union will be anxious to contend with a second Cherokee Nation. Any succeeding administration will again break earlier promises and force your people to remove to another western area. Worse, to dissipate or move back into John Ross's established Cherokee Nation."

Sarah clasped her hands, shifted her stance. "None of those close to me have acknowledged your viewpoint. Will you be advising the delegates of your position?"

"No, I must keep my senatorial focus on matters of other importance. As a fresh senator, it is incumbent upon me to wield whatever power I have on issues concerning Texas and Oregon. I pass this knowledge to you, advising you as I advised your father and John. Your party must negotiate for new appropriations and demand claims of the government for past failures under the old treaty.

"The factions must bury their hatchets. John Ross is plotting to keep all under his control. He must be made to acknowledge the terms of the treaty your father died for. I share my private position with you to advise only your cousin Stand of my view, which is to negotiate a compromise.

Strive for new annuities, for reparations. Take the money. Go home. President Polk, although he means well, has bigger fish to fry."

Sarah nodded, absorbing Houston's wisdom.

"Or better yet," he said, his voice rising, returning to English as if continuing a conversation with an old friend, "Come to Texas! You and your husband can establish a new home. How many babes have you now?"

"Two young ones, a son and daughter, who I have brought with me to the city. An infant boy remains home in Van Buren."

Houston smiled. "I wish you well, Mrs. Paschal. I must circulate now, but I hope our paths again cross before we each depart the capital."

Sarah nodded, returning his smile. As she stepped back, George latched onto Sam Houston as others pressed around her celebrated friend.

Chapter 50

A Letter Received, a Message Conveyed

Washington City

March 1846

On the late afternoon carriage ride from the War Department, the Paschals were accompanied by Ezekiel Starr of the Old Settlers delegation. Sarah answered George's questions about her visit with Sam Houston, but chose to embellish her conversation with stories of old times when The Raven visited at her home on the Oostanaula. Houston's position was for Stand's ears only.

Ezekiel, known as a calm and patient man who never displayed his anguish would be disappointed with an opinion counter to his and other Western Cherokee party members. He rambled on about mountains and vast prairie he saw his exploration trip to the Colorado Territory and the northwest strip of Texas, a good future home. The Cherokee Outlet, he said of that narrow strip of land that the Treaty of New Echota provided for hunters to travel to the western mountains, opened up to a potential homeland free of John Ross's rule.

A quarter-blood Cherokee in his mid-forties, Ezekiel was brother to James Starr, one of the treaty signers; upon Ezekiel's return home from the expedition, he had found his brother and nephews dead, his family scattered, hiding from Ross's marauders across the Arkansas line.

Sarah watched him as he talked. He kept wiping his face with his handkerchief. When the carriage pulled to a stop in front of Mrs. Hamilton's and the coachman stepped down to open the door, she removed her glove and touched Ezekiel's hand.

"You are burning with fever!" she said.

"It's the erysipelas, Mrs. Paschal. Don't you fret over me. It comes and goes." The man seemed to have wilted from the strong delegate she'd observed earlier at the reception.

"Can you ask Mrs. Hamilton to refer a physician tomorrow? Perhaps he can offer you relief."

"Thank you. I will do that," Ezekiel answered, and bid the Paschals a good evening.

The carriage crossed The Avenue and drove north on Sixth Street past a line of parked buggies and coaches fronting Coleman's National Hotel. The popular establishment bustled with evening tea guests and diners. Sarah had seen advertisements for bed suites that included bathtubs! Such an elegant residence for her friend The Raven!

Several blocks on they turned left onto E Street and two blocks farther to Eighth Street. Mrs. Terry's girl Venita came down the steps of the lovely Federal-style brick home and accompanied Sarah from street to steps. While George paid the driver, Sarah paused in the foyer.

"A letter done come for Mr. Paschal, ma'am," Venita said, pointing to the marble-topped entry table. "Missus Terry said to tell y'all she paid the post an' will add it to your 'count. Is there any else you need from me now?" Sarah shook her head and Venita walked down the hallway to the back.

Stepping to the table Sarah lifted the letter. The script was clear; the handstamp smeared. She made out "Van Buren." Turning to the backside fold, she saw Dr. Frank's name as the sender.

"George!" she said as he entered. "A letter. From Dr. Frank at home!" Her voice shook.

He took her arm and ushered her to the stairway. "We shall read it in our room, dear."

They stood before a west window where sundown rays lit the dim bedroom.

"Ridge!" Sarah said, trembling. "Something must have happened to Ridge!"

"Calm, my dear," George said loosening the seal, his hands shaking. He uncurled the creases and read silently. A shudder, he trembled. "Oh, no!"

Sarah called out, "Ridge!"

She grabbed the letter as George heaved and shook his head. "No, no—" he mumbled.

Sarah read the first line. "I regret to inform you that your beloved brother has passed from this world—"

She looked up. "A.B. died?"

George stared out the window as Sarah read. "Your girl Eliza came for me two days hence . . ." She looked at the date: March 10. "His fever raged. He bore early symptoms of smallpox, yet even before eruptions appeared he succumbed. I spare you his final hours, but can assure you, his death came quickly—

"Oh, George! Smallpox in our home!"

She read on. "Fear not for your infant. Upon first notice of your brother's fever, your nursemaid Milly removed the babe to the quarters behind your residence. All others, of course, I previously vaccinated. All are free of symptoms."

Sarah closed her eyes and took a deep breath of relief before continuing. "The town grieves for one in his prime of life, one respected in the community, manifested with principles of honor and character."

George collapsed onto the side of the bed. He held his head in his hands. Sarah moved beside him, stroking his hair.

Time passed in the stillness of the room. George raised his head and leaned against Sarah. "I failed Augustus. I failed to insist he take the vaccine."

"No, dear," she said. "I'm so saddened for his passing, but his decision was his own. Your guilt is misplaced in your grief."

"It is, yet it haunts me." He rose and took his hat where he'd tossed it on the bed. "I know you share my sorrow, but I feel a need to walk and recall memories of my older brother."

Sarah nodded. "I understand. Please, take your time to mourn."

George embraced her, then slipped out the door. Sarah sat in the chair near the window. Waves of sadness for her brother-in-law heaved through her body and settled into her chest; calming, she bowed her head in relief that she still claimed three dear children born of her body.

Rising, she walked to the mantelpiece where leaned the excellent portraits Mr. Young had delivered. She removed her gloves and laid a hand on each, feeling their small spirits. Then she went to the children's room where she told Lettie the sad news and embraced George Walter and Soonie.

"We will speak again soon, George," Stand said. "Again, my condolences on the passing of your brother." He took his hat from the foyer tree.

While George arranged his papers on the settee where the men had talked, Sarah gathered her light drape around her shoulders. "I'll walk you to The Avenue where you can collect a carriage." Stand had mentioned he would meet later with the Commissioner of Indian Affairs.

Mid-day sun beat down as the cousins walked Eighth Street. Sarah repeated her private conversation with Sam Houston and his desire for her to pass on his position only to Stand. She shared the news that Texas would not cede its northwest strip.

"He said that his power as a fresh senator is limited, he must use what influence he can muster for issues concerning his state and the Oregon boundaries. He advises us, Cousin, as he did with Father during the times of negotiations to fight for appropriations, and demand claims for past failures under the old treaty.

"He said our factions must bury our hatchets. He knows John Ross is plotting to keep the nation under his control. For that to come to pass Ross must acknowledge certain terms of our treaty signed at New Echota. Strive for reparations, our friend told me. Negotiate for the most money we can get."

Stand stopped as they came to D Street. He took Sarah's arm as they crossed. Shaking his head he said, "I thought we could enlist Houston's help, but I understand his position.

"Emotions run too high, Sallie. Our counsel and those Ross hires are preparing documents President Polk requested. It is rumored he suggests giving the Outlet to us, leaving the remaining present territory boundaries for Ross to rule."

Sarah lifted her hem as they crossed. "That validates what Houston said," she exclaimed, "that Ezekiel and others cannot expect to get a portion of northwest Texas! The President wants to give us what we have claimed since the treaty was signed in 1835. How generous!"

"So it seems," Stand said, "And yet, we are here to reach a compromise. I must keep that principle forefront. Too many of us have died."

He turned to her. "Thank you for this information, for making this trip with George. I know you must miss your babe. I'm pleased with his name, Ridge Watie. How goes it with George Walter and little Susan?"

"George Walter inherited his father's intellect. He thrives, seeing the city. Soonie has a touch of fever. I'm certain she'll rally, though, under Lettie's good care."

They walked to a carriage. Stroking the horse's forelock, she bid him *donadagohvi* and wished her cousin success, then hurried back to the boardinghouse to check with Lettie on Soonie's fever.

Chapter 51

Sarah Speaks

Again, I had no mourning crepe. My brown twill dress was not black enough, even covered by the black-weave shawl Lettie had hurriedly purchased for me. The long weeping veil she stitched to my black bonnet covering the deep-red roses could not cover me in the manner I wished to be covered. I wanted to be draped in widow's weeds. I wanted to run away, to hide, to scream in the forest of my youth. I wanted my mother. I lifted my gloved fingers beneath the veil and dabbed my eyes with my black handkerchief. My tears would not stop.

I tell you now, sitting on that church pew between George and George Walter was as dark a moment as all the dark moments I had yet endured.

Soonie melted away.

The doctors who came to our rooms—I sent for a second after the first could give me no answer—were perplexed. They applied mustard plasters to her chest and prescribed warm drinks concocted of words I had never heard. They questioned us. Could she have sipped tainted water? Picked up, as little ones do, a stone that might have been unclean? We recalled no event when such could have occurred. Influenza? Yellow fever?

My herb basket proved futile. Mrs. Terry's hired man drove Lettie to a black spirit healer who sent back rhubarb, ginger, and camphor remedies. We soothed the child in ice, yet on the third morning, my hand resting on her chest, a tiny voice uttered, "Etsi." My Soonie lay still.

Three years old.

I mourned double deaths. My innocent girl babes wrenched from me, denying me my years of love and pleasure with them beside me, growing, excelling as women and mothers. Why? Pointlessly, needlessly gone. My heart knew no peace.

George's faith and convictions comforted him and allowed him to subdue his emotions throughout the service at the Presbyterian Church near the Capitol and cortège to the Congressional Cemetery. The commissioners considered us members of the Indian delegation, thereby allowing our daughter a plot in that august burial ground on the west bank of the Anacostia River.

The afternoon, bright sun with blooming trees and bulbs belied my dark place. I suffered not the cold rain of Emily's burial, but rekindled my pain. Stand and members of friendly delegations stood around, associates of George's, and our companion Ezekiel, looking weak. From beneath my veil, I summoned all the grace I could muster to thank each for his presence.

Sam Houston who had been busying his hands during the church service, stooped and presented George Walter a tiny dove he had whittled. His compassion touched me deeply.

Before I left Soonie's grave, I removed my glove and again pressed my handprint into fresh soil covering a daughter of mine. Lettie joined me from where she had stood at a distance; I laid a branch of lilacs across the mound.

Upon returning to our rooms, I felt not the animosity toward George that I did following Emily's burial. He had written a short obituary for the *Daily Union* earlier, stating her death on the 4th of April, describing Susan Agnes as "a lovely child with intelligence and reason far above her attained age of three years."

His heart ached as dearly as mine, but I understood that he, unlike I, must get on with our nation's work. I felt no inclination, though, to share our combined grief in the bedroom; I feared bearing another child whose potential passing would again rip my heart.

My two daughters I buried; George Walter and Ridge Watie remained.

This time, though, I could see the angel face of my Soonie in Mr. Young's portrait. What excitement it had been to watch my two laugh as they remembered their sittings! Those memories revived me as I returned from the burial ground and clung to her painting while George took our son for a walk with a promise of a bowl of ice cream at the National Hotel.

Lettie sat with me in our room as I stared at my baby's image. I told my friend I wanted to go home to Mother at Honey Creek.

"I know ye grieve, Sallie. Yet ye cannae leave," she replied. I had shared Sam Houston's warning with her. "Th' purpose of yer trip is nowt finished."

"I have no desire to continue in this city of strangers."

"Ye have Senator Houston."

"Yes. Though having passed on his position to Stand to do with that information as he sees fit, my job is done."

Lettie reached across and took my hand. "Perhaps. But ye know not how John Ross intends to wield his wicked power. Ye once cared so deeply for the nation that ye acted to avenge yer family's deaths. To leave now might leave a door unopened.

"Mayhap there be a way for closeness to yer mother." She stood and led me to our sitting suite where George kept a desk. Pulling out paper and writing instruments, she left me to write my grief in a letter to my mother, advising me not to make mention of the politics in which I was involved should my post fall into evil hands. My friend allowed me to soothe my soul with words of sorrow.

The following day George brought home news that Ezekiel Starr had died. My grief found no escape. The warrior's passing, though, rekindled in me my need to see negotiations to an end through any means I could. Lettie arranged a fitting with the dressmaker for a mourning crepe ensemble so I could return to a public setting, should one be required.

I found such a reason in early July when I forced myself to accompany a War Department tour given for delegates to visit a gallery display in the Capitol Rotunda. My mission was personal.

The walls were hung with paintings of landscapes and nature; a large colored folio of John James Audubon's fowls and flora lithographs lay open on a table. I turned the pages of magnificent images imagining shrieks and birdsongs bordering streams in my homeland.

As I had hoped, displayed as well were selections from the National collection of Indian portraits commissioned over the decades. The paintings of chieftains in feathered headdresses dressed in beaded deerskin, flamboyant as they were, paled for me as I stood before the face of my father, painted by Charles Bird King. His flying gray hair, cravat, and elegant coat and vest validated the level of command he achieved in life. Through his dark eyes and firm lips, he spoke to me. I clung to my bereavement for my baby, yet vowed to my father for his death not to be in vain.

I remain eternally grateful for my stamina. Many works of science and art were lost in the vicious fire several decades later in the castle built on the Capitol Mall, the scientific and cultural Institute endowed by the Englishman James Smithson. My father's portrait was among them, though lithographs survive.

Yet it came to pass that my father's death—those of my loved ones and friends murdered for signing the Treaty at New Echota and the years of internal war—was in vain.

Yes. In vain.

Into the long-simmering soup termed "the Cherokee problem," President Polk and Congress dropped a new ladle: a commission was appointed to read the voluminous documents presenting each historical viewpoint. Three men representing various government agencies decided the stock was rancid, threw it all out, started over with fresh drippings.

In our room George daily reported to me the swirl of the boiling pot. The commissioners, appointed in July, wrote and negotiated a treaty that was affirmed by Congress for signing by all parties a month later, named the Treaty of Washington, August 6, 1846. Neither the Western Cherokee nor our Treaty Party received a new country. John Ross remained Principal Chief of us all.

I simmered, also.

A general amnesty was declared; all difficulties and differences previously existing were settled, "to be forgotten and forever buried in oblivion," this new treaty read.

The new soup contained bitter weeds, though still palatable.

Reparations were issued for our Ridge and Boudinot families' losses, the Western Cherokee agreed to quit their claim to rightful ownership of the land that they were given decades before in return for compensation, funds were bestowed for schools and for replacing the printing press so long ago destroyed.

On Thursday, that sixth day of August, I stood outside the circle of signers in the War Department assembly room and watched John Ross write his name on the parchment, finally admitting the validity of the Treaty of New Echota and its remaining articles.

All these years and deaths later.

I positioned myself near the doorway to the foyer. Lettie and I had planned this moment to the last detail. The President was not a signatory; the delegates, Secretary of War, and commissioners were to reassemble at the White House where he would congratulate them on their conclusion of agreement. George, signing as a witness, would attend, but I chose not to accompany them.

After the ceremony, Ross and Stand shook hands. It was a sight I never dreamed I would witness. Yet I marked Stand's comment that he was here to compromise.

I busied myself as the group around the table broke up and the delegates gathered for the short walk across the street for their meeting with the President.

It being four months since my Soonie's passing, I wore but a short veil draped across my bonnet; the large sleeves of my crepe concealed my weapon.

When John Ross gained the doorway I stepped forward as if to shake his hand. Did I see fear in his eyes?

I pulled from my sleeve a thorny rose. I looked straight into his face and softly said as I had on his rose-covered porch, "Your arrogance killed my family and our people!"

I raked the short stem across his outstretched hand. His face blanched. I turned and walked away before he could respond. Glancing back, I watched him shove the rose into his trousers' pocket, wipe his seeping palm with his handkerchief, and continue out the door.

George smiled as I joined him and Stand at the table. "How gracious of you to shake your nemesis' hand, dear."

"Thank you, George," I answered, smiling.

Leaning against Stand's shoulder I stated in a hushed tone, but loud enough for both to hear. "Our statement is made."

Neither knew what I meant.

Chapter 52

Pursuit of a Dream

The Paschal Home

September 1846

The house on Thompson Street rekindled family losses, shrouded with Soonie's and A.B.'s empty places at the dining table. Sarah found joy in Ridge's care, doting on her year-old son's antics. George grieved his daughter's and brother's losses in work at his and John Ogden's partnership. Little George carried Sam Houston's whittled dove in his pocket.

From the stack of newspapers William had saved for George at the office, one evening he brought home an issue of the local *Intelligencer* dated the 5th of September to share with Sarah. She sat mending socks on a porcelain darning egg from her sewing basket that she kept next to her rocking chair and bright lantern as they sat after supper in the parlor, a pattern they established after returning from the capital.

The paper's editor commended the Cherokee delegates for shaking hands in amity and hoped all feuds would be forgotten in his foreword to a piece reprinted, an August article from the *New York Commercial Advertiser*.

"It was such a mess, wasn't it George?" Sarah commented. She had lived each delay observing political maneuverings; the Cherokee treaty was finally attached as a rider to a bill of little consequence.

"Yes. The wheels of government were bogged down in the mire of waging war with Mexico over Texas annexation and preventing war with the British over the Oregon boundary."

Perhaps to make amends for his Congress's failure to approve funding before adjourning—which necessitated advancing funds by a private bank—on August 14th, President Polk had invited the delegates to meet with him following a review of amendments and receipt of their advances in the War Department. Other sums appropriated would eventually be paid accordingly with interest.

George shifted the paper to catch lantern light, telling Sarah how each of the delegates was described, lingering over the passage about his own role:

> ...As the delegations were leaving, the President inquired of Judge Paschal whether all the parties were satisfied with the treaty and whether the orphans of the Ridges and Boudinots had been provided for. The judge answered that all were seemingly now satisfied, and that there was nothing more gratifying than the remembrance of these orphans in the treaty.
>
> He further remarked that his services as advocate of the Cherokees were now closed, and that from his heart he was thankful to the President and Secretary of War, and the Indian commissioner, for the favorable result; that he fondly hoped the Cherokees would be a happy and prosperous people.

"President Polk certainly was impressed with you, it seems," Sarah commented while fixing a skipped stitch.

"And with your cousin. Listen."

> ... In taking leave of Stand Watie the President said, 'I hope, Mr. Watie, that your people have forgiven each other and that all will yet be well.' Watie replied, 'I have entered into this treaty of amnesty in all sincerity; I intend to be peaceable, and have no doubt that others who have less to forgive will follow the example which all the leaders have set.'

Sarah paused her darning. "Stand's willingness to compromise is proof of his commitment to peace. He, among all, has lost most."

"Yes. Now here is a testimony of the President's devotion to your peoples' cause," George said.

> . . . There have been matters of far greater general importance during the President's administration than the settlement of the Cherokee difficulties, but there is none which reflect more credit upon his head and his heart, than his successful exertions to save an interesting people from extermination.
>
> From the day when he came into office he has turned much personal attention to the subject, and no doubt thoroughly mastered it. In speaking of the orphans of Ridge and Boudinot to Judge Paschal today, the President paid a very just compliment to the Rev. William Potter and the Rev. Cephas Washbourne, who have used their utmost exertions, since retiring from their missionary labors among the Cherokees, in behalf of the families. These are the gentlemen who attended the funerals of their murdered chieftains—

Sarah interrupted, her tone tense. "Those who had the opportunity to be properly buried. Not Father. Nor John."

"Now, dear. The angry days are behind us." George said. "Here is the portion of the article I most admire."

> ". . . The President warmly congratulated Judge Paschal upon the successful results to his clients, the Treaty party, and expressed a hope that a like success might attend his professional career to which he would now return in Arkansas.'"

Sarah smiled as she fingered a sock to find the hole. "Quite the compliment to you."

"Which, my dear, I have taken as the President's support of a future for me in Congress. I intend to pursue the nomination for Congressman Yell's vacated seat in the United States House of Representatives."

The darning egg slipped from Sarah's hand into her lap, hit the floor with a *thump!* and rolled to the edge of the rug. She didn't even try to conceal her surprise.

George folded his paper, stood, and retrieved the egg. Handing it to her he said, "I hope I have your blessing. Although I know you maintain spiritual beliefs that do not include attending regular church services with me, I would be grateful if you would assist me in the societal portion of my endeavor."

Sarah nodded, rolling the egg in her hands. Not "doing her duty" as his wife sitting next to him at services had at times been a point of contention between them. As their life evolved in Van Buren, she stood her ground with only irregular attendance. She did, of course, accompany him on occasional social gatherings, bringing a dish for shared tables under the trees in summer. In answer to outside inquires of her absence from services, though, Sarah replied she remained home Sundays to allow the servants their day off to enjoy fellowship at the coloreds' church.

"However," George said, "for me to offer myself to the public as their preferred candidate, I will need to move in congregational circles as well as organize stump speeches to draw in the general masses. I watched you recently present yourself with grace and composure in governmental and political circles. I do not doubt your ability in those assemblies, as you were sought out by the President as well as our friend, Sam Houston. Will you join me as my helpmate and companion for this journey that will eventually return us to Washington City?"

Sarah looked across at her framed sampler hanging on the wall—created almost a decade ago while she considered George Paschal's marriage proposal—and absorbed the whitewashed house, the dun horse, the draping willow, and the urn embellished with the word "Home."

She created a new home here on Thompson Street.

Yet she *had* enjoyed this recent venture into recognition as a woman of influence. As well, she and Lettie had enjoyed the freedoms offered in the city. Foremost, Soonie was there. The move would not be forever. She had read this election would only fill Congressman Yell's few remaining weeks of office. "Surely, you'll go alone for the end of this term?"

"Yes, dear. Time is of the essence since this session ends on the third of March. Already the Governor has dawdled in refusing to appoint a successor, causing this rushed balloting. And then, as holder of the office, I shall seek reelection and we will return together."

Noting Sarah's distant gaze, George added, "Shall I ask Eliza to bring coffee?"

"Yes, please." Sarah continued to stare at the sampler. Here she was identified as the daughter, sister, and cousin of slain loved ones, but those wounds were now healing. In Washington City, her family role would be less known. She would live as the wife of a congressman in the cosmopolitan city where she could raise her sons and gain for them educations not afforded locally.

As the orphans of Major Ridge to which President Polk referred, she and Watty had received five thousand dollars to share, as did John's and Elias' heirs. Another hundred thousand dollars was spread among the Treaty Party for claims for murdered relatives and property taken by the Rossmen. The Nationalist coffers were filled with money drawn inappropriately from the original removal fund. George received a sizable payment for his services as counsel, and now his business with Ogden boomed as did the town.

But could George find backing for his pursuit of Congressman Yell's seat? He had many friendly associates in his legal sphere, but he also had enemies. She remembered the rumors surrounding his resignation from the Supreme Court after Stand's trial. Positioning himself for such a lofty federal office would naturally bring out opposition from those who had grievances against him or who merely wished to attack his doctrines. She knew so dearly discord between politicians.

And she herself? Theirs had often been a marriage of discord. After Emily's burial, she called him a fraud and a fake. Had George changed? Had her opinion changed? She had gained a recent respect for his negotiation skills, watching him in his element with the delegations. This, she assumed, would be the persona he would present in running for Congress. Could she support his new snakeskin?

George returned carrying the coffee tray and set it on the table between their chairs. Sarah dropped in a lump of sugar and stirred; in his new snakeskin, he stooped to servants' duties.

She looked again at her sampler. "We would, of course, keep our home here? Not sell?"

"Yes, dear. Of course. I will be representing my constituents. We would return periodically. We'll find a pleasant house to let during sessions. We will bring our sons. Abundant opportunities for them."

"Lettie?"

"She has redeemed herself in my eyes, so yes. Certainly. And Milly."

"Not Milly. Her child and Isaac are here. I feel Lettie and I could care for the boys."

"As you wish."

"Are you prepared for opposition, George? Candidates and their cohorts sling mud as well as political arrows. Do you have the support of the Democrats?"

"From many, I've been told. I wanted to ask first for yours."

Sarah paused her stirring. "Then yes, I will accompany you to your political events in any meeting place you select, churches or public squares. Your years of placing yourself in the public light should serve you well for election to Congress. President Polk will be pleased to have a fervent Democrat to back his causes. I will help and encourage you in your goal."

"Thank you," he said. She noted his smile, the warmness of his eyes.

He repeated, "Thank you," and stood, bending to kiss her on her lips.

She returned his kiss. As the moment ended, she smiled and said, "We shall excite the voters at your stump rallies, but I will ask Isaac to build you a portable step-riser for when the proverbial stump is not available."

They laughed.

CHAPTER 53

Eggs & Barbs

Van Buren and Fayetteville

Winter 1846

With the ratification of the treaty by Congress, prosperity and peace—or avoidance—spread across the Cherokee Nation.

In the state of Arkansas, political upheaval erupted when Archibald Yell resigned from Congress to enlist soldiers to fight in the Mexican War. The vacant congressional seat left only one representative to pursue funding for Arkansas.

It was vital for the citizens to send another man to represent their interests; however, voting for "my man" to win was often more important than the policies they promised. In Arkansas campaigning served as entertainment. Supporting a favorite candidate was like betting on a favorite racehorse, and truly at times was a blood sport; in the past, duels were fought over political insults with occasional adversaries killed.

Undaunted, George tossed his hat into the ring. Sarah, her six months of wearing mourning apparel having passed, engaged a dressmaker for daywear of burgundy and deep blue with matching bonnets. She sat next to her husband in church and brought Milly's sugared pecans and dried apple slices to local rallies. George's speeches in Van

Buren and Fort Smith gathered tradesmen, farmers, and merchants with their ladies, most of whom knew George or at least knew of him.

Women, of course, had no vote, but wives could wield influence over their husbands. Children ran around the campaign areas as if at a fair; George, in affirming his stance on temperance, allowed no keg of cider or beer set out to attract voters as did most candidates. In late November, Sarah traveled north with him to Fayetteville hoping to find time for a visit with her brother John's widow and orphans at their home.

George's supporters tacked up circulars and sent boys throughout the town as criers announcing his two o'clock speech. Families left their homes, merchants their businesses; saloons emptied of patrons. The street in front of the courthouse filled.

Sarah smiled and nodded to familiar faces—Treaty Party and Old Settlers friends of her family—as she moved through pockets of applause and cheers while George spoke. She handed his circular to outstretched hands; topped with a design of the State seal, his flowery text ended with a quotation from the Little Rock *Democrat* newspaper: "Judge Paschal is well known in the state as an energetic business-man, whose information in regard to all matters concerning the state and the west, is second to no one; and his general acquaintance with the present Congress and affairs at Washington, would eminently qualify him to enter the duties of the station at once."

Sarah reached the edge of the group not having seen her brother's widow, when a man wearing a bowler hat shouted, "Who you representin', Paschal! The Cherokees you got all that money for in Washington City? Or white folks?"

A man next to him yelled, "How much you got for yo'self? Runnin' for a legit job now you's through bleedin' the Injuns?"

George shouted, "The results of my negotiations with President Polk have brought peace to the Cherokee Nation! And thereby peace to this troubled northwest area! I will now use my influence in Congress for you! For trade! Build up Fayetteville to rival Little Rock!"

Sarah noticed a nearby couple; the woman held a basket draped with a checkered napkin. "Prattle, Paschal! All you do is prattle in th' papers. I seen you in court. You waylaid my brother on the stand. You're all pomp and prattle!" He reached into his wife's basket and grabbed an egg. Rearing back, he threw it at George, hitting the porch post with a *splat*!

A man next to the egg woman reached in at the nod of her head and threw another, this one landing near George's feet. People holding circulars wadded them and tossed them at supporters who shouted for quiet. One rowdy grabbed a man's circular and ripped it. Chants of "Paschal-prattle!" followed. Hats fell as men shoved others, ladies cried out and husbands ushered them to safety.

"Paschal-prattle!"

"Paschal-prattle!"

George yelled for calm.

Sarah edged farther from the crowd when suddenly buckskin arms grabbed her. She clung to her stack of circulars as she spun around into the arms of a tall Indian.

"Let's get you out of here, Mrs. Paschal."

In her shock, it took a moment for Sarah to recognize Youngdeer, the Cherokee farrier who had ridden with her to kill John Ross. He pressed his hand on her bonnet, protecting her, and guided her to an alleyway beside a dress shop.

Glancing back, Sarah saw the sheriff jump on the courthouse porch and stand beside George. The lawman yelled for quiet. Slowly the crowd took notice. Shuffling and guffawing, the rabble-rousers snuck away. George's supporters jeered them off and shouted for him to continue.

"Youngdeer! Thank you!" Sarah exclaimed. A smile replaced her surprise.

"We have little time, but I've wanted to speak to you." He started to remove his wide-brimmed hat, then pulled it lower and turned his back to the street knowing they should not be seen together.

Shortly after their attempt on John Ross's life, Youngdeer had sent word by Robinson that he was leaving Van Buren. Sarah always regretted not having an opportunity to thank him for his help; their secret demanded they never meet.

Youngdeer smiled now. His handsome pock-marked face had matured over the four years since their parting at Sallisaw Creek; Sarah sensed sureness in his bold expression, confidence in his words.

"I read in newspapers you accompanied Mr. Paschal and the delegations to meet President Polk. I've wondered if you met up with John Ross?"

"I did. I've wished so much I could share with you the resolution to our desperate day of revenge." She quickly told him of her and Lettie's scheme, her ruse of a handshake, embedding the thorny rose in their enemy's hand.

"Good! You have taken the final act of drawing John Ross's blood as he did against our people. I've always regretted doubting your avenging words."

"Youngdeer, don't. Together we repudiated his evil lies." Sarah reached to touch his shoulder, then caught herself. "And what of you? Are you plying your farrier trade here?"

"Yes, but not for long. I've learned that with the settlement for the Cherokee now established, I can claim my aunt's long-delayed removal allowances as her heir. When I get the money, I am going to Texas when the war ends." He smiled. "Many a horse needs 'a shoeing in that new state!"

"I'm happy for you. I know you'll find success."

"Thank you. And for all you've done for your family and our people." He touched his hat. "We must part."

"Yes. *Donadagohvi* and fare thee well, my friend." Not daring to shake Youngdeer's hand or hug him as she truly wished, she watched him walk down the alley and then slipped into the nearby dress shop.

Realizing George might miss her in the crowd that still gathered, she asked the keeper if she could view her mirror to straighten her bonnet after the melee, then returned to her post on the edge of George's supporters.

Sarah clapped not only for her husband's confident words but for her fortuitous encounter with Youngdeer.

George's campaign stumping avoided further egg-throwing; however, barbs in the press cut deep. Even so, supporters flocked to his speeches. Rumors of contentious campaigning in counties across the state filled the papers as voting took place on Monday, December 14.

Not having seen her mother in more than a year, Sarah arranged for Susanna and Watty to spend Christmas in Van Buren to help celebrate George's impending election. Tom drove them from Honey Creek and they were met with tears of joy and sorrow.

Rumors of vote tallies trickled in from across the state: George leading his Democrat opponent, Albert Rust. Whig Newton leading Whig Noland; Whig Newton ahead of George; George ahead of both Whigs. Days crackled with anticipation.

Lettie and Milly prepared a Christmas Eve supper of roasted goose, mashed turnips slathered in gravy, and beets pickled in Eliza's special cloves-brine. Sweet memories of those missing from the table substituted for campaign chatter. Sarah shared stories of the journey and their time in Washington City as well as the anticipation of a future return.

As dusk fell, Sarah saw Watty's eyes flash as neighborhood firecrackers interrupted conversations. He lowered his head but showed no fear; the dear man had witnessed so much gunfire in recent years. Taking the bowl of turnips Sarah passed him, he filled his plate until overflowing.

With the dining room cleared and the house silent, Sarah and Susanna sat drinking the last of their coffee.

"Watty seems to have reached a place of composure. I am so pleased," Sarah said.

"Yes. I'm glad you could witness his self-control. The Lord has bestowed a peaceful home for my dear son's tumbled thoughts, for serenity from the tragic events He has placed before us."

"I see that," Sarah said, sipping the last of her coffee. "Etsi, there is a matter I wish to share with you."

"Of course. Anything, Sallie, always."

Her mother's seventy years showed in lines that furrowed her face, but now with softness. Her lips no longer formed a line of pain from the suffering witnessed throughout her decades.

Sarah searched for Cherokee words to explain her story. "The legislature in Little Rock recently adopted a Married Women's law, stating that going forward property owned at the time of marriage or acquired afterward by gift of descent shall be her separate property."

"I had not heard!"

"I've thought of the money you and Father gave me—gave George—to build our home. In my musings and casual conversations with other wives, though, I do not see how this law can include me. The rule requires a woman to record her deeds or inheritances at the courthouse in her county. George, of course, placed the deeds and lands he's purchased in his name."

Susanna tapped her fingers on her saucer and frowned. "Naturally."

"Yes. George is a lawyer in all aspects of our lives." Sarah pushed her cup aside. "I'm telling you this because my portion of the orphan repatriations from the federal government has come to me, but George deposited them into his bank. He allows me, of course, any purchases I wish. Our life is comfortable. But should any future allocation come to me through you, I wish that you—we—avoid George's knowledge of any gift."

Susanna nodded. "Thank you, Sallie. This is good for me to know."

Sarah gathered their empty cups. As Susanna stood she laid her hand her daughter's head. "Such travails we have shared. May we now share an end to them."

The Saturday after Christmas with the joy of watching the boys playing with their new toys, Sarah joined George for a walk to the wharf. A steamer from Little Rock was scheduled to dock, perhaps carrying news of an official tally by the Secretary of State.

Calling out Christmas wishes to passersby and waving to disembarking passengers, Sarah stood aside as George sought out Colonel Drennen's boy offloading crates for the mercantile. A stack of *Arkansas Gazettes* lay on a nail keg; George gave the boy some coins for payment and to cut the twine for an issue.

With the newspaper tucked under his arm, George suggested stopping in at his office. The empty room was the perfect place to begin a celebration for the future Congressman Paschal.

Sarah drew her cape tighter in the unheated space. George sat at his desk and opened the paper to page two, the editorials and letters page. Smoothing the creases he gasped, "No!"

"George?"

"This cannot be! Listen:

> We are inclined to the opinion that Arkansas has for once, elected a good and true Whig to Congress. Mr. Newton is still nearly one hundred votes ahead of the foremost Democratic candidate, who has heard for all his strong-holds. The counties yet to hear from will scatter their votes upon Newton, Paschal, and Noland. Paschal is two hundred votes behind, and is even unpopular in his own section of the State.

"How can that be?" Sarah walked behind him and looked over his shoulder. The five candidates' names headed columns with county totals listed below.

George didn't move as he stared at the figures. She reached around him and ran her finger down the list. "You're *not* unpopular in our county! Rust has but thirty-three. Newton one hundred forty-six to your two hundred thirty-five! The other two are minimal. And look at those blank lines!" She quickly counted. "More than fifteen counties have yet to report, many are listed as not official tallies!"

She bent in closer. "Washington County. Oh. Fayetteville—"

"Yes," George read, his words monotone. "One hundred ninety-two for Newton. A mere sixteen for me."

"Well, those Whigs must have turned out on election day. Probably a Newton man brought a keg of beer to the polling place!"

"Perhaps. But Little Rock. Pulaski County."

She read, "One hundred eighty-seven for Newton. Sixty-six for you. Oh, no . . . . "

"Totals," he said, pointing.

Sarah leaned in and saw the figures: *Newton 1,549. Rust 1,437. Paschal 1,280. Noland 766. Haralson 123.*

"I am in third place!" George's voice rose until it filled the room. "Third! Even behind the other Democrat, Rust! Why? Why, Sarah, why? I had support. I had promises from friends and associates!"

She patted his arm.

"I also have enemies." His voice drifted off. He shifted to another section of the newspaper.

"These figures are not official, dear. Please. Let's go home. The incomplete totals mean nothing."

"They do, Sarah. My abilities are not appreciated."

His shoulders slumped. He stared out the window. She felt for the first time her dreams, too, of a return to Washington City fade.

"Let's go home. You don't want to have curious visitors stopping in as the *Gazette* makes its way into subscribers' hands."

"I cannot hide, Sarah. The news will out. It's the risk I took standing for election."

"True. But this will give you time to prepare for tomorrow's comments as news spreads."

At home, George and Sarah opened the front door to a warm room and boisterous boys. Leaving George to entertain, she went out to the kitchen. Susanna followed; Sarah gave the women the sad news. Lettie sighed with no comment; Susanna bustled around the room shaking her head.

"Milly!" Eliza said. "Let's whup up some cream an' suga'! Get out a jar of yo' pickle' peaches. Miss Sallie? You's and Mister George needs cheerin' up. We'll serve y'all a special supper!"

Sarah and Susanna laughed at the boys' antics during the meal. Watty, not understanding why so soon after Christmas the family enjoyed another feast, chuckled and teased his young nephews. George joined in with tales from a Bible storybook he promised to read to them later.

As evening passed into night, Sarah realized, perhaps, that once again her perceived future would end in disillusion. In bed that night her supportive passion provided consolation to George, though her fading dreams mirrored his own.

CHAPTER 54

An Eagle Flies

The Paschal Home

January 1847 - April 1848

Politics, Sarah thought. The art of the inexplicable. The parlor sat empty as she read the local *Intelligencer*. Susanna and Watty's return to Honey Creek several weeks ago had left a void in her world. On this last day of January, she felt restless. When Milly suggested taking the boys on a stroll, Sarah readily agreed.

Her sewing failing to entertain her, she set her embroidery hoop aside and picked up the local newspaper thrown earlier on her porch to read the advertisements; perhaps a new bonnet could calm her.

Yet a column caught her eye: William Newton was on his way to Washington City carrying the Whig banner to represent Arkansas. He would join in Congress another conservative neophyte, the Whig Congressman from Illinois Abraham Lincoln.

The paper quoted a Little Rock letter that stated post-election results:

> By these returns, Newton leads Paschal by 23 votes, and thus in the opinion of the Secretary of State, Newton is elected. But if we add to Paschal's vote of a 26 majority received in Sugar Loaf and

Big Creek Townships, but which were not sent to the Clerk here within three days from the election, and were, if we understand the reasons assigned, excluded by the Secretary of State, it will be seen that Paschal's majority is THREE over Newton.

We should certainly feel it our duty to comment upon the outrage upon the peoples' rights in excluding these votes—

Sarah heard footsteps on the porch; George opened the door.

"George! I just read of the late votes! You truly did win!"

"Yes. But it's over." He hung his hat and slumped in his chair. "Newton's gone to Congress. My letter declining to contest the results will soon be published. And for what, this furtive loss? What future lies before me? Now my sources in Little Rock tell me that when the session ends on March third, Newton will *not even run* for the following term!"

"Then *you* shall! The paper validates that he has gone to Congress against the will of the people!"

"No. My spies have word that Benjamin Johnson's name will be placed forward. His wife's family connections to leading Democratic powers guarantee his success."

Sarah felt the door slam on her dreams of a return to Washington City.

"Today, though," his voice shifting to a firm tone, "I received a letter from San Antonio. Both my brothers have read of Newton's assumed win. They encourage me to consider Texas. Isaiah tells of his active law practice. Franklin, though no longer sheriff, is a leader in city affairs."

"But the war? Mexico has not yet conceded."

"True. Isaiah writes of General Santa Anna's double-cross in his return from exile in Cuba. Rather than negotiating an end to the war as he promised, the general is leading his army into battle at Buena Vista, far south of the Nueces Strip. The Rio Grande River, some two hundred miles southwest of San Antonio, will outline the shape of the state once the Mexicans are overcome."

Sarah could not picture any of the locations of which George spoke. "How thoughtful of your brothers to write."

"They ask for me to visit them. Travel south soon, next week, perhaps. If I feel an affinity for what I see, their lives and stature, I can submit my petition for practice before the Texas Supreme Court."

"George? Remove to Texas? I cannot take my sons into a state *at war*!"

"No, dear. Nor would I ask you to enter an untamed land. I shall prepare my petition and leave it with Isaiah. When the time is right, when peace is attained, he will present my application before the Court at the appropriate session, possibly at the end of this year. He, of course, is a friend to the jurists."

George straightened; he leaned across and took her hand.

"Sarah. What does Arkansas offer us now? We have but your family keeping us here. I'm asking you to consider removing—"

"Leave our home? I welcomed extended trips to Washington City, George. But move forever from my aging mother? Watty? Stand?"

"Yes. Not until safe, certainly. A year from now, perhaps. Will you consider this?"

"I'll think about it, George. But—"

"That's all I ask of you for now. Think how our lives can be born anew in a new city. San Antonio. Or Galveston, a growing port city on an island."

Her eyes left George's and focused on her sampler, the only home she'd known other than here on Thompson Street. Her restlessness amplified as she stared at her needlework painting that represented home and family. She grappled with those notions as she realized her menses had not yet flowed this month.

Friday, April 7, 1848, finally arrived.

While George directed household crates loaded onto the steamboat, Lettie oversaw the family and servants boarding the *Deborah*. Sarah took her leave and stepped off the wharf. She walked to a vacant rise near the river.

My past, she thought, is buried here in this land of graves: Father, John, and Elias. Thomas Watie. Andrew Campbell. So many.

She planned to briefly disembark while they docked in Little Rock to visit Emily Oolootsie's grave, but she bore the sadness of not returning to say a last *donadagohvi* to Soonie in distant Washington City. Most troubling, Mother and Watty would remain at Honey Creek under Stand's watchful eye.

Last fall her mother and Watty had driven down, arriving for Sarah's confinement. Her unfounded anxiety over her fifth birthing on September 23, was soothed by the comfort of Susanna as midwife. Having named Ridge Watie as her own, Sarah allowed George to name his new daughter: another Emily for their dearly departed, and Agnes in memory of his mother. Dark of hair with a delicate cream complexion, Emily Agnes resembled no family member and would grow, Sarah hoped, to be her own person.

During the winter George traveled to Texas. At the December session of the Texas Supreme Court, his petition was accepted by the State Bar. He met with his brothers in San Antonio and a young relative. They discussed a partnership: J.A. Paschal would open an office in San Antonio and George decided to establish a law office in the booming port of Galveston. The new partners took a trip to the island city where they met with cotton merchants and established lawyers.

All plans hinged on Mexico losing the war, of course, but upon his return to Van Buren, George shared his proposal with Sarah. She, in turn, waited to give her consent until receiving a reply from her mother who answered with a few words, "Go, my daughter."

George, enthused though not yet sharing his plan with anyone other than Sarah, lit the firecracker for leaving. As the wick burned, Sarah vacillated between excitement and reluctance. Mother supported her. Sam Houston had invited her to move to Texas. George spoke about how his famous new acquaintance Samuel Maverick had a finger in every San Antonio pie as well as across the state. Having never mentioned Sam to George, Sarah wondered if he had ever mentioned to Sam his wife's family name. Probably not.

George viewed Texas as a legal land to conquer when on February 2, 1848, after almost two years of savage battles, the Treaty of Guadalupe Hidalgo was signed establishing the Rio Grande as the U.S./Mexico border. Mexico recognized the annexation of Texas and agreed to sell California and the remaining territory north of the Rio Grande for fifteen million dollars. For years the newspapers reported death and battles to acquire new territory for the Union, but gory headlines soon would be replaced by glory: the discovery—a mere week before the treaty signing—of gold nuggets found at Sutter's Mill in the Sierra Nevada mountains of California.

George chased nuggets of his own crafting: he implored the Crawford County courts to move forward with legal cases to receive his clients' fees; he sold his acreages; he sold the house. Whether he considered selling any of the slaves, he wisely made no mention to Sarah.

Requesting that William stay on as clerk he dissolved his partnership with John Ogden. The editor of the local paper had composed a notice of the Paschal's removal to Galveston for publication in tomorrow's issue, as well as word of the dissolution of the Ogden partnership and establishment of the new Texas partnership of George W. Paschal, Esq. and J.A. Paschal, Esq. representing clients in Galveston and San Antonio.

Sarah had wished good-bye to Mrs. Ogden and several of her women friends, but the family's removal, she felt certain, would be the talk of the town when made public. The Catholic Diocese purchased her large and lovely yellow-brick home on the Van Buren Heights for a Female Academy to be conducted by the Sisters of Charity, but that transaction would be mentioned in a later issue.

Two weeks ago Susanna arrived unannounced at the Thompson Street house. Sarah glanced up from helping Lettie wrap china plates in rags to see Tom draw the carriage in front. He helped Susanna step down and assisted her up the porch steps. Sarah grabbed the door and embraced her mother. Taking the carpetbag from Susanna's hand, after greetings by Lettie and Milly and the boys, Sarah settled her mother in the parlor to cradle her new granddaughter while the servants watched over her other children and packed other rooms of the house.

Rocking and cooing, Susanna asked Sarah to pull her chair close. In a hushed voice her Cherokee words did not leave the room. "I thought it best that Watty not travel with me. He is in a content period now. I feared seeing you ready yourself for departure might upset him. Memories of our visit at Emily Agnes' birth will sustain him when I tell him you have removed to Texas."

"Etsi! I'm so conflicted!"

"Please, don't be, Sallie. The nation is now peaceful, though John Ross still rules. I want you to build a new life for yourself and your children in Texas. You must go."

"To the city of Galveston, George has decided. I feel I can settle there. I've found it on a map he has in his office. It lies on a bay of an ocean called the Gulf of Mexico."

"Then I shall write to you at Galveston City." Susanna paused her rocking. "I am old now. Watty and I enjoy what comforts we need. I brought you this to help you as you seek a new life." She patted the carpetbag beside her chair. "Do not let George know of my gift. Always, my daughter, always know you are the hereditary head of our Wild Potato Clan, no matter what laws white men establish."

Sarah's eyes moved from her mother's face down to the valise. When she set it there earlier, she noted the weight; now she knew what it contained.

With this gift, Sarah felt that her mother was abdicating her headship of the family clan to her daughter. Responding in kind—to solidify her leadership and reassure her mother of the trust placed in her—Sarah leaned back in her chair and said, "I accept your gift and now I want to tell you a story I have kept secret from you."

In the time that followed Susanna smiled and cried and smiled again as her daughter proved to her that she was worthy of clan leadership, how she and Stand had plotted to kill John Ross, how she and Youngdeer rode into the Nationalist encampment, of her standing on the rose-covered porch and firing her pistol at the chief's heart, of her failure to kill him, finally wiping Ridge blood across his face.

Susanna slowly shook her head, her tone serene. "You failed not, my daughter. You stained him with the blood of our family. It lies there with the stain of the blood of our people who died for his stubbornness."

Her mother laughed as Sarah related the scene at the War Department reception, her final statement of revenge. "Oh, Sallie, I only wish I had been there to see the murderer's expression as you pretended to shake his hand! You have stood in for me and made good our family's revenge. I can now rest in peace for the balance of my days. Thank you, my daughter."

Now from her viewpoint on the vacant lot, Sarah remembered the tears as her mother left the following day. Would she ever see her brother again? Had she held her mother for the final time?

Sarah took a deep breath remembering this landing eleven years ago, sitting on a keg, straining to see what lay ahead as her flotilla fought the Arkansaw, the river saying, "No! I do not willingly receive these uprooted people seized from their homes!" Yet from each overflowing flatboat crawled the Cherokee, the Real People renamed "Immigrants," exiled to a Promised Land of fraud and murder. Here she lived as a member of a family sacrificed for truths sworn to them by Great Fathers who lied, who merely wanted land for white people to settle, to chop down trees, to plow rows, to establish towns.

Sarah saw the *Deborah's* funnel smoke rise and watched the boat tug at its mooring lines as if as anxious to leave as she was. This time Sarah was traveling with the current, to the confluence of the Mississippi and downriver to New Orleans. There her family would board another steamboat to edge the Louisiana and Texas coastlines west to Galveston Island.

A brush of shadow. A *whoosh*! of wings. She followed the flight of an eagle, the white of its head and tail, its broad wingspan with feathers fanned like fingers pointing. Unlike those golden threads of eagles embedded in fabric as she sat in President Monroe's Elliptical Saloon almost a quarter century before, this eagle—the sacred bird of her people—circled, then soared downriver.

Uwohali. Leading her way.

Infused with the spirit and strength of Susanna, here on this riverbank Sarah vowed to bury her titles of vengeful daughter, sister, cousin. She would live free of politics. Texas would be her salvation, her opportunity to begin anew.

She wore with pride her remaining title of mother. And with trepidation, that of wife.

The End
Book One

AFTERWORD

Thank you for reading Book One of *A Woman of Marked Character*, my imagined portrait of Sarah Ridge, a biographical novel. Sarah's great-granddaughter Kathryn Agnes McNeir Stuart who shared with me a correspondence and a long interview (which I tape-recorded in 1991) was the source for family tidbits that I would not have known otherwise: Sarah was born during an aftershock of the New Madrid earthquake; Sam Maverick had "courted" Sarah, and George Paschal was "sweet on" a woman named Anderson in Van Buren, hence Emily Oolootsie's middle name written as "Anderson" in the family Bible, which was lost in a housefire. She also told me George had written a romance novel, but that no copy of it remained. Thank you, dear Kathryn.

I used a typescript from the Bible records for Sarah's daughters' deaths, placing Sarah in Little Rock and Washington DC for those chapters. Knowing Sarah was in those cities, I gave her reasons to be there. For Little Rock, I found newspaper notices of George being burned on the *Marietta* at Pine Bluffs, his Temperance Society speech, as well as the advertisement for his "Auction and Sale of a Negro Man."

I also found the newspaper article "George Paschal and his Lady" in Washington City in 1846 where Soonie is buried. Her portrait remains, so I show Sarah having paintings made of both children, but there is no record of one of George Walter.

Hester is fictional, as are Lettie and Robinson. Sarah's slaves' names are all listed in various legal documents and I hope I do them justice in bringing them to fictional life in her story.

John Ross: his long friendship with Major Ridge is well documented, as is the split between them before the signing of the Treaty of

AFTERWORD

New Echota. As Sarah says in Chapter One, "In the final moment of accepting the government's promises we believed our truth. Principal Chief John Ross, as I shall tell you, believed his."

Ross's beliefs for negotiating a separate treaty are his own, and I endeavored to present his side as well as the Ridges. History shows, however, but for his delay of the inevitable, the final forced removal might not have been as tragic. As well, the Western Cherokee welcomed the tribe from the east, and opportunities were missed to live as one.

Sarah's rumored attempt on John Ross's life was recorded by Colonel Hitchcock in his diary, yet discounted by him; I allow her to her avenge her family's murders, as well as make her final statement to Ross at the War Department with the rose. (To write accurately of "cap and ball" long guns and pistols, I joined a black powder shooting group and learned the process.)

The assassinations are well-recorded; I was fortunate that my good friend Barbara Lea Gibson's family farm was not too distant from White Rock Creek where Major Ridge was murdered. Her father showed us the exact spot in the creek where it occurred. That was over twenty years ago and Barbara Lea has passed, but I will never forget my emotions standing in the creek, imagining the sound of rifle fire, the horse rearing, Sarah's father falling. Thank you, Barbara Lea.

Sarah did accompany her father to Washington City in 1824 and was refused schooling by the Quakers. Did he take her with him to President Monroe's soiree? I'd like to think so. The Cherokee delegates were presented with Indian Peace Medals, and therein lies my story of the talisman that will play such a powerful role in Sarah's future.

In the "Holy Bible, Holy Moccasins" chapter, I've already mentioned George having Miss Anderson write her name in the Bible. I found a letter in one of George's letterbooks to the New York merchant saying he was mailing a gift of John's moccasins. When I read that, I was surprised that Sarah would part with such a precious memento. Did she give George permission? If not, how would she react if she found out? I let her rip!

Later when Emily dies in Little Rock, the cause of her death is unknown with "chills and fever" noted in her obituary. My newspaper research led me to an article about traveling invalids who accidentally left packets of morphine at a boardinghouse and a person died, so that sad story evolved.

Sarah's cousin Stand Watie's exploits have been written about in many books and he left many letters. He was a Cherokee warrior through and through; he too avenged his family's murders, yet shook hands with John Ross at the final treaty signing in 1846.

So as Sarah and her family and slaves board the steamer for Galveston, I invite you to travel with them as she becomes an independent woman and builds a rewarding life while confronting the death of another baby, hurricanes, and yellow fever epidemics. Marrying a man much her junior and bearing another son, Sarah trades her city property for an isolated 500-acre ranch across Galveston Bay where this woman of remarkable ability endures a bitter land encroachment and the Civil War, then is faced with a tragedy of dreadful magnitude.

Look for *A Woman of Marked Character - The Imagined Portrait of Sarah Ridge Paschal Pix 1812-1891, Book Two 1848-1891* coming soon.

ACKNOWLEDGMENTS

In a writing project spanning thirty-three years, there are many along the way to thank. First and foremost are my sister and brother-in-law, Sharon and Claud Bramblett of Austin, Texas. Their love of Sarah's story and encouragement and support have been unending. Sadly, Sharon passed away a few months before publication.

Five years ago when I was traveling to Houston to visit my son Jarret Webb and grandson Thatcher, my daughter Jessica Webb Frank said, "Why don't you visit Sarah's grave again?" She set me off on the final race to the finish line. Not only did Jess encourage me during my writing times, over the months during my self-publishing saga, she continually came to my aid whenever the tightrope broke, picked me up and brushed me off, retied the rope and sent me on my way again.

Barbara Daly, long-time friend and romance writer, listened to first versions and has been with me through evolving iterations, always believing I could do it and bringing me back when I wandered off.

During this past period of writing, my friend Lease Plimpton, my first reader for every chapter I printed off as Sarah spoke to me, helped me turn research into a biographical novel. During endless evenings discussing WWSD—What Would Sarah Do?—Lease's years of interest in the untold stories of women combined with her intuition to help sharpen my thoughts; her pen ejected a multitude of "ands" and "buts."

Sue Vandal, my other primary reader, brought to Sarah's story fresh eyes and unique insight. In the final rewrite, I heard Sue's comments that expanded and validated the woman I created for my imagined Sarah's walk through life and history.

Donna Stewart has been steadfast in her interest in my writing, and along with her husband Bill, we've spent many a dinner and cabana time discussing my progress and plans.

I'm grateful to Pam Peckham-Chace and Martina Halsey for reading, and my good friend Steven Dulude for listening to my ramblings over the years.

Jackie Gantt, dear friend and Galveston aficionado, and I had so many fun times searching for Sarah's house in the island city. Sean McConnell, Special Collections Manager of the Galveston and Texas History Center at the Rosenberg Library, has always been helpful above and beyond, as has Marie Hughes, Director of the Chambers County Museum at Wallisville.

My special thanks to Paul and Dorothy (Doyen) Ridenour for furnishing photographs from their McNeir Family Collection. They have been most helpful in offering their family research on Sarah, Dottie's 3rd great-grandmother. More information on the Ridge family is available on their website paulridenour.com.

My good friend and artist Gale Fogarty took my many rough sketches for locations relevant to Sarah's history and turned them into clarity on her detailed map for readers to follow the trail of Sarah's story.

The winsome song "This Good Life" was written by my neighbor, fellow writer and mentor Luke Wallin, and is included on his CD *When You Try to Steal the Blues*. You can hear Luke's melody on YouTube Music, read his lyrics on Spotify, and learn more at lukewallin.com.

My deep appreciation to Jace Weaver (Cherokee Nation), Ph.D., Professor of Religion, Adjunct Professor of Law, and founding director of the Institute of Native American Studies Program at the University of Georgia, Athens. Dr. Weaver was historical advisor on the PBS series *We Shall Remain, Trail of Tears* episode, as well as author of many books. His gracious editing and comments on Cherokee history in my manuscript were invaluable.

I'm so very grateful to my Texas editor Liz Clare for her eyes on my final manuscript. Her clear vision—Liz's Lens, I call it—for seeing Sarah within the maze of Cherokee history, strengthened and honed my story. I take responsibility for any blemish on Sarah's imagined portrait that slipped by.

ILLUSTRATIONS &
MAP CREDITS

Maps

The United States 1840
Florida Center for Instructional Technology

Cherokee Nation & Removal Routes to Indian Territory 1838 with Sarah Ridge's Locations
Gale Fogarty, Artist

Illustrations

President Monroe Peace Medal 1817 *United States Mint*

Major Ridge (circa 1820s) *Archives of American Art, Smithsonian Institution*

John Ross (circa 1820s) *National Archives*

John Ridge (1825) *National Archives* (Portrait by Charles Bird King currently hangs in the Crystal Bridges Museum of American Art, Fayetteville, Arkansas)

Sarah Ridge (1826) *Chambers County Museum at Wallisville, Marie Hughes, Director*

McNeir Family Collection, digitized by Paul Ridenour:

Elias Boudinot (circa 1830s)

Stand Watie (circa 1840s)

Sarah Ridge Paschal (from original painting, circa 1842)

Susan Agnes "Soonie" Paschal (1846)

George W. Paschal (circa 1850s)

Ridge Plantation House (now Chieftains Museum, Rome, Georgia, National Historic Landmark)

SOURCES & FURTHER READING

Books

Thurman Wilkins, *Cherokee Tragedy: The Ridge Family and the Decimation of a People* (My primary source for the Ridge family story through the time of the assassinations.)

Edward Everett Dale and Gaston Litton, *Cherokee Cavaliers: Forty Years of Cherokee History as told in the Correspondence of the Ridge-Watie-Boudinot Family*

Donald Davidson, *The Tennessee; Vol 1; The Old River: Frontier to Secession*

John Demos, *The Heathen School: A Story of Hope and Betrayal in the Age of the Early Republic*

Allen W. Eckert, *A Sorrow in our Heart: The Life of Tecumseh*

John Ehle, *Trail of Tears: The Rise and Fall of the Cherokee Nation*

Grant Foreman, *A Traveler in Indian Territory: The Journal of Ethan Allen Hitchcock*

Frances Griffin, *Less Time for Meddling: A History of Salem Academy and College 1772-1866*

Steve Inskeep, *Jacksonland: President Andrew Jackson, Cherokee John Ross, and a Great American Land Grab*

Marquis James, *The Raven: A Biography of Sam Houston*

Paul Kelton, *Cherokee Medicine, Colonial Germs: An Indigenous Nation's Fight against Smallpox, 1518-1824*

Paula Mitchell Marks, *Turn Your Eyes Toward Texas: Pioneers Sam and Mary Maverick*

Rowena McClinton, *The Moravian Springplace Mission to the Cherokees, Vol. 1 & 2*

Tiya Miles, *Ties That Bind: The Story of an Afro-Cherokee Family in Slavery and Freedom*
George W. Paschal letterbooks, Arkansas State Archives, Little Rock, Arkansas
George W. Paschal, *Ninety-Four Years: Agnes Paschal*
Theda Perdue, *Cherokee Women*
Marion L. Starkey, *The Cherokee Nation*
Jace Weaver and Laura Adams Weaver, *Red Clay, 1835: Cherokee Removal and the Meaning of Sovereignty*

Newspapers

Saturday, September 9, 1843. Advertisement "Auction and Sale of Negro Man." *Arkansas Intelligencer* (Van Buren AR). p. 3.

Thursday, March 12, 1846. "Another Cherokee Delegation." Daily Union (Washington City). p. 3. ("The delegation is accompanied by George W. Pascall, [sic] esq., of Van Buren, Arkansas, as attorney. Judge Pascall is accompanied by his lady, who is the daughter of the late Major Ridge, the lamented Cherokee chief, who lost his life for *signing a treaty under the direction of the President of the United States.*")

Hon. J.W.H. Underwood, Mar. 26, 1885. "Reminiscences of the Cherokee, The Treaty of '35," Chapter III. *The Cartersville Courant*, p. 1. ("... Mr. Boudinot ... and Sallie Ridge were there ...")

Theses & Dissertation

Jonathan Filler, *Arguing in an Age of Unreason: Elias Boudinot, Cherokee Factionalism and the Treaty of New Echota*, 2010, Bowling Green State University

Jane Lynn Scarborough, *George W. Paschal, Texas Unionist and Scalawag Jurisprudent*, 2010, Rice University

Stephen Watson, *If This Great Nation May Be Saved? The Discourse of Civilization in Cherokee Indian Removal*, 2013, Georgia State University